Greenpoint Doughboy

Greenpoint Doughboy

—

Peter McHale

ISBN-10: 069282023X
ISBN-13: 9780692820230

This novel is dedicated to: My great-uncle John McKay
And the men of the Fighting Irish 69th Regiment of New York

1 Private = 1 Doughboy

5 Doughboys = 1 Squad

4-5 Squads = 1 Platoon

4-5 Platoons =1 Company

4 Companies = 1 Battalion

3 Battalions or 12 Companies = 1 Regiment

2 Regiments = 1 Brigade

2 Brigades or 4 Regiments = 1 Division

3-4 Divisions = 1 Corps

3-4 Corps = 1 Army

CHAPTER 1

Thanksgiving Day, 1911

———

"MA'LL BE HERE SOON," ANNA announced. She looked around the parlor and saw her brother John sprawled on the sofa.

"Who are you? The bishop's cat?"

John had collapsed after a long morning at Saint Cecilia's. He had served four special Thanksgiving masses with Father McGolrick, the pastor. The day started at 6:00 a.m. Father preached one Mass after the other with great vigor, but by the fourth go-around, even John knew the Latin verses by heart.

"Ah, shut it," John muttered, eyes closed.

Anna leaned in, flitted her big blue eyes, and pressed her lips against her brother's ear. "Did Father let you finish the wine and help you with yer cassock Johnny?"

"It's the sixth ring for you, Anna McKay, I swear it!"

Across the living room, Alex McKay put down his pipe and his newspaper, changing his thoughts from world affairs to his children.

"Enough from the both of yers," he demanded. He repacked his pipe, lit it, and puffed until a cloud of smoke formed around him. "Leave yer brother be, Anna."

"You're a pest," John added.

Anna flitted her eyes again and stuck her tongue out at John. She was surely a beauty, with flaming auburn curls that fell down around her soft pale face and large clear eyes. But at just fifteen, Anna, the youngest, acted more a holy terror than sweet angel.

"Yer ma will be here soon, lass," Alex said. "Help yer sister, Catherine, in the kitchen."

The sun was soon to set on this Thanksgiving Day, 1911, the last Thursday of November. About an hour earlier, Alexander McKay had a rather unique and unexpected visitor—a dapperly dressed man, a newspaper reporter from the *New York Herald*. He was writing a story about the McKay household of Brooklyn on this the American day of thanks. "The article will run in tomorrow's morning edition," he told Alex.

Alex led the reporter on the grand tour of the rather unique house he rented from his employer, Standard Oil Company of New York. "It was built in 1640," said Alex, "constructed by Dutch settlers. The first Europeans to arrive in Brooklyn, you know." Alex lit his pipe, took a toke, ran his long spatulate fingers over his handlebar mustache, and explained that *Breukelen* was a Dutch word meaning "broken land."

"She has four-foot-thick walls," Alex boasted as the men stepped down into the dank cellar. "Those are turret windows," he said, pointing to the front wall of the house, "fer aiming and shooting Indians—at least that's what my two boys think."

The reporter took note of the huge beams holding up the main floor and was impressed by the floor's wide wood planks.

"Cut from original Long Island woodlands," Alex said. "British army officers quartered here."

The *Herald* reporter was keenly interested in the architecture, but he had come to Greenpoint to write a different tale. The McKay family home, the reporter explained, was at the exact center of New York City. The reporter wanted to know how Alex McKay and his family fared this Thanksgiving Day, considering parents Alex and Mary were immigrants to America and were busy raising four teenage children.

"I am deeply grateful," Alex said to the reporter. He removed his pipe and held it by the tips of his long fingers. A distant gaze washed over his thin, angular, pointy face. "I am very grateful for all that America has given my family," he added somberly.

Before the two men left the cellar, the reporter opened his leather case and removed a sketch pencil and a pad. He asked Alex to stand still for a moment while he sketched a quick portrait of the Irish immigrant father. Although using only a charcoal stick, the reporter managed to catch Alex's pensive stare hidden behind his long mustache, and then almost magically, the reporter captured the lustrous bright shine in Alex's very green "Irish" eyes.

The two men went up the cellar steps to the kitchen where Catherine, Alex's oldest at nineteen, prepared dinner. Once the reporter saw the young beauty, he was so taken by her youthful glow that he sketched a portrait of her on the spot. Catherine had pulled her hair back for cooking, bunched it tight, and held it by a brooch. Her roundish pale face and striking blue eyes—big blue eyes just like Anna's—evoked a natural warmth and grace.

———

John finally awoke and sat up on the parlor sofa, stretching and yawning as Alex put down his pipe to tell his son about the recent visitor.

"Turns out we're at the center of things here in Greenpoint," Alex cheerfully boasted. "A *Herald* reporter told me this house is the very epicenter of our fair city. The story will run in tomorrow morning's paper."

"I knew you were the 'hub of the wheel,' Dah," John sassed. Soon to be seventeen, he'd begun to feel his oats.

"Don't be a wise one, son. Nobody likes a wise one."

"You'll get a trip to the pokey, like Archie," Anna blurted out as she flew back in from the kitchen, her long auburn curls bouncing.

"No more talk like that, Anna," Alex warned.

Catherine emerged from the kitchen behind Anna. "The turkey's done," she said softly, removing the brooch that held her hair, letting her thick locks fall free. "We're ready to sit."

John headed to the bedroom that he shared with his older brother, Archie, eighteen, and put away his cassock. The original Dutch house had three bedrooms. Sisters Anna and Catherine shared one, parents Alexander and Mary shared the second, and John and Archie shared the third. The house was new inside, having been renovated by the Standard Oil Company of New York (SOCONY), and it even included indoor plumbing.

John went into the bathroom to wash up and peered at himself in the mirror. He'd begun athletic training at the local Antrim Society Club gymnasium. The club's managers had just hired a new trainer, and they purchased a slew of new exercise equipment. John started regular athletic training six months ago, and he could feel his body had changed. He'd gained muscle and felt himself getting stronger. He was shedding his boyish build, and that suited him just fine. He was eager to become a man.

———

John went back into his bedroom and stuck his head out the window to see if the Meeker Avenue trolley car was making its way down the street. His ma would be arriving home that way.

The Meeker Avenue stop was just outside his window. Every day, hundreds of passengers rode the streetcar to the end of the line at Penny Bridge and traveled across Newtown Creek to the sprawling Calvary Cemetery. The memorial trade in Greenpoint, Brooklyn, and Blissville, Queens, on other side of the bridge was vigorous with business. The Catholic cemetery was giant, housing thousands of graves.

Penny Bridge was actually Greenpoint's Meeker Avenue Bridge, but everybody in Greenpoint used the old name. Penny Bridge was the name for the Long Island Rail Road station on the Queens side along the cemetery, so that's the name everyone used. Meeker Avenue Bridge replaced the old wooden Penny Bridge that had burned in a fire.

A trolley conductor once told John the story of the old Penny Bridge. He said an oil tank at a nearby yard had ignited one night, and flames quickly spread to the dry wooden bridge. When firemen ran to the creek, one of them plunged waist deep in the creek's muck-filled muddy banks, and he became stuck. After the fire was over, they found him in that very spot singed to death.

"The bishop made sure a statue was erected for that poor soul," the conductor told John. "He wanted everyone in Brooklyn to know that an Irishman will do his duty, no matter what. If you pass the main gate at Calvary, you'll see his statue, first thing."

John heard the trolley car in the distance. The rattle grew louder, and then he heard the familiar sound.

Clang! The conductor struck the bell.

"End of the line!" he shouted. "Penny Bridge. Cross over for the cemetery."

"Ma's home!" John yelled, bringing his head back inside and running across the wood-planked floor into the parlor.

Mary McKay got off the streetcar and slowly walked to her home. The chicken coop was clean, the walkway swept, and the rosebushes were bare but in order. Her stems produced wonderful blooms, a true miracle considering the torrid soil in which the flowers were planted.

The wind kicked up, and Mary grasped her coat to stop her shivering. *A crisp, clean day,* she thought. Fresh air. The brisk breeze kept the smelly smoke from the nearby Greenpoint refineries from settling over her house.

Mary was a proud woman, but not boastful. She was proud that she made a life for herself, proud of her husband, Alex, and her four children. She had left Antrim with nothing. Her family's farm had been bequeathed to her older brother, not her. Glen Ariff, Ireland, was like Eden on earth, its sloping glens gliding to the sea. Nevertheless, there was no life for her there, no future, and at sixteen, like a million others before her, Mary sailed to New York City and began a new life as an American.

She was proud, but she had her troubles, too. *Like anyone,* she considered, *nothing that can't be straightened in time.*

Archibald, her second child and older boy, was pure trouble. "Born with the devil in him," she would say. She had spent her Thanksgiving morning at the downtown Brooklyn jail on Adams Street making sure Archie was fed a decent Thanksgiving meal. He had been arrested for brawling on Metropolitan Avenue and was sentenced to three days. Consequently, Mary left the holiday cooking to her daughters, Catherine and Anna.

Just as well, she thought when entering her house. Catherine had been introduced to a young man, the brother of her boss at the Greenpoint Candle Company. His name was William.

"He works for Standard Oil, too, but he wears a suit," Catherine oft repeated.

"An office man." Mary snorted silently. "Not a laborer. That's good."

Alex gazed at his wife as she entered the parlor and removed her winter coat. The cold air put a pink blush on her cheeks. She was petite and thin with delicate, fine features, like a nose and eyes painted on a porcelain doll. Yet, Mary was a feisty woman, too. She could take charge, and Alex knew when to get out of his Mary's way.

"How is our boy?" he asked her.

"Incorrigible." She sighed, looking to John, her rock. "I love Archibald dearly," she professed openly, "but I pray for him to become more like you, Johnny." She reflexively ran her fingers through John's light-brown hair.

"Two eejits?" Anna sassed.

"Like Johnny, Anna," said Catherine. "Not like you."

"Ha! Funny."

"Like yer face," John retorted, curling his arms like an ape.

Alex raised his hand like an old king. "Enough of that," he ruled, and there was silence.

———

Thanksgiving dinner was a masterfully prepared banquet. Anna covered the table with the family's good tablecloth and put out her mother's fine plates. She and Catherine lit candles and placed them in Mary's holders, the crystal ones that Alex had given her as a wedding gift. The turkey, moist and tender, was roasted to perfection, and the mashed potatoes and creamed onions made by Anna were as good as any found in a fine New York hotel.

"You girls will make blessed wives," Alex offered, both content and full of great thanks for his handsome, healthy family seated around him. "You're just like your mother, girls," he coyly added. "And Mary…" He peered adoringly at his pretty wife, bathed in soft candlelight. "You've taught them well."

"The face on you, Alex McKay," Mary gushed, embarrassed by the open display.

"It's the truth, dear." Alex was adamant. "The truth."

The family was together, minus Archie. Alex and Mary were at wit's end with him. Archie preferred Greenpoint's street life above parish life, and although still not twenty years old, he drank alcohol and gambled. He had a mischievous gleam in his eye, and he openly cavorted with older women.

"Full of the blarney and horny as a hare," Anna whispered to Catherine.

"Indeed," Catherine replied softly, so as not to be heard.

The family sat together all afternoon and into the evening, but when the Thanksgiving dinner was finished, the girls got up to clear the table, and Alex went with his son down to the cellar under the main floor. Alex installed an oil burner in the house. Boiler making was his trade, but Alex manufactured and repaired large industrial burners for SOCONY, ones used to refine gasoline and kerosene.

Mary wasn't fond of the new oil burner machine, "firing off with no one tending it." She preferred a wood fire. Alex thought fireplaces belonged to the past century, but he didn't fight his wife.

The men headed to the cellar to fetch the wood needed, and John was eager to get his dah alone.

"I was trading words with that big-mouth Martin McSweeney at Antrim Hall," John began. "He was boasting, you know, nothing new there, how Mayo men brawled with the English. He said, 'Erin Go Bragh' are a Mayo man's words and not for all the Irish to say."

Alex pressed tobacco into his pipe and struck a match on a stone wall. He had wanted to chat with John about Ireland for some time now but always considered the boy too young. Tonight, however, as Alex peered across the dim cellar and through the hanging smoke, he saw the clear eyes, broad shoulders, and square jaw of an earnest man. *How did my boy grow so fast? It's time*, he thought, *and what better day than Thanksgiving?*

"Johnny," he began, "when folks say, 'the Irish, they speak the Gaelic,' it's akin to sayin', 'the French, they speak the romance.'" Alex toked his pipe and flattened his mustache with his fingers. "We're Irish, son. Our language is Irish, not Gaelic. And since the time of Patrick in four hundred, we Irish have been Catholic, too. We're Irish Catholic in Ireland, north, south, east, and west. Nothing more—and no other thing! It's not *who* we are, son, it's *how* we are."

The pungent tobacco smell filled the dank room.

"From time beginning," Alex went on, "the English have stepped on our land, stepped on our religion, stepped on our language, and worse, stepped on our throats. For no reason, Johnny, but to enslave our people—make us royalist-loving Protestants, nothin' more."

He shook his head vigorously. "It'll never be!"

"All over Ulster and Antrim, John, the Irish Catholics decided to 'take it no more,' and they stopped those English devils dead in their tracks. No more of them, us Ulster men said!" Alex had to control his passion.

"A real grudge, eh, Dah?"

"A grudge that isn't over. In Ireland today, Catholics till English plantations subjected to English law. No different than for the Negro slaves here in America. They want us Irish to speak English and be English citizens…Swear allegiance to an earthly king and watch our culture die. I for one say no to that!"

Alex tapped his pipe against the window turret and reached for his tobacco.

"Ya sound like Corcoran before Bull Run or like Meagher frothing at the Know-Nothings."

Alex looked at his son earnestly. "Corcoran was right, John. How do you think he got so many Irish to volunteer for the Union? It wasn't for no reason, son. Those Irish immigrants knew exactly *who* and *what* they were fighting against, and they came to Corcoran in droves."

"And Ma's family, Dah, in Glen Ariff? How'd they keep that farm?"

Alex gave his son a knowing pat on the shoulder. "Someone on ya ma's side 'sipped the soup,' son, but don't ever let her know I said as much. There'd be hell to pay, for sure." He laughed and coughed.

"We better get, Dah."

"Yeah, we better, but I wanna say one more thing before we're done here."

John listened.

"We Irish are taking our place at the table here in America, and America is going to give us Irish a lot more say in this world. The time of elitist English rule is no more. When we march down Fifth Avenue, we're stickin' it in the eye of those bastards. We show them who Americans are, and it's us! You are not Irish American, son, you are American through and through and above all things. Your ma and I made sure of that. America is a great land, John. We have much to be thankful for. So remember America first, America foremost. Forget the old ways. Forget the old country. You're an American."

"Indeed, Dah, indeed."

CHAPTER 2

1911- April 1917

———

THE SPRING AIR WAS A bit cooler than William had expected, so he donned a waistcoat over his dress suit and peered into a nearby reflective window to adjust his tie. Once in order, he set out on his journey from the high corner of Calvary Cemetery near his parents' Blissville home. He trekked downhill through the giant graveyard, over the grass and mud, and passed thousands of modest tombstones and castle-like mausoleums of deceased Irish immigrants until he reached the cemetery's rear gate near Penny Bridge Station at the Meeker Avenue Bridge. His shortcut to the McKay home across the Newtown Creek was now a well-worn path, but before completing the last leg of his trip and crossing the bridge, William stopped to wipe the mud and dirt from his shoes and give them a quick buff shine. William never showed up at the McKay house without looking tip-top. He was an office man, not a laborer, and he wanted the McKay family, if not all of Greenpoint, to know it.

William had become a regular at the McKay household since 1911, when he officially began to court Catherine. By 1914, he had watched the McKay siblings mature grow into adulthood, and come of age. Catherine's sister Anna, no longer behaved like an impish brat. She had become a charming, beautiful woman, but still with a sharp tongue and devilish wit. Young brother John, now twenty, stopped assisting Father McGolrick at Saint Cecilia's and put his focus on athletics.

William heard rumors that John had become an accomplished pugilist, but young John never said a word about his boxing, so William never broached the subject. John talked a lot about getting a full-time job, possibly at Standard Oil like his father. Brother Archie had work, but nothing career minded, and he continued to get into skirmishes up and down Greenpoint's Metropolitan Avenue. Catherine was mortified.

Over the years, William had joined the McKay family for Sunday dinners and attended all the holiday parties. In time, Alex and Mary McKay got to know William well, and they approved of him. Mary McKay was especially pleased. Although William was demure in stature and a rather short man, he had a commanding presence that suggested he was a successful sort no matter what. William wasn't one who merely eked out a living; he had a good office job, and he saved his money. He was thrifty, and he modestly imbibed alcohol, which Mary believed was the Irishman's curse.

The McKay's found William to be a planner, too. He'd been courting Catherine for the better part of three years, and he was sure he could afford marriage before asking Catherine to be his wife. He took promotions at SOCONY, and he was financially secure. He could offer Catherine a good life; a modern, clean home; and a chance for Catherine to raise any future children full-time and not have to work like so many Irish women.

Anna, on the other hand, thought William was too much the planner. One afternoon she cornered him in the family kitchen and pointedly suggested that he "get off the pot."

A few weeks later, on a warm, sunny spring afternoon in 1914, William made his way downhill through the cemetery into Greenpoint and found father Alex McKay at the SOCONY yards. William asked Alex for his daughter's hand in marriage, and Alex gave William his full blessing. William then strolled over to the nearby Greenpoint Candle Company and found Catherine at her work. William had shared his intention with his sister, Margaret, and because Margaret was Catherine's supervisor, William begged Margaret to make her self and the other decorators scarce. He wanted to be with Catherine alone.

The workday ended, and William escorted Catherine out of the factory gate and back to her home by the creek. They strolled along a tree-lined street under a white flower canopy bloom, and William asked Catherine to be his bride. Catherine said yes, and the three-year courtship ended in marriage on a showery morning four weeks later.

Father McGolrick presided over the wedding ceremony at Saint Cecilia's Roman Catholic Church in Greenpoint, and young John McKay assisted as his altar boy.

"The last time!" John insisted. He felt he was much too old for the altar boy job. He was twenty, after all, and most of Saint Cecilia's altar boys were no older than thirteen or fourteen, but John had promised Catherine he'd do it, and being the sort who always kept his word, John followed through. Father McGolrick didn't object, since he regarded the mature John McKay to be one of Greenpoint's finest young men.

Older brother Archibald, on the other hand, left the Roman priest a bit more perplexed. *It's a matter of nature versus nurture,* McGolrick mulled. Mary McKay had been to his confessional many times. The poor woman didn't know what to do about Archibald.

Father McGolrick discovered no impediments in the McKay household. Alex and Mary were fine parents. He finally settled the case, concluding that Archibald McKay was troubled by nature and not by nurture.

The spritely bridal party burst through the church doors onto the shallow steps under a misty gray rain. Father McGolrick's tulips were in full bloom, and they splashed color on the church's otherwise pale stone façade. McGolrick tended the stems himself, believing the natural beauty softened Greenpoint's otherwise industrial pallor.

The drizzle stopped long enough for William and his sisters—
Margaret, Mamie, Sabine, Sara, Agnes, and Loretta—to stand on the church steps and join the four McKay children—Catherine, Archibald, John, and Anna—and pose for a photograph. Thomas McHale, William's father, owned a Brownie, and he snapped the picture.

"What a brood," John whispered to Anna.

Anna saw a horrific contortion on John's face.

"Sara McHale all but undid my britches," he said with a cringe "right in the middle of Mass, Anna. Did ya see that?"

"Not only the soul needs nourishment, dear brother," Anna swooned. She did her best to roil him.

John sighed. "I should've saved myself the grief."

———

By 1915, a year after William and Catherine's wedding, the newlywed couple welcomed a baby boy into the family. They named him William Joseph, after his father. McKay brothers Archie and John were quick to call the new babe "Little William," explaining that they didn't want to confuse the father with the son. Actually, the devilish McKay boys couldn't resist taking a potshot at their small-size, stuffed-shirt brother-in-law, whom they now relished calling "Big William."

In 1916, one year after little William was born, Catherine and Big William welcomed a second child, a daughter. They named her Catherine. William's youngest sister took to saying baby Catherine was soft "like a kitty cat," and soon enough everyone in the family called the new baby girl "Kitty."

Since her daughter's family was growing ever larger, Mary McKay thought it was time to move. She gently twisted Alex's arm, suggesting the family leave the old Dutch house on the creek and move to a larger apartment in the middle of town. Mary wanted to be closer to

Catherine, and she thought that she could keep a better eye on Archie. Alex had been taking young John to the yards, so he didn't mind making the slightly longer walk to work.

New parents Catherine and William moved to an apartment of suitable size: a two-bedroom, second-floor flat at the corner of North Henry Street and Nassau Avenue in Greenpoint. The apartment was exactly midway between the McKay home, which was on Meeker Avenue at the end of Russell Street, and the McHale home, which lay on Pearsall Street in Blissville.

"An easy walk, either direction, good and fair," William obliged Catherine. He said he'd keep her close to her mother, and he kept his word, but Catherine couldn't help but notice that William made his fair share of walks back to his home, too.

Catherine was very content living at North Henry Street. The apartment overlooked the expansive, leafy Winthrop Park, and if Catherine stood at the edge of her portico window and peered down the street, she could see what seemed like all of Greenpoint. She so loved her perch that overlooked the park that every morning and afternoon she could be seen sitting in the portico window, rocking her child. North Henry Street was a magnificently peaceful place.

———

By 1916, John McKay began an apprenticeship position and worked with his father at Standard Oil. Archie got work driving a delivery truck around Brooklyn. Alex had considered Archie for the apprenticeship job, but he worried the bustling refinery was too dangerous a place for Archie's unfocused mind. Archie could get hurt—or worse, killed—and Alex had to spell out the reality to his oldest son.

"You'll need to find employment elsewhere," Alex said curtly to Archie before offering the apprenticeship to young John.

Archie's pride was cut. He knew he had misbehaved one too many times, and he knew his father didn't trust him, but the rejection was painful.

Johnny's a perfect bloke and I ain't, he thought.

Alex's concerns could be justified, but closer to truth, Alex feared Archie would embarrass him. Alex could ill afford to parade an intoxicated Archibald under the noses of SOCONY bosses. Everyone in town knew Archie hung out in gin mills and associated with dregs. Archie was one who drank until drunk. He soaked his brain to a stupor, and once ossified, he would either use his money to buy the house a round of drinks, or he'd come to blows with whomever was in his way. It all depended on his mood. Usually, after mixing it up with the Greenpoint police, he'd get a good baton beating and wind up in jail. By the youthful age of twenty-three, Archie McKay was well on his way to becoming a lost soul.

———

When his boys were younger, Alex took them to the SOCONY yards so they could see firsthand how hard a man had to toil to earn his living. John was no novice to the refinery's noise, but when he began full-time work, the bone-rattling, nerve-shattering clamor and clang shook him to the core.

Thunderous booms bellowed out from under gas tanks as steel-on-steel thuds reverberated from steam-driven hammers that strained to jam giant pilings into the Newtown Creek's banks. Whenever the high-pressure steam valves released, deafening shrieks of superheated steam spewed, and John had to hold his hands over his ears. The cacophony came from all directions, and confusion abounded.

"Keep yer head on a swivel, son," his father yelled over the din. "There's no getting used to it. You have to focus and concentrate."

The men on Alex's crew showed John how to negotiate the twisted pipes encasing the enormous refinery vats.

"Hold this piece of wood at all times." They stuck a wood stick out in front of themselves. "If one single pipe has a tiny leak," they warned him, "you're a goner."

"Be'fer ya ever knew what happened…" A man groaned and warned. "So take me word."

"Light the torch," Alex barked to his welder. "Keep that arc on that fitting."

The constant hammering above them was deafening.

"You've got to concentrate and stay with the job in front of you, son," Alex yelled into John's ear. "Put the noise behind you."

John thought that impossible.

The welder kept his arc on the pipe as sparks flew from the torch at the bottom of the tank. Alex diligently kept watch, nervously twisting his mustache with his long fingers while looking for mistakes.

"Get in closer, Mullin," Alex ordered. "Hold that pipe for him, Grady."

Suddenly, there was a giant popping sound and a huge bang. A super-heated shockwave blasted past their bodies. John looked down around his legs; he thought he'd been burned, but he wasn't sure. The flames went by so fast. He looked to the other men and saw them all laughing.

"One second in the throes of hell is 'nough fer me," said one convulsing, cherubic Irishman with a heartily chortle.

"Trapped vapor on the bottom," said Alex, his long fingers now wiping soot from his eyes.

They looked one another over and made sure no one's hair was aflame. Once people were sure they were all OK, the welding job continued.

"You've got to complete the job, son, no matter what task you're given."

John soon adapted to the booming and crashing sounds of the re-finery and demonstrated to his father and the bosses that he could com-plete small tasks on his own. He learned welding and pipefitting and learned how the larger refinery operated. Union bosses at SOCONY were pleased, and they told Alex as much. John would get his union card soon.

"He's a fine young man," the shop boss said to Alex. "We'll be hiring him as a pipefitter."

Alex was very pleased. Young John would have steady work—union work. Work that would allow him to get on in life and get settled, get married, raise children, and maybe someday have a home.

The 6:00 p.m. whistle sounded, signaling an end to the first shift. Alex and John plus a group of men assembled near the SOCONY main gate, milling about until everyone collected and could walk up to Meeker Avenue together. They were all friends. Some had worked with Alex for years and some were recent emigrants from Ireland's Ulster Province in the northeast. All were members of the Antrim Hall Society Club and were Catholic men.

John was by far the youngest and certainly the most agile among the group, so as a favor to all the men and to his dah, he collected each man's lunch pail and carried the laden sack up to Meeker Avenue. John was honored he could help his father's coworkers, but more, John was happy he made his father happy.

The everyday banter while strolling up to the Avenue usually cen-tered on refinery work, or sometimes someone told a funny story about the old days in Antrim. But for the better part of a year, the easy banter was rarely heard, and all talk focused on the gruesome war news out of Europe.

All the men had a father, brother, or in some cases a son who'd been scooped up by the British army to fill its desperate need for more men to feed the carnage in Flanders.

Irish males of proper age were conscripted by the British and sent to France. Irish families in America had good reason to worry. In 1916 alone at the Battle of the Somme, 420,000 British army soldiers were either injured or killed. Nearly 25,000 died in one day of fighting. Some 680,000 German forces met the same fate.

"It's a feckin' meat grinder over there," one of the men said to John, and that kind of talk scared him. John was just getting started in life, and he liked the idea of becoming his own man, a man who could earn his own way. He had no interest in military life. All the guys at Antrim Hall gym talked about the war. Some guys wanted to go to France and fight, but most thought the war had nothing to do with America. America is boundless, they said, and the new century was about promise, not war. Why get bogged down in Europe's troubles? President Wilson promised he'd keep America out, and he was reelected in November saying so.

Wilson had managed to calm the trumpeters of intervention when the *Lusitania* was sunk in May 1915. Now in 1917, German U-boats began sinking every ship on the Atlantic, warship or passenger. How could America possibly remain neutral? Day after day, newspapers blared bold headlines of horror and mayhem. Death tolls had gotten so exorbitant that the French and British governments began to lie about the actual numbers. It was only a matter of time before they'd need more men. Where would they look?

Then there was the matter of Mexico. Germany was stirring up trouble on the border, and President Wilson had to warn Mexican nationalists to stay out of Texas. He'd already dispatched the US Army, including New York's "Fighting Irish" 69th Regiment, to the Rio Grande border.

Very few Irish in Greenpoint supported America getting involved in the European war. Certainly they had no interest in fighting to protect the English. Neutrality was the prevailing sentiment, and Wilson used it to run his successful reelection campaign. "He kept us out of war" was his popular slogan.

Wilson played the politics, and he hedged his bets. His Republican opposition, led mostly by former president Teddy Roosevelt, barnstormed the country by clamoring for greater war preparation and warning voters the United States was woefully unprepared. President Wilson acted only to shut Roosevelt up and got Congress to pass the War Preparations Act, a spending bill that bolstered the navy fleet and developed better armaments for the army. However, once the 1916 election passed, Wilson's administration put the War Preparations Act on the back burner.

Alex McKay had read all the horrific news accounts, and he was deeply concerned that his sons, John and Archie, and maybe Catherine's husband, William, were of the right age and would be the men called to serve. William was married and a breadwinner; perhaps he would be exempt. But the last time there were exemptions to the draft, Irish immigrants ended up burning down half of Manhattan and lynched hundreds of innocent Negro men.

"No," Alex said, shaking his head and flattening his mustache, "there will be no exemptions this time."

———

Big William sat in Winthrop Park across from his home wearing a work shirt and tie, but no jacket, enjoying the park's peace and serenity, seemingly without a worry in the world. The sun warmed his back as little William and Kitty played underfoot. He read his newspaper, page after page of news about the European war. Like every man in Greenpoint, William was profoundly worried. "What would happen if America got in?" The question was on everyone's mind.

After the *Lusitania*, William was much in favor of the president's decision to stay out. Wilson was a man of theory, not action. As William understood from supervising the loading of boats, sometimes when working in treacherous waters, little or no action is best.

Nevertheless, conditions out on the Atlantic had gotten much worse. The German kaiser began to sink all ships. There was no way Wilson could keep America out. War was only a matter of time.

William and Catherine hadn't discussed the war, but Catherine knew if war came, her husband and brothers would be the first men conscripted. That thought sickened her. Newspapers reported stories of young men dying by the thousands from gas bombs and machine guns, tank warfare, and airplanes dropping bombs and shooting men from the air. She couldn't imagine anyone she loved so dearly embroiled in such a calamity. She stopped herself from thinking about it.

William felt the same and remained silent on the subject.

As the sun-filled afternoon hours passed, Catherine kept her eyes out over the park and the street below. Earlier, she had noticed a truck parked on Russell Street, and it caught her attention. The truck sat parked just beyond the corner bar Farrell's, and it hadn't moved all day. Something told her that the truck belonged to Archie. Archie never wandered very far beyond Greenpoint. The police usually let him alone if he was quiet.

Catherine opened the bay window and quietly called down to William.

"I'll take the children now," she said softly. William folded his paper and collected the kids. In a moment, he was at the top of the stairs and in the kitchen.

"He's all yours," he said, handing little William to Catherine. "I'm exhausted from all the work." He smiled at his wife.

"Well then, you should take a nap." Catherine reached over and straightened his tie.

William sauntered to the bedroom. "I just might."

Archie strolled out of Farrell's bar on Russell Street and walked the short distance down Nassau Avenue to his sister's apartment on the corner of North Henry. Singing aloud to himself, he darted up her staircase and popped into the open kitchen without warning.

"Little William!" Archie cheered. He grabbed the toddler and spun him up in the air. He smelled of beer.

Catherine quickly took the child from his arms before her husband heard the commotion.

"Hey, Katie," Archie said to Catherine, "would ya have a coin or two for your hard-working brother?" Catherine was always a soft sell. "At least till payday," he added. "I'll get ya back."

William heard Archie from the bedroom and stormed back into the kitchen.

"You've still got deliveries, Archibald?" William was annoyed. He knew what the answer would be. He bristled at Archie's drinking. How many times did he and Catherine have to hear from the Jewish baker, the German butcher, or the English shopkeeper about the Irish problem of drink?

"Ach, William, saving the world again, are you?"

"If yer put yer coins on the collection plate and not on the bar they'd multiply like the fishes."

Archie scoffed. "So that's the bullshit McGolrick's peddling now, eh?"

"Archibald!" Catherine scolded. "Enough!"

"So you've heard the news, I suppose?" Archie changed the subject.

William was skeptical. "What are the pub scholars tellin' you now?"

"Tomorrow, President Wilson will announce America's in the war."

Catherine's heart sank. She fell back into a kitchen chair and grasped little William.

"Stop upsetting your sister!" William shouted. Baby Kitty began to cry.

"And what if I *did* hear from the 'scholars at the pub,' *big* William? Don't mean they're wrong."

"It's not true, Catherine." William held his wife's hand. He stared angrily at Archie and spoke in a calm but commanding voice.

"Get out of here, Archibald!" he demanded. "And don't ever come back."

———

John thought Antrim Hall's gymnasium was the best part of the society hall, period. None of the other county society halls in Greenpoint or in Brooklyn, for that matter, had a gym with the same equipment. Antrim Hall was surely the best.

The hall's directors hired an ex-pugilist Irishman named Ennis O'Shea to run the athletics program. Ennis did a great job attracting young athletes to the gym. He set up a boxing ring and had punching bags, boxing gloves, a wrestling mat, steel weights, medicine balls, and jump rope—everything a young man needed for physical fitness.

John had been going to Antrim Hall since he was a small boy. The first time was with his mother and father, and then eventually he went by himself. Archie stopped going when he was a teen, and Anna and Catherine only went on special days like Saint Patrick's or Easter.

Alex McKay and Mary Black met at Antrim Hall at a dinner dance in 1889 and married one year later. Antrim Hall was an important part of their lives, and it was imperative to share it with their children. Regardless, only John kept going regularly. He attended the dinner dances and the functions, and he met a few nice, marriageable girls, but since he was sixteen, John went to Antrim Hall mostly to use its gym.

John never considered himself a real boxer, but he loved to get into the ring. Ennis O'Shea had taken a liking to the studious, athletic John McKay, and he willingly gave the teen a few lessons. O'Shea also set up sparring sessions for John, and on one Saturday night every other month, O'Shea held a boxing tournament.

John boxed twice in the tournaments, winning once and losing once, but he never dared say anything to Anna or Archie about his fights. If they ever knew that he fought—and if they ever found out he lost—they'd never let him hear the end of it. *Our perfect Johnny got whooped!* He could hear Anna's joyful crowing.

"Jab, jab, jab, left," O'Shea prodded.

John stabbed the heavy punching bag, *rat-ta-tat-tat*.

"Keep your chin up. Keep your eyes on your opponent," O'Shea instructed.

There was an echo at the end of the hallway near the gym entrance. Someone was yelling John's name.

"McKay!" John could hear the echo in the distance.

Martin McSweeney burst into the gym, out of breath.

"Great," John whispered to O'Shea. "It's Greenpoint's mouthiest Mick."

"McKay, have you heard?" McSweeney asked, excitedly.

John and O'Shea stopped to listen.

"The war is on," McSweeney told them. "It's here. America is in. We're in."

CHAPTER 3

April 1917

———

JOHN TURNED ONTO BUSY METROPOLITAN Avenue and joined the crowds of people, horses, wagons, and motorized trucks cramming through Greenpoint's main fare. It was a warm May afternoon, and everyone was outside on the street. Bakeries, butcher shops, fish stores, and fruit and vegetable stands teemed with people.

John weaved around elderly women, prams, and carriages, and past the corner newsboys and the neighborhood goons. *Goin' nowhere, doin' nothing*, John could hear his dah say. He waved hello to the shopkeepers his ma used, and they yelled back over the crowded sidewalk to "say hello to yer ma fer me." John spotted a local police officer standing at his corner beat, and John knew the police officer practiced boxing with Ennis O'Shea. John made a mock fighter's stance as if ready to fight. The police officer laughed and asked John, "How's your dah doin'?" He added, "Alexander McKay is a fine man, John, always remember that."

"My dah's good, Officer McKenna, and we promise we'll keep a better eye on Archibald."

The police officer knowingly smiled and tapped the brim of his hat with his baton.

———

John was in great spirits. He had been offered a permanent job at SOCONY. It would be steady work and a steady paycheck. Now he could consider marriage and children. "But not so fast up that avenue." He laughed to himself.

He sauntered uphill and east toward Meeker Avenue toward home, then he saw Archie's truck parked off the side of the street and half up on the sidewalk. "Why's he so damn defiant?" John loved his brother dearly, but never truly understood what made Archie tick. From outward appearances John and Archie looked very similar, both boys having their dah's bright-green eyes (the girls had their ma's big blues), but inwardly John and Archie were completely different men. John considered most people to be decent and honest, while Archie was convinced everyone had an angle or a scheme, and they couldn't be trusted. And if the subject of the Catholic Church ever came up, forget it. John was filled by deep faith, while Archie thought the church and its litany of rules was a bunch of horseshit.

John dodged across the busy avenue behind an ice wagon and past a cart, then he waited for a motorcar to pass as he made his way toward Archie's truck, a modern GMC flatbed with a polished maroon cab and shiny gold letters on the door.

"McGiven's Parts and Repair," it read. Archie spent the day shipping broken and repaired machine tools. He was free to roam Greenpoint all day, and that kind of work suited him well.

John had to give it to Archie. He learned to drive a truck, he was good with motors, and he'd become a pretty good mechanic. "He'll always have work," said their dah.

And roamin' 'round Brooklyn, John thought, *ain't too bad, neither.*

John approached Archie's truck and saw a dozen or so men hunched shoulder-to-shoulder in a circle, raucously laughing. Some guy in the middle of the circle wore a colander pot on his head and held a mop handle over his shoulder like a rifle. He marched up and down the sidewalk shouting, *"Ein, schvie, tri..."* while stiffly swinging his arms like a Kraut soldier. The men around him roared with laughter.

John broke into the circle and saw Archie. Archie had everyone rolling.

"Guten tag, Kaiser Johann," Archie shouted upon seeing John. He saluted John with the mop and the men laughed even harder.

"You're a loon, Arch." John shook his head and smiled. Archie could be very funny drunk or sober, and John assessed Archie hadn't had a drink yet thank God.

Archie kept up his Teutonic persona and spoke to John in pigeon German.

"Herr bruter," he yelled, *"du vant der vide zie vagon machine?"*

John had never driven a motor vehicle. He rode on a motorbus once before, but *vide der vagon machine?* Yessireee!

Archie tossed the colander and mop into the back of the flatbed as the brothers climbed into the truck's cab. Archie showed John how to start the engine and put the weighty vehicle into gear.

"Push down the choke," he instructed. "Let go of the brake, a little bit on the gas. Ease up on the clutch. You got it, Johnny. You got it."

John drove the shiny motor truck up Metropolitan Avenue to Meeker Avenue and turned north. The McKay brothers made quite a sight driving in the modern machine. Two dashingly handsome young men rolled past the horses and carts with graceful ease and sped under the tree-lined street. The sun flickered its light down upon them. They looked like the very image of a new, modern America and the twentieth century.

"Johnny," Archie shouted over the rumble, "have you seen Chaplin's new picture?"

"Nah," said John, his eyes fixed on busy Meeker Avenue. "Any good?"

"You've got to see it, Johnny. It's called *The Immigrant*. Oh, you'll laugh. It's very funny. Chaplin's on an immigrant ship and he's sailin' fer New York. The ship's rockin' back and forth, and Chaplin keeps slidin' across the deck, bumpin' into all the pretty ladies. They get all indignant with him—ya know how that is?"

John drew a wide smile. "I'm *sure* you do."

Archie went on. "Chaplin is hanging over the side of the ship, and yer think he's sick to his stomach from all the rockin', but then he turns 'round, and he got a big fish wigglin' in his mouth, caught with his bare teeth…It's so funny, Johnny, ya gotta see it."

"He's always good fer a belly laugh."

"I asked Ma if her ride was like that, like Chaplin's," said Archie.

"What did she say?"

"She said it was worse."

"What about Dah?" John asked.

"He said he slept all the way."

The brothers laughed aloud. The thought of their dah snoring away in the middle of an ocean monsoon was no surprise. He could sleep through anything.

————

John stepped into the parlor, then Archie. Their father, Alex, sat alone in his chair, his pipe unlit, the afternoon newspaper folded on the low table beside him. His eyes were red, and he stared blankly into the dark parlor, repetitively rubbing his long finger across his mustache. He'd been weeping.

"Dah?" Archie called out. They'd never seen him look so grim.

"My boys," Alex said, mournfully. He let go of his mustache and brought his hand up to his eyes; he could not stop his trembling. The boys didn't know their mother was sobbing inconsolably in her bedroom. She too had read the news.

John picked up the folded paper from the low table and read from the headline.

"A proclamation establishes conscription," he read aloud, "whereas, Congress has enacted and the president has on this, the eighteenth day of May, one thousand, nine hundred and seventeen, approved a law…all male persons between the ages of twenty-one and thirty, both inclusive, shall be subject to registration for the purpose of conscription into the Armed Forces of the United States."

"Let me see that." Archie took the paper from John and began to read for himself.

"It'll be OK, Dah." John put his hand on his father's arm. "It's just the Huns, Dah, not the devil. We'll get there, and they'll run before we fire the first shot."

Alex patted John's hand but didn't speak. He understood what was about to transpire. This war, which so greedily reaped Europe's youth in its bloom, was once in a distant place, far away, but it was now firmly planted at his doorstep.

His sons, boys at the cusp of manhood and soon to flourish in marriage and fatherhood, would be ripped away by the roots. Their lives would be circumvented and thwarted only to satisfy the bloodthirst of old men. The European war had arrived in America, and the McKay family could not avoid it.

"Well, looky here," said Archie. "They've got us broken up into groups."

He flipped and folded the paper and kept reading.

"Category One," he began. "Eligible and liable for military service. That's me and you, Johnny." Archie smirked. "And Category Four," he said, his face changing to a sneer, "exempted due to extreme hardship. The poor fellow, who is married and has a kid. He'd be too broke to fight, they claim."

Archie cocked his head to the side and feigned an Irish brogue.

"Somebody musta' told Big William a war was brewin'."

"Don't worry about William," said John. "Do you want Kitty without her father?"

Archie threw the paper onto the sofa.

"I've got to go, boys," said Alex, excusing himself. "Ya ma needs me." He rose slowly from his chair.

"Is Ma home?" John asked.

Alex didn't answer. The two brothers watched their father wobble across the parlor like an old, broken man. They'd never seen him like this before and it scared them. Archie put his hand on his brother's shoulder.

"He's afraid for us," he said.

"Yes, brother," said John. "So let's make him proud."

CHAPTER 4

April 1917

———

William Donovan (left) and Father Francis P. Duffy

JOHN CARDINAL FARLEY SAT AT his desk and shifted his rotund body toward his secretary. Raising one stubby finger, he motioned to have his window shut. A motor vehicle accident on the street below had become too distracting, and he couldn't think. *The automobile has changed Manhattan forever*, he mused.

"Is Father Duffy here?" he asked.

"Yes, Your Eminence. Father is waiting."

Cardinal Farley was satisfied making Duffy wait. He didn't care much for the "high-minded" priest or his New York literary friends. He thought Father Duffy was a little too elitist and self-serving and not particularly obliged to the drudgery of parish life.

Farley read his predecessor's report on Duffy and knew all about his *New York Review* magazine crowd. The old archbishop didn't stand much for modernist Catholic views, and he disbanded the *Review* writer group by exiling them to the farthest corners of the New York Diocese. Duffy was unceremoniously sent to a storefront church in the Bronx, a place for spiritual conquest, maybe, but intellectual death for sure.

Cardinal Farley was suspicious of Duffy's brandished Americanism. Duffy was a Canadian, after all, not even an Irish American. He was certain that Duffy came to New York strictly to make a name for himself.

Oddly enough, Cardinal Farley ended up thrusting Father Duffy onto the front pages of New York's newspapers. In 1915, when Farley assigned Duffy as chaplain to the New York National Guard's 69th Infantry Regiment, also known as the Fighting Irish, President Wilson had professed neutrality in the European war, and the 69th Regiment had dwindled in size to five hundred men. Farley assigned Duffy to the 69th to give the high-minded intellectual priest a good dose of the confounding perplexity that the stubborn and plebeian Irish working class was famous for.

Now Duffy was back from Mexico. "With the dust still on his boots, no doubt," Farley earlier remarked to his inner circle.

In 1916, Poncho Villa and other Mexican nationalists were creating havoc on the Texas border, and President Wilson needed a ready army to counter the trouble. Just like when President Lincoln relied on the Irish 69th Regiment to repel the Confederates at Bull Run, Wilson deployed the 69th to Texas on very short notice. Duffy found himself in the dusty, wind-driven Lone Star State, corralling a rough-and-tumble

Irish regiment that was short on discipline, lacked morality, and, in his mind, included very poor representatives of Irish Americans in general.

In the first week of the 69th's Texas deployment, anti-Catholic New York newspapers extrapolated upon minor accounts of disobedience and bad behavior and splashed headlines detailing this Irish debauchery onto every street corner newspaper in New York.

Chaos was the expected norm for the "Irish hooligans in uniform." Anti-Catholic editorialists hastily joined in and accused the Catholic regiment of taking its orders from Rome. "What respect for American values should we expect from a garrison of papist legionnaires?" questioned a writer at one unscrupulous gazette.

Duffy was quick to take action. He contacted his newspaper-writing friends in New York and Brooklyn, and they published his eloquent rebuttal letters that refuted the scandalous reports. He argued that the Irish were patriots serving at the behest of the president and protecting the nation's border.

At the same time, Duffy cracked down on the "confounding" Irish and demanded discipline. He enlisted help from Colonel Haskell, the commanding officer of the 69th, and forced sobriety on the men. Duffy reminded the soldiers of their fine regimental heritage and sternly accused them of besmirching the memories of the regiment's Civil War honorees.

"You represent the Irish and America wherever you go," he scolded them. He threw down his garrison cover and kicked it across the dusty ground. "Act like men, dammit. Not boys!"

The men of the 69th responded, and soon Duffy had them under his potency. Confessions went up, attendance at Sunday Mass went up, and imbibing alcohol was no longer a highly celebrated daily ritual.

Esprit de corps in the 69th Regiment soared.

John Cardinal Farley heard all about the 69th in Texas. He realized that Duffy, his Bronx exile, understood better than anyone what was at stake for the Irish Catholic Church and the archdiocese of New York City in the upcoming European war. Farley needed Duffy and his connections to the press, the politicos, and the people for Farley's New York archdiocese to succeed.

By 1917, events were moving quickly. Imperial German diplomats in Mexico urged Mexican nationalists to invade US southern border states. British government intelligence intercepted a telegram sent to Mexico's German ambassador, Zimmerman. In the dispatch, the Germans encouraged Mexico to attack Texas. The story leaked to the press, and the Zimmerman episode quickly became the final straw for most Americans. President Wilson was compelled to act.

On April 6, 1917, Wilson made his case for America's entering the European war and spoke before a joint session of Congress. Shortly afterward, the Conscription Act was signed, and the draft began.

Back in 1863, the then New York archbishop, John Cardinal McCloskey, took the reins of the New York archdiocese, right in the middle of the Civil War. Irish Catholic immigrants strode down gangplanks of immigrant ships and proceeded directly to the Irish 69th Regiment of New York. They donned Union uniforms and, without reservation, fought for the Union. By the end of the war, the Irish as a group received the most Medals of Honor and had the highest number of casualties. Archbishop McCloskey had good reason to be confident that his church would benefit greatly from such unflinching Irish Catholic demonstrations of patriotism, but then the Civil War Conscription Act was passed, and the New York City draft riots erupted. Any goodwill toward the Catholic Church or its new Irish citizens evaporated.

During the Civil War, Irish men were dying in much greater numbers than any other group of fighters. Irish immigrants began to become suspicious of Know-Nothing partisans, who were numerous in New York City's politics. It was believed that the Know-Nothings were the ones who conspired to send Irish men before any others into the slaughter fields of Maryland, Virginia, and Pennsylvania.

The Conscription Act was the final blow for the naturally suspicious Irish. The act allowed for a conscription exemption. A man paid a simple sum and avoided being drafted into the Union army. For wealthy men or those who had regular work, the sum needed to purchase an exemption was within reach. However, for the destitute Irish men who scrounged for every morsel of survival, the amount might well have been a king's ransom.

Upon the passage of the Conscription Act, Irish immigrants in New York City convulsed. A large portion of Manhattan was burned to the ground, and upward of two hundred free Negro men were apprehended by riotous Irish marauders and hanged.

After the riots, there was no goodwill left for the Irish or their papist church. Most of the heroic Irish actions performed on the battlefields of the Civil War were left forgotten or relegated to Irish self-memorials and self-celebrations to this day.

———

"Ask Father Duffy to come in," said the cardinal.

The tall, lanky priest with alert, observant eyes entered the archbishop's office. Duffy leaned forward and reached for His Eminence's plump hand. Clutching it, he kissed the cardinal's ring.

"Look at you," said the cardinal.

Duffy was wearing his 69th Regiment uniform, the Texas dust still on his boots.

"Thank you for seeing me, Your Eminence."

"Sit, Francis, sit." The cardinal motioned to a set of wingback chairs in the corner.

"Tea, Francis?"

Duffy raised his eyebrow before responding.

"Mine comes with Irish whiskey."

"Francis," the cardinal continued, "I want to thank you for your quick response to those slanderous reports the newspapers printed. It could have become a rather large problem had you not nipped it in the bud."

"Yes, Your Eminence," said Duffy. "I saw the dangers and implications rather quickly."

"I understand what can happen," the cardinal said, nodding. "I was a secretary priest for Archbishop McCloskey in this very office during the draft riots."

"I see," said Duffy. "I assure you, Your Eminence, such behavior will not flourish on my watch."

"The 69th, Francis. What is the status of the regiment? I would suppose that after Mexico, many of the men were discharged and returned to civilian life."

"We are at five hundred men, Your Eminence, down from two thousand."

"Has Colonel Haskell received correspondence from the army concerning the recent conscription order?"

"We desire to remain an Irish regiment and to keep our Irish complexion. I have made my opinions known to the senior staff that I do not wish to reenlist the majority of the men we took to Mexico. Some are suitable, but I'd just as soon leave the majority of that lot at the pier."

"Exactly, Francis," said the cardinal. "I believe my concerns and yours are very similar. I think this European war will have grave consequences for our country and for our church. Who we send to represent Irish Catholics will be of utmost importance."

"I've considered the issues," said Duffy, "and if I may offer suggestions…"

"All ears, Francis."

"While in Mexico, I met an army officer named William Donovan. He was with a militia unit out of Buffalo. He's our man, Your Eminence, and I beg of you to correspond with the governor to get him to the 69th. He's keenly interested."

"His qualifications?"

"He earned an undergraduate and a law degree from Columbia. He was a varsity footballer and captain of the team. He is a very fit and athletic man, a natural leader, someone who will set a very high standard. He's connected to Governor Al Smith's people, and he's a savvy fellow who is interested in propagating the faith and advancing the Irish. He's deeply patriotic. His love for the United States is unmatchable."

"The Union and the Constitution serve to protect us, Francis. Our patriotism must be unquestionable. This country must know we are Americans first and foremost."

Farley received his tea.

"The fathers of the Holy Cross at Notre Dame College," he continued, "called in every favor to erect that statue of Father Corby in Gettysburg. No establishment organization would recognize him, not after the riots."

Duffy had planned to craft his chaplaincy after Corby's. He wanted to use the Civil War chaplain's service as a blueprint for his own.

"I need Donovan, Your Eminence," Duffy pleaded. "He doesn't want a high rank and would rather serve among the men. He feels he'd be much more effective there."

The cardinal nodded silently.

"We are reviewing our recruitment efforts," Duffy continued. "We want to focus on the county societies and look for upstanding athletic young men there. No more with the old sods. It's the youthful sort we can train and impress upon."

"I will send a dispatch to the parishes and have them each make a list of ten or more suitable candidates. That should give you a leg up."

"Thank you, Your Eminence," said Duffy. "The army requires us to be manned at two thousand before they will federalize the regiment. Colonel Haskell and his staff are pushing to be the very first deployed to France. He says it's important to keep the reputation of the 69th intact. Sort of the exuberance of Corcoran and Meagher, without the politics."

"Ah, rascals they were."

"I've been assured the conscription will be implemented without any shenanigans this time. No exemptions. It will be straightforward and clear."

"For that much we should be grateful, Francis."

———

The brass band marched down Metropolitan Avenue while flags and banners waved. Uniformed soldiers with bullhorns shouted from the sidewalks, urging men to sign up and fight against the kaiser. "Stop the imperial Germans. Be the first to fight!"

"They're killing women and children with gas bombs," some of them shouted through the bullhorns.

"They're sinking every ship on the sea!" shouted others.

"American men must fight. Show the Huns who's tough."

Recruitment posters got plastered all around Greenpoint. Men handed out flyers on street corners, and some spoke at movie houses before the picture. Army recruiters stood around anyplace young men congregated, sometimes even outside the church on Sunday.

However, inside the heavily ethnic Irish neighborhood of Greenpoint, not all the anti-German rhetoric settled on receptive ears.

"Why would any Irishman fight for the English?" was the strongest and most pervasive sentiment. It was a good question. The Irish had a long history of squabbles with the constitutional crown. Why should Irish blood be spilled to defend it now?

The recruiters of Irish men heard the rebuttals and readily adapted their slogans. The message on the streets, the flyers, and the posters quickly changed.

"Defend America's honor! Defend liberty!" was the new somber conveyance. The sinking of ships on the sea and the drowning of innocent women and children led to strong, acrimonious feelings about the Germans. In an immigrant enclave like Greenpoint, more than half its inhabitants had crossed the Atlantic, and they had fresh memories of the fearful and turbulent passage.

The kaiser was acting like an international bully, and the imperial German government sounded brutish and smug. Britain and France, on the other hand, were defending free people, a message all freedom-loving Americans could embrace, including the Irish.

Allying with England and France was the only way to stop the kaiser's wrath. "Show us your American pride!" was now shouted through bullhorns. "Show us your Fighting Irish spirit!"

Boxing coach Ennis O'Shea had asked John to come by Antrim Hall on Thursday night "to meet a priest," he said. O'Shea had rounded up a group of Greenpoint men and asked them to come to the club that same night. He told the men that Father Duffy, the chaplain of the Fighting Irish Regiment of the New York National Guard, wanted to speak to them.

"You're in a select group," O'Shea said to each man privately, "and Father Duffy only wants to speak to select men."

Everyone contacted by O'Shea understood it was a recruitment pitch for the 69th, but out of respect for Ennis and the Catholic priest, everyone planned to attend.

Young men were being forced into a rather hasty decision. The Conscription Act passed on May 18, 1917, and the first round of mandatory draft registration for Group One (twenty-one to thirty years old, unmarried, no dependents) was a short three weeks later on June 5. If a man didn't volunteer for a home state regiment by June 4, he would effectively be throwing his name randomly into a huge hat and end up anywhere the army wanted. It made better sense to volunteer for a local regiment, so the question quickly became which one.

Martin McSweeney, the mouthy Mick, insisted the 69th Regiment was the only outfit for an Irishman.

"Can yer imagine," he openly questioned those around him at Antrim Hall, "giving yer confession to an English-born Baptist minister, who, after he's done listenin' to your depravity, turns around and writes a love letter to his wife?"

John knew a little bit about the Fighting Irish Regiment. Everyone in Greenpoint remembered a story or two about Irish bravery in the Civil War and everyone heard of Corcoran and Meagher. John knew Irish fighters were the most decorated men by the war's end and that the brave Irish immigrants of the 69th had the highest number of casualties.

John remembered, when he was a kid, seeing an old man from the 69th whose left leg was missing below the knee. He spent his last days sitting quietly in Winthrop Park. Sometimes he had a cup out for coins, but mostly he just wallowed away the hours, rekindling old exploits if another veteran happened to be around. All the neighbors in Greenpoint knew him as a hero in a great war, but mostly nobody took the time to interrupt his silence.

John knew about Father Corby from Father McGolrick. "He was a priest's priest," McGolrick said, and John thought if he had to go to war, going to war with Catholic lads would be good.

On Thursday night, John took his familiar stroll up Metropolitan Avenue to North Greenpoint and Antrim Hall. O'Shea was there as were about thirty other men John's age. O'Shea led the men to the main ballroom and seated them two rows across in front of the low stage.

"Wait here," he told them, and he left.

The empty stage was filled with American flags and Irish banners, mostly from County Antrim. A minute passed by before a tall, lanky figure wearing a US Army uniform made his entrance through the curtains and onto center stage. He wore a brown leather belt around his waist and a leather harness across his chest. This was a harness worn only by American army officers, but he also had the collar of a Catholic priest.

He stood at attention with red, white, and blue flags laced with emerald-green banners draped behind him. His legs remained tight together, and his arms were straight down except for his left, which held his hat tucked neatly under his elbow. He appeared as if he were saluting his audience.

"I am Major Francis P. Duffy," he began, his voice echoing through the mostly empty ballroom. "I am the chaplain of New York's 69th Regiment in Manhattan. I am a Catholic priest, so you may call me 'Father Duffy' and not 'Major Duffy.'"

The men relaxed in the chairs.

"Men," Duffy continued, "as you know, the president of the United States has called our nation to war. The time has come to mobilize and prepare military regiments across the country and make young men just like you ready to fight and defeat a German army that has been at this game for over three years."

Duffy held his hat over his stomach.

"You will be called to war, men. There is no escaping it. Your fate is set." Duffy lifted his hat high. "Whether you want it or not, you will fight in this European war."

He let that thought sink in.

"What I offer you men," he continued, "is a Catholic outfit, an Irish outfit, and a Catholic priest like myself, who'll stand by you all the way from the trenches of France to the victory parade down Fifth Avenue when you come home a victorious warrior."

Duffy walked closer to the line of chairs.

"I have requested you men," he confided, "because I and the officers in the Sixty-Ninth want to build the finest regiment of Irish fighters America has ever seen."

John felt a pride and excitement shoot through his body.

"Your pastors have told us you are the very best men of your parish. Mr. O'Shea has vouched for each and every one of you. You are the finest, most upstanding young men Greenpoint has to offer—athletic, intelligent, serious-minded Irish Catholic men." Duffy stomped his foot on the stage. "We want to build a regiment teeming with the finest, most upstanding Irish Catholic men New York has to offer, but I need your help.

"I know you've heard of the Fighting Irish," Duffy said. "You've heard of our history, the bravery of Irish men who, just as you shall, stood tall and faced their destinies with confidence and pride."

Duffy's voice lowered.

"Those Irish men put their stamp on America's history," he explained. "Those men, poor Irish immigrants, all rewrote a chapter of this nation's story. They forever changed words many wished interpreted as '*most* men are created equal,' and they fought bloody battles and died so that those words shall forever mean exactly what they say, '*All* men are created equal.'"

Duffy boomed.

"How do you think our God in heaven has judged such men? Poor men, who fought and died to end the enslavement of his children."

Take it, no more, John remembered.

"I believe our God would greatly approve of such men, and I am supremely confident he has bestowed his grace on them in eternity. I need you to join me," Duffy pleaded earnestly. "You are all good Irish boys from Greenpoint, but the Sixty-Ninth Regiment wants to make you great Irish men from America. Put your stamp on history and fight for free, liberty-loving people. I will go with you. I will be by your side. I will return with you when your duty is done. If our Lord calls you, and it is your turn, I will absolve you. I will hear your confession, and I will give you a Catholic burial. No other outfit, no other Regiment, but the Irish Regiment of New York can offer you that."

Duffy walked down the set of steps to the line of men.

"Take this card," he said, giving one to each man. "If you choose to join the Sixty-Ninth on June fourth, show us this card, and we will get you through the process faster."

When Duffy finished dispensing the cards, he addressed the men once more. He stood at attention again, his cover tucked under his elbow, his long legs pinned together.

"Let's close with the Lord's Prayer," he said.

The men stood and bowed their heads. With numerous flags of the United States and countless banners of County Antrim behind him, Father Duffy led the men in prayer. Once finished, the men blessed themselves with the sign of the cross.

John had no doubts. On Monday, June 4, he'd go to the armory on Lexington Avenue at Twenty-Sixth Street in Manhattan and join the Fighting Irish of New York. He tucked the card Father Duffy gave him safely into his back pocket and fastened the button closed.

CHAPTER 5

June 1917–July 1917

———

ERIN GO BRAGH

JOHN SAT ON THE EDGE of the parlor sofa next to his father's chair, beaming with newfound confidence. "When me and Arch are done with this war, the whole world will be a better place. We're gonna beat those Huns till there ain't no more fight in 'em. No more wars, Dah, only peace. You'll see."

John pointed to the toddler. "Little William will know nothin' but sunny days. When we're done with them Krauts, no more rye loaves— just good 'ol Irish soda bread."

Alex sat in his parlor chair, toking his pipe. He hoped his son was right. Whoever was filling his head with these notions of world affairs, he didn't know, but army and guardsmen were everywhere in the city, stirring up patriotism. Some of it must have rubbed off.

All the better, Alex considered. The boys were going "over there," as everyone started to say. Filling them with confidence wasn't a bad thing. In fact, it was a good thing. All Americans needed to get behind the lads. The German kaiser had to be stopped. America's entering the war was the right thing to do.

"You're definitely joining the Sixty-Ninth, John?" Alex asked his son. "No other regiments?"

"Only the Sixty-Ninth, Dah," John said. "The Irish Sixty-Ninth or nothin' else."

"Well, you're in fine company, son." Alex pointed to the afternoon newspaper. "Cardinal Farley is callin' on all Catholic young men to enlist. He says that the 'patriotism of Catholics is to be tested in this war. No doubt who he's recruitin' fer."

"No doubt," John agreed. "Ennis O'Shea said they're workin' to keep the Sixty-Ninth Irish and Catholic. Ennis said Father Duffy's in on it and the Laymen's League is in on it, but who knew the cardinal was the ringleader?"

They laughed.

Archie breezed through the front door, but not before Mary looked at him once over. She suspected that her son did not know she even did it, but Archie always noticed.

Archie was sober. He'd been sober for over a week.

"Army life's puttin' the fear of God in him," Mary shared with Alex. "Very sad, but true."

She had come to terms with the conscription of her two boys. She simply denied the expanding war was a fact. She put it out of her mind as best she could and stopped reading any newspapers. She insisted that

Alex keep his papers and magazines out of sight because she didn't want to see anything about the war or even things that could remind her of it. "The boys are joining the army to get some good discipline, especially Archibald. That's all. They won't even leave New York."

The thought of life in the army *was* putting the fear of God in Archie. He didn't want to end up in France by himself with people he didn't know—or worse, people who didn't know him. Fighting a war with fellow Irish Catholic men had a sudden agreeable appeal. He was going to enlist with his brother. If John wanted to join the 69th, he would join, too.

"You can't just show up, Archibald," Mary said, objecting to Archie's presumption he could join the 69th.

"Yes I can," he answered defiantly, "and yes, I will."

"But Johnny's got a card, Archibald," Mary implored. "They're asking him," she said, pointedly, "not you."

John jumped in. "Anyone can join, Ma. It's not like I've been blessed by the pope or knighted by the ghost of Corcoran."

"Don't be wise to yer ma," Alex warned.

Mary persisted. "Archibald, I don't know why you think you can just stroll off the street and join the most elite regiment in New York."

"Oh, now you're an expert on the elite regiments of New York, are you?"

"No more, Archibald," Alex scolded him. "I won't have that."

Mary had had enough as well. She wasn't about to have another debate with Archie and his crazy ideas.

"What if they don't accept you?" she said sternly. "Then what? Have you thought of that?"

In fact, Archie had thought about it. He had an alternative plan, but he kept it to himself. Drivers at his job told him about the 47th Regiment in Brooklyn. The 47th was for men like him: handy in carpentry or good with motor mechanics.

"The army needs men who ca-n fix a truck, Arch," a fellow driver who joined the 47th told him. "You'd be a natural for that outfit, McKay."

Archie had become a good motor mechanic, and the thought of bettering his skill in the army, war or not, appealed to him. Though he still wanted to enlist with John, he kept his options open to the 47th. Besides, if his mother and father knew he had ideas about motor mechanics, they'd find a way to make his idea sound dumb. He kept the 47th to himself and said nothing about it.

"Monday morning, Arch," John looked at him squarely. "Seven o'clock, sharp, Arch. You can't be late, brother. *Seven o'clock* in the morning. You got it?"

"Yeah, yeah," Archie answered John, but a pugnacious gleam was alit in his eye. "Seven a.m. at the armory, Twenty-Sixth and Lex."

———

For the rest of the day, Archie drank at McGee's on Metropolitan Avenue until he was stone drunk. He boasted to everyone within earshot that he and his brother, John, were "joinin' the "Fightin' Irish," and then he added, "We're goin' to git the kaiser all by ourselves."

"We'll be marchin' down Fifth Avenue," he drunkenly professed, "with medals on our chests. One fer killin' the most Krauts, another fer bein' the most brave, and one big, shiny medal for puttin' a bullet through the kaiser's bean and knockin' that silly chicken pot off his fat head."

"Shut yer gob, McKay," Fergus McMann, a regular, shouted from his barstool.

"The Sixty-Ninth doesn't want the likes of you, Archie McKay," said Berti Mullin, another regular.

"Yeah, they will," retorted Archie. "You'll be readin' about the McKay men of Greenpoint. Soon enough."

"I remember readin' about your surreptitious incarceration, Archibald," Fergus McMann prodded. Everyone in the bar laughed.

Archie became bored and grew tired of the grunts and grumbles from the old sots like McMann and Berti Mullin.

"What in hell do they know?" he reasoned in his addled brain. He thought he should go to Williamsburg. There, he drunkenly concluded, he would tell the Krauts off right to their faces. Archie and Johnny McKay were goin' "over there," and they we're gonna kill Germans.

Archie moved impulsively and stumbled out of the bar and into his truck. He drove down Kent Avenue along the edge of the East River to the south end of Greenpoint below the Williamsburg Bridge, where suddenly Irish names became German names and places like McGee's and Farrell's became Das Stein Haus and Das Bier Keller.

Archie stopped his truck at Das Bier Keller under the bridge and staggered into the Germanic neighborhood watering hole. He managed to get himself to the end of the long bar, stumbling, but without falling down. The men in the quiet Keller immediately noticed him.

The *Bier Meister* kept the peace and handed Archie a stein of lager. Archie gulped the beer and placed his empty glass on the bar.

"Who drinks this piss, anyway?" he shouted loud enough for the men around him to hear.

They ignored him.

Having gotten no response, Archie was dissatisfied. He looked down the bar, hardly able to stand upright and unable to focus on a single face. He only saw Krauts...nothing but Krauts.

"I'm goin' to France!" he yelled, shattering the dead quiet. "And I'm gonna kill Germans!" His voice was now full-throated. "And when I'm done makin' you Kraut pussies pee yer britches," he gloated, unaware that he was outnumbered by much bigger men, "I'll have yer runnin' back to yer Mutti's teat."

"Surprise, surprise," piped a patron from the corner, his Teutonic intonation sounding naturally sardonic. "An Irish drunk. This one must have fallen off his barstool."

Everyone in the Bier Keller laughed.

"Yer a bunch of pussies," Archie shot back. "Why won't yer go home and fight fer yer lovin' kaiser?"

A tall man got in behind Archie and wrapped his muscular arm around Archie's neck. Two others joined in and the men lifted Archie off his feet. Holding him like a battering ram, they carried the rambunctious Irishman to the front door and tossed him into the street.

They wiped their hands of him and went back inside. No point disrupting the peace or foregoing their *gute Bier*, no need to beat up an ossified Mick.

Archie lay in the gutter, aching all over. He became dizzy and vomited down the sewer drain. He rolled to his side and, without getting up from the scum-filled street, he passed out, his truck parked a few feet away.

———

John was up early, washed and dressed in his Sunday clothes. The trip to the Manhattan Armory from Greenpoint was a labyrinth of trolleys, a ferry, and a train. He couldn't afford to miss any connections.

Archie was nowhere to be found. *He's screwing up,* John thought, but he said nothing to his parents, who were both awake and now in the kitchen.

Alex and John were typically out the door before sunrise, and Mary normally made her men breakfast before they left for the yards. This morning's routine was no different, and so far, neither Mary nor Alex asked about Archie. Anna too was awake and stirring. She wanted to wish her brothers good luck before they went off to the Manhattan Armory.

"Where's Archie?" Anna whispered from John's bedroom doorway.

John shrugged and cinched his belt. He didn't know, and he didn't have time to delve into Archie's mayhem. *No foolin' around now,* he thought to himself. Sorry, Arch, you'll have to fend for yer self.

John came into the kitchen and kissed his ma on the cheek, no different than any morning of any day. Mary made eggs and toast and put a few extra strips of bacon on his plate.

"It'll keep you," she said.

John saw the redness on the edges of her eyes, and it made him sad. He didn't want to upset his mother—he never did—but here he was, enlisting to protect the whole world, and he couldn't even protect his own mother from a broken heart. He hated the feeling.

Neither Alex nor Mary said a word about Archie. They decided before John came down not to upset him or give him anything more to think about. It was simply a matter of time before Archie would turn up.

Anna came to the breakfast table, and John could see that she too had her turn with the tears.

"I'm very proud of you, John," Anna said, putting her hand on his. "Seriously, my brother, I am so deeply proud of you."

"Thank you, Anna," said John.

"Truth be known," Anna added, batting her eyes, "if us women could pick up a rifle, I'd go over there and shoot those Kraut fuckers, too."

"Anna!" Alex barked.

Mary looked to her husband and shook her head vigorously. "Where does she get it?"

"It's just how I feel," said Anna, unashamed.

"As do I," John said with a laugh, amused at Anna's brashness. "As do I."

———

By 6:45 a.m., a crowd of young Irish men had gathered outside the 69th Regiment Armory on Lexington Avenue. They filled the sidewalks and spilled onto Twenty-Sixth Street. They were twenty-one to thirty years old, unmarried, and no dependents. These men wanted to be the first to enlist in the regiment and be the first to go "over there."

Many came with friends, and some had the invitation cards that Father Duffy handed out. They stood quiet with nervous excitement. The bullhorn shouts of "Stop the Kaiser" and "Defend Liberty" had now died down, and in what should have been a boisterous and rowdy collection of brash American youth, there was total silence.

The men began to self-organize and lined up along the imposing stone armory walls and down the sidewalk, eager to commence with military-style order and discipline. All the men wore suit jackets, ties, and shined shoes. Their hair was trimmed short, and their faces were clean-shaven. They were ready to join the Fighting Irish of New York.

John jumped in line and scoured the crowd. There was no sign of Archie. *Not this time, Arch,* he thought, *no more childishness.* The thought of abandoning his brother upset him, but John sensed that enlisting in the 69th and preparing for the war in France meant he could no longer be part of Archie's recklessness. From this day forward, John knew he had to be a man, stalwart and reliable. For once, he traversed the ramparts of the National Guard Armory—there would be no going back. He and Archie were now on divergent paths. The regiment would demand all his time and attention, and he could no longer avail himself the time to help his beloved, troubled brother.

"You're one to wear yer thoughts on yer face," said a singsong Irishman in a wispy brogue. John was surprised by the intrusion.

"Daniel Buckley," said the singsong man. He wore a wide smile on a cherubic, almost effeminate face. He put his hand out for John to shake.

"John McKay," said John. He recognized the brogue as southern Irish, not from the north like his mother and father.

"Whar ya frum?" Buckley asked.

"Saint Cecilia's, Brooklyn," said John. "You know it?"

"I've been in America five years now," Buckley answered, "but I can't be firm and make claim I am familiar with all the parishes of this grand city."

"Greenpoint," John added. "And you?" he asked.

"Daniel Buckley of Ballydesmond, near Cork in the south. Are you familiar with it?"

"Only what my folks have said."

"Never in Ireland, for you?"

"I'm an American, Buckley."

"Aye, an American signing up for an Irish regiment."

"And you, Buckley? An Irishmen signing up fer an American regiment?" *Not who we are, but how we are,* John remembered.

"Aye," said Buckley, "I suppose we're both in a conundrum. Who is it yer lookin' fer, McKay?"

"My brother."

"Aye, McKay. We all have one in the family. The wayward soul, the black sheep."

Spotting Archie from the corner of his eye, John popped out of the line so Archie could see him. Archie was badly disheveled: his face unshaven, his hair uncombed, and his shirt untucked and stained with beer.

John pulled Archie into the line. "Arch, you can't come here lookin' like you've been out with the alley cats." John didn't bother to ask Archie where he'd been. John knew where Archie had been.

"They don't give a shit what I look like," Archie barked, spewing a sickly odor. "They just want my ass to sign up and fight."

"I'm not so sure, Arch," John warned his brother. He grabbed Archie by the shoulders and tucked in his shirt, fixed his collar, and flattened his hair. In comparison to the dapper, bright-eyed applicants lined up and down the city block, Archie looked as fit as a flat tire.

The front doors of the armory swung open, and a New York National Guard sergeant in a crisp, tailored, olive-drab uniform lifted a bullhorn to his mouth and shouted the first set of instructions to the throng of men.

"Candidates, if you are in possession of a card given to you by an officer of this regiment, including Chaplain Major Duffy, line up before me at this doorway."

Hundreds of men broke out of the lines along the walls and made their way to the sergeant at the doors. Two privates came down the steps, and the sergeant ordered them to organize the applicants in rows of forty.

"Well, that's it, brother," Archie, said to John while extending his hand. "The next time I see you, we'll both be New York Fighting Irishmen."

"Until then," John said to Archie, shaking his hand and patting his shoulder. John turned to the singsong Irishman.

"And best of luck to you, Daniel Buckley."

"The best of luck I have," Buckley answered, "and good luck to you, John McKay of Greenpoint."

John hustled over to the growing formation, leaving Archie and Daniel Buckley behind as he fell into one of the forming rows.

A sergeant came down the steps to supervise.

"Count to four," he ordered the candidates, "then start again." The candidates in the formation began to count—one, two, three, and four—and the count started again. The pattern continued until each man was assigned a number.

"If your number is one," the sergeant shouted through the bullhorn, "fall out and follow me through the doors."

When John got inside the armory, he was shocked by its vast size. The armory was cavernous, bigger than any building he'd ever seen before. Rows of giant steel girders rose from the sides over a highly polished wood floor until they met at the top of the ceiling, at least a hundred feet or higher.

American flags hung from every crossbeam. John saw the famous emerald green banner of the Fighting Irish 69th Regiment: the gold Irish harp with its gold lettering, "Erin Go Bragh," or "Ireland Forever."

John recalled stories he'd heard of General Corcoran and the battles of the Civil War, stories of Irish heroics and Medals of Honor earned by Irish immigrants. He read the banners overhead: Bull Run, Malvern Hill, Antietam, Fredericksburg, Gettysburg, and Appomattox.

Where will our place be? he wondered.

The sergeant barked directions.

"To the table that has the first letter of your last name," he pointed. "Micks, if your name starts with 'Mc,' go to the Micks. We need a special table for dumb Micks."

The privates around him laughed.

Along the edge of the armory were long tables. Staff sergeants sat at each row, ready to complete the paperwork needed for each candidate's enlistment. "Get it done fast," said the regimental master sergeant, "but get it done right." The process was well organized and methodical.

"Full name?" the staff sergeant snapped.

"John Joseph McKay."

"Permanent address?"

"Four sixteen Meeker Avenue, Brooklyn."

"Age?"

"Twenty-one."

"What month where you born?"

"February."

A private behind the table turned dials on a token press machine. He slipped a metal disc the size of a quarter into a slot and pulled hard on a lever. The disk then fell out, he caught it, and he pulled the lever again to make a second one.

The staff sergeant looked carefully at the disk, inspected it for defects, and once satisfied that it was good, he handed both disks and a leather lace to John.

"Slip the lace through the holes and put it around your neck. These are your tags, McKay," the staff sergeant said. "You are number 91539. Memorize that number and know it. Never take these tags off. Never separate the two tags. If you're blown to smithereens, the army will know who owns your stinking corpse."

The privates laughed again. The staff sergeant tried to upset new candidates as they came through, but John didn't give him the benefit.

"You're in Kilo Company, McKay. You'll take your oath with them."

John read the metal disk before he put the chain around his neck. "John J. McKay," it read, "PVT 69th NYNG, K Co. 91539." He slipped the leather string around his neck.

There were two more papers to sign before John was sent to the medics.

"Pick a person the army can contact," said the staff sergeant. "Somebody who's always home."

John thought for a minute and considered his mother was always home. "Mrs. Mary McKay," he said, "four-one-six Meeker Avenue, Brooklyn. She'll be home."

"This is your government life insurance, McKay," the sergeant said while holding the final form. "Pick a person you want to get the money in the very likely event you die over there." The sergeant then added, "It's ten thousand bucks, McKay, so give it to you mother and father. They can buy a house with that kind of dough."

A house? His ma and dah always dreamed of a house.

"Mrs. Mary McKay," he said again, "four-one-six Meeker Avenue, Brooklyn," and he signed the form.

———

The process moved swiftly for John. The medics told him he was five feet nine inches tall, he weighed 163 pounds, and he had an athletic build. The dental officer reported John was missing a lower molar and that he had six silver fillings and one gold filling. He had two active cavities needing repair and undeveloped wisdom teeth.

John couldn't help but notice that many men who had entered the armory were now leaving rejected. Some were given an outright "no" from the staff sergeants, and some got the bold red stamp, "not qualified," from the medical examiners. A failed candidate had to walk down the middle of the armory past all the incoming recruits. Most kept their heads down and scurried out, dreams of joining the elite 69th Regiment gone for good.

"John McKay!" Daniel Buckley called from across the armory floor. Buckley had a grimace on his face as he hurried over to John.

"There was a bit of a donnybrook, John," Buckley began. "After you departed, a regimental sergeant came along who seemed to know Archibald. I learned later the sergeant is employed as a police officer in your Greenpoint neighborhood. And, John," Buckley continued, "the sergeant tapped yer brother on the shoulder with his baton and told yer brother to find another regiment—that he had no place in the Sixty-Ninth of New York."

"Where did Archie go?

"Well, John, I'm sorry, I must add to the tale, because the story doesn't end neatly. Apparently, Archibald, yer brother, isn't fond of being touched by a baton. He got into a wee bit of a shovin' match with the sergeant until a couple of other fellers jumped in and helped the sergeant sway the outcome. Those men held Archibald while the sergeant gave him a couple of fine blows to the stomach. Archibald ran off, but I don't know where he fled."

Buckley saw two officers approaching, and he snapped to attention. John turned to see who was there, and he snapped to attention as well. Just then, Father Duffy and another regiment officer, Maj. William Donovan, approached.

"Good morning, Father," Buckley said.

"At ease, men," Duffy ordered, and Buckley and John relaxed.

"Is it 'Private Buckley' yet?" Duffy asked.

"I take my oath later this day, Father. And proudly, I may add."

As Buckley spoke, John noticed Buckley also had a K stamped on his tags—the same K that he had. Buckley must be in Kilo Company.

"Buckley," said Duffy, "this is Major Donovan. I've told him of your experience on the *Titanic*." The archbishop had answered Duffy's plea and pulled the needed strings to get Bill Donovan into the 69th.

"We'll give you a fair shake," said Donovan, his intense blue-eyed stare cutting through Buckley. "Show us you're brave and honest as any man, and we'll be happy to call you a proud Fighting Irishman of the Sixty-Ninth."

"Thank you, sir." Buckley saluted.

"And who are you?" Duffy turned his attention to John.

"John McKay, Saint Cecilia's, Greenpoint."

"Ah, Father McGolrick," said Duffy. "How is he?"

"No one gives an Irishman a finer homily," John said. He had heard a parishioner say that once and liked it.

"Are you one of our selectee candidates, McKay?" Duffy asked.

"Yes, sir."

Duffy's mind ran through the lists of names given to him. He remembered McGolrick's list and ran down the list of names.

"John McKay, you were an altar boy for Father McGolrick, no?" Duffy asked.

"Yes, Father, ten years."

"Good, McKay," said Duffy. "I'll keep you in mind."

Duffy dismissed John and Buckley, and the two men double-timed it across the armory floor, out from under Donovan's stare, and up to the second-level seats above the main floor.

"The *Titanic*?" John asked Buckley as they ran up the stairs. "What's that about?"

"How old were you in 1912?" Buckley asked.

"Sixteen."

Buckley looked at him squarely. "Do you remember the young man who survived? The third-class passenger?"

"You're Daniel Buckley from the *Titanic*?"

"In the flesh before your eyes."

"Mother of God," John exclaimed. "Jesus, Mary, and Joseph!" He blessed himself with the sign of the cross.

John had read all the stories about the *Titanic*. Twenty-one-year-old Daniel Buckley got on the ship in Belfast. After the ship hit the iceberg, water began to pour into his berthing compartment. Buckley climbed the stairs to the main deck of the ship as a lifeboat was being dropped. He got on the boat, but shortly afterward, a group of older men jumped in. Star Line officers stopped the lowering and ordered those men out. One officer fired a warning shot. A woman next to the boyish Buckley put a shawl over his head, and Star Line officers thought Buckley was a young woman, not a man. Not until survivors were on board the SS *Carpathia* did anyone realize Buckley was a male passenger.

"As you can imagine," Buckley explained earnestly, "I have been subjected to much ridicule. Many think of me as a coward. I am not a coward, and I shall prove it. I went to Father Duffy for his guidance, and I asked to join the Sixty-Ninth Regiment. Father is a strong believer in redemption of souls, John. Father is a great man that way. He's giving me a chance to redeem myself, to redeem my soul before God, and I need to do that. This is my chance."

John remembered reading the newspaper accounts of Buckley's saga, and he recalled how everyone in Greenpoint called Buckley a coward. They said that he should have stayed with the other men. Then, John considered how Father Duffy was willing to give Buckley a second chance, and John thought that he himself had no right to judge Buckley. He shook Buckley's hand.

"We'll be in the trenches together, Daniel," John said. "I'll pray for you, and you can pray for me. Stick together and we'll be brave enough."

"And let's pray we're out of France a day before the devil knows we're gone."

———

I, Daniel Buckley, do solemnly swear that I will support and defend the Constitution of the United States against all enemies, foreign or domestic; that I will bear true faith and allegiance to the same; that I take this obligation freely, without any mental reservation or purpose of evasion; and that I will well and faithfully discharge the duties of the office on which I am about to enter. So help me, God.

Daniel Buckley, Kilo Company, 69th Fighting Irish

CHAPTER 6

July 1917–September 1917

———

JOHN AND ARCHIE GOT DRESSED in the back bedroom of their parents' apartment, donning their military uniforms for the first time. Atop the two beds, the brothers laid out their shirts, slacks, belts, boots, and collar insignia as sisters Anna and Catherine, Big William, and their ma and dah waited in the parlor.

"It's an overseas cap," John explained to Archie. "You got the campaign hat, 'cause you're stickin' 'round."

"The leggin's are different, too." Archie unraveled his brother's wool leg wrap and let it spill to the floor.

"They're puttees," said John. "Your leggin's are canvas. The sergeant said puttees are better fer the mud. He says there'll be lots of mud."

"Boots, then leggin's?" Archie asked. "Or the other way 'round?"

"Shirt, pants, socks, boots, then leggin's," John said. "Your leggin's lace up along your leg."

Both brothers tucked in their olive-drab shirts and donned their boots. Archie pulled his leg wrap up to his calf, tucked in his pant hem, and laced it tight. John took the long, scarf-like, wool wrap and carefully wound it tightly over each lower leg, pulling it snug before he tied it secure.

"Got yer collar buttons?" Archie asked.

"I got a guard and infantry," said John. "Pin 'em fer me, will ya? The guard one goes on my left side."

Archie pinned his brother's collar and handed his buttons to John.

"Engineers!" John crowed, reading Archie's insignia. "Archibald McKay, New York National Guard engineer. You'll be buildin' them motorcars soon enough, Arch."

"Gotta get my ass shot first. Fine world, ain't it?"

John pinned Archie's collar and patted his arm. "Ready to show Ma and Dah?"

The budding men pushed out their chests and straightened their shoulders before marching into the parlor. Alex was in his chair, and Mary sat on the sofa with Catherine, holding the children. Anna and Big William stood at the kitchen door. When John and Archie entered, Mary instinctively brought her handkerchief to her face and gently sobbed. The tapered olive-drab uniforms hugged the McKay brothers' frames and transformed them. No longer did they look like carefree boys on a Greenpoint Street; rather, they now resembled serious men with the weight of a troubled world on their shoulders.

"You are so handsome," said Catherine. "My word. I can't believe it, how mature you both look."

Big William came to attention and saluted his brothers-in-law.

"You're fine-looking men, and you'll be fine soldiers, too. The army should be proud to have you."

"They'd be proud to have you too, William," Archie sniped.

"Mary," Alex asked his wife, "have you ever seen such handsome men as our boys?"

"Boys, Dah?" said John. "We're grown men now. Ready to go fight fer our country."

"That is true, Johnny. You are both grown men, but you're still handsome boys in our eyes. Right, Mary?"

"Indeed, Johnny," she said, "you'll always be our boys, and I'll always be your mother. Don't ever forget that." Mary began to cry. "I'm much too young for this," she moaned to Catherine. "The boys are being yanked away, and I have no say at all. How is that right?"

Alex held her hand. "Our boys are being called by the nation, Mary, called to do their duty. We must be strong."

Mary became bitter. "As everyone keeps telling me." She shot up from the sofa and headed to the kitchen. "The whole damn world wants me strong!"

"Ma!" John followed her.

"Ma, you have to understand." John put his hand on her shoulder. "I want to go over there. I want to fight. I'm in the top regiment in America. We have the smartest officers in the world. Our captains are Princeton men, and the majors all graduated from Columbia. Father Duffy says Major Donovan is the finest military man in the country. I'm in good hands, Ma. I'll be OK. When I get back home, I'll take ya to Gage and Tollner. We'll order clams and crab cakes and finish up with pecan pie. All yer favorites."

"That's a promise I need you to keep, Johnny McKay." She hugged her son, kissing him on the cheek.

"I will, Ma. I promise I will."

"Archibald?" Catherine queried. "Why is your hat different from Johnny's? I thought you were joining the Sixty-Ninth too?"

"Now, Catherine, why would I join an outfit that's got a commanding officer who's too fat to fight? The elite Sixty-Ninth has no rudder, you know. Nobody's in charge. God only knows where the poor fellers of the Fightin' Irish will end up. No, Catherine, I joined the Forty-Seventh because it's a fine outfit that needs a man like me: one who's good with his hands and can fix a truck."

Archie parroted a rumor he'd heard on the streets. Many local Irish, envious of the men picked to be in the 69th, started unflattering false rumors.

Archie was correct, however, when he said the Forty-Seventh Regiment needed men who could fix trucks. As usual, though, Archie only told half the story. Archie skipped his confrontation on the steps of the 69th's armory. He said nothing about being held by two men and getting punched in the stomach. Archie fled from the 69th and ran to the 47th Regiment in Brooklyn because he had no choice.

"Good for you, Archie," said William. "You'll have a trade when the war is done."

"And he'll be far from the guns while the war is on," Anna added.

––––

From June to August 1917, the New York National Guard 69th Regiment expanded from five hundred men to its full complement of two thousand men. The US Army, now commanded by Gen. John Pershing, doubled in size. It grew from a paltry one hundred twenty thousand officers and enlisted men to a force of two hundred twenty-four thousand.

National Guard regiments around the country grew much faster than the regular army, as men opted to join local regiments by a factor of four to one. Not until the spring of 1918, a year after national conscription began, did the US Army finally enlist four million men.

By July 1917, the 69th Regiment was eager to get organized and federalize into the US Army, but the Irish regiment was still without a permanent commanding officer. Internal fights ensued, and bitter rivalries among the officers threatened to derail the 69th's preparedness plan. However, before anything detrimental transpired, the War Department soothed all hard feelings and appointed a commanding officer that nobody in the 69th wanted.

Col. Charles Delano Hine, a fifty-year-old West Point graduate and a professional railroad man, had absolutely no connection to New York's Irish community. Hine was not Irish Catholic, nor did he know anything about the regiment's exulted Civil War history. Nevertheless, once

Hine took the regiment's reins, he suppressed all the strong personalities, and the regiment settled down and focused on federalizing to join the US Army.

Both the officers and the NCOs of the Fighting Irish considered the 69th a burgeoning elite regiment. They saw they had "good clay" to work with, and they could make quick strides training the carefully culled recruits. Good order and discipline came naturally, and all the recruits exuded great pride after having been selected for the 69th.

"We saved the Union at Bull Run," a staff sergeant said, pounding his foot on the armory's gigantic floor during a regimental meeting. "Our Irish men held the line, held the Confederates. The Union line crumbled, the soldiers ran, but our men did not retreat!" His voice boomed and echoed across the cavernous room. "We shall never retreat!"

Esprit de corps soared. The unique nature of an all-Irish, all-Catholic regiment, eager to prove its patriotism and prowess on the battlefield, caused the men to quickly coalesce. Nevertheless, non-Irish and non-Catholic men joined the regiment for the same reasons: they wanted to fight for a superb outfit. The makeup of the 69th Regiment was 95 percent Irish Catholic, and 95 percent was good enough for Cardinal Farley, Father Duffy, and Major Donovan.

Training at the Manhattan Armory quickly became too confined. Once the men were issued backpacks and kits, it was impossible to assemble all two thousand together on the armory floor.

Each man had a poncho, blanket, knapsack, entrenching tool, steel helmet, water bottle, haversack, ammo carrier, bayonet, mess kit, first-aid kit, sewing kit, and tent rope, all rolled inside a single over-the-shoulder harness that secured around the waist. The pack weighed eighty pounds and made each man way too bulky, even for the spacious armory.

Still not issued were gas masks, rifles, or any type of assault weapon other than a bayonet. Because the New York Guard unit couldn't get ammunition, grenades, or any types of rifles, they trained using wooden firearms. With this method, there was no way they could conduct effective training.

Major Donovan wasn't deterred. If the regiment couldn't practice shooting weapons, he'd concentrate on tactics. He divided each company's platoons into small groups. In every company, Donovan created squads of rifle grenadiers, riflemen, automatic riflemen, and hand grenadiers. All squads were assigned runners and were commanded by a company lieutenant and a sergeant.

The squads were mixed into small groups, each designed to have different infantry capabilities. They were fast moving and agile. They coordinated with machine gunners and the light artillery guns, and they moved swiftly across the battlefield to have a deadly impact on the enemy.

Donovan clearly stated the regiment's objectives to the men during training. "You will advance under offensive gunfire. You will make it to Hun positions. You will penetrate the Hun line. You will jump into Hun trenches. And you will jam your bayonet down every Hun's throat. Make no mistake, men." He gazed at each man, his eyes beaming a natural intensity. "We will teach you how to kill Germans and destroy the German army."

After an afternoon with Donovan, the regiment's spirits soared higher than the steel-girded roof. The men loved Donovan. They loved his strength, intelligence, and leadership. Considering he was an Irish firebrand and a faithful Catholic man, the men of the 69th loved that, too.

On one occasion, Donovan called in some favors from Governor Al Smith's people and pulled a few strings at the US Military Academy. He, Major Stacom of the regiment's 2nd Battalion, and Major Moynahan of the regiment's 3rd "Shamrock" Battalion commandeered a Hudson River ferry transport and took two hundred 69th infantrymen up to West Point.

At West Point, Donovan arranged for the regiment's three battalion commanders to get weapons and live ammunition and the use of the campus's shooting range to put the 69th's tactical concepts into motion. Each of the majors selected two company captains and two squad lieutenants. Those officers selected company men of varying ranks who were considered exceptional.

Captain Hurley of Kilo Company in the 3rd Battalion chose Dowling and Martin for his lieutenants. The lieutenants chose Daly, Hughes, and Meade as their sergeants, and those men chose a handful of corporals and privates. PFC John McKay made the cut.

At West Point, each of the three battalions conducted fire practice using mostly the older American-made Springfield 1903 rifle, but also the British-produced, American-modified Enfield 1917 rifle—the rifles they'd be issued in France. West Point possessed two styles of automatic rifles: the French-made Chauchat and the Browning automatic. They also carried numerous French-made Hotchkiss machine guns, but they had only one of the brand-new Browning water-cooled light machine guns—a firearm all the officers had read about, but no one had ever seen. Captain Seibert of Machine Gun Company implored Major Donovan to exert his influence and get the Browning, which was by far a superior weapon. Donovan couldn't make any promises; how US forces would be trained and deployed once they arrived in France was still an open question.

John's shooting performance stood out at the West Point exercise. He was an excellent natural shot with perfect aim. He never missed one target. The only other private to shoot the Enfield rifle and Chauchat automatic rifle better than he was a pimple-faced, lanky private in Alpha Company in the 1st Battalion named Dick O'Neil. O'Neil showed himself to be a natural student of Donovan's agile military tactics, and Donovan took an immediate shine to the tall and lean O'Neil. John and O'Neil worked together as part of a four-man Hotchkiss machine-gun crew, and both participated in a mock assault on German trenches using automatic rifles. John and O'Neil had so much tenacity and shooting ability that they put wide smiles on all the battalion majors' faces.

Dick O'Neil and John McKay became fast friends at West Point. They were the same sort of men, similar in many ways. Both were quiet and eager to learn. They were athletic and excelled in military discipline. Each exuded an innate confidence and, although both men got notice from their superior officers, neither man boasted or acted cocky like some others who earned similar acclaim. John McKay and Dick O'Neil were studious, serious men who realized early on that every demand conveyed by regimental leadership, no matter how petty or trite, was meant to teach them how to defeat the Germans and stay alive.

Later that afternoon, on the ferry ride back down the Hudson, the men became better acquainted.

"I can't make the trip from Greenpoint anymore," John said. The trip from his Greenpoint home to the 69th Armory had become too arduous.

"Same for me," said O'Neil. "I'm up in Harlem."

"An Irishman in my company says I can rent a room where he lives. It's a boardinghouse run by an Irish widow close by the armory. He says it's clean and the housemother's a good cook. There're extra rooms."

"I don't know," said O'Neil, "I've got a steady girl in Harlem. She'd get a bit knotted up if I moved downtown and ate another woman's cooking. Unless it was my mother's, of course, but she's long gone."

John wondered how his mother would take the news. She wouldn't be happy when she found out he planned to live in Manhattan, but he had no choice. The demands were too great. Every day started before sunrise. Each began with close-formation drills, classes devoted to regimental history, and then hours and hours of tactics.

Like all new recruits, John had to learn military organization and the differences between ranks when reading a collar insignia. He learned never to call a fellow enlisted man "sir" and to always salute those with a higher rank. A was now alpha, and B was bravo. Six a.m. became zero six hundred hours, and three p.m. was now fifteen hundred hours. He never walked anymore; he double-timed it to everything.

The men in Kilo Company, John's company, grew close during this period and began to coordinate and operate as a single unit. They stood guard duty with one another, close-order drilled together, stood inspections, and were assigned cleaning and KP duties.

John and Daniel Buckley were in the same squad. John was assigned as an automatic rifleman and machine gunner, and Buckley was assigned as a runner. Runners not only relayed messages from senior officers to the front line, but they also carried the heavy cartridge cases of automatic rifle ammunition to the shooters. At the armory, John and Buckley trained together, but so far, Buckley only had to carry rolled-up puttee leggings as a substitute for the weighty automatic rifle ammo.

John took a liking to Buckley, even though Buckley didn't excel at military life. Buckley wasn't one who exuded innate confidence. He once shared with John that he was deeply fearful of getting back on a ship again and crossing the Atlantic, especially since German U-boats were sinking transports. John cared about Buckley and decided he'd stick by his Irish underdog friend no matter what, but John also made sure Buckley was a proficient soldier. After all, he might have to rely on Buckley one day.

Buckley's boardinghouse was ten blocks away from the Lexington Avenue Armory, sitting mid-block on West Eleventh Street. The trip from the boardinghouse to the armory was ten minutes by foot, and John figured that if he lived on Eleventh, he could get a lot more needed sleep. O'Neil lived in Harlem and had a steady girl, but it didn't take him long to convince his sweetheart he needed to live closer to the armory, too. O'Neil's girl wanted him to move downtown. Up in Harlem, he did nothing but sleep.

"It's clean," Buckley repeated to John and O'Neil. "And Mrs. Hickey would love to have two handsome devils like you donning her doorway."

John promised his parents he'd come home to Greenpoint every weekend, and Alex impressed upon his wife that their son had no choice but move closer to the Armory.

"We must be strong, Mary," he told her. "We can't send our boy off with a mixed mind. We can't fill him up with our troubles. We have to keep our emotions inside from here on."

A few days later after a long day of drill, John and O'Neil followed Daniel Buckley to his boardinghouse and arranged to let rooms from Mrs. Hickey. The cost was two dollars per week. The rooms were small but adequate. A bathroom was on the third floor. John and Dick O'Neil slept on the fifth floor. In the mid-July heat, Mrs. Hickey's boardinghouse sizzled hot. They opened every door and every window—anything to get a breeze.

"No overnight guests, Mr. O'Neil," Mrs. Hickey hollered up the staircase, chiding O'Neil in advance. Buckley told her Dick had a steady girl, Estelle.

"Never, Mrs. Hickey," O'Neil hollered back. He turned to John and whispered, "Who could do it in this heat?"

Mrs. Hickey loved having the young Irish infantrymen in her boardinghouse. Every morning before sunrise, Buckley, O'Neil, and John sat at her table and devoured her breakfast. Mrs. Hickey didn't mind waking early or spending a few extra cents on eggs and bacon, knowing her boys would have an arduous day at the armory. Mrs. Hickey made a small show at the corner grocer, telling anyone who'd listen she had to buy extra groceries to feed her hungry, handsome, young Irish fighters. When the men came back in the evening, Mrs. Hickey cooked an equally hardy and hot supper. She was deeply proud of her three fine soldiers, and she boasted this to everyone.

One day, in a burst of pride, Mrs. Hickey strolled down to the 69th Armory Regiment shop and dropped three dollars to purchase an emerald-green Fighting Irish flag. She hung the flag from her front window, next to her Stars and Stripes. That flag never came down.

———

Kilo's sergeant called close-formation orders, and the soldiers stomped their boots on the armory floor and executed an abrupt, right-facing turn.

"Parade, rest," he barked, and the men uniformly widened their stance and crossed their arms behind their backs.

The close-order drill clamor echoed loudly inside the cavernous walls of the armory, and the noise traveled all the way up to the officers' planning room on the second level. The business of the 69th Infantry Regiment started at 0530 hours, and by 0730 hours, regimental training was in full swing.

In the planning room sat the 69th's executive officer, Col. Latham Reed. To the right of Reed were his headquarter captains: sanitary, supply, and machine gun. Across the table were the regiment's heavy hitters, Majors Donovan of 1st Battalion, Stacom of 2nd Battalion, and Moynahan of 3rd Battalion. Sitting at the end of the table between both sides was Chaplain Duffy. The officers awaited Commanding Officer Hine's arrival. Executive Officer Reed said Colonel Hine had important news.

"A-ten-hut!" exclaimed Reed while standing. Colonel Hine was at the doorway.

All the officers reflexively stood, their legs pushing the chairs behind them.

"At ease," Hine commanded. He adjusted his thick black-frame glasses and then mumbled, "Seats."

The men sat as Hine opened his folder and shuffled through papers.

"I have a few agenda items before I get to the main business," he began. "First, I'd like to hear about West Point. Major Donovan, this was your effort. Would you start?"

"Yes, Colonel," said Donovan. "It was an enormous success. We had two hundred men and were able to shoot five thousand rounds—plenty of experience for everyone. We have some fine shooters throughout the companies, a welcome surprise, considering we have mostly city men."

"A dead-on eye is a dead-on eye," said Hine, "country or city."

"Yes, sir," Donovan agreed. "We would like to schedule more excursions to West Point or out to Long Island. We need more room to train. We think we can make readiness improvements if the men get time in the field."

"Major Moynahan." Hine turned to the Shamrock Battalion commander. "What is the status of our company and platoon organization?"

Donovan, Stacom, and Moynahan, along with Captain Seibert of the Machine Gun Company, had worked diligently for days to develop the regiment's offensive attack plan, deciding to split the battalion companies into small teams.

"Each company will have four infantry platoons, Colonel," Moynahan said. "Each infantry platoon will be led by a lieutenant and a sergeant. We break the infantry platoon into four parts. Three hand-grenade teams, six rifle grenadiers, sixteen riflemen, and four automatic riflemen. Captain Seibert's company will provide machine-gun support, and we intend to cross-train all automatic riflemen to operate in machine-gun teams."

"And this has been shown to work?" Hine asked.

"Yes, sir." Donovan jumped in. "We are growing more confident every day, but we need the weapons to train the men."

"I heard you last week, Major." Hine bristled. He tilted his head back to peer at Donovan through the bottom of his eyeglasses perched at the end of his nose. "Perhaps the army will rectify our shortage."

Hine turned to the young Captain Seibert of the Machine Gun Company. "My sources at the railroad tell me Browning Company will be slow to deliver its machine gun. We won't know exactly which weapon your gunners will use once we are in France, but my intuition tells me you should focus your training on the French Hotchkiss gun and not the Browning."

"Yes, sir," said Seibert.

"Chaplain Duffy," Hine continued, "do you have any items for us?"

"Yes, Colonel," Duffy began. "When the regiment prepared for the Mexican deployment in '16, sir, we had great difficulty separating the men from everyday home life. We were inundated with mothers, fathers, wives, and girlfriends, all forlorn for love or money, and we had infinite familial strife."

"You have an answer for us, Chaplain?"

"Yes, sir."

"Good, Chaplain Duffy, but I'm going to ask you to brief us after I address the main business. We'll be able to form a plan when I'm through."

"Yes, sir."

"Gentlemen." Hine shuffled his papers and pulled one from a folder. He read it aloud. "We have received our orders from the War Department," he said. "We are assigned to the Forty-Second US Army division, Major General Mann commanding. The Forty-Second Division is comprised of two brigades, designated the Eighty-Third and the Eighty-Fourth. We are assigned to the Eighty-Third Brigade, Brigadier General Lenihan commanding. Our Sixty-Ninth Regiment has been redesignated the One Sixty-Fifth Infantry Regiment. All references to the Sixty-Ninth Infantry shall be deleted immediately. We will join two other regiments in the Eighty-Third to include the One Sixty-Sixth Infantry from Ohio and the One Fiftieth Machine Gun Company from Wisconsin. The One Fiftieth is training on the Hotchkiss now, Captain Seibert."

"Yes, sir."

"The Eighty-Fourth Brigade will be comprised of the One Sixty-Seventh and One Sixty-Eighth Infantry regiments; Alabama and Iowa, respective."

"When are we joining up?" asked Executive Officer Reed.

"Camp Mills, Long Island, on September fifth," said Hine. "We have ten days."

"I'll write up the deployment orders for your approval," said Reed.

"There is one more part to this, gentlemen, something that affects the One Sixty-Fifth directly," said Hine. "The army has ordered the One Sixty-Fifth's manning level increased to three thousand men."

"We have a waiting list," said Duffy.

"No, Chaplain." Hine shook his head. "The War Department has ordered four local city regiments to provide three hundred fifty men each. Those regiments have already received the order."

"Wait a minute," Donovan said, slamming his hand on the table. "We've spent two months cultivating our men. The Sixty-Ninth has a waiting list a mile long of outstanding candidates. Why should we dilute the quality of the regiment? Colonel, you need to vigorously protest this decision."

"I'll carry a shillelagh to the War Department and sing a song of protest. Tell General Pershing our Irish pride is bruised."

"That Irish pride," Donovan spewed, "is the only reason *your* men will fight, Colonel. I respectfully request *you* honor your men and ask the army to change the order."

"The War Department has spoken, Major. The order is written."

Duffy saw the despair on Donovan's face. The War Department's order was completely counter to an all-Irish charter. The order was dismissive and directly opposed the very principles that motivated the men. Duffy decided he'd visit John Cardinal Farley at Saint Patrick's.

"Those regiments are going to send us their bottom-feeders," Donovan continued to rage, "and if the War Department wants the Sixty-Ninth to sift shit, I will personally make sure the Sixty-Ninth is the best shit-sifting outfit the army has ever seen."

"I won't oppose you, Major. If a man is inferior to your standard, discharge him."

The colonel's seeming compromise calmed Donovan down, and Father Duffy used the quiet moment to move away from the new orders.

"Colonel," he said, "we have a standing invitation from the Irish American Athletic Club of New York City…"

Hine removed his glasses, wiped his eyes, and grimaced. *More Irish.*

"There's a fine fellow there named Martin Sheridan—"

"The Olympian?" Hine interrupted.

"Yes, Colonel, from the '08 London games."

Martin Sheridan was a well-known celebrity among New York's Irish. Not only did he garner two gold medals, but he also did so under the nose of his English hosts. The staunchly anti-English, Irish-born athlete forged an American tradition that has been repeated ever since.

At the London games in 1908, each country team marched into the stadium behind a flag-holding athlete. When the lead athlete passed the English sovereign sitting in a review box high above the field, the flag bearer dipped his nation's colors as a sign of respect to the king.

When the American team strode into the London stadium and passed the English sovereign, American athlete Ralph Rose, convinced by Martin Sheridan, refused to dip the American flag as he passed the English king. Instead, he raised Stars and Stripes even higher. Later, Martin Sheridan was credited for the obvious snub because he was famously quoted as saying, "This flag bows to no earthly king." Any man or woman who carries the American flag leading the Irish in New York's Saint Patrick's Day parade down Fifth Avenue swears to this oath today.

For Irish Americans, Martin Sheridan gave the mercantilist Protestant crown a good public drubbing, but more importantly, it reinforced the Irish's burgeoning belief that their newly found country gave them an abundance of prestige. Irish American pride soared.

Sheridan's slight was not spur of the moment; rather, Martin Sheridan recalled the Fighting Irish 69th's commander, Michael Corcoran, who in 1861 refused to avail his regiment and refused the orders of New York's governor to line the sidewalks along Broadway to honor the visiting Prince of Wales. Corcoran's refusal left an enormous gap on the parade route and caused the New York governor major embarrassment. Furious at Corcoran, the governor charged him with court-martial, but after Fort Sumter was attacked, the southern states seceded, and the American Civil War began. Lincoln needed the Fighting Irish Regiment.

Lincoln overrode the New York governor and dismissed all charges against Corcoran. Washington was imperiled. The Confederates were a short distance away across the Potomac at Bull Run.

"Sheridan would like to speak to the regiment, give our men a pep talk," Duffy continued. "And Captain Archer of Gulf Company is a New York Athletic Club man, too. They'd like to give Captain Archer a send-off."

"An Irish wake?" mused Hine.

"Defined finality can be a good thing, Colonel. We Irish are experienced with it. Martin Sheridan has suggested the regiment attend a New York Giants baseball game and enjoy an afternoon of good cheer at the Polo Grounds. I believe it would be an appropriate place for our families to say final good-byes."

"Approved, Chaplain Duffy," Hine said. "Executive Officer Reed, make it happen."

Hine stood and the men stood. The 165th Infantry Regiment, the 83rd Brigade, and the US Army 42nd Division were born.

———

Four New York City Infantry Regiments surrendered 350 men each and sent them to the 165th. One of them sent its hooligans, criminals, and overall worst men to the 165th. Another, a distinct non-Catholic, non-Irish regiment, formed to counter the many Irish regiments springing up in New York, sent only their best. The other two asked for volunteers and found enough willing to transfer. The sudden influx of outsiders strained the insular Irish, but officially and publicly, the new regiment did its best to welcome the newcomers.

Behind the scenes, Major Donovan feverishly worked to discharge undesirables as soon as they walked through the door. Any excuse was used to drum a man out. Donovan put the regiment's medical and dental staffs to good use.

Hard feelings between those who considered themselves true Fighting Irish and those who were outsiders could not be assuaged. The men of the original 69th took it upon themselves to publish an address book, and none of the outsiders were included. Once published, it was distributed to original 69th Infantry members only.

The battalion majors blended the outsiders into established platoons and soon realized that they had a much more effective fighting force. Once the men began to train together, which outside regiment they came from or whether or not they were Irish became unimportant. Father Duffy stumbled on a new motto for the regiment's new infusion of men.

"Irish by adoption, Irish by association, or Irish by conviction."

Changing from a state National Guard outfit to a US Army infantry regiment required many changes. First, every man needed to be dressed uniformly, and now that the US Army was supplying uniforms, each man in the regiment was issued an army olive-drab jacket, a campaign hat, leather leggings, and leather walking shoes.

The regimental sergeants were briefed about the Polo Grounds outing and a subsequent march down Third Avenue to the ferry terminal.

They had the immediate task of making the large and unwieldy regiment look like one disciplined unit. They paraded the cumbersome companies around the Armory streets until they got the standardization and precision they wanted.

Everyone in the regiment needed US Army insignia and needed replacement dog tags, too.

John's sergeant handed him the new 165th insignia buttons and gave John two new dog tags. John carefully looked the tags over before he removed his old set. "John J. McKay, PVT 1/C, Co. K, 165th INF, 91539." The information was correct. He pulled off his old set and dumped them in a bin, then slipped the new tags over his head.

"Never take them off," the sergeant, instructed.

————

Invitations for an afternoon baseball game at the Polo Grounds to watch the New York Giants play the Cincinnati Reds were mailed out to all the regiment's families and guests. Dignitaries were invited, including Charles Whitman and Alfred Smith, New York governors; Franklin Delano Roosevelt, assistant secretary of the navy; John Purroy Mitchel, New York City mayor; John Cardinal Farley from the New York Dioceses; and Charles Francis Murphy from Tammany Hall.

John knew an invitation was sent to his parents' home. He knew he'd have to explain to his mother that, after the Giants game, he'd report to formation and march to the ferry terminal for a ride out to Long Island and Camp Mills. The staff sergeant briefed the company men and told them, "Don't plan on no more visits home." He added, "Next stop after Mills is France."

"Get your personal affairs in order, men," the platoon sergeant added. "Shake your mommy's hand and kiss your daddy good-bye. Don't send no money to ya girlfriend. She'll spend it on her boyfriend, and he ain't you. September fifth, men, that's it. We ship out to Mills."

Mrs. Hickey was brokenhearted hearing the news. She loved having "her" boys in her home. They made her feel needed again. Her husband and son had passed, and her daughter married an Australian. She was alone in New York. Boarders had come and gone, but none changed her house like her boys.

"I'm alone again," she would say. "Left alone with my prayers." She found herself sobbing fitfully in the middle of the day. "Aye, my dear boys, you give me many more reasons to pray."

———

The weekend rolled around, and there wasn't any drill. On Saturday morning, John set out from Mrs. Hickey's house in Manhattan for Greenpoint and an afternoon supper with his family. He was eager to see Little William and Kitty; the toddlers were sprouting up so fast.

John strolled over the Williamsburg Bridge, looking down at the busy boat traffic through the morning mist. The piers on both sides of the river were crowded, filled by steamers, barges, tugs, and sailing vessels. *It won't be long,* he thought.

In the distance, through the haze, John could make out the spire of Saint Cecilia's and his Greenpoint neighborhood. Once on the Brooklyn side of the bridge, he jumped onto the Meeker Avenue trolley and rode it north to Oakland Avenue, just past Metropolitan Avenue.

"No fare for brave Irish men." The conductor patted his shoulder.

From the time John started out on Eleventh Street in Manhattan, as he made his way through the Italian neighborhood south along the Bowery and east to the Jewish neighborhood along Delancey Street, everyone in his path cheered and saluted him. Complete strangers thanked him for his service. Men reached out and shook his hand. Closer to

Greenpoint, with its Irish citizenry, many recognized his 165th Infantry insignia and knew he was a member of the Fighting Irish Regiment.

"Go get 'em'!" he heard some say.

"Shoot a Kraut fer me!"

"Show them Huns how we Americans do it," they said.

He jumped off the trolley car and walked down Meeker Avenue. Just before he reached his family home, he heard Anna scream from the third-floor window.

"Johnny's home!"

John sprinted up the stairs to see his ma standing in the doorway. She looked so sad. Alex stood behind her. He too seemed melancholy. John's heart sank. He knew this was his last visit home. He'd have to tell her that the regiment was shipping out to Camp Mills and then France.

Mary wrapped her arms around her son, giving him a deep embrace. She didn't want to let go.

"Let him in," Alex gently chided, and Mary relented.

Anna ran up to John, kissed him on the cheek, and pulled his campaign hat off his head. "I could kill Krauts," she said, putting the campaign hat on her head while holding a broomstick like a rifle. "Pow, pow, pow!" she pressed.

"You have all the firepower I have," John told her. He pulled Anna in close. "This is it, Anna," he said. He looked at Anna sternly. "Time's up."

Anna's eyes welled, and she grabbed John and hugged him tightly. Crying softly, she said, "You'll be OK. I know it."

Mary looked at Anna and asked what was wrong, but Anna couldn't answer her without bursting into tears. John finally answered.

"You got the baseball invitation?"

"Yes," said Alex.

"Well, after the game, I'll be mustering with the men. From there, we'll ship out to Long Island."

"The railroad stops right here at Penny Bridge," said Mary.

"No, Ma," John said. A lump grew in his throat. "There'll be no more visits. This is the last time. We'll get one more good-bye after the game."

Mary exploded indignantly. "Who says good-bye to a child at a baseball game? Clearly, no mother came up with that one."

"Armies and mothers don't mix," said Alex. "We'll be at the game, son, as will Catherine, William, and Anna. I asked Archibald, but he said, 'Tell Johnny I'm a Dodger fan.'"

Archie burst through the door. He too was dressed in his olive-drab uniform and campaign hat.

"Tell me, brother," he started out, "are you sick of them leprechauns yet? Tellin' yer how the old country was so dear and singing them ditties. I'd puke."

"It's all tactics and stormin' Hun trenches, Arch. Infantryman stuff, not shamrocks and pots o' gold. You should meet Major Donovan; he'd take the blarney out of ya fast enough."

Archie was defensive. The 47th Regiment was nowhere near ready. His unit was completely disorganized, and for the immediate future, he was going to sit in Brooklyn and live off an NYNG private's salary of thirty-three dollars per month.

Rumor around Greenpoint was that the 165th Regiment and the 42nd Division would be the first New York outfit to leave for France. Archie was deeply proud of John, but he never showed that pride unless he had a few drinks. He boasted the loudest then.

"My brother is toughest man in Greenpoint!" he'd yell from atop his barstool. "He's fightin' with Wild Bill himself."

Brooklyn newspapers began to refer to Major William Donovan as "Wild Bill," a name Donovan earned when captain of the Columbia University football team. The name was quickly adopted and it served to enhance the cream-of-the-crop reputation of the 165th. Everyone in

Brooklyn had heard about Wild Bill Donovan. It might have been media-savvy Duffy who passed Donovan's old college nickname on to his newspaper friends.

John got his father alone in a back bedroom, and they spoke privately.

"I'm earnin' thirty-three dollars a month, Dah, and I don't need all of it. The army will take ten dollars every month and mail it to you and Ma."

"That's very generous of you, son. I'll put the money aside."

"No, Dah, it's for you and Ma to use. Keep it."

"You're a fine man, son." Alex instinctively reached over and hugged John. He hadn't hugged his son since John was fifteen.

Alex was nervous. "Many fathers don't have to send their sons to this war, John, but I've thought it over. This is a rare opportunity for a young man like you to shape events. America stands for fairness and freedom, John. No one knows that better than us Irish. You are fighting to defend fairness and freedom, and you are not an idle observer. You are part of a larger force for good. You are in the fight, son, forging a future Little William and Kitty and your children shall live. Go forward with a clear mind, son, and know you are deeply loved by your family."

"I love you too, Dah."

Catherine and William arrived for dinner, and John rushed out to greet the children. Kitty, at one and a half years, could only patter across the floor, but Little William, at almost three years, bolted excitedly and jumped into John's lap. John grasped each child in his clutches and lifted them onto the sofa. The children pecked his cheeks, and he kissed them back. He squeezed them until they laughed and giggled at their silly uncle.

"Such beautiful babes," John cooed. "Such beautiful babes, you have, Catherine."

———

Alex sat in his chair and lit his pipe. His entire family was around him. He was satisfied and content, happy to have this simple moment but saddened knowing he'd never have it again. As his Mary had said, the family was being pulled apart, and he had no control to stop it. No promises could be made, and no promises could be kept—not until the war was done. He had never experienced his fatherhood like this. He was filled with happiness, surrounded by his four grown children, but at the same time, he was forced to chew a bitter pill. He didn't know how he should feel, but once again, his Mary had it right. "We are much too young for this."

———

Father Duffy's plan for a day at the Polo Grounds went off without a hitch. The regiment mustered at the armory at zero six-hundred hours, marched over to the east side of Manhattan, and boarded three ferryboats to transport the men upriver to the Polo Grounds.

Martin Sheridan of the New York Athletic Club came out and addressed the regiment. Sheridan was a natural rabble-rouser, but his message of unflinching American patriotism was compelling. He explained the Irish regiment was not going to war to help the English or the French. This European war had broadened beyond Europe's continent and was now in the open oceans.

"America is an island nation," he told the crowd. "America relies on the seas for free commerce and safe passage of immigrants seeking work, just like you and your parents."

He relayed the story of the 1908 Olympics and got a rousing cheer when he once again proclaimed, "This flag bows to no earthly king." Then he reminded the men of their Fighting Irish history and goaded them to "do no less than those who went before you."

After Sheridan was finished, the men remustered, and they marched into the stadium as a single regiment. The crowd of family, friends, and dignitaries roared and cheered.

The regiment halted and the men were dismissed. John and Buckley joined up with Dick O'Neil and found the McKay family and O'Neil's girlfriend, Estelle, sitting above the Giants dugout.

John sat next to his ma, and she held his hand as the game was played. As the innings passed one by one, the inescapable, teary good-bye grew closer and the festive afternoon began to fill with despair.

When the game finally ended, Buckley excused himself and joined with Kilo Company men. O'Neil and Estelle disappeared for a final good-bye smooch.

"All men muster immediately," a regiment sergeant, shouted through his bullhorn.

"I gotta go," John said to his family.

Alex grabbed his wife's hand and held it tightly. "No emotion," he had warned her earlier. "Remember, John's safety," he told her. "No tears."

As Mary hugged John, she did everything to keep her composure. She held him tightly and instinctively recalled how he smelled when he was a newborn baby in her arms. She ran her fingers through his soft brown hair and peered directly into his clear green eyes. *Remember him,* she said to herself. *Remember everything about him and never forget.*

"I have to go, Ma," John said. "I love you, Ma."

Tears poured down Mary's cheeks. "I love you too, son. Forever and eternal."

Alex closed his eyes. Anna buried her face deep in her handkerchief, sobbing. Catherine and William hugged tightly as John came to attention, performed an about-face, and turned away from his family to join up with his company.

———

Third Avenue in Manhattan was teeming with onlookers from the Polo Grounds to the Thirty-Fourth Street ferry terminals. Thousands of New

Yorkers came out to watch the Fighting Irish Regiment march. Women ran out to the street and gave men flowers. Many others stood shoulder to shoulder, lining the street and cheering the Irish infantrymen.

In the distance, at the corner of Third Avenue and Fiftieth Street, stood Archie. He was alone and in uniform. As John's platoon marched by, Archie came to attention and saluted his brother. John smiled broadly, broke rank, and saluted Archie—then he ran back and rejoined his squad.

CHAPTER 7

September 1917–October 1917
Camp Mills

———

"A-TEN-HUT!" THE PLATOON SNAPPED UP straight, shoulders back, and chests out. "Forward…march!" They moved down the dirt road in unison.

"McSweeney," the platoon sergeant barked. "Cadence."

From the rear of the formation, Marty McSweeney began the now familiar rhythmic verse, "Garryowen."

Let Bacchus' sons be not dismayed
But join with me, each jovial blade
Come booze and sing, and lend your aid
To help me with the chorus

The men moved in perfect modulation, their voices booming and echoing across the muddy plain to the far edges of the camp.

Our hearts so stout have got us fame
For soon tis known from whence we came
Where're we go they dread the name
Of Garryowen in Glory

The platoon reached the shooting range and halted.

"Fall out and fall in," the range master shouted, and the men double-timed it to the rifle stack, each plucking a weapon before proceeding to the firing line. At the far end were two automatic riflemen and their runners. Next, a hand-grenade team, then four riflemen followed by grenadiers and another four-man rifle team. The pattern continued until the last two men on the line were automatic riflemen.

John was at the far left end of the line, and when he looked over his right shoulder, he could plainly see all the faces in his infantry platoon. First, there was dour Ed Rooney. Rooney was an automatic rifleman like John and was one of John's tent mates. Rooney hailed from the Bronx and was the type of guy who sensed the worst in everything, always sounding doom and gloom. After Rooney, were runners Daniel Buckley from Ireland and Bergan Morgan from Long Island. They also bunked in John's tent. After them was hand-grenade thrower Luke Boyle, who could toss a grenade forty yards and hit a target dead-on. Beyond Boyle was the four-Mick rifle squad—McSweeney, McElroy, McKenna, and McCoun—and then more grenadiers. John knew every man by name, especially mouthy Mick Marty McSweeney, who hailed from Greenpoint like John. McSweeney bunked in John's tent too, along with Ed Rooney, Daniel Buckley, Bergan Morgan and a fellow rifleman far down the line named Jim O'Conner.

The platoon squad shot one hundred rounds per man. "Make every bullet count," the instructors would yell. "One bullet, one Hun."

The instructors taught the infantrymen to be calm and take careful aim before shooting. They were taught to lie flat and shoot and to shoot while on the run. The men learned control signals, when to fire, and when to stop. Sometimes it was a whistle, sometimes a flag, and occasionally a pistol flare. The infantry platoon, led by a first or second lieutenant and a staff sergeant, soon became a highly disciplined and coordinated unit.

After two hours at the shooting range, the men formed up again and marched into the giant mud field for trench digging. Every man carried an entrenchment tool in his backpack. For the time being, the entrenchment tool was considered more important than a rifle.

"Dig faster, dig deeper, dig wider, dig more," the sergeants yelled over and over. "It'll save your life. Dig a hole and get in it. Dig a trench and get behind it. Dig more, dig faster."

Every platoon of every company practiced digging trenches every day. The mud fields around Camp Mills had been dug up, buried, and redug a thousand times over. That still didn't stop the sergeants from making the men even more proficient at using an entrenchment tool.

After digging, the platoon marched to the bayonet range. Early out in training, they stabbed static objects. After two weeks, however, training shifted to piercing pads worn by a moving man. Half the platoon wore the pads while the other half jabbed blades at necks and groins, and the slashing and stabbing movements became rote and mechanized.

After the morning's drill, the platoon sergeants mustered the men into formation and distributed the new "Rainbow Division" shoulder patch. Col. Douglas MacArthur, a 42nd staff officer, either through a stroke of brilliance or simple happenstance, nicknamed the 42nd Division "Rainbow Division," and the name stuck. MacArthur claimed the division's regiments came from every corner of the nation and arched over the country "like a rainbow."

By the summer of 1917, the regular army had already sent its four divisions to France, and General Pershing, commander of American Expeditionary Forces Europe, was hungry for more divisions to arrive as soon as possible. The War Department needed to quickly federalize National Guard units. They scrounged through outfits from every corner of the country to find ones suitable to fill the 42nd.

The sergeants distributed the patches and ordered the men to have them sown on to their uniforms by 1300 hours, after the midday mess. They then dismissed the company. John, Daniel Buckley, dour Ed Rooney, and mouthy Martin McSweeney, plus Long Islanders Bergan Morgan and Jim O'Conner, ran back to the tent to retrieve their backpacks and sewing kits from under their cots.

The company's tents lined up in rows along a dirt footpath designated "Kilo Street." There were fifty tents to a company; 276 men were crammed under a canvas-covered labyrinth of poles and taut, crisscrossed ropes. Getting in and out made for some fancy footwork.

Kilo Street was one of twelve streets inside the camp's Section 165. All of 42nd Division was assembled at Long Island's Camp Mills on the flat Hempstead plain. Next to Section 165 was Section 166, the Ohio Regiment. They made up the division's 83rd Brigade. Across the camp's flat grass avenue sat Section 167, the Alabamans, and next to them Section 168, the Iowans. Those regiments made up the 84th Brigade.

"I joined the army and whaddaya know?" Ed Rooney bellowed sitting on the edge of his cot, pricking his uniform shoulder with a sewing needle. "In this man's army, I'd learn how to sew."

"I, for one, have learned to dig rather grand ditches," said Buckley.

"No one shovels it like you, Bucks," said Martin McSweeney. He threaded his needle like a skilled seamstress.

"I never expect but a grunt from a pig, Martin," said Buckley.

"Kiss my ass," said McSweeney.

Tent mates Jim O'Conner and Bergan Morgan sat on their cots sewing, too. They laughed, and so did Buckley. The tent mates had become friends.

"Hey, Bucks," Martin McSweeney called from across the tent.

"Sergeant says we're shippin' out on the HMS *Gigantic*." McSweeney looked to the others. "Have ya heard, fellers?"

They all nodded their heads yes, except for John.

"She's the sister ship of the *Titanic*, Bucks. At least that's what the sergeant said."

"My arse in your face, McSweeney. I have no fear as you think."

But Buckley shifted nervously on his cot. He could barely hide his trepidation. He didn't want to cross the Atlantic Ocean again.

John sensed Buckley's unease, and he raised his hand. "Enough," John said. "No more of that."

John was the natural leader, the most respected man in the tent. Whatever John said went, and John didn't like it when mouthy Martin McSweeney decided to taunt Daniel Buckley. John respected Father Duffy's decision to encourage Buckley, and John decided he should encourage Buckley, too.

"Oh, fellers!" McSweeney snorted. "King John has ruled. No more fun." But none of the men joined in with McSweeney, and the razzing stopped.

They sewed their patches and double-checked one another to make sure the patch was sewn on right and suitably for inspection.

John's friend from Alpha Company, lanky and tall, pimple-faced Dick O'Neil, popped in, originally saying he had a camera and wanted to take some pictures. But O'Neil was all excited and had some news he wanted to share.

"Have you heard Major Donovan is lookin' for smokers, John?" he asked, taking a seat on a cot.

"Boxing?" John asked.

"Yeah, mate, they's goin' to have a smoker between the 165th and the 167th. Major Donovan and Colonel Hine got a wager goin' with Colonel Screws. He's the CO of the Alabama 167th. They was an old gray-coat outfit in the Civil War."

The tent mates gathered around O'Neil.

"Them Southerners talk a lot of shit about us Irish," said O'Conner.

"I heard 'bout that too," said McSweeney.

"Yeah, mate," O'Neil continued, "the 69th of New York and the 4th Infantry of Alabama fought each other at Bull Run, but the 4th Infantry then is the 167th Alabama now. Can ya believe that?"

"We're shippin' to France with Confederates," McSweeney said unhappily.

"They love them English ways," said O'Conner.

O'Neil continued. "I heard old Alabama Screws told Colonel Hine and Major Donovan his Alabamans beat the Irish at Bull Run. And I heard Major Donovan told old Alabama Screws to go feck himself. Then he told that old southern hick the Fightin' Irish of New York never lose! 'Specially to no backwater cotton farmers."

"We're gonna show them barn balers whose boss, right, Johnny?" demanded McSweeney.

"Remember what Martin Sheridan told us, fellers?" Ed Rooney peered around the tent. "Dem One Sixty-Seveners fought against our flag."

"Ya gotta sign up for the smoker, Johnny, show them southern fellers who the Irish are."

"I didn't mean to start nothin'," O'Neil said, "but how 'bout I give yer name to Major Donovan? The One Sixty-Fifth could use you."

"I've heard the bunk them Sixty-Seven fellers say," said John, holding a stick in his hand, "and I ain't gonna listen to any more of that kinda talk about us Irish." He flicked the stick onto the dirt floor and stomped on it. "I'm in," he said. "You can tell Major Donovan."

The tent mates went wild, jumping up and down.

"Get 'em, Johnny!"

"Hit 'em fer me!"

"I must confess," said Buckley, "although not of American birth and a true Irishman at heart, I feel obliged and proud to defend the American flag."

John and McSweeney grabbed entrenchment tools, and Rooney picked up a pickax.

"We'll make a real American out of you, Bucks," said O'Neil. He tossed Buckley his camera. "Snap a picture fer us, will ya?"

Left to right: Marty McSweeney, John McKay, Ed Rooney, and Dick O'Neil

———

Major Donovan sat at his desk inside the 165th Division's 1st Battalion headquarters at Camp Mills, devouring the division's latest intelligence report. Donovan was desperate to know what the 165th would face once in France, and he read everything he could get his hands on. This intelligence report was penned by his old pal Col. Grayson Murphy of the division's intelligence arm, a man Donovan knew from his days on Wall Street. Grayson Murphy was a J. P. Morgan man who traveled extensively through Europe representing J. P. Morgan himself before the war, and Murphy maintained his personal relationships with all of Europe's top bankers.

Murphy's report delved into the details of the war's origin, and he offered insightful observations on the conditions that led to the fighting. Murphy was convinced the Germans wanted the European war all along, needing to capture and control the port cities of Ostend, Dunkirk, and Calais near Flanders to gain access to the Atlantic Ocean, but the Germans also needed to confront the growing Russian army amassing on the German border. Murphy explained that Archduke Ferdinand and his wife were shot on June 28, 1914, and in a short span of thirty-seven days, the Germans managed to move one million men, tanks, guns, and ammunition to attack Belgium and roll through France. Murphy believed the attack—known as the Schlieffen Plan—was in the works for some time. Even so, after heavy fighting, the French army and the British Expeditionary Force managed to stall all German advances by the fall of 1914. The Germans became stuck in place, stalemated, unable to move, and the fluid but very casualty-ridden open warfare tactics of the German army became the static trench warfare fighting—the environment the Americans would encounter upon arrival.

———

"Hello, hello." Father Duffy lifted the canvas flap and bent down low so that he could enter Donovan's tent.

Donovan turned back to look who was there, and saw his tall priest friend in collar and uniform.

"I pray to the man upstairs for guidance," Duffy said, taking a seat, "and He keeps sending me to you, William."

"You should pray to Douglas MacArthur. He has better answers."

Duffy laughed but spoke in a serious tone.

"What's the latest, William? We must be nearing deployment. I see our boys in the field. They are gaining a great deal of proficiency."

"I just read the division intelligence summary," said Donovan. "We're walking into a cauldron of crap over there. The president's war preparedness plan is nonexistent; we'll be on French and British schedules crossing the Atlantic, not our own. There's the word 'amalgamation' that French and British staff officers have been throwing around. They want to pillage our division ranks and refill their trenches with our men. I'm told General Pershing is on the ground at Allied headquarters in Chantilly, pushing back very hard. Supposedly, he has Wilson's support."

Donovan stood up and walked to a map of France he had propped up on an easel. "We're going to occupy what's called the Lorraine sector," he said. He pointed to the village of Saint Mihiel and slid his finger down to Basel, Switzerland. "The American Expeditionary Force will occupy the land south of that line," he added. "The Kriemhilde Stellung, or Hindenburg Line, as the Brits call it, runs along the same line, but the Germans sit to the north."

"Doesn't sound too horrible," said Duffy.

"Well, there's one more thing." Donovan handed Duffy the report. "The Russians are a basket case. They've lost five million men already, and Czar Nicholas abdicated in March. If the Russian government collapses or pulls out of the war, the Germans will be able to move one point seven million men from the eastern front to the western front. If we have to face three point eight million Germans before we get our men trained and our divisions organized, they'll annihilate us."

———

The night of the smoker was like no other. Soldiers were on edge all day, waiting for the much-touted bouts to start. The atmosphere around the camp was stoked ecstatic, driven by boundless youth and raw adrenalin. From Alabama privates to New York colonels, everyone had a wager on the outcome.

The pugilistic confrontation was more than a matter of mannish regimental pride. The confrontation was a clash that would forever determine the superiority of North over South, Union over Confederacy, Catholicism over Protestantism, and finally answer the question, who won Bull Run?

There would be four bouts: bantamweight, lightweight, middleweight, and heavy. One side needed a decisive count over the other to claim victory. The referees were chosen from the 42nd Division headquarters staff.

Each regiment had ten days to prepare a team. Father Duffy had the wherewithal to contact Father McGolrick in Greenpoint, and he summoned Ennis O'Shea at the Antrim Club. When O'Shea heard about the Alabama threat to the Fighting Irish's tenacity, he traveled to Camp Mills and stayed on as a guest of the 165th.

O'Shea broke up his fighters by weight class and made them spar fight over a two-day period. After a few sessions, he made determinations of skill and talent and culled four boxers he thought were good enough to defend the regiment.

The 118-pound bantamweight fighter selected was Patrick Clancy, a scrappy sergeant from the Bronx and an original Sixty-Niner who fought Poncho Villa in 1916. Most of the men in his platoon thought Clancy was an angry little shit, but O'Shea relied on Clancy's toughmindedness and his wiry grit, and he couldn't help but notice Clancy had unusually long arms and reach.

The lightweight fighter was 135-pound Cpl. Daniel Dooley from Manhattan. Dooley had some training and appeared to be a solid performer. O'Shea was confident Dooley's technical skill would win him his bout.

Next was John McKay, the middleweight at 165 pounds. John was O'Shea's protégé. O'Shea knew John had the "killer" instinct, but he had never seen John use it. He knew John wouldn't make any mistakes. He wouldn't get himself caught on the ropes, and he had the ability to strike a knockout punch. O'Shea considered John his best bet.

Finally, there was Pvt. Thomas Ahern of Brooklyn. When Donovan saw Ahern standing near the boxing ring, he called Ahern a big, dumb ox. Ahern was huge at over two hundred pounds, and he was all muscle. O'Shea was troubled. Ahern's boxing skills were lacking, so he sent a few men on a scouting mission, searching for anyone in the camp who was as big as Ahern. The scouts peered all around, but mostly up and down the company streets of Section 167, the Alabamans. They couldn't find anyone bigger or stronger than Ahern, so O'Shea chose Ahern for the team, thinking his brute power would act to counter his lackluster skill.

Opposing the Irish, O'Shea only knew the fighters' names. Eldrich Stubblefield would fight Patrick Clancy at bantam, Strickland Crawford would take on Daniel Dooley at lightweight, Marsden Price would fight John McKay at middleweight, and Shay Mott and Thomas Ahern would be in the heavyweight class.

The October air was cool and crisp, and strings of electric lights brightly illuminated the wooden stage holding the raised boxing ring. At 5:00 p.m. on a cloudless fall day, the evening sky still offered plenty of light.

Attendance wasn't mandatory, but a full turnout was expected. A good number of onlookers from the 166th Ohio and the 168th Iowan were also expected.

The officers sat in cordoned-off sections close to the ring. Major General Mann, the 42nd's commanding officer, and many of the headquarter staff officers came, including Colonel MacArthur. Brigadier Generals Lenihan of the 83rd Brigade, Brown of the 84th, and Summerall of the 67th Artillery were there. The four regimental commanding officers, including Charles Hine and Preston Screws, attended. All the battalion commanders, company captains, and platoon lieutenants from every regiment in the division came to watch. Company staff sergeants marched the rank-and-file men onto the open field surrounding the ring, and they filled in behind their respective company officers. In all, twenty thousand attended.

Alcohol consumption was prohibited, and rowdy behavior was unacceptable. Major General Mann insisted on an evening filled with divisional spirit and nothing more, but it was difficult to keep a cork on the ebullient men. The Irish arrived in the fiercest of fighting moods, and the Alabamans of the 168th came locked and loaded.

HQ for the 165th squad was a tent on the north side of the ring, and the 167th squad occupied a tent on the south side.

First up was Patrick Clancy, the bantamweight. Clancy tore out of the 165th tent wearing a pissed-off look on his face. He was so revved up that he was oblivious to the thunderous roar that swooshed all around him. Ennis O'Shea escorted Clancy up to the elevated canvas ring, patted him on the back, and went to the corner. He hoped to give Clancy a last-minute pep talk, but the raucous noise drowned him out.

Eldrich Stubblefield was even wirier than Clancy, but O'Shea saw that Stubblefield did not have Clancy's unusually long reach. The referee brought both men to the center of the ring. A rumbling wave of shouts and jeers washed over the proceedings, and the two men could hardly hear the referee's instructions.

"Three rounds, five minutes each," he said, "no hitting below the belt." They patted gloves in lieu of a handshake.

Clang! The bell sounded and the fight was on.

Clancy was all energy. He came at Stubblefield ferociously, rapidly pounding on the Alabaman's midsection and chest. Stubblefield was stunned and found it hard to recover. Clancy kept on him: punch, jab, jab, jab, and Stubblefield couldn't land a single counterpunch. Just as Ennis O'Shea had foreseen, Clancy's extra-long reach allowed him to pound on Stubblefield and not get hit. In the last seconds of the first round, Clancy unleashed another rapid succession of deadly jabs, this time hitting Stubblefield's forehead. The referee, seeing Stubblefield go weak in the knees and wobble, called for a standing ten count. Clancy rolled back to his corner, and Stubblefield stood dazed in the center of the ring. The referee counted to ten. The Alabaman never recovered, and the referee reached for Clancy's arm. He pulled Clancy to the center of the ring and raised his arm, indicating victory.

The crowd exploded. Donovan jumped on Colonel Hine, and Duffy lifted Major Moynahan into the air. The men in the surrounding field convulsed into a raucous mass of humanity, and before they could settle down and regain a semblance of calm, the next two fighters emerged from the tents.

Corporal Daniel Dooley shook nervously. O'Shea attempted to calm him, but the near riotous noise and powerful energy made Dooley tense up. He couldn't hear any of O'Shea's confident words and advice. On the other hand, Strickland Crawford, the Alabama 167er, was relaxed and loose. Crawford had experience. He had boxed once at a Marti Gras bout in New Orleans. Crawford won that match, and he was ready to win another. O'Shea knew Dooley had technical skills and was confident Dooley would defend himself against the swaggering Southerner.

The two men were called into the center and tapped gloves, and the bell clanged. The second fight was on.

Crawford immediately went on the offensive, but Dooley managed to block every combination Crawford tossed. Dooley gained his footing and threw a cross, but Crawford moved in and clinched Dooley. The men danced and struggled and the referee had to break them apart. Both Crawford and Dooley stayed defensive and hesitant and used the remaining time of the first round to land meaningless pat punches. Time on the first round ran out.

The bell sounded for the second round and Crawford lunged at Dooley to score a quick victory. He threw a haymaker punch at

Dooley's head. Dooley, seeing the large red glove careening down from the corner of his eye, instinctively pulled back. Crawford's punch smashed into Dooley's head, the glove ripping across his face. The laces slashed Dooley's skin and tore a deep laceration above his eye. The referee spotted the injury and separated the men for a moment. He determined Dooley was still fit to fight, and the ref let the bout continue.

Blood poured from Dooley's gash wound and flowed down over his brow and into his eyes. His vision became blurred, and he had to squint to see Crawford across the canvas. Crawford grew even more confident and knew that now was the time to attack his weakened opponent.

Dooley got his arms up in a defensive peekaboo stance, but Crawford, elbows bent, came under Dooley's arms and threw a merciless right hook, slamming his bunched fist into Dooley's jaw. Crawford followed the devastating hook with a left-handed power punch on Dooley's forehead, and Dooley collapsed to his knees.

"Get up!" O'Shea screamed from the corner of the ring, but his words were drowned out by the wild clamor. "Get up!" he screamed again.

Dooley bravely got up on his feet again, unwilling to surrender, but the referee looked Dooley in the eye and used his thumb to wipe his bloody socket clean. The referee saw that Dooley's pupils were no longer equal size, and he called the bout. He raised Crawford's arm victoriously.

Strickland Crawford of Birmingham, Alabama, sacked a Yankee. The 167th Regiment went insane, and the 165th sat silently. Victory for the Fighting Irish was not an option. Victory was inculcated into the minds of every man, and any notion of loss was inconceivable.

O'Shea got back to the regiment tent before Dooley was able to crawl out of the ring. He wanted to speak to John before they got outside, and he could no longer be heard.

"Johnny." O'Shea entered the tent revved up by the desperate fight. He grabbed John by the shoulders and stared him in the eyes. "Kill him," O'Shea implored. "Don't hold back. Wait for the right moment. Wait for the opening and take the shot. Kill him."

"Yes, sir," said John.

"You've got the punch, McKay. Wait for him to make a mistake, then pull the trigger. Got it?

"Yes, sir."

John left the tent and made his way to the ring. He slipped through the ropes and climbed up on to the canvas. O'Shea was right behind him. John couldn't believe the intensity of the noise. It jarred him. "Keep your head on a swivel," he could hear his dah say. "Focus on the task at hand."

"Kill 'em!" he heard O'Shea bark from the corner.

John peered across the mat and made a quick assessment of his opponent, Marsden Price. Seeing Price, John was confident he would win. Price was nervous. He kept bouncing up and down and pulsing his arms, trying to shake it out. John felt no apprehension. Price kept his head down and made no eye contact, and John thought Price wanted to be anywhere but in the ring. He understood that feeling, but now there was no retreat.

"Wait, then kill!" he heard O'Shea yell from the corner. The men tapped gloves, and the bell rang.

John took his time, and Price seemed a bit absentminded, lacking the usual concentration. John threw a combination of punches, and Price seemed to wake up. Price leaned into John and threw a few jabs at John's ribs. Rata-tat-tat! They landed, and John failed to block the barrage. Price's punches stung and hurt, and any empathy John felt for his southern opponent quickly vanished. John jabbed Price with his left hand, then followed it with a left hook. Just as Price winced leftward, feeling the lower jabs, John drew back and off-loaded his right-handed power punch. It landed squarely on Price's nose and forehead. The punch sounded like a dull thud—a sledgehammer pounding rock.

Marsden Price's body went stiff as if electrically shocked. He instantaneously swooped downward, unconscious before he hit the mat. He fell flat on his back. The referee raised John's arm in victory.

In less than two minutes, the fortunes of the Irish rebounded. The officers and men convulsed a second time. O'Shea went crazy. He squeezed John and lifted him so everyone at the far reaches of the field could see the Irish victor.

The skirmish between the Fighting Irish of New York and the Alabama Confederates had reached pandemonium. It was up to the heavyweights: the Brooklyn bruiser, Thomas Ahern, and his opponent, the son of a cotton farmer, Shay Mott.

The heavyweights looked much bigger and much more muscular than the lighter-weight boxers. Shay Mott, wherever the 167th managed to hide him, was every bit as big as Ahern, and that caught O'Shea off guard. O'Shea soon realized the heavyweight bout would be a slugfest, a barn burner, and the man who prevailed would be the one still standing after three savage rounds.

The referee called Ahern and Mott to the center, shouted the instructions, and made them tap gloves. The bell clanged, and the final, most decisive bout was underway.

The heavies moved slower. Neither man was a trained boxer; neither had a specific advantage. O'Shea figured Mott would hit Ahern a few times, Ahern would grow angry, and his Irish ire would make the brute explode. It wasn't a great strategy, but O'Shea knew for sure that triumph was often grasped through brute force. At the end of round one, the fight was indecisive.

Round two began and Ahern and Mott traded one-for-one head and body blows, sending the crowd of infantrymen into an adrenal frenzy. Mott pounded Ahern's jaw and followed it with a series of chest jabs.

Ahern continued unfazed but began to feel the sting from the blows and became angered. Ahern lashed out at Mott and landed a punch on Mott's face.

The blow slashed Mott's skin, and Mott began to drip a mix of blood and sweat that trickled down the center of his face. Mott exploded and countered like a wild beast. He landed two viscous thuds on Ahern's nose, breaking it wide open, and now Ahern too dripped blood and sweat. The bell clanged, and the second round was over.

In the corner, O'Shea wiped Ahern's face and pinched his nose to stop the bleeding. Ahern breathed a frothy bloody mix through his mouth. In Mott's corner, his coach put antihemorrhagic powder on Mott's laceration, and Mott flinched from the burn.

"Plant that southern fucker!" O'Shea yelled into Ahern's ear.

Mott's coach yelled advice as well. "The South is watchin', Shay," he said. "It's time to gut that Yankee and make Alabama proud."

The bell clanged, and the third and final round began. It was all-out mayhem. Both men fired punch after punch as if pounding a practice bag. The crowd was lit up and wild. All the officers were on their feet; the soldiers in the field were in a rage. Clancy, Dooley, and John stood outside the 165th's tent, cheering on Ahern to land the final blow and clinch victory.

The men pounced and pounded. Ahern hit Mott so hard that sweat flew from his head, but Mott would not surrender. He came right back and smacked Ahern equally hard. As O'Shea had guessed, it was a barn burner, a slugfest, a complete standoff and stalemate. Neither side would cede an inch. It was Bull Run all over again.

Finally, the clock ran out. The third round ended, and the referee saw it no other way. He raised the arms of both men and deemed the contest a tie.

———

Dick O'Neil ran down Kilo Street, leaping over the taught crisscrossing ropes and into John's tent.

"Donovan wants to see you."

John sat up in his cot.

"Major Donovan wants to give you a seventy-two!" O'Neil shouted.

Nobody got passes to leave the camp. There was no such thing as a five-minute pass, much less a seventy-two-hour pass.

"You gotta report to First Battalion, HQ," he added.

"See Donovan?"

"Yeah, mate, don't worry. He don't bite hard."

"Better bring yer mitts, Johnny," McSweeney swooned. "Donovan will want to go at least three rounds with ya."

"Gotcha self a sweet deal, eh, O'Neil?" Rooney sneered.

"Sergeant told me to fetch Johnny—no more."

"When do we report?" John asked.

"Now."

John reached under his cot and rifled through his backpack to fetch his polish kit. He unhooked his campaign hat and uniform jacket hanging above his cot, and he whisked off dust and dirt. He popped open a can of shoe polish and used his lighter to light the polish aflame. When the waxy mixture began to melt, he brought the tin tray up to his mouth and blew out the fire. He removed his dress shoes from a burlap potato sack and used a wet cloth to dab the melted wax. He rubbed the mixture on his shoes in tight, concentric circles.

He slipped off his boots and replaced his puttees with his leather leggings. He stepped into his shined shoes, donned his jacket, buttoned the buttons, then put on his campaign hat.

"Am I ready for the major?" he asked O'Neil.

"You were born ready, McKay."

John and O'Neil made their way across the busy camp, jumping over the crisscrossing ropes out onto Kilo Street and then onto the grassy main avenue separating the regiments. Thousands moved up and down the company streets. Even though everyone knew John's name, few outside Kilo Company recognized his face.

Chaplain Duffy, Major Donovan, and Sergeant Joyce Kilmer, the regiment's official recorder, were in the 1st Battalion tent waiting for John. Duffy had spoken to Ennis O'Shea after the smoker and learned that the McKay boy was from a good family in Greenpoint and that his father was a boilermaker at SOCONY—a respectable trade, not a laborer. O'Shea reminded Duffy that John had served Mass for Father McGolrick at Saint Cecilia's for ten years.

Duffy made sure Kilmer got all the facts. The smoker made for a great first Fighting Irish story, but Duffy didn't know Kilmer loathed pugilism. Kilmer's *Here and There with the 69th Infantry*, his book deal with the *New York Times* publishing arm, wouldn't include a tale about boxing.

A staff sergeant summonsed John and O'Neil inside Donovan's tent. They marched with perfect military precision, and they came to attention.

Donovan, Duffy, and Kilmer saluted.

"McKay," Donovan began, his blue eyes beaming. "I wish I had a thousand like you. I want every man in the One Sixty-Fifth to be like you. Job well done, lad. Job well done. I don't think I've experienced a moment of pure spontaneous jubilation like I did when you clocked that Confederate cotton baler right through his barn door."

John didn't know if he should laugh, smile, or stay still. He stood still.

"Bring that spirit to France, son, and we'll win this war in no time."

"Yes, sir."

"Corporal O'Neil, good job getting us the right man."

"Yes, sir," said the lanky O'Neil. O'Neil had been a favorite of Donovan's since West Point.

"Men," Donovan continued, "as you know, there have been no passes granted here at Camp Mills—no leave given. So I award you both this seventy-two-hour pass, commencing at zero six hundred hours tomorrow morning, as recognition of your accomplishment. We expect many things from our soldiers, and you two fine men have demonstrated the traits we want."

"Yes, sir," O'Neil and John said in unison.

Donovan saluted, as did Duffy and Kilmer, and John and O'Neil saluted back.

"Dismissed," Donovan barked, and John and O'Neil hightailed it out of the tent.

Early the next morning, after muster, John and Dick O'Neil left the camp and hitched a ride down Nassau Boulevard to the Long Island Rail Road station in Mineola. John planned to get off at Penny Bridge, then walk up Meeker Avenue to his parents' apartment and surprise them. O'Neil was going into Manhattan and heading up to Harlem to surprise Estelle.

The train wasn't coming for another hour, so John and O'Neil had time to kill. They strolled around the Mineola train station and came upon a brick building with a red-tiled roof. "New York Guarantee Trust," said the title over the door. John saw a stone pedestal and hopped up on top.

"John McKay," he shouted into the cool morning air. "Here he stood, the greatest of them all, the Fightin' Irish hero.

"Hold it!" O'Neil pleaded. He got his camera from his pack. He had one more picture before he could mail it back to Kodak. He'd get Estelle to do it.

"A-ten-hut!" O'Neil yelled to John, still standing on the riser. John laughed and came to attention as Dick O'Neil snapped the picture.

CHAPTER 8

October 15, 1917–November 10, 1917

___

SS *Amerika*, a German-owned ship built in
1905, renamed SS *America* in 1917

ARCHIE TURNED THE TRUCK ON to Horace Harding Boulevard and drove east along the edge of Calvary Cemetery. In three miles, he'd reach Motor Parkway and drive out to Long Island and Camp Mills. John had a few hours before his seventy-two-hour pass expired, and the middle-of-the-night ride to Mineola would take about an hour. Archie insisted on driving; this way, John didn't have to worry about the Long Island Rail Road.

Cool autumn air flowed through the cab, and John and Archie hunkered under blankets that Archie had stowed. By the time the brothers got halfway along Motor Parkway out east on Long Island, all the lights and markers of civilization had faded and the roadway became pitch-black.

"Look after Ma for me, Arch," John shouted over the blowing wind.

"She loves you more than me, Johnny. You're her favorite, ya know."

"She loves us both, Arch. Ma and Dah both do. Imagine how they feel seeing us leavin' for war."

"And leavin' them alone with Anna."

They laughed.

"I, for one, wanna get over there and stick it to those Huns," said Archie, "but my regiment ain't nowhere near ready. Talk is the Forty-Seventh is gonna roll into the Fifty-Third and become one big outfit."

"We're ready, Arch. You should see how we drill and practice in the trenches. Major Donovan and Major Moynahan have been teaching us a lot about tactics. We're gonna make those Huns wish they never saw the Irish."

Archie's truck passed a reflective black-and-white road sign illuminated by the truck's headlights. "Hempstead/Mineola one mile," it said. Archie spotted the exit and slowed the truck to make the turnoff. In the distance, tiny lights from the camp flickered on the horizon. They were glad to get off the dark, desolate parkway, and Archie drove south down Nassau Boulevard toward the camp.

The truck slowed and the noisy wind died down. Archie's emotions began to well. He had wanted to tell John how he felt all day, but he didn't want to say anything in front of their ma, dah, or even Anna. He couldn't yell it out over the noisy parkway ride, either. He swallowed a lump in his throat and spoke.

"I'm glad you got confidence in your officers, Johnny, and it's good you think you got a fine outfit going over there. But you gotta look out for yourself, brother. Them officers ain't looking out for you. They don't care about Ma or Dah or me and Anna. You gotta make it back home, brother. You just gotta." Archie choked on his words. "If for no one else—"

John stopped him. "I'll make it back, Arch, but I'm going over there to do my duty. The duty I swore to. The world has changed right under our feet, Arch, and there's nothing the same no more. America's in the fight, and that means I'm in the fight." John patted Archie on the shoulder. "When this war's done, let's make Little William and Kitty some cousins. Is that a square deal?"

"That's a square deal."

Archie stopped the truck outside the Camp Mills front gate, and John jumped out onto the dirt road. Archie climbed out to join him, and both brothers stood hugging in front of the flatbed's beaming lamps.

"See you in France," said John.

"The first cancan girl's on me." Archie smiled, and the brothers shook hands.

John came to attention, saluted Archie, made a sharp turn, and faced the gate sentry. John saluted the guard and marched through the gate, disappearing into the giant camp.

———

When John got to his tent, Daniel Buckley was still awake, lying flat on his cot.

"Welcome home, John McKay," Buckley greeted him. "I suppose you've heard the news."

John shook his head. He hadn't.

"We're shipping out, October twenty-sixth. Next stop, Brest, France."

No surprise. The news was about to come sooner or later. John was glad he got home one more time.

"Are ya ready, Bucks?"

"For the Krauts or the Atlantic?

"One thing at a time, Bucks. No use worrying."

"John McKay, my friend, few fellas you've ever met in your life, such as a fella like me, knows a certain truth learned from experience, and that's just how fast things can go completely to shit."

John laughed. "True, Bucks, but no sense fretting. It's OK to be scared, Bucks. I read one time that all brave men are scared. They just face the fear when the time comes. When they have to. They don't fret about it. Besides, we got no choice. This war is happening in our time, and ain't nobody else is gonna fight it for us."

"Have you thought about killing a man, John?"

"Yes, Bucks, I have, and I believe our faith will keep us on the right path. I pray God will forgive me."

"Then I suppose I shan't fret anymore," said Buckley.

"That's right. Now let's get some shut-eye, Bucks."

John hung his campaign hat on a peg above his cot and took off his olive-drab jacket. He opened the side pocket to grab his billfold and felt an object buried deep inside. He reached down, pinching two fingers, and plucked out a row of beads—a rosary. He recognized the set immediately. They were Anna's. She must have slipped them in his jacket when he wasn't looking. These rosary beads were a gift from their ma. She gave them to Anna for her confirmation, and they'd belonged to Grandmother Black from Antrim. None of the McKay children ever met Grandma Black, so her "Crown of Roses" was always considered special.

John unbuttoned the upper pocket of his jacket, slipped the beads inside, and fastened it closed. They'd be safe there, and he could feel them against his chest whenever he wore his jacket.

———

One week had passed, and a postman who worked the Greenpoint neighborhood and delivered the mail along Meeker Avenue ran up the stairs to the McKay residence and banged on the door. Mary was home alone.

"Mrs. McKay," the postman called out, and Mary opened the door. He was out of breath having climbed the steps. "I just spoke with a Long Island Rail conductor."

Mary was confused.

"The conductor is heading to Long Island this morning, Mrs. McKay. He said he was moving the Sixty-Ninth soldiers to Long Island City this afternoon. He said he'd be passing through Penny Bridge at three p.m. Said he thought some of the Greenpoint families would like to know and asked me to pass the word. He said he was moving Kilo Company of the One Sixty-Fifth Regiment. That's your boy, Mrs. McKay, isn't it?"

"Oh, dear God," Mary gasped, grateful for the surprise news. "Thank you so much, sir. Yes, that's my boy. Thank you for thinking of us. Three p.m. at Penny Bridge?"

"Yes, Mrs. McKay. That's what the conductor said."

Mary thanked the postman again, and he left. She grabbed her coat and headed down Russell Street to Catherine's apartment by the park. On the way, she saw a girlfriend of Anna's and asked her to pass the word to Anna at work.

Mary cut across Winthrop Park toward Nassau Street and, when in front of Catherine's apartment, she saw her daughter sitting in the portico window with Little William on her lap.

"Catherine," she called from the street excitedly, "the boys are leaving today. John's train is coming through Penny Bridge at three o'clock."

Mary hurried up the stairs and got to the door just as Catherine opened it.

"Three p.m., Catherine." Mary scurried into the kitchen. "Can you have the children ready?"

———

The men in John's tent had their backpacks laid out on their cots. Each man had conducted an inventory for himself, counting all his personal possessions, and then double-checked his tent mate. They were to have everything needed for France, and all the required gear for the pack had to be properly stowed. The pack weighed eighty pounds when full, and it was difficult to balance on one's back. It had to be rigged just right.

"I got more shit than an East-Side peddler," McSweeney moaned, carefully stepping over the tangle of tie-down ropes.

The men were ordered to assemble in formation on the grassy main avenue at the top of Kilo Street. Once in line, the sergeants conducted one more final inspection.

"Helmet?"

"Yes, Sergeant."

"Entrenchment tool?"

"Yes, Sergeant."

"Bayonet?"

"Yes, Sergeant."

"Mess kit?"

"Yes, Sergeant."

"Ammo belt?"

"Yes, Sergeant."

Every man was checked for every item, and nobody moved until the sergeants were completely satisfied that Kilo and every other company was ready to ship out.

The sergeants called the entire battalion to attention, and the long rows of 3rd Battalion Shamrock men marched down the camp's main avenue through the main gate and out onto Garden City's Commercial Boulevard. The Long Island Rail Road train was already in the station. It was the longest train any of them had ever seen, and its cargo doors were pulled wide open, ready for the load up. All four companies were moving. The entire Shamrock Battalion totaling over one thousand men.

When the battalion exited through the camp gate, the men did not sing a marching cadence. There was no "Garryowen," just a deliberate pace akin to a soulful lament. The men were keenly aware they were leaving home for good; leaving their wives and children, mothers and fathers, girlfriends and friends. Everything left behind, recalled now only by memory.

A team of staff sergeants tagged each man's pack, and another team of privates loaded the packs onto the train. The men were permitted to ease up to the passenger cars and await departure. The transit time to Long Island City was fifty minutes. Once arrived, the battalion would transfer onto ferryboats and transit over water to Hoboken, New Jersey. The SS *America* was berthed on the main pier there.

"Bucks!" John motioned for his friend to sit with him at the end of the train car, by the door.

"Ya think they'll be waitin' fer ya, John?" Buckley asked.

"If they know we're coming, my ma'll be there," John assured him.

"The Irish can pass the *craic* faster than Marconi."

The train finished loading, and a distant whistle at the front locomotive sounded. The cars snapped tight, then lurched forward as the powerful steam engine grabbed the rails and dragged the massive weight away from the camp.

The entire 42nd Division was in transit. The 1st Battalion, Companies A, B, C, and D, led by Major Donovan, left Camp Mills overnight and were now railroading up to Montreal for embarkation on the *Tunisian*, a French-flagged ship. The 2nd Battalion, Companies E, F, G, and H, led by Major Stacom, left Camp Mills before dawn. They were scheduled to transport with the 3rd Battalion out of Hoboken. Major Moynahan was already in Hoboken preparing for his Shamrock Battalion, companies I, J, K, and L to arrive by ferry in the late afternoon.

Eight ships were needed to transport the Rainbow Division's twenty-five thousand men. Four ships berthed at Hoboken, and four berthed at Montreal. Once the different transport ships sailed out into the open Atlantic Ocean, each one joined a unique convoy escorted by US Navy combatant ships.

The convoys sailed different shipping lanes and headed to different debarkation points, some in France and some in England. Dispersing convoys successfully countered German U-boats. The U-boats might sink some ships, but not all ships. Eventually, the entire division would regroup in France at the American army training camp located far east in the Lorraine sector.

Only the transport SS *America*, the ship used by the Shamrock Battalion, was a US-flagged ship. Up to America's declaration of war, the *Amerika* belonged to the German imperial government, but after the war declaration, the Wilson administration absconded the vessel and put the sizable German *Schiff* to good use.

————

Word spread among Greenpoint families, and hundreds of people made it to Penny Bridge. The crowd lined up along Newtown Creek or stood on the Meeker Avenue Bridge. Mary, Catherine, Little William, Kitty, and Anna lined up alongside the rail tracks at Penny Bridge station to get close.

Mary was sure John would peer out a window or door and was certain he'd want to take one last look at Greenpoint as the train passed through. John would see the old Dutch house, the busy Newtown Creek, and the smoky refineries where he and his dah worked. He could spot the spire of Saint Cecilia's and think of Father McGolrick, and he'd certainly see the Meeker Avenue trolley and recall the clang of its bell. The conductor would yell, "End of the line!"

The troop train chugged along, passing familiar crossings in Queens, and John recognized the train would soon approach Greenpoint and Penny Bridge Station. He got up from his seat and went to the open window of the train's doorway. He could see inlets and flatboats on the interior waterways that fed the larger Newtown Creek, and in the distance, he spotted Saint Cecilia's high spire. The Meeker Avenue Bridge and Penny Bridge Station weren't far off.

"He's here! He's here!" Anna yelled. The train rolled around the bend, nearing Penny Bridge.

Mary nervously grasped Anna's hand.

Catherine held Kitty and leaned down to speak to Little William. She gave the three-year-old explicit instructions. "Stand up straight, put your chest out, and put your shoulders back. When the train comes, Willie, stand tall and salute your uncle John."

John saw his ma, Catherine, and Anna standing at the edge of the tracks near the Meeker Avenue Bridge. He could see Little William. John removed his campaign hat and began to wave it wildly. Mary and Anna saw him, and they started to cheer. Tears flooded Mary's face, and the train conductor blasted the locomotive's booming whistle. Loud roars and cheers from the surrounding crowd bounced back and forth among soldiers and family members.

"Salute, William," Catherine said.

The sprite toddler stood upright, pressed out his chest, and held his shoulders back. He gave Uncle Johnny a perfect salute.

John saw William, and he too stood at attention in the train's doorway and saluted his nephew.

"I love you, Johnny!" Anna screamed at the top of her lungs.

Mary was displeased, but she too ended up screaming at the top of her lungs so John could hear her.

"I love you, son!" she called out over the noisy din.

"I love you too, Ma!" John yelled back.

Mary felt her chest tighten, and Anna and Catherine instinctively slipped their arms under her shoulders and drew her in close. John waved his hat as long as he could.

The women stood silent watching the heavy train ease its way around a bend, and finally Johnny was gone.

———

Long Island City ferries, their decks brimming with doughboys, motored in loose formation down the East River. John stood at the forecastle on an outside deck, and he peered down the river. From this low viewpoint, the steel cables on the modern bridges spanning Manhattan to Brooklyn shimmered in the autumn sun, appearing majestic.

As the ferry passed beneath the Williamsburg Bridge, John looked up to see the narrow footpath. He recalled his walks from Mrs. Hickey's apartment to his home in Greenpoint.

The ferries glided under the Brooklyn Bridge. The men marveled at the high skyscrapers. The Woolworth building, the cathedral of commerce, was by far the tallest.

The loose formation motored south to the mouth of the East River and rounded lower Manhattan. The Statue of Liberty, solitary in the middle of the harbor, came into view. She appeared aqua-green, but glowed softly while bathed in the late October golden sun.

Men on the deck began to cheer, and the cheers grew louder as more and more men could see the golden lady in the harbor. She represented everything these young Irish Americans were willing to fight for, and the eruption of patriotism was spontaneous. John's boat captain heard the boisterous soldiers below and blasted his ferry's horn. As each ferry rounded Manhattan's battery, loud cheers could be heard from those decks, too, and the ferry captain blasted his ship's horn.

"She was a gift from the French," John heard an officer yell over the cheers, then he heard a second officer answer the first. "And to France we go, to keep her torch lit."

John felt proud. "Defending liberty," he thought. "Liberty is certainly worth defending."

A thousand Shamrock men formed up on the Hoboken pier ready to embark the SS *America*. The process was gangly but organized. Company men fell into single file; platoon after platoon they marched up the ship's brow. One by one, they stopped and saluted the American flag, masted on the ship's fantail.

"She's an Irish-made ship," boasted Buckley. "Built in Belfast."

The men stepped off the pier and onto the gangplank leading up to the *America*'s main deck.

"Irish made, eh, Bucks?" McSweeney goaded Buckley. "How did the last one work out fer yer?"

"Pipe down, Martin, and face the stern. Salute the flag," John barked.

"Don't got yer brother no more, McKay—you gotta protect Buckley?"

John burned with anger. None of his squad mates except Buckley knew anything about Archie, and John thought McSweeney had no business mouthing off about his brother, but John kept his cool and let big-mouthed McSweeney's comment pass.

The sergeants led the men across the main deck, and they climbed down ladders into the ship's deep cargo hold many levels below. The cargo spaces had been reconfigured and made into berthing compartments. Hammock-style bunks hung between poles welded to the decks and the overhead. Between each set of poles draped an upper, middle, and lower hammock.

The men were assigned "bunks" as they came into the cargo hold. The backpacks came off their shoulders, and they were stowed on the deck floor below the lowest hammock. John, Daniel Buckley, and Marty McSweeney bunked atop one another, and across the narrow row were Ed Rooney, Bergan Morgan, and Jim O'Conner. The six men went from living in a small six-man tent to an even smaller space on the ship.

"We'll be bunkin' in a milk wagon next," sniped Bergan Morgan, who like McSweeney got stuck with the hammock closest to the deck floor.

"Gettin' us ready fer the pine box," grumbled Rooney.

When the men came down the ladders and filed into the berthing compartment, Daniel Buckley took note of the hatch door at the top of the ladder. He'd read a lot about ships and shipping since the *Titanic*, and he understood if the SS *America* was threatened by U-boats, then the ship's crew was ordered to close all hatches and lock them.

Buckley saw the acronym QAWTD stenciled on the hatch door, just like he had read. It stood for Quick-Acting Water-Tight Door, and Buckley knew if the ship had an emergency, then a crewman would slam the hatch shut quickly, turn its wheel, and it would lock shut. No one in the compartment below deck could open it. All the infantrymen bunked in the deep hold would be locked in.

Buckley thought about his fellow *Titanic* travelers. After the ship impacted the iceberg, the crippled vessel began to flood with frigid ocean water. The water encroached compartment after compartment and threatened to readily sink the "unsinkable" RMS *Titanic* until the ship's crew scurried to stop the torrent. They executed emergency procedures, trying in vain to hold off the rising water level, and the crew closed all the ship's hatches. But by closing the hatches, hundreds of third-class passengers remained trapped below, condemned to drown.

It was a furious fight to compartmentalize the *Titanic*, to avert further flooding, but compartmentalizing the *Titanic* proved a futile task. The huge below-surface prong jutting out from the massive iceberg ripped an elongated gash just above the ship's keel, and the mighty liner was doomed from the moment of impact.

Buckley thought those who were trapped below deck were treated no better than sewer rats. He could still hear their pleas. They begged Star Line crewmen to unlock the hatches, but the officers wouldn't allow a single hatch to be opened.

Simple curiosity saved Buckley's life. When he saw a trickle of water roll through his berthing compartment, he climbed up to the main deck to see what had happened. Before he could return to his compartment, the ship's crewmen had shut and locked all the hatches, and Buckley had nowhere to go. He boarded an empty lifeboat ready for launch.

"Hey, Bucks." McSweeney poked Buckley from the hammock below. "You gonna use yer bunk or are you sleepin' in a lifeboat?"

Daniel Buckley had had enough of McSweeney's badgering, and he shot back, chiding the mouthy Mick. "McSweeney, you faker." Buckley was furious. "I have supreme confidence, Martin, when the kaiser's U-boats are circling this ship, working to torpedo us and send us all down into the deep and murky—after our ship's crewmen shut and lock those hatches above us and leave us down here to drown—it'll be you, Martin. You will be the first man to shit himself with fear. Not I, Daniel Buckley of Ballydesmond."

———

By nightfall, the SS *America* had tugboats pressing against her bow and latched across her stern. She was maneuvered off the pier by the harbormaster's crew and positioned in the middle of the Hudson River. It was still twilight, and the ship wouldn't sail through the Verrazano Straights until total darkness.

The men got a chow call in the evening and were able to go topside to the ship's mess deck for a meal. The ship could feed 250 men every half hour, and it took two hours to get both battalions fed.

During mealtime, the SS *America* sailed north up the Hudson and dropped anchor. At midnight, she set sail out of the harbor and joined up with a US Navy-led convoy heading for Brest, France.

———

Ten ships steamed at twelve knots through a calm North Atlantic Ocean, and most of the infantrymen on the SS *America* spent their time topside on its main deck enjoying the cool, clean ocean air and bright-blue clear skies.

They were filled with good spirits and laughter. No sign of worry or dread. No U-boats. Some gambled, using dice carved from soap, and others played with cards they'd gotten from YMCA volunteers on the Hoboken pier. The ship's geedunk sold many sundry items like candy, but most men wanted the cartons of inexpensive cigarettes. They loaded up on cheap smokes because nobody knew if cigarettes would be available in France.

John never smoked before, but while killing some time, he bummed a smoke off Buckley. John liked the taste of the cigarette, went to the geedunk, and bought himself an armful of smokes, as many as he could fit in his kit.

"Planning on a lifer stint, McKay?" McSweeney ribbed him.

John took no chances and filled up his pack up with cigarettes. His sergeant told him back in 1916 on the Mexican border that cigarettes were like money and a soldier could trade for most anything for a simple cigarette.

On the ship's fantail, a group of men sat singing popular songs. One song was new, but heard everywhere around Brooklyn's beer halls and theaters. The song was George M. Cohan's "Over There." The musical group got every man out on the rear deck singing at the top of his lungs. Others cheered and hollered or waved their campaign hats.

Over there, over there
Send the word send the word over there
That the Yanks are coming, the Yanks are coming,
The drums rum-tumming ev'rywhere
So prepare, say a pray'r
Send the word send the word to beware
We'll be over we're coming over,
And we won't come back till it's over over there!

Suddenly an alarm bell clanged and the singing stopped. Ship crewmen came out on the upper-deck platforms bullhorns cupped to their mouths, and began shouting.

"General quarters! General quarters!"

The doughboys scrambled and scurried. They ran forward and up-ladder on the ship's port side and astern and down-ladder on the starboard side. Every man headed to his assigned berthing compartment.

They had drilled this before, every day since leaving Hoboken. They could make the *America* watertight in three minutes. This time it seemed different. It wasn't a practice drill. As the men ran to the ladders, they could see the destroyer USS *North Carolina* break hard starboard and away from the convoy. Black smoke billowed from her stacks. Her three-inch gun turrets swung wildly until perpendicular to the ship's bow. They pointed low to the horizon.

U-boats!

John, Buckley, and McSweeney slid down the ladders, hands on the rails and feet on the edges, never touching the steps. In a matter of seconds, they dropped three decks until below the waterline and into their berthing compartment. A navy boatswain's mate stood at the top of the hatch ready to close it. At three minutes sharp, he'd turn its wheel and lock the men below.

In the berthing compartment, men lay flat in their hammocks in complete silence. Buckley prayed on his rosary, and John brushed his hand over his jacket pocket.

"Courage, Bucks," John whispered.

"It's all fun now!" moaned Ed Rooney. He looked across the row and saw Marty McSweeney. A single tear rolled down his cheek.

Ka-boom!

A powerful sonic thud hit the side of the ship, and her thick metal sidewall plates buckled inward and then back outward. A follow-on pressure wave shot across the berthing compartment.

"Holy fuck!" screamed a frightened soldier.

The ship leaned hard to port, its twin screws spinning faster, straining to scoop ocean water. The ship shook and rattled and then moaned as if dying or about to fall apart, rivets straining, ready to pop. The bridge crew executed a second hard left turn, and the ship's metal frame twisted and groaned—then the ship listed steeply to the left. All the backpacks stowed under the hammocks slid across the steeply tilted deck and smashed into the portside bulkhead. Any object not fastened down went airborne, and objects flew across the compartment until they smacked into the metal deck. The soldiers hung on tight, clinging to the edges of their hammocks, nerves shattered.

Ka-boom! A second explosion!

The *North Carolina* bore down on the U-boats and launched a series of depth charges. The high-explosive underwater concussions reverberated through the ocean water, hitting the ship convoy with violent shockwaves.

Bang! A metal wobble, then *bang, bang, bang!*"

The *North Carolina* was firing her three-inch guns.

The *America* pitched downward, rapidly rolling hard right, reversing its list. Backpacks and piles of refuse that had piled up on the port bulkhead careened across the slanted deck floor and slammed into the starboard bulkhead.

The screw propellers groaned like an injured animal, but eventually the groaning eased and the grinding, twisting metal and straining rivets lessened. The *America* righted herself to center, even on her keel, and the guns and depth charges of the *North Carolina* ceased fire.

A boatswain's mate popped opened the hatch, and brilliant light shined down into the compartment.

"All clear!" he yelled down the hole.

CHAPTER 9

November 25, 1917–December 25, 1917

"MOVE YOUR FECKING FOOT, MARTIN." Buckley kicked McSweeney in the leg. He was annoyed. Nobody had room to stretch in the tightly packed train car. Everyone was squeezed, and McSweeney had taken it upon himself to sprawl out.

"They'll be crammin' us in boxes next." Ed Rooney groaned.

"You're dark, Rooney," said McSweeney. "I, for one, plan to march down Fifth Avenue."

"Your three-year plan to get laid, Martin?" Bergan Morgan butt in.

"When the Huns git you, Morgan," McSweeney was broiling, "the army's gonna ship you home ass up in a box, and when your ma and pa open it, to see if it's you, your ma's gonna say, 'Oh yes, that's my little asshole, Bergie.'"

"You stink, McSweeney. Is your diaper full?"

"You aren't a spring breeze, either, Bergan." Buckley waved his hand across his nose.

They hadn't bathed or changed clothes since Hoboken. The SS *America* didn't desalinize enough fresh water, and water use was limited for drinking and the ship's galley; no bathing except shaving one's face.

Jim O'Conner, a Camp Mills tent mate, sat balled up in the corner, shivering. He coughed and hacked, one spasm after the other.

"Cover your mouth, O'Conner," Rooney barked at him. "You'll be puttin' the influenza on us."

"I ain't got no flu," O'Conner insisted, his voice gravelly and full. He covered his mouth and convulsed again. Many men fell ill with lung infections, fevers, and bad colds, but so far, the 1917 flu pandemic hadn't reached the AEF troops.

"McSweeney!" Bergan Morgan finally retorted. "Your ma is such a dumb Irish donkey." He snorted. "After the Huns blow your gob off, the army's gonna ship it home in a box, and when the sergeant holds it up by the hairs and asks your eejit ma if dat's you, she'll say, 'Oh no, Sergeant, can't be. My Martin's much taller."

"Feck off, Morgan."

"Such talk," Buckley warned. "You'll stew in purgatory."

"Martin's goin' to hell, anyhow," said Morgan.

John raised his arm. "Enough from all of yers," he said.

"Oh, oh, boys! King Johnny raised his arm again," McSweeney sneered. "Everyone must behave."

John ignored him.

The men had been cooped up, traveling in the overpacked train car for two days and still had one more day of transit before reaching the American army sector in the east.

They had started out on November 25 in a misty rain and fog at the Brest piers. The battalion was scheduled to travel via French cargo trains and ride all the way to the village Vaucouleurs in the Lorraine sector. There, they'd join up with the 1st and 2nd Battalions.

The cargo train stretched out long across the depot platform, but it was nothing like the Long Island Rail Road with its comfortable seats, windows, and lavatories. French cargo trains had white-stenciled markings on each car: "40 Hommes/8 Cheveaux," or forty men/eight horses.

Seeing that, the men chuckled, amused they were traveling like horses, but the laughter ended when French army officers ordered each car crammed with forty men in full pack. It made for a miserable three-day ride from Brest to the US Army training facility in Vaucouleurs.

The men shivered in the cold and became soaking wet. The foggy mist was now a steady rain, and the widely spaced slats of the hommes car floor sucked up rainwater from the tracks below. Before the first day, everything was saturated. Men resorted to sitting atop their packs. Water was everywhere.

They had little to eat, too. The 42nd Division Sanitary Company, responsible for commissary supply, meted out three days' rations of canned meat and hardtack—dry flat bread, like a cracker. Each man filled two water canteens to the brim, leaving only a half-gallon supply to drink for the three-day trip. At layover stops, the American Red Cross provided hot coffee and bread, and the men had a few hours to get off the train and stretch.

Crammed inside the rail cars en route to Vaucouleurs, they had no idea their fates had already been set. At General Pershing's Chaumont headquarters, American Expeditionary Force staff officers promulgated an elaborately detailed general organizational plan outlining every component of training and deployment for American forces.

The plan outlined which portion of the western front line AEF would occupy and how those forces would occupy it. The plan outlined divisional organization and the larger corps organization and delineated how AEF corps would communicate while on the battlefield.

The Americans were assigned the southeastern end of the western front. It was considered neither a good nor a bad location. The British had insisted on access to English Channel port cities and deployed their forces north of the Somme River. The French demanded that they themselves protect the direct routes into Paris, and they deployed their forces south of the Somme River but north of the Marne River. The Americans were left with the eastern Lorraine sector, south of the Marne River, the Meuse River running north/south through its middle.

The American sector line began at Saint Mihiel in the northwest and ran southeast to Basal, Switzerland. Pershing reconnoitered the sector. He determined that nearby German coal and iron mines and two resupply rail conduits in the city of Sedan just north of the Hindenburg Line were his primary targets.

In November 1917, Pershing's general organizational plan called for the American Expeditionary Force to be manned at one million men, or forty divisions. There would be one US Army made of ten corps. Each corps would be manned at four divisions, and each division would be comprised of four regiments. Regiments varied in size, but divisions totaled twenty-five thousand men each, a number double that of a German or French division and a size decided upon because the American army lacked a sufficient number of trained officers.

By the spring of 1918, however, Pershing's general organization plan numbers had changed radically. Pershing needed a four-million-man army to meet the AEF's needs, and he urged Secretary of War Baker to get his Department of War better organized—and fast.

Pershing was short on divisions, tanks, artillery, small weapons, ammunition, replacements, vehicles, uniforms, and food. He needed more of everything, and time was running short. He refused to send any of his new conscripts into harm's way until he was certain they'd received proper training.

By the time the 42nd Division arrived in France in the fall of 1917, General Pershing already had his four regular US. Army divisions embedded inside French army divisions at the front. Pershing used embedding to gain frontline proficiency, but embedding also quelled the British and French generals, who ceaselessly clamored for force amalgamation.

Pershing dismissed any thought of amalgamation and made sure his American army remained intact under his command.

His general organizational plan called for stand-alone American operations, and Pershing planned for the American army, once ready, to conduct relentless offensive assaults on the German line—a doctrine the more exhausted Allied generals had long abandoned. Nevertheless, Pershing held his ground and used his warfare doctrine as an excuse not to abandon his army.

Pershing was confident that he could uproot the Germans and force them out into the open battlefield. He was certain the Americans could successfully pursue and destroy them using overwhelming force once out on the battlefield.

However, without American men and matériel at the ready, able to perpetrate his offensive strategy, Pershing's open warfare doctrine was impossible to execute. His tactics might have looked winnable on the planning table, but to French and British commanders, Pershing was wishfully thinking and unrealistic. They regarded his plans a colossal waste of time.

All the Allied planners had agreed that a massive German spring 1918 offensive was in the wings, so British General Haig and French General Foch thought it was time for the American general to face reality and supply the Allies with the riflemen and machine gunners they needed and stop making nonsensical, grandiose plans.

General Pershing held his ground.

———

The 165th Infantry Regiment arrived at Vaucouleurs at the US Army's primary warfare training facility, and the men were split up and sent to schools specifically associated to the weapons they would use in the field.

The regiment still billeted together, and John and his platoon mates were assigned to live in a roofless, artillery-shattered ruin of a barn along Vaucouleurs's muddy and meandering main road. The mission for them now was to get enough small-arms training so that each man was an expert marksman and was ready for the next phase of training: making squads, platoons, and companies operate as one coordinated unit.

As automatic riflemen, John and Ed Rooney were sent to the Chauchat automatic rifle school followed by Hotchkiss machine-gun school. Riflemen were issued their British-made Enfields that were modified for American ammunition, and they practiced shooting at the army's rifle ranges until mastering marksmanship. At the light artillery school, mortar teams and grenadiers spent days plying their deadly trade, learning to seek out and destroy Hun encampments and machine-gun nests.

December's cold, wet weather had settled over the Lorraine, and the men shivered and bundled themselves under layers of clothing to stay warm. They weren't permitted to light fires for hot water to shave or bathe, but the sergeants still insisted on clean faces. Uniforms and underwear, on the other hand, quickly tattered and frayed or just fell apart.

Senior officers felt the Vaucouleurs training facility was much too close to the German line. Artillery rumbling could be heard in the near distance. They prohibited lighting fires or creating any smoke until they were convinced German reconnaissance aircraft were unable to spot the American encampment. Tattered uniforms became the norm.

John, Ed Rooney, Daniel Buckley, and Bergan Morgan billeted atop a thick layer of hay piled into a stone-walled, roofless barn behind a farmhouse. Temperatures dropped to near freezing during the overnights, and the four men slept by donning their newly issued winter coats and gloves. Daniel Buckley figured out if he wrapped his puttee leggings higher up on his legs he'd stay warmer. His practice eventually became the norm for everybody.

To build beds for sleeping, the men collected hay from the surrounding farm, but after a day or two they realized the fluffy, dry chaff was completely infested with lice. Soon they were infested with lice, and within a week, every man in the company was infested with the "cooties."

Exposed to bitter cold, men started to fall sick and get ill with infection. Every day, five to ten men were shipped by horse-drawn cart to the Vaucouleurs field hospital. Jim O'Conner, the tent mate who suffered from a bad cough on the train ride east, went to a field hospital and was never seen or heard again.

John asked a bray driver to look for O'Conner and to see how he was fairing, but after three trips to the field hospital, the driver said he couldn't find O'Conner anywhere. There was no sign of the sick infantryman, but the bray driver did say the hospital was loaded up with hundreds of men, all sick with influenza.

"And lots is sick with the tuberculosis, too," he added.

———

"*Messieurs, A-merry-kanz,*" the French sergeant began. He held a French Chauchat automatic rifle over his head for all the automatic riflemen in the classroom to see. "*Le Sho-sho ree-fell auto-mat-teek,*" he added, introducing the weapon to the American newcomers.

John gazed at the rifle. His task was to learn the weapon and become an expert, but looking at it, he wondered about the rifle's apparent haphazard design. The rifle wasn't sleek; in fact, it was rather ugly, as if it had been slapped together. John read in the operator's manual that the Chauchat was manufactured in Paris and was used in France, Poland, Italy, Russia, and now by the Americans, so he guessed it must work good, and it just looked bad.

The Chauchat instructors were a combination of French army officers and regular US Army privates, corporals, and sergeants culled from the regular army and who had gone through the course earlier.

The Chauchat rifle was rated at three hundred rounds per minute and had a twenty-round magazine. The French used 8 mm Lebel rounds, but the Americans modified the gun to use standard .306-inch American ammunition. The Americans modified the British Enfield rifle the same way, but the American version of the Chauchat automatic proved to be a complete failure and made the rifle virtually unusable junk. The American army ended up rejecting almost half of all the modified Chauchats manufactured, and the 42nd Division stuck to using the French version with French ammunition. The far superior, but still-on-the-drawing-board Browning automatic was due to arrive in the spring of 1918, but by war's end, the much-touted Browning automatic rifle was never used by AEF units in any offensive action.

The French sergeants kept telling American trainees the "*Sho-sho*" was a "*ree-fell, chez superior,*" but American instructors countered their French hosts by putting sharp focus on the weapon's defects. The instructors knew the Chauchat's design was flawed, and it was going to get American soldiers killed. The American instructors aimed to lower the casualty toll by making each Chauchat operator proficient at maintaining the weapon and making him fully knowledgeable of the rifle's unreliable characteristics.

In the field, Americans referred to the French automatic rifle as the "damned jammed Chauchat," even though it was arguably primarily the modified American .306-inch caliber version that was guaranteed to jam. The spent shells would not eject from the chamber, and the rifle barrel was apt to overheat. The French 8 mm version jammed less, but its twenty-round clip-casing magazine was of poor design. Since it was opened on one side, the shooter could peer at the magazine case and see how many rounds he had remaining. The magazine's open-face design, however, invited dirt and mud, and in the mud-filled trenches of France, the chamber frequently jammed, and this was a fatal flaw.

John remembered shooting the Chauchat at West Point and remembered it had nasty recoil. He ended up with a large bruise on his shoulder. At the automatic rifle school, John heard a French sergeant say the rifle's recoil was "*la gifle*," or "a slap," and in this case, the Frenchman meant a slap from an angry woman.

The rifle's violent recoil required the shooter to keep his face away from the chamber and at the same time keep the stubby butt of the rifle pressed firmly against his shoulder. Spent rounds flew out of the chamber a mere inch from the shooter's face. Taking good aim and making a good shot with the Chauchat was awkward. The rifle was rated to 1,500 feet, but successfully hitting the intended target usually happened somewhere inside three hundred feet.

Each man in the rifle class was issued his own weapon. There were four automatic riflemen per platoon and four platoons per company.

The 165th Infantry had twelve companies, so the French meted out 192 Chauchat rifles to the Irish American regiment. An automatic rifleman, like all riflemen, was responsible for maintaining and cleaning his rifle. He was to have the weapon in his possession at all times. American instructors gave implicit orders and demanded that novice riflemen never refer to a rifle as a gun. A man could find himself counting off fifty push-ups if he ever committed such an inexcusable error.

"This is your rifle," a sergeant barked to the class of students. He held a Chauchat above his head. He lowered the rifle, moved his hand below his waist, and grabbed his crotch. "And this is your gun! Never confuse the two."

The rifle weighed twenty pounds and was easy to transport. The Chauchat's lightweight and easy transportability was its best feature and made the weapon invaluable on the battlefield. The Chauchat was the lightest automatic weapon available, and the Allies had a small tactical advantage using it.

At the shooting range, the instructors ordered the riflemen to line up along a makeshift trench. The men spread out down the line and prepared their weapons for shooting. It was the first time with an automatic rifle for many, but all the men had some shooting experience using the Springfield back at Camp Mills.

John situated himself in the trench next to Ed Rooney. Both men were eager to fire the weapon, believing they were on the cusp of big change. No more classroom theory, no more wooden weapons, no more mock practice; this was the real thing.

"Raise your weapon," the instructor barked to the men. "Lift the rifle barrel parallel to the ground. Make it equal to the height of the tripod. Place the butt plate firmly against your shoulder. Flip your trigger switch."

When the instructor was sure every man was in position and ready to shoot, he blew his whistle in two long-winded intervals—the American signal to "commence fire."

The line exploded. Rounds cooked off in a rapid rat-a-tat-tat succession, leaving a smoky trail. The empty cartridges flew from the chambers and down into the dirt. In less than five seconds, a twenty-round magazine was depleted.

"Flip your trigger switch," the instructor shouted. "Flip your magazine release. Catch the magazine in your hand. Do not let it touch the ground. Place the empty magazine in your container and reload with a full cartridge."

He counted thousand one, thousand two, thousand three, then blew the whistle for two long blows.

Again, the rifles exploded. Sulfur smoke from the combusting gunpowder flowed down into the trench and settled like a fog. Downrange, high-velocity bullets ripped into the dry mud ground between fifty-foot and thousand-foot distances, throwing clumps of dirt high into the air.

The instructors shook their heads. They had much work laid out before them. These riflemen were the best shooters in the regiment, and to a man, they shot the Chauchat poorly. By afternoon, every gunner would have to hit targets at one thousand feet or better and be proficient at loading and reloading the rifle with timed precision.

The instructors instilled repetitive action into the riflemen. Each man developed his automatic muscle memory and learned to fire the Chauchat with predictable precision and very little forethought. In the heat of battle, acute muscle memory equaled survival, and repetitive learning was the only way to help a man overcome fear and keep him shooting even when he was paralyzed by terror.

The French sergeants knew from experience that a man could get lost on the battlefield, disoriented by exploding mortars and loud artillery concussions pounding beneath his feet. An automatic rifleman had to shoot without thinking.

"Again!" the instructors yelled into the trench line. "Again! Again! Again!"

———

Although full of lice and stinking of pig urine and cow dung, the squad mates' roofless stone barn was a paradise compared to most of Kilo Company's private first class billeting. Daniel Buckley acquired a table and a metal basin for washing. He found two stools for sitting, and one day he returned to the barn carrying a burlap sack packed with fresh bread, cheese, and two bottles of homemade red wine.

After primary weapons training was over, the platoon friends gathered inside the barn. They sat around, scattered on clumps of hay while carefully cleaning their rifles. Their attitudes had changed greatly since school had ended. They all gained proficiency using their weapons, and each man regarded himself more as a veteran than a newbie. Even the runners, Buckley and Bergan Morgan, were trained to shoot the Enfield.

"Hey, McKay," McSweeney called out. The easy banter around the open barn quieted. "I learned a new word in French, McKay. Do you wanna hear it?"

"Do we have a choice, Martin?" Ed Rooney grumbled. He dabbed gun oil on his rifle barrel, took a clean cloth from his kit bag, and carefully spread the liquid.

McSweeney reminded John of Anna: both were absolute ballbusters. "Why not?" John surrendered. He lifted his rifle, put the butt against his shoulder, and practiced taking aim.

"It's the French word *shoo-shoo*." McSweeney smiled.

McSweeney mimicked a French instructor's pronunciation for the Chauchat automatic. The French sounded like they said "shoo-shoo," and "shoo-shoo" quickly became a popular American nickname for the rifle.

"*I,*" McSweeney began as he lifted his rifle and aimed it, "*shoo-shoo.*" The men laughed nervously.

"And *they,*" he continued, pointing to the riflemen seated about the barn, "*shoo-shay.*

"And *you,* John McKay," McSweeney finally said as he pointed his rifle crazily about the barn, "shoot-*shit!*"

The men in the barn burst with laughter. Even John rolled back on his hay bed laughing. Word was out to all the infantrymen. The French-made Chauchat automatic rifle was a piece of crap.

"Not Johnny," barked Ed Rooney. "Johnny's, hitting everything."

"I find it rather remarkable," Buckley opined, "that our Fighting Irish Regiment went out of its way to determine who was the grandest of shooters only fer the American army to give him its worst rifle."

"Bucks!" McSweeney kept on. "I heard you couldn't hit the side of an iceberg." McSweeney silently counted *one, two, three.* "Oh wait, fellers," he said, "Bucks done that already."

"Not very funny, McSweeney," said John.

"Cul tona! Martin," Buckley cursed McSweeney in Irish.

"The Hotchkiss gun will be better," said John. "Me, Rooney, Buckley and Bergs Morgan start class Monday. We're a team."

"I've already learned my way around ammunition," said Buckley. "Black canisters of thirty-oh-six bullets to the Enfield, green canisters of eight-millimeter Lebel bullets to the automatics, and the big brown boxes of eight-millimeter feeder clips for the Hotchkiss. The Hotchkiss are particularly weighty."

"You'll be strapping like Valentino," said McSweeney. "When you're marching down Fifth Avenue. All the girls will be eyeing you."

"Aye," said Buckley smiling, "and so they will."

―――――

American machine-gun team firing the French Hotchkiss gun

John and Ed Rooney thought the Hotchkiss machine gun was a shit-hot machine—a far cry from the Chauchat. They loved shooting the Hotchkiss. The gun fired fast, it fired far, and it was deadly accurate.

In the classroom, all four men—John, Ed Rooney, Daniel Buckley, and Bergan Morgan—learned how to break down the weapon and clean it. Both Rooney and John were given the kits for the field, and a small wrench was needed to take the weapon apart.

The shooter, either John or Rooney, held the gun with two hands. The left hand held a D-ring on the gun's butt, and the right hand was on the brass trigger assembly. The D-Ring allowed the shooter to point the gun in any direction by swinging it side to side. It pivoted on the tripod thirty-seven degrees either way.

It had an air-cooled, gas-operated barrel. Five metal vents near the shooter's end allowed for air to flow and dissipate the heat. Beneath the barrel was the gas compression chamber. The gun was rated at five hundred rounds of 8 mm Lebel bullets per minute, but the men learned that at a rate of 120 rounds, the barrel wouldn't overheat, and the gun's reliability was greatly improved.

The four men worked closely as a team. One shooter shot the weapon, the second shooter spotted targets. One runner fed the rigid magazine clips into the gun's breach while the second runner ensured that a steady supply of ammunition got to the gun team.

In the field, moving the gun from one position to another while under enemy fire was of utmost importance. They choreographed the move with timed precision. The nonshooting gunner donned asbestos gloves while the shooting gunner unlocked the gun from the tripod. The nonshooter lifted the fifty-three-pound gun and carried it to the next position while the shooting gunner collapsed the eighty-pound tripod and, with the help of a runner, carried the tripod to the waiting gun. The fourth man, a runner, carried ammunition.

The men learned they had a slight advantage over the German MG-08 Maxim gun. Because the Hotchkiss was much lighter, it had a slightly better range. Buckley and Bergan Morgan were warned that German machine gunners aimed for the lower legs of runners. If the runner fell to the ground, machine-gun fire would hit a runner's head and kill him.

In one week's time, the four Shamrock men were fully qualified on the Hotchkiss gun. Once deployed back to the trenches with the regiment, however, John and Rooney were expected to shoot the Chauchat automatic. Buckley and Bergan Morgan would be ammunition runners. The independent 165th Machine Gun Company supplied machine gunners to each platoon, but someday, John and Rooney would augment the MG Company, if needed.

Rumors always flew that the Germans aimed for machine-gun crews. The casualty rate for French and British gunners was much higher than for ordinary riflemen, and there was an enormous shortage of trained MG teams. Pershing's planners accounted for such eventualities, and the American army cross-trained automatic riflemen.

———

Father Duffy entered the 165th's bullet-ridden command post off the Vaucouleurs main road and made himself known to the sentry. He came to see Colonel Hine, but the colonel was busy in a meeting. Duffy used the delay to visit Major Donovan, and he sauntered over to the major's office a few doors down. He rapped his hand on Donovan's wall.

"I'm hearing confessions," Duffy said, and Donovan looked up and laughed.

"I confess, Father." Donovan put his hands up to surrender. "I'm stealing everything I can put my Irish paws on."

"Absolved."

"That easy? I should steal more."

"How are we doing, William? Is the regiment up to standard?"

"We are vastly outperforming the others," Donovan explained. "Division staff is ecstatic. General Lenihan and Colonel MacArthur are in Chaumont briefing Pershing's staff that we're ready. We'll join the rest of the division in Langeau in the first week of January. Once we get a handle on our command and control and hone our artillery folks, I expect we'll be at the front by March."

"So the regiment is moving south to Langeau?"

"December twenty-sixth. That's the current plan. Colonel Hine's planning a Christmas Day stand-down and ordered sanitary to prepare a holiday mess."

"And the Eucharist? Has the colonel considered Christmas Mass celebration?"

"That's your department, Padre, but some simple advice?"

Duffy laughed. Simple advice? Donovan was anything but simple.

"The French are refusing us rail transportation," Donovan began. "Our trip to Langeau will be by foot, and it promises to be a difficult move. The route takes the regiment directly over the Vogues mountain range. There'll be lots of ice and snow this time of year. Sanitary has warned Colonel Hine that they can't guarantee that mess carts and pack animals will make it up the slopes. We could find ourselves at the top of the mountain freezing with no food at the most critical time."

"Then Colonel Hine will move before Christmas?"

"No, no. He plans to start out December twenty-sixth, and that's where I see an opening for you."

"I see."

"My ears on the ground tell me you've been lurking around the old chapel at Grand. Measuring the nave, I take it?"

"Infantry or espionage, William? Which is your calling?"

"Not mutually exclusive, Father. Intelligence and reconnaissance are essential elements of warfare."

Duffy smiled.

"I would suggest you offer the colonel an early departure from Vaucouleurs with a scheduled stop in Grand. That will cut the regiment's march into two parts. You'll get Grand, a great location to celebrate the Eucharist, and the men will get a Christmas Mass they'll certainly write home about. Maybe you can get that Kilmer character off his keister and finally scribble a dispatch."

"He swears to copious notes." Duffy laughed. "But he has yet to produce a single written word."

"Ah, poets." Donovan sighed, and they both laughed.

"The chapel at Grand would be perfect. It can handle the regiment, no problem."

"You're a padre with a plan, Father. Don't let the colonel know we spoke."

The sentry knocked on Major Donovan's wall and said Colonel Hine was ready.

"I expect to see you in the front row, William." Duffy stood up. "And in the 'state of grace'!"

Donovan laughed. "I'd have to stop stealing from the French!"

Colonel Hine saw Duffy coming down the hall and stood up behind the cluttered table that he used as a desk. Duffy saluted Hine, and Hine saluted his chaplain.

"How may I help you, Father?" Hine took his seat and Duffy followed.

"Christmas, Colonel. We are two weeks until Christmas, and I believe the regiment is ready for some seasonal cheer—a spiritual lift."

"Sanitary Company is planning a full Christmas field banquet, Chaplain. The men will have plenty of rations. Good army mess. Ham, potatoes, hot coffee, plenty. And I intend to order a twenty-four-hour stand-down for the holiday."

"A bountiful banquet, Colonel, yes, but as you know, sir, I am a man of the cloth, condemned to soulful nourishment. A task our Sanitary Company, God bless them all, is ill suited for."

Hine was used to Duffy's ways. He knew Duffy had already lined up his dominoes. Duffy was here to get him to tap the first one.

"Now, Father," said Hine, revealing some exasperation, "I know there's an elaborate plan up your sleeve, something to promote our regimental Celtic pride, fully worthy of Catholic gravitas and pomp?"

Hine realized he sounded patronizing and gave Duffy a wide smile. "I support Irish life inside the Fighting Irish Regiment, Father. So let's have it: What do you need?"

"Midnight Mass in the village Grand."

Colonel Hine assessed the offer silently and voiced no objection. Hine calculated the regiment's scheduled march by foot to Langeau and realized it could be broken into two parts. A stop in the village Grand, he reasoned, could ease the difficult foot slog. Duffy didn't mention Donovan, and Hine didn't confide to Duffy that a stop in Grand could help alleviate some of the burdens the march to Langeau placed on the regiment.

"There's a seven hundred-year-old church at the center of the village," Duffy continued with his pitch. "A group of French nuns are nearby. Soeurs de la Miséricorde. They have ovens large enough to make bread, and they have a ready supply of wine to meet our regiment's Eucharist needs. I believe I can put the entire regiment inside the church for one midnight Mass."

Hine waved for Duffy to stop. "Very good, Father, very good. I'll speak with Executive Officer Reed and we'll form a plan. A grand Christmas in Grand," he said contently. "I like the sound of that very much."

———

On December 18, the regiment packed up camp at Vaucouleurs and began a sixty-mile march to Langeau. The first stop was Grand to celebrate Christmas. The regiment uneventfully traversed the flat ground portion of the trek in three days and managed to reach Grand before heavy snow began to fall across the region. The regiment settled quickly and was comfortable bunking on French-supplied army cots inside closed structures. Father Duffy's elaborate Christmas preparations had stirred great interest among the French villagers and from the local clergy. They were ecstatic the American army wanted to use their Renaissance church, and they did everything possible to help Father Duffy create a joyous Christmas celebration.

Father Duffy worked feverishly to prepare the chapel for Christmas Eve Mass, but the sight of a seven-hundred-year-old Renaissance chapel ensconced inside a Romanesque village freshly blanketed by clean white snow evoked more Christmas emotion and feelings than Duffy could possibly create himself. Suddenly, the old French village didn't look like a mud-filled, dreary hellhole; rather, the blanket of bright snow made the decrepit but picturesque Grand seem almost new.

On Christmas Eve night, officers and soldiers of the 165th Regiment tramped through knee-deep snow and piled into the Grand Village Catholic Cathedral to celebrate midnight Mass with Father Duffy. Three thousand men packed the church. It was filled to capacity. Officers sat in the sanctuary on either side of the altar, and the enlisted men sat in the rows of pews and alongside the nave. Those who arrived an hour before midnight found themselves standing outside in the cold air.

Father Duffy had the chapel ready for the midnight celebration, and he expected virtually every man in the regiment to attend. Hundreds of candles lit the altar. Duffy liberally dispersed candles along the nave and down the center aisle. The church glowed warm and homey while bathed in a soft, flickering yellow light.

Soldiers filtered into the Renaissance church as their French hosts from the local parish choir sang Catholic hymns in Latin. The mood was somber, spiritual, and prayerful. Men silently filed into the pews, knelt in prayer, and buried their heads inside their hands. Many shed tears, missing loved ones. Some cried for fear, and some cried out of loneliness, but others cried after seeing the sheer beauty and hearing the sounds inside the marvelous church. Father Duffy had outdone himself.

At the rear of the church, bells rang, announcing the commence-ment of the Mass, and Father Duffy led a procession up the church's center aisle. Brigadier General Lenihan carried a staff bearing Christ on the cross. The choir sang "Onward Christian Soldiers" in English, a song none of the Irish men knew. Joyce Kilmer convinced Father Duffy that the hymn, English and Protestant, was appropriate for the wartime Mass celebration. Father Duffy, feeling a bit more Christmas spirit than usual, thought the Protestant hymn a generous gift to the regiment's non-Catholic commanding officer and agreed to use it.

Duffy towered over Brigadier General Lenihan and made the impish French priests seem downright tiny. Duffy blessed the soldiers in the church and said the requisite prayers to begin the Mass. The young Irish Americans, regular churchgoers all, followed his every word and, to the great surprise of the local French, the youthful American men repeated every Latin verse in Latin.

Father Duffy climbed the pulpit and opened the Bible. He read the traditional Christmas Gospel and, as per Catholic custom, every man stood.

"A reading from the Gospel of Luke," Duffy began. The men made the sign of the cross by blessing their foreheads, their lips, and their hearts.

In those days a decree went out from Caesar Augustus that the whole world should be enrolled. This was the first enrollment, when Quirinius was governor of Syria. So all went to be enrolled, each to his town.

And Joseph too went up from Galilee from the town of Nazareth to Judea, to the city of David that is called Bethlehem, because he was of the house and family of David, to be enrolled with Mary, his betrothed, who was with child.

While they were there, the time came for her to have her child, and she gave birth to her firstborn son. She wrapped him in swaddling clothes and laid him in a manger, because there was no room for them in the inn.

Now there were shepherds in that region living in the fields and keeping the night watch over their flock. The angel of the Lord appeared to them and the glory of the Lord shone around them, and they were struck with great fear.

The angel said to them, "Do not be afraid; for behold, I proclaim to you good news of great joy that will be for all the people. For today in the city of David a Savior has been born for you who is Messiah and Lord.

And this will be a sign for you: you will find an infant wrapped in swaddling clothes and lying in a manger."

And suddenly there was a multitude of the heavenly host with the angel, praising God and saying:

"Glory to God in the highest and on earth, peace to those on whom his favor rests."

Duffy closed the Bible and walked to the center of the altar.

"Do not be afraid, men," he shouted full-throated. "Have no fear. A Savior has been born for you. What a great gift from our Lord on this Christmas Day.

"Men," he continued, "we are not prideful enough to believe God is on our side. We are the Irish! *We know* God is on our side!"

They laughed.

"Is God with me?" Duffy thundered, and the rows of men listened. "It is a question on every man's mind. Will God be with me at my time of need, or has God forsaken me? After all, I am a sinner.

"First, men, be confident God will never abandon you. At times, you may not hear God's voice when you need to hear it, but be assured, you are a spiritual being, born with a soul and imbued with the Holy Spirit. God *can*, *does*, and *will* speak to you. When your heart is pure and your mind is clear, you'll hear Him, plenty good.

"Our God is the truth and the light, but it is a light that can be blocked and darkened when we men put barriers between ourselves and our Lord. It's we who cause God's pure light to be bent and corrupted. Not God.

"Some of us are so deeply buried behind barriers, we've become incapacitated and can't see the Lord's light at all. We've become blinded and make bad conclusions like 'God has abandoned me,' or worse, 'God doesn't exist at all.'

"The shepherds of Bethlehem on the night of Jesus's birth received the greatest message any man could ever hear. God proclaimed the birth of His only Son. Those shepherds greeted that message openly, with a pure heart and a clear mind. They were ready to hear the Lord's word, and they heard the angels loud and clear.

"As democratic men who profess free will, we are in France to defend our right to freedom and liberty, but only through freedom and liberty can a man choose to remove the barriers lurking deep in his heart.

"Our enemy is *not* in this fight to protect freedom and liberty, men. Our enemy fights for the glory of his race and his nationalist pride—both godforsaken principles.

"During this war you will exercise your freedom through free will. You can get yourself right with God. If you want our Lord to be on your side, if you want God to be on *our* side, then every man here needs to remove all barriers before himself and God and enter the state of grace. You need to get square with the man upstairs. Do *not* call on our Lord to help you if you are not ready to hear His message."

Spring 1918

———

THE 165TH REGIMENT ARRIVED AT the Langeau training facility, decimated. Men suffered from frostbite and some had pneumonia. Influenza
spread through the ranks, and many were starving. Inferior-made US
Army boots issued at Camp Mills fell apart under the austere mountain
conditions, and men were forced to track through deep snow and ice
barefoot. Soldiers hadn't changed or cleaned uniforms since Hoboken,
and their US Army-issued olive-drabs wore threadbare or fell apart.

The regiment's Sanitary Company failed at its mission. Just as
predicted, during the planning phases for the sixty-mile Vaucouleurs-
to-Langeau trek, pack animals pulling heavily loaded mess wagons
couldn't climb the steep slopes of the icy Vosges mountain range. The
165th's Sanitary Company got stalled at the base. No food reached the
regiment. Each man, now loaded down, carrying his weapon and ammunition, lugged more than a hundred pounds over the rugged hills.
Colonel Hine insisted the march go forward, and he ordered the regiment to slog through the frozen highland even without food or drink
for three days.

Morale was near mutinous. Soldiers fell out of rank and collapsed
in the snow. Company captains had to fall back to the rear echelons
and make sure stragglers didn't give up and quit. Those who suffered
pneumonia were returned to the Vaucouleurs field hospital. The men

became disgusted. For the first time, they began to question the decisions of the regiment leadership.

The long trek exposed massive ineptitude inside the 165th's officer ranks. The commanding staff knew pack animals might not make it over the steep mountain pass, and they knew critical food shortages could starve the troops at the worst possible moment. Yet, no one thought to issue reserve rations for each man to carry in his pack. In lieu of proper planning, the men on the icy mountain were damned to starvation. They collapsed in the snow.

Charles Hine, ever the railroad man, apparently respected schedules above all other things and made every decision based on his determination to deliver his 165th Regiment to Langeau on time, even if he had to lose 10 percent of his men.

Hine's decisions came under furious scrutiny by AEF HQ staff. General Pershing was enraged when he heard what happened to the 165th Regiment. When Hine arrived at Langeau, Pershing relieved him for incompetence. Hine was sent to a backwater supply outfit, and Col. John Barker, a West Pointer from General Pershing's Chaumont HQ staff, temporarily took the reins.

New commanding officer Colonel Barker was a calm and deliberate sort, but after taking on the 165th Regiment, he found himself in the middle of a bees' nest. The Irish were livid over their maltreatment, and now lesser issues like no hot water, lice, and infected billets suddenly became big issues. Disciplinary infractions soared, and the highly touted esprit de corps of the Fighting Irish 69th became strained.

Regiment officers acted quickly to alleviate the anger and began issuing replacement uniforms. What they didn't realize, however, was that the new jackets, pants, shirts, and boots meted out to the infantrymen were British army issue and not American. Hell would freeze over before any Fighting Irishman donned a loyalist jacket, and the men flatly refused to put on the new clothes.

When Colonel Barker got word of the insubordination, he didn't crack down. Instead, he ordered two regiment majors to conduct a detailed review of conditions. Colonel Barker's first act was to ensure the 165th's men no longer slept in roofless barns atop lice-laden hay; he made sure every man's billet was inside an enclosed structure on top of an army cot.

John, Buckley, Marty McSweeney, and Bergs Morgan made it through the Vosges march OK, but dour Ed Rooney got a case of frostbite on his foot and had to be treated at the Langeau field hospital.

———

The 165th Regiment men finally settled down, satisfied, that overall conditions were improving. They had indoor billeting, and every man was issued a dry cot. As usual, senior officers got the better, more-coveted billets inside Langeau village, and the enlisted men in each of the four regiments got dispersed out into separate hamlets scattered around Langeau village proper. The 165th Regiment landed in the small hamlet Baissey, a short walk to town over a rolling meadow. All the regiments were connected to Langeau via narrow dirt paths that soon widened into bustling thoroughfares.

The Langeau camp was more than 150 miles from the Hindenburg Line and well beyond range of German reconnaissance aircraft. Colonel Barker allowed his men to light fires, and they now had hot water to bathe in and delouse, and bathe they did! The Sanitary Company wagons finally arrived from Vaucouleurs, and Colonel Barker made sure hot mess was served every day.

The men were issued liberty passes and had free time to travel into the Langeau village. Colonel Barker ensured that every man was paid in cash, and he made sure the commissary had items men could buy. Simple items like shaving kits, shoeshine kits, sewing kits, and cigarettes kept everyone content. The Young Men's Christian Association set up shop in Langeau and offered a cozy place to get free coffee and experience small reminders of life back home.

Colonel Barker had plenty of time to address the regiment's morale problem. Langeau's Advanced Training School was not ready for the Rainbow Division, and field-training maneuvers had to be delayed.

Ammunition for artillery guns hadn't arrived. Small-arms ordnance was scarce. There were no mortars or hand grenades, and the men hadn't received gas masks. Only a handful had a chance to don a device and walk through a chamber.

The unceremonious change of command between Hine and Barker proved no worse than a short-lived administrative hiccup. General Pershing's general organization plan shifted training away from company and regimental capabilities and emphasized training for the much broader battalion, division, and corps levels.

The still disparate, separated, and uncoordinated 42nd Rainbow regiments came to Langeau to train and mold into one capable fighting division. General Pershing's instructors had the colossal task of corralling all two hundred separate regiments, creating forty separate divisions and making those divisions coordinate operations on the battlefield at a corps level. Pershing's ultimate goal was to form ten corps of four divisions each using twenty-five thousand men, or 1.2 million men in total: one giant US Army war machine.

The 42nd Division's training concentrated on honing its command control and communications capabilities. The division's leadership needed to learn how to move light infantry companies across an open battlefield and simultaneously coordinate light and heavy field-artillery firepower.

Langeau's instruction emphasized open warfare tactics, and Langeau instructors avoided teaching any trench warfare doctrine. General Pershing planned for the American army to saturate German fortifications with artillery shells and pepper enemy front lines with grenades, mortars, and machine-gun fire. Yet, oddly, once a division departed Langeau, it was immediately embedded into a French division that only practiced trench warfare tactics.

As a stark reminder, Pershing planned to ceaselessly barrage German trenches, trap German troops in place, and charge over the top into no-man's-land to assault Krauts inside their trenches. Every man in the division was issued the murderous-looking trench knife.

A handheld bayonet, the trench knife had a ten-inch serrated blade and a brass knuckle handle. The knife looked ominous and deadly, and it served to remind every soldier that survival in the trench could be as debased and inhuman as shattering another man's skull with one's fist.

Every officer and enlisted man was also issued a gas mask, but the division got little training on how to don the lifesaving filter. Not only did the advanced training school fail to teach the men how to quickly don the device, they never trained the men to shoot rifles, fire mortars, or run across an open field and attack enemy lines while wearing it.

John thought the gas mask was uncomfortable and difficult to use. Marty McSweeney and Buckley thought the facemask looked like a pig's snout. Everyone in the division got a quick lesson on the mask and learned that the breathing device had two parts. The rubber and canvas portion strapped tightly over the head, and the respirator canister dangled down over the chest. Everyone thought the mask was too bulky to use. When a soldier pulled the mask over his head, nose clamps slid down and clipped his nostrils shut. The user then inserted a scuba-like mouthpiece and breathed through a hose connected to the respirator. By 1917, the British army had greatly improved the gas mask, but no matter how well designed the mask had become, it was only as good as a soldier's ability to don it quickly and correctly.

Germany first began using chlorine artillery gas shells against the French at the second Battle of Ypres in Flanders in 1915. Gas-borne irritants were always around and used by both sides earlier in the war, but when the Germans switched to deadly chlorine gas and used it wholesale against Allied troops to terrorize them in the trenches, the rules of the war changed for everyone.

Chlorine gas first scorched a man's lungs and immobilized him, and the side effects that followed left him slowly struggling for breath. His lungs filled with body fluid and the victim lingered until he drowned. Allied soldiers had strong opinions about gas; they said they'd rather take a machine-gun bullet to the head than die from gas poisoning.

———

John McKay, Daniel Buckley, Ed Rooney, Bergan Morgan, and Marty McSweeney walked together along the dirt path from Baissey across the grassy meadow to Langeau Village. The village was astir and busy. It was mostly filled with American soldiers, but Langeau was still a different kind of town. Better than any of the shoddy villages they'd seen, Langeau was alive. It had shops and cafes. A soldier could buy a beer or wine or get a good meal, and there were women—plenty of women. McSweeney knew exactly what he wanted.

"A million dames," he pleaded. "We gotta get us some."

John flicked his cigarette into the dirt and stamped on it. Using a prostitute was far outside his faith, unquestionably sinful, and he remembered what Father Duffy said at Christmas. John tried his best to stay square with God, as Father Duffy had asked, and John didn't want to disavow the priest.

But he hadn't been with a woman yet, not fully anyway, and John realized he might not survive France. If he clung to the rules of the Church, he might never be with a woman, and that prospect didn't seem right. He saw the places the women worked. Soldiers lined up outside the doors. At first, he didn't think he would ever visit one of those places, but he mulled it over and considered his situation.

"You comin' along, Bucks?" John asked.

"I see your troubled face, John," Buckley chimed in, "and I must say, we've been told it's perfectly OK to stick a bayonet down a man's throat and drain the bloody life out of him, but God won't condone a single moment of pleasure, feeling the warmth of a woman?" Buckley shook his head side to side. "I believe God shall forgive us, John."

John smiled and released a cloud of smoke into the air as Buckley continued. "Now as for Father Duffy. Get yourself a French priest for your next confession. He won't understand a single word you say, and all will be forgiven."

McSweeney, listening, reveled in the thought. "And you'll relive the whole damn thing in splendid detail."

The five friends got in line outside a saloon. The women were on the second floor, and each man waited his turn. Out of nowhere, Buckley pulled out a bottle of homemade French wine he had purchased from a French priest behind a monastery. Buckley popped the cork with his pocketknife and took a swig of the earthy swill, then winced.

"To us!" He saluted his platoon mates and passed the bottle to McSweeney.

"To us!" said McSweeney, cheering and taking a swig. He passed the bottle to John, who drank it and cheered, and then he passed it to the next man until it was emptied.

The entire month of January 1918 passed before the 42nd Division began full-fledged field training, but at dawn on a cold February morning, just as the sun broke over the horizon, the entire division stood in place on Langeau's practice battlefield, ready to go. The artillery shells had arrived. Tons of small-arms ammunition was available, and all the preparative classroom training was completed. Every man had a trench knife, and every man had a gas mask.

The 165th Irish Infantry Regiment of the 83rd Brigade and the 168th Iowan Infantry Regiment of the 84th Brigade were lined up along the frontline mock trench and, in accordance with the general organizational plan, the 166th Ohio Infantry Regiment backed up and replenished the 165th while the 167th Alabama Regiment backed up and replenished the 168th. The setup: two regiments forward backed up by two regiments in the rear. This was the called the "box pattern."

The box pattern was standard for the US Army in France. It enabled both General Pershing's staff at the corps-headquarters level or division staff officers at the division-HQ level to quickly move troops and bolster replacement manpower at the front. The box pattern allowed for a continuous cycling of fresh fighters to the front and enabled the American army to put relentless pressure on the Germans.

Also at the Langeau practice field, far behind the infantry trench line, was the 42nd Rainbow's 150th Field Artillery Regiment. The Field Artillery unit dispersed stokes mortar squads close to the front line and deployed its 75 mm howitzers slightly forward of the rear backup regiments. The larger guns, the 155 mm howitzers, went farther back, closer to the 42nd Division HQ command post.

The Brigade commanders and all the regimental officers were on the front line with the infantrymen. The chain of command kept Brigadier General Lenihan and Brigadier General Brown in face-to-face contact with their regiment's officers. Any orders or information received from division headquarters came to the brigadier general via telephone. The general then disseminated that information to his regiment commanding officer they in turn used runners to pass it to the battalion major and company captains.

Company captains were positioned on the front line with the infantrymen platoons and used runners or one of the many signaling devices to pass the information to the numerous platoon lieutenants.

The 165th's CO, Colonel Barker, was never too far away from Brigadier General Lenihan, and the battalion majors, Donovan, Stacom, and Moynahan, were only a short dash away from Colonel Barker. Command control and communications for the 42nd Division proved very effective from the outset of training, and the 42nd Rainbow Division demonstrated a high level of coordination and discipline on the training battlefield.

Occasionally, however, communications got crossed or misunderstood and a bewildered company captain or lieutenant would soon see a battalion major charging down the trench line coming directly his way. Nobody wanted to see Wild Bill Donovan on the warpath, fearing the "raging major" might show up to keep stricter discipline in the trench.

The 42nd's intelligence unit also participated in mock battlefield training. Intelligence Company members, including poet Joyce Kilmer, dispersed across the zone of action and sent progress reports back to Division HQ by using runners or men on bicycles.

John took his position at the left end of the trench line and looked over his right shoulder. The lineup was the same as it was when training at Camp Mills. Dour Ed Rooney was next to John, and behind Rooney were runners Daniel Buckley and Bergan Morgan. John was comforted seeing familiar faces. All the way down the line he recognized every man: the hand-grenade team thrower, Luke Boyle, and his team, the four-mick riflemen including mouthy Marty McSweeney; the grenadier team; and the stokes mortar squad. Gone was Jim O'Conner. Word had it O'Conner got sick and died from influenza.

One change from the days at Camp Mills was a machine-gun nest perched at the far end of the trench line just off John and Rooney's left side. The gunners were from Machine Gun Company, not Kilo

Company. They operated the Hotchkiss with a four-man crew just like John, Rooney, Buckley, and Bergs Morgan, but nobody knew any of the MG Company men.

John heard a percussive "pop" shot from a small cannon behind the trench line. He recognized from the signal that artillery batteries were about to commence fire.

In less than one second, soaring shells began to zoom overhead. The supersonic warheads flashed across the sky and hit the ground, unleashing a hellish fury. Ferocious detonations, one after the other, ripped open the earth and threw a curtain of molten rock and mud high into the air. The ground shook as shells whistled or shrieked and then slammed into the ground like a hundred crashing asteroids hitting the earth all at once. Adrenalin raced through John's veins.

Keep your head on a swivel.

The bone-rattling explosions caused everyone's nerves to pulse. It was impossible to hear anything except shells thumping the ground and then exploding. No one could think or speak as the shockwaves slapped against every man's face and pounded dull thuds against their chests. Most were frozen by fear.

John brushed his fingers across his breast pocket to feel Anna's rosary.

Crack! He heard a single pistol shot. The signal: "Prepare to fire."

Captain McKenna fired the round, and every man in the trench instinctively stood up, readied his weapon, and took aim.

Crack! Crack! The second signal sounded.

Artillery shells exploded one after another, and the ground rumbled and shook. A curtain of toxic sulfur smoke hung across the green meadow, and Kilo Company's infantrymen took aim and opened fire on the targets that were laid out in the field.

The sound of rifles cracking and artillery exploding was deafening. Luke Boyle tossed his first grenade at a set red X in the field and scored a direct hit. Grenadiers shot their weapons as mortar squads fired round after round. *Thump, thump, thump,* the mortars sounded. Riflemen shot, reloaded their rifles, and shot again. John and Ed Rooney let loose their Chauchat automatics, laying waste to the wooden targets in the grass. Buckley and Bergs Morgan fed the riflemen magazine after magazine with nary a glitch. The entire Kilo Company platoon roared to action as the Hotchkiss machine-gun spit bullets and ripped up everything in its path. The small-arms fire and artillery enfilade were so intense that none of the Kilo Company men had a sense that two full regiments of the division were offloading at once.

Crack! Crack! Crack! The men heard three pistol shots from Captain McKenna's pistol.

"Over the top!"

Every man moved, climbed over the low trench berm, and ran across the flat field while firing his weapon. Platoon lieutenants and the sergeants led the charge shouting, "Attack, men! Attack!"

Adrenaline gushed as the platoon careened across the flat, grassy land toward the mock German trench. The artillery explosions thrashed the earth under their feet as scorching, heat-filled sonic booms flew past their bodies. The infantrymen pressed on! John got ahead of Buckley, who was carrying the heavy ammo cans, and he eventually ran out of ammunition. He kept moving forward toward the mock trench, running at top speed. He then reached behind his back and retrieved his knife. He brandished the huge blade and slipped the brass-knuckle grip through his fingers before charging with all his might to the mock trench.

When John reached the "straw" German target, he lifted his knife in the air and leaped into the pit, tackling the enemy and tearing its canvas body to shreds. He slashed at the straw man, fomenting a rage he'd never felt before. He jabbed the straw soldier's chest and stabbed it over and over. He then bashed its head with his brass knuckles and stood up victorious, peering down over his vanquished enemy.

He was out of breath, his heart pounding wildly. Sweat beaded up on his forehead and rolled down his face. Just a short year ago, he was a carefree young man in Greenpoint, working the SOCONY yards as a pipe fitter. Now, he'd been taught to hate an enemy he had never even seen. John knew his life had changed dramatically, and he understood hating another man for the sake of hate or pride was morally wrong, but he also understood he'd been called by his country to defeat the enemy. If he had to foment a rage to kill Huns, so be it; he could do this again.

———

Archie scooted up the steps of his ma and dah's Greenpoint apartment and burst through the door.

"Ma!" he called, entering the parlor, but there was an eerie quiet in the house.

"Archibald," Mary whispered from the parlor sofa. She was dressed in her bedclothes and sat, unable to get up. Alex and Mary hadn't seen Archie since Christmas. He never got a pass to leave Camp Upton out east on Long Island.

"Look at you," said Alex, joining them in the parlor. Archie looked fit and trim. He had lost weight and gained muscle, and he looked older and more mature. He had lost his boyish way. "Army life has been good to you, Archibald," Alex added.

"Not so sure about that, Dah, but take a look." Archie pointed to the patch on his shoulder. He'd been promoted one rank to corporal. "Five more dollars a month, Dah."

"Good for you, son!" said Mary, concealing her surprise. Archie seemed clean and sober. He looked healthy and alert and now, seeing he'd been promoted, she was full of hope for her son.

"Are you feelin' OK ma?" Archie asked. Mary hadn't gotten up to hug him and Archie quickly discerned she couldn't.

"I'm fine, son, I get dizzy spells once in a while. When my blood pressure is high. I have to sit here and rest."

"Keep resting, dear," Alex said to his wife. "I'll speak with Archibald in the kitchen."

Archie got right to business with his dah.

"The 47th Regiment is part of the 53rd Division now, and I'm shipping out with them," he said. "We're leaving New York at the end of the month."

Alex shook his head disappointed. He harbored a crazy notion that perhaps Archibald would remain in America—that, Archie wouldn't deploy to France. Now, he had to tell his ailing wife that their second son was soon leaving for the war.

The two men went into the parlor and Archie knelt down by the sofa to kiss his ma on the cheek.

Tears welled in Mary's eyes.

"You're leaving for France, aren't you?" she asked.

"Yeah, Ma, I am," said Archie.

Her tears rolled down her face.

"Here, here, dear," said Alex. He sat next to his wife and put his arm around her shoulder. "Things will be OK, Mary," he said. "Let's be strong for Archibald."

"I can't," she whimpered. "I can't be strong anymore."

CHAPTER 11

Spring 1918
Luneville, France

———

THE 42ND DIVISION BROKE CAMP at Langeau and embedded into a French army Division at Luneville. Rank-and-file soldiers were glad to be done with mock battles, straw enemies, and tedious training, and were eager to get to the real action at the front. However, many of the 165th's midgrade officers openly questioned the seemingly rash and ill-timed orders. They wanted more time to train.

Captains McKenna of Delta Company and Hurley of Kilo Company were the most vociferous. They complained, demanding their infantrymen get more time practicing before deploying to the trenches. Three weeks on a mock battlefield in Langeau, they openly argued, was not enough.

Major Donovan called the young officers to his office and set them straight. "The Russian government has collapsed," he explained. "Czar Nicolas and family are in exile. The Bolsheviks have signed a nonaggression pact, and the Russians are out of the war. The Krauts are moving everything to the western front. The AEF needs to take control of the Lorraine sector and allow the French to redeploy along the Marne River and reinforce the Brits along the Somme. It's 'Here we come, ready or not,'" Donovan said flatly. "Luneville is our orders, gentlemen. Do you understand that?"

"Yes, sir," said McKenna.

"Captain Hurley?"

"Yes, sir."

Donovan dismissed them both.

Four French VII corps divisions had already redeployed from the Marne River sector and were heading north to the Somme River to bolster British forces. Intelligence reports indicated the Germans intended to attack BEF and French forces at the Somme as early as the spring of 1918. The 42nd Rainbow had to fill the gap created by the French exodus in the east sector. Luneville at least, Donovan calculated, was quiet, and he was grateful the 42nd wasn't simply shoved into the breach and forced to fight the Germans at the Somme. That coming clash promised to be a bloodbath, and Donovan thought, if sent, the untrained and inexperienced 42nd Division would end up as cannon fodder for the Krauts.

"We'll still have time in Luneville," he reconciled.

Senior French army staff at the AEF's Charmont headquarters assured General Mann that his 42nd Division would transit from Langeau to

Luneville by rail, and the French made good on that promise. The train trip wasn't comfortable. Loose slats on the forty hommes cars did little to shield soldiers from the howling, cold winter air. The men were crammed together and kept warm, but the close man-to-man proximity allowed lice to spread and, by ride's end, every man twitched and scratched.

The 165th Infantry train plodded through the French countryside over the midnight hours and eventually arrived at Luneville's main station at daybreak. The men quietly disembarked, badly fatigued from the persistent cold and bumpy ride, but none dared to complain. Travel by rail was a luxury and, since the bitterly harsh trek from Vaucouleurs in December, it was hard to find a single soldier who would say a bad word about a French hommes train.

The 165th Regiment slowly formed up in long lines along the main road, abutting the rail station. When finally called to attention and ordered to march, they moved methodically and half-asleep. Some men grumbled but kept the brisk pace and marched up to Lunesville's main thoroughfare on their way to King Stanislaus's castle. The castle would serve as the regiment's quarters, and the men were eager to bunk down and get some rest.

As the morning sun rose behind them, a newly awakened Celtic pride replaced midnight yawns and grumbles. Although only a few minutes into the new day, Luneville's citizens were awake and astir, ready to greet the American doughboys as the Yanks marched through their town. French men, women, and children jammed the sidewalks and crammed open window boxes while cheering wildly and waving American and French flags.

The New York regiment men swelled with pride and then began smiling and waving.

"Can you beat this?" yelled the normally dour Ed Rooney.

John wore a wide smile on his face.

The unexpected celebration put a confident "top-of-the-morning" swagger in every man's step. The esprit de corps between French partisans and the Irish American soldiers was electric. The Americans instantly fell in love with the exuberant French and felt assured they were fighting for the right side.

King Stanislaus's castle was an enormously imposing structure, and the soldiers couldn't believe they'd been assigned to billet in such high quality and comfort. The castle was the best lodging they'd experienced, and Luneville's town looked even more inviting than Langeau's. McSweeney kept whispering while they stowed their kits and set up cots, *"free time" in the new town was sure to be fun.*

The men got mail call and spent hours huddled inside the castle's warm barracks rooms, pouring through Christmas cards and letters that had finally caught up to them. They read and reread every letter from home—from family, girlfriends, and loved ones—gleaning the slightest tidbits of life back in New York City.

John got a package from Anna. He shook its contents onto his cot and out fell two small, metallic pins and a letter. One pin was a shiny, emerald-green shamrock, and the other was a brightly painted red, white, and blue American flag. John smiled seeing the pins, and when he unfolded the letter a photograph landed on his cot. It was a picture of Little William and Kitty wearing Saint Patrick's Day hats.

"We took this picture in the fall," Anna wrote. "We wanted you to have it before for the holiday. So please forgive. Happy Saint Patrick's Day, brother!"

John studied the photo carefully. Catherine's babies had gotten so big. They weren't babies anymore. They were toddlers. John missed their playful giggles and the endless pecks on the cheek. He could hear Kitty's tiny voice—"I love you, Uncle Johnny,"—and he recalled Little William's salute at Penny Bridge.

What will life bring them? John mulled silently. *No more war*, he prayed. *We'll fight the good fight, we'll beat the Huns, and we'll get back home. All this will be over soon.*

John tucked the photo into his jacket pocket with Anna's rosary, then unbuttoned the jacket's upper lapel and fastened the emerald-green shamrock pin and American flag pin inside the flap. Wearing pins outside one's uniform was strictly prohibited. Metallic objects reflected sunlight, which made a soldier easy prey for a sniper.

Anna's letter was four sheets in length and filled with her humor. She recounted Christmas night dinner and wrote how Archie "was very attentive to Ma." She wrote, "He filled her house with great spirits and laughter in the hopes she wouldn't think about your being gone. Then he had a little too much sauce and knocked over her living room lamp. Needless to say, Ma remembered you were missing, immediately."

Anna went on to say Archie got his orders and was scheduled to deploy with the 53rd Pioneer Division, leaving New York City by ship on March 8. "We will all be at the pier handing him over to the army," she quipped. "Arch said he'd be in the Lorraine sector, so look for him when he gets there. Should be by April."

Anna didn't say that their ma had gotten very ill since John left. Anna was very worried about their mother's high blood pressure, but she decided there was no point telling John; it would only upset him. She left out any word about their ma's illness.

———

The good life in Luneville didn't last. After seven days of lounging in King Stanislaus's Castle barracks, orders arrived for the 165th to move closer to the frontline trenches. The entire 42nd was joining a French Division near the village Nancy to provide a counterweight against German units camped on the other side of the Kriemhilde Stellung, the name for the Hindenburg Line in the Lorraine sector.

The 165th Regiment moved northward into a densely wooded, muddy subsector, officially marked on maps as the "Chaussailles-Rouge." Unofficially, the subsector, a huge collection of covered earthen berms dug out by French soldiers earlier in the war, was dubbed "Camp New York." Why the camp got named after the New Yorkers' fair city, the men of the 165th didn't know. Some said the comparison was obvious. Both were dirty shitholes.

The French name, Chaussailles-Rouge, loosely translated to "fitted red," and that accurately described the woodlands' natural reddish hue. A month prior, one New York newspaperman followed an American regiment into the Rogue woods and observed that the reddish hue of the trees resembled the color of dried blood.

As the month of February passed, temperatures rose, and a warming thaw took hold, turning Camp New York into the world's worst mud-filled mess. Wooden walk paths got laid down over the saturated ground so soldiers could get around the camp. Moving from one end to the other was a tricky game. If a soldier brushed up against a fellow soldier when walking the narrow boardwalks, he could easily land in a two-foot-deep pool of wet mud.

The camp was set back from the actual frontline trench and was where the reserve, or the "backup," infantry troops bunked. Men slept in dugouts, numbered "one, two, three…" and so on, constructed from gouged-out hillsides and covered by the huge felled trees. Atop the massive tree-trunk beams was a twenty-foot layer of mud and rock. Sometimes a dugout could be a deeply excavated hole in the ground, and soldiers had to climb down rickety ladders to reach the floor bottom.

Living conditions inside dugouts were horrible. Dugouts were wet, muddy, dank, filled with stale air, and dimly lit. The men didn't bathe or change uniforms or heat water for washing. Twenty-five to fifty stinking bodies overwhelmed even the hardiest man. Only rats seemed attracted to the stench.

Adequate sanitation was an immense problem. Infantrymen defecated into handheld pots, then tossed the excrement into a giant, open trench. Once a week, a few soldiers were ordered to pull out an entrenchment tool and cover the fecal mound with a fresh layer of earth. The job was always done halfheartedly, but once in a while, when the smell became unbearable, sergeants cracked down and made sure the job was done right.

Conditions inside the trench weren't much better. Bathing was out. Shaving was required and done with ice-cold river water. Urination and defecation were the same as in the camp but, depending on the direction and velocity of the wind, an unbreathable, foul odor could waft over the trench and incapacitate a squad.

The 42nd Division spread out on the Chaussailles front using the American army box pattern. The 165th Regiment of New York and the

166th Regiment from Ohio took the front. The 167th and 168th took the rear as ready replacements.

Inside the 165th Regiment, Major Donovan's 1st Battalion took the initial turn, manning the frontline trench alongside French army troops. The 2nd Battalion and 3rd Shamrock Battalion remained billeted at muddy Camp New York.

Donovan eagerly impressed upon his French army instructors that the 1st Battalion was ready for reconnaissance missions or small raids. The French appreciated the American commander's aggressive style and sly use of small squads, but the Irish regiment's open warfare tactics ran afoul compared to the doctrine promulgated by French and British generals.

Frontline French army officers and NCOs weren't necessarily in sync with their senior command policies. Trench warfare was the doctrine of the French and British, not open warfare. Allied leadership was convinced that the open warfare doctrine was unsustainable, a conclusion they reached only after amassing monumental casualties. However, French officers assigned to teach survival in the trench and how to fight real battles saw things a bit differently than their superiors and grasped that the 165th's infantry tactics were pragmatic and useful.

Major Donovan developed a hybrid version of trench warfare. This involved using artillery guns to suppress shorter-range, light infantry weapons and machine guns and conduct clandestine open warfare; over-the-top attacks using a small, light infantry squad and those tactics appealed to Donovan's French hosts.

Camp New York was considered to be in the rear section of the forward deployment area. The trench line was considered the actual front line. Once German artillery guns opened fire, however, any distinction between forward and rear was hard to make. German artillery shells pelted every part of the Chaussialles-Rogue sector, and every man was vulnerable to flying shrapnel from high-explosive shells that could land and explode without much warning. No man was safe anywhere.

In dugout number one of Camp New York, John, Daniel Buckley, and the rest of the platoon squad prepared to rotate out of the rear echelon dugout and move up to the frontline trench. Buckley's habit of squirreling every empty burlap sack sure paid off. This time, John and Ed Rooney kept their temperamental Chauchat automatics clean, dry, and away from the mud by wrapping the guns in Buckley's burlap.

Captain Hurley gave Buckley a well-earned, public attaboy, and the Irishman quietly beamed with justifiable pride.

Buckley proudly recalled why he was frugal. The Buckley family was destitute, and Daniel had worked feverishly to save the money needed for his *Titanic* passage. The RMS *Titanic* was his ticket out of a meager life in Ballydesmond, and Daniel Buckley never forgot the lessons he had learned from his parents. "Everything has at least one good use," his mother would say, "and most things have at least two good uses." Wastefulness in the Buckley family was the gravest of sins.

The Shamrock Battalion collected on the high road above Camp New York and readied for the short march to the trench. They could hear German artillery guns drumming in the distance. It sounded like a distant thunderstorm, but unlike thunder, the exploding artillery concussions made the ground under their feet tremble. Men still inside the dugout saw loose mud from the dugout's earthen walls cascade down and splatter on the floor, and they wondered how much longer the huge tree-trunk roof would hold up.

The atmosphere in the Rouge Woods was tense and apprehensive. The men could hear shells land, and they smelled sulfur smoke drifting uphill through the forest. They were anxious to get out of the dugouts and, quicker than usual, everyone had his pack packed and ready and the men lined up on the flat dirt road ready to go; no delay.

The sergeants shouted "fall in," and everyone formed up behind the lieutenants and the sergeants into their respective platoons. The four companies of 3rd Battalion stood ready behind Major Moynahan, and he called his battalion to attention.

"Forward, march!" the major shouted, and in one moment, all the men moved in unison away from Camp New York and down the slope to the trenches. The Shamrock Battalion would finally confront the Kraut enemy face to face.

————

In the Chaussailles-Rogue forest, at the center of the 165th sector, 2nd Battalion, fell under heavy artillery fire all morning. The barrage continued well into the afternoon, and 42nd Division staff officers concluded that the Krauts were sending a "greeting card" to the newly arrived AEF Division. The Germans wanted the Americans to know that they'd found 2nd Battalion's encampment.

During the morning assault, 2nd Battalion's Major Stacom wanted his men out of harm's way and ordered them to hunker down inside the dugouts. Men crammed into the deep, earthen shelters as high-explosive shells tore into the forest, ripped up ancient trees, and rattled the ground all around them. After four hours of incessant shelling, one single artillery round landed directly on top of 2nd Battalion's dugout number three.

The violent direct hit threw the dugout's heavy, weighted, tree-trunk roof high into the air and caused the twenty-foot protective mud-and-rock cover to break loose and fall. Tons of mud and stone dropped directly into the dugout and onto the men trapped below. Behind the falling earth, the massive tree trunks fell to the ground, slamming down on the men. A dozen were killed instantly.

Major Donovan was near the 2nd Battalion dugout when the ordnance hit. He spontaneously organized a recovery team culled from un-injured 2nd Battalion men. Soldiers climbed onto the heap of debris, indifferent to personal safety. They feverishly dug through the mud, using only entrenchment tools and their hands, and worked to lash ropes around the huge fallen tree trunks, attempting to pull the heavy girders off the trapped men.

The rescue effort didn't go smoothly. German artillery shells continued to pound the ground, and when shells landed too close, men had to leave the collapsed dugout and take cover. Nobody quit the rescue effort. Muffled pleas for help could be heard down deep under the pile.

Donovan's team had no machinery, no plows, no cranes, or mechanical diggers. His men had to rely on inadequate entrenchment tools, and time was not on their side. The muffled, desperate pleas began to fade, and the trapped men began to suffocate. No one knew how much time remained, but rescuers continued to dig.

Two of the trapped were extricated near the dugout's entry, and Donovan's team could see the top rungs of the wooden ladder used to descend into the deep hole. When the rescuers scooped out mud to widen the entryway, more wet mud filled in behind. The effort was valiant and tough, and the rescuers were relentless, but in the end, the effort was futile. Twenty-two Americans died; twelve succumbed instantly and ten suffocated.

Adding to the day's general state of confusion, Major Moynahan's 3rd Battalion had arrived at the forward trench line and was ready to take the reins from the 1st Battalion. Once again, Major Donovan took command of the situation and sent a team of his best men to help organize 3rd Battalion.

Donovan encouraged Major Stacom to focus on his own 2nd Battalion, and Stacom took over the rescue effort. The ten trapped soldiers, although most likely dead, had to be recovered. All twenty-two needed to be identified and buried in properly marked graves.

One of the 1st Battalion men selected by Donovan to help the Shamrock Battalion get settled was lanky Dick O'Neil, and O'Neil used the opportunity to seek out his old Camp Mills buddies, John

McKay, Daniel Buckley, Ed Rooney, and Marty McSweeney. The men of the Fighting Irish Regiment were rocked back by the sudden loss. The attack on 2nd Battalion was first blood, and the New Yorkers swore revenge against the murderous Krauts.

"They're fuckin' bastards." O'Neil frothed. The men were hunkered down low inside the trench. "They'll trick you and then shoot you."

French soldiers warned 1st Battalion infantrymen. German soldiers would wave white flags or don Red Cross garb in an effort to dupe Allied fighters. Once an allied soldier relaxed his defenses or let his guard down, a German soldier waving a white flag of surrender would pull out a pistol and open fire.

"We're gonna git them, Dick. You wait and see," John said, roiling. He pressed his cigarette into the dirt floor. "Ed and I are gonna rip 'em in half."

"They drew first blood on us." Rooney spit. "No mercy."

"I'm gonna stick this bayonet up their asses." McSweeney jammed his bayonet into the wall.

O'Neil explained that perhaps the guys in the 2nd Battalion had gotten sloppy. They didn't want to wash or eat in the unsanitary, smelly dugouts, so some started to leave their personal gear and kits on the ground outside at the base of a tree or next to a fortification. Neil explained how any reflected light helped German spotters figure out positions.

"They'll pass your longitude and latitude to the artillery," he said, "then all hell will break loose. You gotta be careful," O'Neil warned them. "Always think. The Krauts are watching everything we do."

The sergeants of 3rd Battalion signaled for the Shamrock men to drop their large packs in the nearby dugout and report back with their squad mates in the trench. Each man was assigned a permanent position along the row; the order was just like it was at Camp Mills and Langeau.

"It's yours," the sergeants growled, showing each man his area of responsibility along the trench line, "so get to love it."

By nightfall, Dick O'Neil and the rest of 1st Battalion's assist team departed, and 2nd Battalion's rescue mission was completed. They had recovered twenty-two bodies and hurriedly reburied them on the high ground over trenches near division HQ. Father Duffy announced that he planned a memorial Mass by week's end, and somehow Daniel Buckley knew that poet Joyce Kilmer was writing a poem to commemorate the fallen Chaussailles-Rouge infantrymen. The poem would be read at Duffy's Mass.

Over a week's time, 3rd Battalion settled into the trenches and received the much-needed training from the French instructors. The French worked diligently to morph the American infantrymen from being proficient and technically adept to being experienced soldiers, steeped in practical skill and flexibility, replete with defensive and offensive capabilities.

The mission in Luneville was "defend the line," and in the trench at the battalion level, French instructors taught the Americans how to set up in depth-tiered and layered defenses. The Germans could assault one set of trenches, but not two or three trenches at once. The French imbued basic survival techniques too, and they impressed upon their American trainees the importance of keeping one's head down and keeping one's location undetectable.

Majors Moynahan and Donovan actively colluded and conveyed to their hosts that American squads needed to run some raids. The majors also argued emphatically that American infantrymen needed a morale boost and to exact retribution from the Krauts.

This time, the French instructors capitulated and, in the spirit of Saint Patrick's Day just around the corner, they allowed the Fighting Irish Regiment to plan and execute a raid.

Majors Moynahan and Donovan organized a clandestine reconnaissance mission for 0300 hours across no-man's-land to map out enemy defenses and machine-gun positions. The reconnaissance team, handpicked by Donovan, was charged with clearing a sortie route for a later attack squad. The elite recon team set out and crossed over the Kriemhilde Stellung, sliced through rows of barbed wire to clear a foot-path, and sabotaged German early-warning devices.

The majors then hashed out a modest plan along with Machine Gun Company Lieutenant Seibert and passed the plan up the chain of command to Colonel Barker and Brigadier General Lenihan at the 83rd.

The plan was approved.

Moynahan and Donovan chose infantry squads from Captain Hurley's Kilo Company and briefed those select infantrymen, includ-ing automatic riflemen John McKay and Ed Rooney on the tactics they intended to use to "hit the Krauts in the trench." The handpicked squad learned the tactics like one, two, three—Major Donovan had been drill-ing them into everybody's head since Lexington Avenue.

The plan required absolute silence and no use of any audible sig-nals. The raid was timed out, and each part of the attack squad was ordered to execute its portion of the mission using a hack time. The entire assault would last fifteen minutes, no more. Killing and injuring Kraut soldiers was the primary goal. "Let the bastards know we're here," Donovan urged his team. The Americans planned to be in and out be-fore the Germans understood a raid was underway.

Donovan and Moynahan planned for a nighttime raid and waited for an overcast sky. By happenstance, the night of the attack they ben-efited from a thick fog that settled over the forest. The covert assault team wiped mud over their faces and wore gloves to darken their skin, anyhow.

Thirty minutes before go-time, Father Duffy arrived at the Kilo trench and offered the men confession, absolution, and Holy Communion. John hadn't seen Father Duffy since Christmas at Grand, and he took comfort seeing the tall priest in the trench.

At Antrim Hall a year before, Duffy had promised the Greenpoint men he'd be with them during the fight in the trenches and in harm's way. He offered a Catholic regiment, an Irish regiment, and here he was at the very moment they were primed to execute the first mission. Duffy had kept his word.

Ed Rooney gave John the once-over to make sure all his gear was secure. John looked Rooney up and down as well and, just as John finished inspecting Rooney's gear, the American machine-gun nest on the far right side of the line opened fire, spewing a hellish fury of lead across no-man's-land.

Rooney gave John a silent thumbs-up signal, and John returned the same. The squad lieutenant locked and loaded his rifle, a signal it was time to move. Behind them, down the trench line, American mortar teams and grenadier teams shot a volley of salvos as hundreds of light infantry warheads landed on the German line.

At the far end of Kilo's trench, Father Duffy stood at the jump-off point. He blessed each man as he climbed over the berm and crawled out onto the open no-man's-land. The squad lieutenant and sergeant led the way. The light infantry followed, and all the men disappeared inside the nearby forest in mere seconds.

John's heart pounded. He could feel Anna's beads through his shirt but he maintained focus and kept his head down, following Ed Rooney's footsteps. American machine-gun fire, mortar fire, and the grenadier enfilade made the Germans turn their attention away from their right flank, and they redirected their hellish Maxim machine guns at the American gunners on their far left side. As hoped for, the German right flank was now open and made vulnerable for the fast-approaching American squad.

The Americans spread out, taking positions inside the foggy woods. Only the hand grenade team continued forward along the trench edge.

Luke Boyle, the dead-on ace, tossed grenade after grenade. All his tosses landed directly in the center crevice of the narrow German trench.

The grenades exploded under the Krauts' feet, shocking the soldiers and causing panic. Those not immediately injured by the shrapnel fled the trench, unknowingly charging directly toward American riflemen waiting inside the misty woods.

"Fire!" yelled the lieutenant, and the American riflemen unleashed a torrent of bullets at the fleeing Germans.

"Screw you!" John yelled at the top of his lungs, the crackle of gunfire drowning out his shouts. An intense rage rushed through his body. He swooped his Chauchat, took aim at the trench edge, and fired on German soldiers trying to escape.

"You killed my friends!" he screamed, his finger never leaving the trigger.

He swung around and aimed his Chauchat at German soldiers scurrying across the ground and trying to dive back into the trench. He loaded his second magazine and looked over at Ed Rooney, who had already depleted his reserve mag. John then saw Martin McSweeney ram his bayonet into the chest of a German soldier who lay on the ground pleading, "Red Cross, Red Cross!" McSweeney would have none of it.

The Germans were in a state of shock, their commanders unable to discern the direction of the American attack. The Americans were everywhere all at once, and by the time the three-minute ambush assault was over, twenty German soldiers lay dead. The American team didn't take time to survey the damage and hightailed it out via the sortie route, never looking back.

Right on time, the second American machine-gun squad opened fire on the German line, suppressing any return fire. Kilo Company's stealth squad was back inside the home trench in a matter of minutes—no casualties, no mistakes. The Fighting Irish had carried out their first raid, near Saint Patrick's Day no less, with perfect precision. The raid was a huge success, and Major Donovan's Indian-style assault methods were no longer regarded as interesting textbook theory, but were rather very deadly, effective, and practical.

———

Kilo Company soon learned that the German army was not too tired or lying prostrate waiting for the fresh-faced American Irishmen to plunder their position. Twenty-four hours after what was now known as the Saint Patrick's raid, German artillery guns roared to life, slamming Kilo's position with thousands of high-explosive projectiles.

American artillery batteries shot back, and the American and German field-artillery guns traded fire for the better part of two days. The American 155 mm Howitzer was on par with the German Morser 16 gun, so neither the Americans nor the Germans had any advantage. Little could be done for men caught in the trenches on either side. They simply hunkered down and prayed.

Nobody wanted to be inside a dugout, and nobody wanted to be buried alive like 2nd Battalion's Echo Company. The Shamrock lieutenants agreed and never ordered a single man to seek shelter inside the deep holes.

John, Daniel Buckley, Bergan Morgan, and Rooney stayed safe during the first assault by tucking under the forward wall of the trench. The wall was six feet high, and the trench was three feet wide, small enough to provide a snug enclosure.

When the two-day artillery exchange eventually abated, German reconnaissance airplanes flew low passes over 3rd Battalion's camp. The 3rd Battalion infantrymen got antsy and paranoid, expecting a second German artillery assault at any moment. The men grew weary, and nerves became frayed. But a few days passed, and there were no more low passes or signs of another impending attack. Life along the Luneville trenches returned to a normal routine.

John, Buckley, Morgan, and Rooney were positioned at the far end of the squad's line, and there was little reason for platoon mates to walk past their posts. For soldiers positioned at the middle of the line, however, like rifleman Marty McSweeney, an endless parade of soldiers using the latrine or wanting to bum smokes made for a steady stream of foot traffic over his post.

The trench was too crowded and way too tight. Tempers routinely flared.

John looked down the trench line and saw mouthy Marty McSweeney acting irritably, almost irrationally. His arms flailed, and he was shouting incoherently. Platoon mates had been crisscrossing over his post all day, and McSweeney had reached his boiling point. He had had enough.

"Bucks!" McSweeney yelled down the line. "Did you take my smokes? You were the last to have 'em."

"Absolutely not, Martin. Nary, I have them. Nary, I've seen them."

"Here's one." John threw a single cigarette at McSweeney.

"Not the point, Johnny boy." McSweeney sneered. He was angry and adamant. "We can't be livin' in a trench with a thief, can we?"

"Thief, Martin? Are you serious?" Buckley was furious.

"I've seen how you work, Buckley." McSweeney snorted. "You're no simple leprechaun, are you?"

"I resent that, Martin."

"That's enough!" John yelled to McSweeney.

"Fuck off, McKay. I don't take orders from you."

"I said that's enough, Martin." John warned again.

"Oh, fellers," McSweeney shouted aloud. He was filled with vile. "Has our perfect soldier, King Johnny, ever told you about his drunken bum brother? Huh, Johnny?" McSweeney goaded. "Have yer told them, Johnny?"

"Shut your mouth, McSweeney!" John grew furious.

"I'll say what the fuck I want, and your stupid brother is nothin' but a gutter drunk, McKay. Everyone in Greenpoint knows it."

"Stop it!" yelled Ed Rooney.

"I didn't take your cigarettes, Martin," yelled Buckley.

John raised his fists. "Why don't you come over here and open your big mouth McSweeney?" he warned.

"I ain't scared of you McKay." McSweeney stood up inside the trench as he charged at John.

Tha-wump!

A single high-velocity bullet cracked and tore through McSweeney's skull. The force threw his body against the trench wall, and blood spilled everywhere. His lifeless body landed directly on top of Bergan Morgan, and Morgan was soon soaked in McSweeney's blood.

"Get him off me! Get him off me!" Morgan panicked. "Get him off me!"

Ed Rooney crawled toward Bergan Morgan and yanked on McSweeney's limp arm until Morgan was able to slide out.

John fell back to the trench wall. He was in shock. He couldn't believe McSweeney had been hit, and he blamed himself for getting into a fight with McSweeney.

"It ain't yer fault, Johnny," Rooney yelled. "His big mouth did him in."

Buckley slid over and grabbed John by the shoulders. "Don't matter what words got said." Buckley looked John square in the eyes. "We're all doomed here."

Two company sergeants and a lieutenant arrived, scurrying through the narrow trench.

"Call the medic!" the lieutenant barked.

"No use," said the sergeant. "He's dead."

———

The next night's trench duty began normal enough, but by 0300 hours, German artillery guns roared to life and high-velocity projectiles began to rain down on the trenches. Kilo Company was under attack once again.

The men hunkered down, but they soon noticed that the shells hitting the ground were not high explosive; rather, the detonations created a dense mist and smoke. Nobody recognized the type of ordnance, and they were caught unawares until a warning bell sounded over the trench line.

"Gas!"

Kilo's men scurried for their masks. Hardly a man had one at the ready. Many kept the mask stowed far away inside the dugout.

Buckley had his mask donned in seconds, and he dug through John's pack, looking for his mask. John kept his face pressed low in the trench, trying to suck trapped air in the corner crevices, but the gas seeped in and settled almost everywhere.

"Hurry, Bucks!" John called out. He could taste the chlorine.

Buckley got John's canister and pushed the face mask against John's mouth. John grabbed the straps and secured his mask tightly to his head, but it was too late. He had breathed the deadly gas, and his lungs started to burn. He filled up with mucus, and his eyes started to flood, filled by thick tears.

Buckley grabbed John and dragged him out of the trench. Hundreds of Kilo Company men, all gasping for breath, screamed that they'd been blinded or couldn't breathe, and none of them could find the battalion dressing station. The gas attack was full on. Men fell to the ground choking, their hands pressed over their eyes as they tried to protect them from the burning vapor.

The forward trench line emptied out, and the division field hospital was soon overfilled. Ailing infantrymen spilled into the medical depot fraught with panic and desperation. Kilo Company was completely incapacitated and out of commission.

Of the 296 Kilo men assigned duty in the trench, 290 were injured during the gas attack. By daybreak, all of them had been removed from the battalion dressing station and taken to the US Army hospital in Luneville. Injuries varied; some had minor lung burns, and some were gravely ill. Most men were able to return to the company after a few days, but for some, recovery lasted over a month.

The 167th Alabama regiment hurried to the front and replaced the Irish in the trenches. The attack put the entire Kilo Company out of commission for two months.

by the E. W. Bliss Company.
    Private John I. McKay—Company K, 165th Infantry, slightly wounded. Private McKay was carried yesterday among the list of those believed from Brooklyn, but not positively identified. His identity among the slightly wounded is now positive, his family having received an official telegram to this effect. Private McKay is the son of Alexander McKay, and his home is at 416 Meeker avenue. A brother, Archie, is a member of the former Forty-seventh Regiment. Private McKay is on the honor roll of the Standard Oil Company.

———

Workers inside the Western Union office in downtown Brooklyn stared at the Tele-type machine.

"Injured, injured, injured," the War Department telegrams read. "Injured, injured, injured."

They were grateful and thanked God the telegrams didn't say, "Killed in Action."

As American soldiers began to pour into France, the newspapers now reported ten thousand soldiers per day were arriving in Europe. Western Union workers knew it was just a matter of time before telegrams relaying the horrible news of a young man's death or serious injury would arrive back home. They dreaded such inevitability. The telegrams had to be hand delivered, face-to-face, and they loathed the thought of delivering such sorrowful news to a mother, a father, or a wife with child.

The Western Union messenger assigned to deliver the telegrams in Greenpoint made his way north along Meeker Avenue, trying to go unnoticed, but everyone in the clannish Irish neighborhood watched him make his way up the avenue. He had ten deliveries, and Mrs. Mary McKay at 416 Meeker Avenue, Brooklyn, was his first.

Bridget O'Leary, the McKays' downstairs neighbor, gasped when she saw the Western Union messenger stop outside the front of her house. She grabbed her five-year-old son and clutched him tightly as she watched the messenger climb the stairs and knock on the McKay family door.

"Not Johnny McKay," she cried. She hugged and kissed her son and then remembered Mary McKay was home alone. She quickly ran up the stairs behind the messenger.

As the Western Union man handed Mary the envelope, Mary started to hyperventilate and became dizzy. Bridget and the messenger caught her as she collapsed, and they pulled her limp body to the couch.

"Do they have whiskey?" the Western Union man asked.

Bridget's oldest son, Daniel, was at the bottom of the steps in the street. Bridget yelled down to him. "Fetch Mr. McKay at SOCONY. Tell him there's an emergency at home."

Mary was having a panic attack and could not control her distressed breathing. She lay helpless, almost unconscious on the couch.

"Your son has been injured in action, Mrs. McKay," the messenger assured her. "He has not perished."

Bridget patted Mary's hand trying to revive her. "Johnny's alive, Mary," she said. "Did you hear the messenger? Johnny's alive."

Mary's breathing slowed slightly, and she was able to open her eyes. "My blood pressure," she whimpered. "The doctor says I'm sick with the blood pressure."

———

Father Duffy celebrated his memorial Mass for the twenty-two Echo Company men of 2nd Battalion killed in the Chaussailles'-Rouge woods dugout. The Mass was held on a flat, grassy plain high above the trenches and away from any artillery strikes. Most of the 165th men attended.

John suffered no residual effects from the gas attack; he fully recovered. He and Buckley went to Mass. The same could not be said for many other Kilo men, and at least twenty had to be sent home.

Father Duffy's Mass was a spiritual spectacle, held on a wonderfully warm and calm spring morning. The Chaussailles's forest trees, far enough away from the damaging artillery salvos, flourished brilliantly in fresh bloom. Northern France's natural and abundant wildflower, the deep red-petaled poppy, was in abundance, too, spread all across the field.

The Mass was a solemn and sad celebration. Every man cried hearing Poet Joyce Kilmer's prose, a poem he titled "Rogue Bouquet."

Father Duffy read the poem at the end of his Mass as two buglers sounded "Taps." One bugler played close by the altar and the other sounded from a distant hill. As Father Duffy read the mournful poem aloud, the mournful bugles echoed melancholically.

In a wood they call the Rouge Bouquet
There is a new-made grave today,
Built by never a spade nor pick

Yet covered with earth ten meters thick.
There lie many fighting men,
Dead in their youthful prime,
Never to laugh nor love again
Nor taste the Summer time.
For Death came flying through the air
And stopped his flight at the dugout stair,
Touched his prey and left them there,
Clay to clay
He hid their bodies stealthily
In the soil of the land they fought to free
And fled away.
Now over the grave abrupt and clear
Three volleys ring;
And perhaps their brave young spirits hear
The bugle sing-
"Go to sleep!
Go to sleep!
Slumber well where the shell screamed and fell.
Let your rifles rest on the muddy floor,
You will not need them any more.
Danger's past;
Now at last,
Go to sleep!"
There is on earth no worthier grave
To hold the bodies of the brave
Than this place of pain and pride
Where they nobly fought and nobly died.
Never fear but in the skies
Saints and angels stand
Smiling with their holy eyes

On this new come band.
Saint Michael's sword darts through the air
And touches the aureole on his hair
As he sees them stand saluting there,
His stalwart sons;
And Patrick, Brigid, Columkill
Rejoice that in veins of warriors still
The Gael's blood runs.
And up to Heaven's doorway floats,
From the wood called Rouge Bouquet,
A delicate cloud of bugle notes
That softly say-
"Farewell!
Farewell!
Comrades true, born anew, peace to you!
Your souls shall be where the heroes are
And your memory shine like the morning-star.
Brave and dear,
Shield us here.
Farewell!"

Joyce Kilmer, March 1918

CHAPTER 12

Ancerville, April–June 1918

———

———

THE 42ND DIVISION RECEIVED HURRIED orders to withdraw from Luneville's Camp New York and march fifty miles due west to join up with five US Army divisions already deployed in the northwest Lorraine.

Content to leave the ominously blood-hued Chaussialles-Rouge behind, the 42nd repositioned itself around a hamlet named Ancerville in the Baccarat and filled in for a French Division that was repositioned to the Marne River in the Champagne sector.

Still reeling from its expedition in the Rouge Forest, the move to the quieter Baccarat sector was an opportunity for the 42nd's ailing regiments to regroup, reman, and retrain. The 165th Regiment suffered serious casualties during the Chaussialles-Rouge gas attack and was precariously undermanned. Unfortunately, tuberculosis and influenza suddenly began to take a hold as well.

Soldiers throughout the Lorraine entered field hospitals, suffering from illness much more than those injured by gas attacks or by machine-gun fire and shrapnel wounds. By war's end, more men died of Spanish flu and tuberculosis than by battlefield injury.

An immediate call went out for replacement soldiers. A dependable supply of fresh troops to refill frontline units was promptly needed. French and British convoys were delivering ten thousand doughboys per day, and the War Department solved its manpower shortage by chopping up freshly landed divisions and reassigning men piecemeal. Newly arrived soldiers were culled from their stateside outfits and assigned haphazardly to frontline divisions—division cohesion be damned.

Inside the Fighting Irish Regiment, men who had succumbed to more serious gas injuries slowly trickled back into the ranks. The 165th's sergeants were eager to get these field-tested men back. If they could harness the experience of the veterans and use them to assimilate the off-the-boat newbie replacements, regiment readiness could be restored quickly.

However, as the freshly minted replacement soldiers reported for duty, company sergeants and lieutenants assessed a huge problem. The newbies were completely unprepared for frontline operations. They barely knew how to don a uniform correctly, much less operate a weapon proficiently. The level of training back in America was abysmal and suffered greatly in order to satisfy British and French convoy schedules. The War Department made no time for effective training, and the onus for preparedness dropped on frontline units in-theater.

———

"When the lieutenant fires his pistol," Buckley shouted at a newbie from Boston, "get on yer fecking feet and aim yer fecking weapon."

The men had been in the trench all morning, and the newcomers still hadn't learned simple trench signals.

"After the second crack—" Buckley spit, the veins in his neck popping—"shoot your fecking weapon! And if the lieutenant fires his pistol a third time, yer arse goes over the top, or the forth shot will be in yer feckin' back."

"Easy, Bucks." John flipped the release on his Chauchat and let the magazine drop into a bucket. He took a deep drag on his cigarette as he and Rooney reached into their ammo canisters, pulled out magazines, and shoved them into the Chauchat's breach.

"Bullocks!" Buckley roiled. "They know what to do. They're just chickenshit eejits. You're Sixty-Niners now!" he yelled over the trench line, his warning heard by all. "Act like Sixty-Niners!"

Ed Rooney leaned into John and whispered, "I believe we've created a trench tyrant."

John exhaled his smoke and laughed, but as he peered down the line, he saw too many faces he didn't recognize. Men he had learned to trust and rely on were gone, either sick with flu or injured by gas. A quarter of the platoon was new, and the trench line was getting remanned by a bunch of off-the-boat, know-nothin' replacements. John didn't know whom he could trust if things got hot. Buckley and Rooney were still close by, and he took comfort in that.

The afternoon's trench training concentrated on basic command-and-control signals, but not much more. Every man in the platoon squad had to know the lieutenant's signals. A platoon had to operate singularly and coordinate its response to the enemy. An unorganized platoon only invited trouble.

"Get comfy, girls," the sergeant bellowed down the line. "I don't care if we're here all night."

John, Rooney, Buckley, and Bergs Morgan pounded their heads against the earthen berm wall. They were disgusted, tired of the monotony, and pissed that the newbies couldn't get the basics right. Rack time is all they cared about—extra shut-eye, a good night's sleep. They didn't want to waste an extra second practicing dumb shit like trench signals.

During a smoke break, Ed Rooney elbowed his way into the middle of a group of replacements who were milling in a circle. They grumbled about how the high-minded old-timers had too much self-regard.

"You're in the Fightin' Irish now, lads." Rooney gazed at them sternly. "We're gonna press up against the Krauts soon, men. So ya better get yer shit square, or dem Krauts will gut you like schweine. Kill or be killed, do you understand that, Mac? Make yer choice."

The men who enlisted at the Lexington Avenue Armory on the very first day had the 69th's bold history inculcated deep into their souls. They couldn't sit idly as their prideful regiment fell prey to a bunch of listless newcomers.

"Learn yer shit!" Rooney barked at them. "Or get the fuck out!"

———

Training also meant reorganization, and in April 1918, the 165th's leadership was reorganized while in Ancerville. Colonel Baker, the well-regarded regiment commander, got called back to a staff assignment in Washington, DC, and Major Stacom of 2nd Battalion and Major

Moynahan of 3rd Battalion were replaced by Echo Company's Maj. Alexander Anderson to command 2nd Battalion and Delta Company's Capt. James McKenna to command the 3rd, or Shamrock Battalion. As for Colonel Baker, he always knew his command assignment was temporary, but he greatly cherished his New York Irish regiment.

Ready in the wings, Colonel Baker's replacement was another West Point alumnus named Col. Frank McCoy, a man destined to make the 165th Infantry Regiment one of the most militarily aggressive outfits of the entire American army.

McCoy was a well heeled and politically connected professional officer who spent his first years outside West Point charging up San Juan Hill with Teddy Roosevelt and the Rough Riders. The then 2nd Lieutenant McCoy sustained a gunshot wound during the San Juan charge, and his heroics eventually landed him a rather prestigious placement as a White House aide, again working for President Theodore Roosevelt. Promoted to the rank of major while at the White House, McCoy was well regarded by the president's inner circle of influential advisors, and Frank McCoy was well on his way to a very successful US Army career.

Although an unabashed anti-Catholic Irish Protestant, the antithesis of the Fighting Irish Regiment's ethos, McCoy was a good fit for the 165th. McCoy was a hard charger who came to the Baccarat sector infused with a ready-to-do-battle ethos and was completely in sync with his equally aggressive 165th officer corps. At the start of the war, McCoy was determined to get in the fray and smash up Krauts. The famously courageous New York City Irish Catholic regiment, he surmised, was the best place to do it.

———

"What's on your arm?" John asked.

Buckley jumped down into the trench and put four canisters of the 8 mm Lebel ammunition at Rooney's feet. He was out of breath.

"I'm proud to say it's a fine green Irish Shamrock armband," Buckley said. "Very exclusive and worthy of wear only by the most proud runners inside Major McKenna's Shamrock Battalion. The major says we runners must wear the band at all times."

"Not proud before, Bucks?"

"I shan't be confounded by your sarcasm, John McKay. 'Tis not my doing, boasting of Irish pride in an Irish regiment."

A pistol shot at the far end of the trench sounded, and John and Rooney instinctively came to attention, loaded their Chauchat rifles, and took aim. Buckley too grabbed his Enfield and took an offensive stance.

Two consecutive pistol shots sounded, and every man on the trench line fired his weapon at the targets laid out across the flat field. *Rat-tat-tat*, sounded the Chauchat automatics. *Pop, pop, pop*, snapped the Enfield rifles, and *thump-thump* went the Stokes mortars. A giant wave of sulfur smoke rolled back into the trench.

Three full months had passed since the Rouge Bouquet gas attack, and Kilo Company's infantrymen demonstrated that they were back and ready for the field. The platoon lieutenant's numerous trench signals were fully understood. Newcomers coalesced with the old-timers, and hard feelings between the Irish and non-Irish infantrymen eased. There was no more confusion and no more griping. Every man knew his job and a new esprit de corps took hold.

Captains of 165th's Companies had been charged with getting their platoons up and ready. The new commander, Colonel McCoy, planned to move the entire regiment up to the front, and he demanded every squad, platoon, and company demonstrate offensive and defensive operations in real-world conditions. He planned to conduct intelligence probes, run raids across no-man's-land, coordinate assaults with the division's Artillery Regiment, and generally harass the Germans until it hurt.

"Be nimble, be flexible, be aggressive, but most of all, be smart" was the strident commanding officer's mantra. This was nothing the Irish Regiment men hadn't heard before, but all of them, officer and NCO alike, agreed as word of an impending major German assault spread through the ranks. The stakes this time around, were much higher.

———

On March 21, just as the Rainbow Division began to settle down in Ancerville in the Baccarat and get accustomed to reasonably dry tent living, twenty-nine German army divisions took siege and attacked BEF positions along the Somme River. Early reports were not good for the Allies. The Germans smashed British defense fortifications, hitting them with a never-before-seen twenty-four-hour, one-million-shell artillery barrage followed by waves of fast-moving storm troops carrying flamethrowers and hundreds of flanking light infantry tanks.

The Germans attacked the Brits with such ferocity that it was impossible for the Allies to anticipate enemy movements. Not even the best intelligence reports had predicted such a powerful onslaught. German General Ludendorff's army had such overwhelming firepower that the Germans readily smashed through British defense lines and mowed through villages that young British soldiers fought and died for by the tens of thousands two years prior. Now, these same hard-won villages were back in the hands of the German army after only one week. The long-anticipated German spring offensive Operation Michael, named by Commanding General Ludendorff himself, was thrust upon the Allies.

For generals on both sides of the line, this was the now-or-never moment of the war. If the Allies could stop or slow the German offensive, the German army would stall and be forced to defend its occupied ground. Conversely, if the Germans were able to compel the British army to move its forces northwestward and abandon the French army at the Somme River by attacking in Flanders and imperiling Belgium's port cities, the Germans could drive their army through the British/ French gap and capture Paris.

In Chantilly, Allied generals worked feverishly to stop the German onslaught advancing rapidly toward Paris. French Generals Foch and Clemenceau and British General Haig assessed that the German army was advancing too quickly and was thusly vulnerable to a broadside attack. General Pershing agreed with that assessment and offered his six American Divisions, four regular US Army Divisions plus the 26th Yankee Division and the 42nd Rainbow Division, to join the French in the Champagne region along the Marne River. Pershing promoted using his American forces as "shock troops," a counter to the German "storm troops."

Supreme Allied Commander Foch agreed, and he gave orders for the American Divisions to conduct stand-alone operations in the field for the first time, but he also hedged and placed those divisions on either side of a battle-hardened French division. The Allied assault on the German 3rd Army was set for July 15 outside the city of Reims in the Champagne sector.

CHAPTER 13

July 15, 1918
Champagne Marne Defense

———

———

"MAJOR MCKENNA SAID, 'WHEN THE balloon goes up,'" said Buckley.

"What in hell does that mean?" asked Rooney.

"I have nary a notion, Edward." Buckley sat up in his cot, his uniform undershirt saturated by sweat. "I simply heard Major McKenna answer Captain Hurley. Captain Hurley asked when the battalion would move closer to the action, and Major McKenna said, 'When the balloon goes up.'"

John lay flat on his cot, staring up at the ceiling, trying to stay cool. The July heat was stifling. He and Buckley agreed the gigantic Camp Bouy barracks were even hotter than Mrs. Hickey's boardinghouse.

"Two days' travel by truck in the middle of the night from Ancerville," John surmised, "and look how big this camp is. The whole damn division is here. Have you ever seen so much ammo and artillery in one place? We're close to the fightin'."

"Don't hear no guns," said Rooney.

"Don't be puttin' your pessimism on us, Edward," said Buckley.

"If it's time for the big show, it's time," said John. "We're ready. The Krauts here can't be no worse than the Krauts in Ancerville."

"One of my fellow messengers overheard Sergeant Meade," Buckley explained. "He said that Sergeant Meade said it was easier to get Luneville's mud off his boots than this white Champagne chalk. He heard Sergeant Meade say, 'Champagne is where the French grow grapes.'"

"And where the Krauts make the war." Rooney rolled to his side, trying to stay cool.

Buckley went on. "He said he rode with Major McKenna on the truck from Ancerville. He said the major had his map out and got real excited when we crossed over a river bridge marked 'Le Marne.' He said Major McKenna called over a group of lieutenants. They all looked at the major's map."

Bergan Morgan sat up to join the conversation. "Fuck, it's hot." He wiped sweat beads from his brow. "Where did dem Frenchies in Luneville says they was goin'? Didn't that corporal say somethin' 'bout Champagne? I thought he said somethin' 'bout the Marne River in Champagne."

"We moved west, that's for sure," said Rooney. "That's gotta make us closer."

"They gotta tell us sometime," said John. "Make sure we're pointed in the right direction."

Buckley groaned and fell back on his cot. "A funny man you're not, John McKay."

A Kilo Company platoon sergeant entered the bunkroom and blew his whistle. All the infantrymen leaped from the cots, landing upright on their feet at full attention. The room went silent.

"Men of the 3rd Platoon," he bellowed, "formation at 1300 hours on the square. Have your notepad and your pencil. Uniform of the day: Bravo."

He blew his whistle again and barked, "As you were," and the 3rd Platoon men fell back onto their cots, trying to escape the broiling heat.

———

Colonel McCoy returned from 42nd Division headquarters, having received a full battle briefing from Brigadier General Lenihan. The 42nd Division was to be split in half. The 83rd Brigade dispatched to the French XXI Corps's at Saint Hilaire near Esperance. The 84th Brigade, led by Brigadier General Brown, dispatched to the French XXI Corps's southwest along the Marne.

McCoy burst into his Regiment HQ office and flattened the battle map out on his table. Majors Donovan, Anderson, and McKenna, eager to learn every detail, carefully studied the map.

"The French have an elaborate defense strategy," McCoy explained, "and we will play an integral part."

Major Anderson stared at the map and noted his battalion was designated as a "Sacrifice Post." His men, along with three French units, would occupy widely dispersed positions along a weakened first line of defense—a line designed to fail and be laid bare for annihilation.

The 1st and 3rd Battalions, on the other hand, were positioned much farther inside the densely fortified blockade called a Center of Resistance. The 166th Ohio Regiment fared better too, assigned as rear reserve in accordance with the American box pattern.

"The mission for Third Battalion," said McCoy, standing over the table with his finger on the map. "Major McKenna, you are to hold position and defend the line. Second Battalion, Major Anderson, you will man the Sacrifice Post and First Battalion. Major Donovan, you will lead the broadside assault on the German flank. Gentlemen, we will travel tomorrow night by rail to Esperance, then proceed by foot to our assigned post. Let your men know how much General Pershing holds the Fighting Irish in the highest esteem. He considers the Forty-Second Rainbow to be his shock troops, able to stop Kraut storm troops dead in their tracks."

———

John peered down the trench line, ticking off names of guys he knew, but he didn't get very far. He didn't know half the faces. The newbies weren't so new anymore. He just hadn't taken time out and learned the new names. He didn't like that he didn't know who was next to him, but thought the newbies had learned their stuff pretty well at Ancerville and figured if they did OK against the Krauts there, they'd be OK in Champagne, too.

French army engineers completed excavating the enormous trench lines needed to quarter the Americans just as the 2 regiments of the 83rd Brigade arrived at Saint Hilaire. Each set of deeply gouged troughs—three parallel rows shoveled out by a monstrous, mechanized excavator—carved out enough earth to hold the entire brigade. Big as the dig was, the American infantrymen crammed in tight, standing shoulder to shoulder. They filled the huge, mechanically dug trenches end to end.

John's position was the middle of the middle. Kilo Company's 1st and 2nd Platoons manned the forward trench line in front of him, and the 3rd platoon, John's platoon, and the 4th filled the rear trench. On John's left side was Lima Company, and on his right side, Mike and November Companies, all Shamrock men.

The 3rd Battalion held the middle Center of Resistance. The French army manned the second Center of Resistance and took position on 3rd Battalion's left flank. The American 1st Battalion, led by Major Donovan, formed the third Center of Resistance positioned at the far right side. The 166th Ohio Regiment, the other regiment of the 83rd Brigade, was assigned rear reserve. The two regiments of the 84th Brigade, the other half of the 42nd Division, took position about fifty miles west along the Marne River, assigned support for the French XXI Corps there.

Once settled in the trench, Kilo Company men noticed they were far back, away from the front line. The Center of Resistance trenches were at least three miles away from the barbed wire no-man's-land and any German fortifications. Emotions stirred up when word spread that 2nd Battalion men who formed behind Major Anderson were marching to a Sacrifice Post, a lure for the Krauts.

No one was happy any infantrymen from the 165th Regiment were being used as bait. The men of 2nd Battalion were going to get the worst of the fighting. When they marched past the CR posts, hardly a man could look. Only quiet prayers were offered. Father Duffy marched with 2nd Battalion, standing shoulder to shoulder with Major Anderson.

"We loaded them up with extra ammo," said Buckley. "I made sure of that. The carriages are filled to the top and then some."

"Only gonna make the pain last longer," said Rooney.

"If you got bullets," said John. "It's a fair fight. Good job, Bucks."

"God be with them all," Buckley whispered.

———

Ten minutes after midnight on July 15, the summer night calm over Saint Hilaire ripped asunder, replaced by a tumultuous rage. The skies over the American trenches burst aflame. High-explosive artillery shells, mortars, gas bombs, and earth-scorching rockets cascaded down on the Americans, landing everywhere.

"Gas! Gas! Gas!" the sergeants yelled, and with the lesson of Luneville still fresh on everyone's mind, every man immediately stopped and donned his mask.

The barrage was massive. It consumed every inch of the sky. The German 3rd Army unleashed a hellish fury. Six thousand artillery pieces blasted at once, pounding Allied defense positions. Phase three of Ludendorff's Operation Michael was underway.

Ten divisions of German storm troops and thirteen more in ready reserve waited in place behind a low ridge, fully mobilized and ready to charge at the twenty-mile-wide Allied front. Ludendorff's objective: use his 1st and 3rd German army's twenty-three divisions to assault the French and American lines east of Reims. Use his 7th Army and its thirteen divisions to push against the French 6th Army west of Reims. If he could achieve a thirty-mile or greater gain and mirror his past advances made during his major drives against the BEF south of the Somme, he'd break the Allied line in half.

For the American 83rd Brigade and the three French XXI Corps Divisions dispersed around Esperance and Saint Hilaire, the thrust of the German assault was limited to a one-and-a-half-mile-wide stretch. The German threat was real and powerful. A short five miles across no-man's-land, two fully manned and battle-tested German assault divisions sat poised, ready to roll over the French and the American 42nd Rainbow.

Ordnance rained down on the Irish and thumped the ground, tossing earth and trees high into the air. The Allied infantrymen hunkered down inside the Center of Resistance trenches and inside the Sacrifice Posts with gas masks on. The men could do little but press their bodies firmly against the earthen walls and pray not to be hit.

Enfilading shells, rockets, and mortars crashed down from every direction. A nearby forest ignited in flames, but most of the fierce concentration of high-explosive mortars, projectiles, and gas bombs landed far forward on the abandoned trenches. Bunkers and dugouts emptied as part of the in-depth defense plan.

The ground under the men's feet rumbled and shook. The clamor of exploding shells was deafening. Impact after impact, shrieking mortars swooped overhead and smashed into the earth, ferocious jolts jarring them as they exploded, and superheated shockwaves flashed across the flat ground mere inches above their heads.

The infantrymen stayed down, crouched in position. Their nerves were frayed, pulsing wildly because of the thunderous claps and jolts. Their hearts pounded hard. Their breathing was strained and deep. Even the most experienced man was overwhelmed, drenched by sweat and riddled with anxiety.

"Keep calm, men. Keep calm." Captain Hurley roved up and down the line, exuding a superhuman-like confidence. He maintained a bold assuredness, seemingly impervious to the fear gripping every man.

Major McKenna came down the line behind the captain and assured his men that the artillery assault was largely ineffective. He forced them to think beyond the immediate, intense bombardment.

"What is your primary mission, men?" McKenna screamed over the crashing booms.

"Defend the line, sir!" the soldiers yelled back.

"Good, men."

The shelling raged for four hours, all through the dark, predawn morning, but just like it had begun, the crashing cacophony of mortars and shells ceased all at once and was replaced by a flat, silent stillness. Sulfur smoke that once filled the trenches and choked the infantrymen had lifted, and they could remove their gas masks. Many of the Irish infantrymen took great relief when the incessant enfilade had stopped, but others braced for the upcoming assault.

"You know the route to the depot?" John yelled to Buckley.

"Yes, John. You and Edward have four extra canisters to start. Bergan and I will maintain a continuous relay: nonstop feed."

"Good." John looked to his side. "You ready, Roons?"

"Kill or die, Johnny. Kill or die."

"Got your trench knife?"

"Right here." Rooney grabbed his holster.

"You?"

"Ready."

John reached for his holster and ran his finger down the serrated blade's sharp edge.

From the direction of the Sacrifice Post, the Shamrock men heard a single gunshot pop. It was Major Anderson, signaling for his 2nd Battalion men to be ready.

"Game's on, Johnny!" Rooney yelled excitedly.

Inside the Sacrifice Post, 2nd Battalion's infantrymen stood up in the trench and took aim. Neither Major Anderson nor his lieutenants could see the ensuing onslaught. They could only hear a thunderous rumble, the roar of men and machines drawing ever closer.

Pop, pop.

The men inside the Centers of Resistance heard Major Anderson's second signal, and there was a sudden eruption of small-arms fire and mortars coming from the American Sacrifice Post. The 2nd Battalion opened fire on the invading horde. Major Anderson aimed high and fired a flare signal that tore straight up and burst bright in the black sky. The men in the CRs saw the Sacrifice Post illuminate brightly under the phosphorescent light, but could only see shadows and silhouettes of men—thousands of them, pressed against one another in a brutal, crushing struggle. Brilliant small flashes of light burst continuously by the millisecond as small-arms fire crackled. Hundreds of hand grenades exploded and a dense cloud of sulfur smoke rolled up the valley and poured down into the CR trenches.

The 42nd Division's Field Artillery Regiment acknowledged Major Anderson's signal flare and fired a single cannon shot in response. The FAR's heavy gunners tilted their 155 mm howitzers low and aimed the deadly enfilade fire squarely at the second German assault line waiting over the low ridge. When the American FAR men fired, they gushed ecstatically, eager to join the fight.

In the Sacrifice Post, 2nd Battalion's machine-gun nests roared to life, leveling a stream of hot lead. The machine gunners mowed down line after line of charging Krauts, but the charging storm troopers, trained to move forward at all cost, leaped over dead comrades and forged onward. Thousands of German soldiers came over the ridge. Shoulder to shoulder, they swarmed into the abandoned Allied trenches, bunkers, and dugouts.

The 2nd Battalion held its ground. Platoon lieutenants maintained strict discipline and it paid off. The Americans began to stem the flow of charging Krauts, firing a steady flow of bullets, mortars, and grenades until the raging storm troops, eager to press forward and not get bogged down in a trench fight, bypassed the American Sacrifice Defense Post and continued.

At 83rd Brigade HQ, Brigadier General Lenihan's staff began to collect intelligence reports from spotters. Motorcycle messengers delivered reports after having navigated crater holes, burning forests, and dead bodies strewn about the battlefield.

As reports came in, General Lenihan grew confident that Ludendorff's assault plan would unravel as expected. One excellent exception: reports from Major Anderson. His 2nd Battalion was successfully defending the Sacrifice Post, and casualties were reported to be low.

American field artillery proved very effective. The second German assault wave was hit hard by American enfilade, and spotters reported much disarray just over the ridgeline. The first German assault wave was confounded, too. German intelligence briefed their officer cadre that the American and French first line of defense would be much closer to no-man's-land. The German officers surprisingly found themselves charging through empty Allied trenches and couldn't figure out why.

German storm troops continued to flood past the laid-bare Sacrifice Posts. They proceeded at a brisk clip, moving deep into

French-held ground. General Lenihan made telephone contact with Colonel McCoy and Majors McKenna and Donovan and ordered his 165th Infantry officers to set a time hack. Lenihan expected the first wave of Germans to be abeam the three Centers of Resistance posts in ten minutes.

"Attack commences at hack time plus thirty minutes," Lenihan told his officers. "French advised signal flare initiates action."

McKenna and Donovan dispatched messengers to company captains saying that a broadside attack was imminent and to look for the signal flare.

German storm troops spilled out from the naturally protective tree line, crossed into the open, unshielded field, and flowed down a shallow, sloping valley out onto the low-lying flat area. The lead thrust line emerged from the trees and passed the 1st and 3rd Battalion CRs situated on ground slightly higher than the open flatland. French and American units observed the charging German line but maintained total silence, allowing the Germans to pass.

At hack time plus thirty minutes, a bright flare lofted above the 83rd Brigade command post, and instantaneously the French army roared to life. The French blasted the German storm troopers head-on. Machine-gun fire, mortars, and light artillery ripped into the German troops, killing hundreds of soldiers instantly.

Storm troop commanders did not buckle amid the chaos of the surprise attack. With characteristic bravery and unwavering discipline, they ordered their columns of storm troops to turn ninety degrees and attack the French Center of Resistance head-on.

"Angriff! Angriff!" the Americans could hear the German officers shout.

Major McKenna lifted his arm and fired a single shot. All four of his Shamrock Companies stood up inside the CR trench, lifted their weapons, and took aim.

John checked the breach of his Chauchat and the magazine. Both were clean and clear. Ed Rooney did the same. Buckley loaded his Enfield and stood at the ready. They'd never seen so many Krauts in one place before.

German officers in command of the trailing columns recognized their flanks were vulnerable to broadside attack and turned their stretched-out rows of soldiers toward 3rd Battalion's Center of Resistance and ordered them to charge at the Americans. John, Rooney, and Buckley could hear the orders shouted from Hun officers urging the German troopers to kill and destroy the American defense post.

Major McKenna fired two consecutive pistol shots. John, Rooney, Buckley, and the whole American infantry line opened fire and blew a tightly aimed, deadly effective small-arms cannonade straight into the belly of the invading Krauts. Hundreds fell at once, but thousands continued up the slope, racing toward the American CR.

"Attack!" the American sergeants screamed, and the Shamrock men fired with abandon. Machine guns pelted lines of Germans, mowing them down. Grenadiers launched mortars deep into the attacking swarm, and arms, legs, and torsos could be seen flying high into the sulfur-choked air and macabrely crashing back down into craters of mud. Still the Germans pressed. With row after row of men, they climbed the shallow slope and made haste attacking the American defense post.

John shot nervously and wildly. He was way too frightened to take good aim. He blew thought cartridge after cartridge and saw he was starting to run low.

"Buckley!" he shouted, but got no answer. He began to fret that he and Rooney would run out. Buckley had left for the depot when the shooting started, and Bergan Morgan was due back soon. John knew he had to slow down, calm his nerves, and conserve.

He heard his father's voice. *Concentrate on the task before you, son.* Then he heard Ennis O'Shea. *Wait for the shot, then go in for the kill.*

John's shoulder stung with pain. The Chauchat's recoil hammered his upper arm. He adjusted the tripod and pressed his body firmly against the trench wall for support, then rested the rifle butt against his beaten shoulder. This time, he was slow and deliberate. He took careful aim and waited until his Kraut targets were less than one hundred feet away from the end of his rifle. He carefully counted down a methodical "four, three, two, one..." He allowed the enemy to approach in close. He aimed and pressed the trigger. *Pop-pop-pop-pop-pop.* He picked off five Krauts with five bullets.

"Shit-hot, Johnny!" Ed Rooney shouted over the raging noise. "Shit-fucking-hot!"

Ed Rooney opened fire, and he too fell three Germans.

"You got 'em, Roons?" John screamed.

A squad of storm troops skirted up slope and closed in on the edge of the American trench. The Germans were shielding two grenadiers and a flamethrower operator, trying to move them into firing range. Every 3rd Battalion infantryman saw the encroaching squad and emptied his magazine trying to stop them, but no one could get a good shot.

The two German grenadiers launched a series of mortars at the Shamrock trench and managed to hit the far end of the line, killing at least ten men instantly. John and Rooney felt the intense heat and the gigantic flash roll past their bodies. They got pelted by rocks and were blasted by flying dirt. After the cloud lifted, total chaos ensued as infantrymen who were badly bloodied or hit by shrapnel ran from the impact zone.

The experienced flamethrower operator was not shaken by the bloody blast. He maintained his calm. He took careful aim at the American trench and spurt an arc of fuel atop twenty Shamrock infantrymen hunkering inside the trench. The men felt the viscous oil hit them, but before they could figure out what it was, the flamethrower ignited the arc and the Shamrock men were scorched by fire.

Riflemen rushed to extinguish the raging blaze, but the sticky, viscous fuel clung to the men's uniform and seared their skin. It was too late.

Major Donovan raised his pistol and fired three consecutive shots. All one thousand of his 1st Battalion men arose in unison inside the deep trench and climbed onto the open field.

"Attack!" Donovan growled, angered by the horrid scene he'd just witnessed.

"Attack!" his company captains repeated.

"Attack!" urged the platoon lieutenants, and "Attack!" screamed all the squad sergeants. The 1st Battalion men roared down the slope onto the open flatland, careening toward the rear echelon German flank.

"There goes Dick O'Neil!" Rooney yelled to John.

The machine-gun nest at John's left side continued to lay down a steady stream of deadly fire. The gunners swung the Hotchkiss's barrel from left to right and back again, almost casually crisscrossing the sloped pitch, wiping out every Kraut in its grizzly path.

The carnage of dead German soldiers began to pile up under the American trench. Some of the dead men were very young and many were very old. Regardless, the German storm troops kept coming— nothing seemed to stop the flow.

Donovan led his battalion while holding his pistol high, his trench knife fastened to his waist. 1st Battalion infantrymen were out for blood. No mercy. Donovan's men swooped down on top the lightly armed resupply regiments and annihilated everybody. Everything in 1st Battalion's path was killed, captured, or destroyed.

At Brigade HQ, spotters reported that the Germans were holding the next assault wave, and that the first wave assault troops had pulled away from the French and were now in retreat. The first and second wave trailing flanks had been decimated by Donovan's attack, and 3rd Battalion's CR trench and Major Anderson's Sacrifice Post were no longer under attack.

Inside Brigade HQ, General Lenihan's operations and intelligence staff hashed over the Germans' next move and considered the enemy's limitations. German artillery fire should be expected at any moment—at least enough enfilade to protect the retreating divisions and allow them to fall back and regroup. German cannons had fired for over four hours nonstop and were still too hot. The Germans had expended an enormous amount of ammunition. There couldn't be much more at the ready. It could never be replaced so quickly. Any second artillery barrage would be limited.

Lenihan's men believed that the Germans would pull back, regroup, and conduct follow-on attacks at some point over the next twenty-four hours. This time they knew, however, that the in-depth defense traps were no longer viable. Lenihan called Colonel McCoy and ordered him to retrieve Major Donovan and move Major Anderson out of the Sacrifice Post. Anderson and his men were to join Major McKenna's battalion and take position inside the center CR.

Lenihan had to move quickly and prepare his brigade for the next attack. He understood the next round would be a direct faceoff between himself and the German 3rd Army commander. His brigade had to be ready for anything, and General Lenihan was sure the German 3rd Army still had a plenty-lethal punch.

———

At dawn in Saint Hilare the next day, after the initial German assault, the 165th infantrymen, bunched together inside the Center of Resistance trenches, finally got a good look at their handiwork. Thousands of dead Krauts lay strewn across the battlefield, their bodies lying in mud-filled, bomb-blasted craters. The German assault drive was a total failure. The Americans and French held the line at every major post, and the Allied in-depth defense strategy proved a great success.

Daniel Buckley and Bergan Morgan spent the midmorning hours hauling canisters filled with 8 mm Lebel bullets back to the trench. They had to refill each expended Chauchat cartridge casing.

Buckley stood at the trench edge and called down to Rooney while pointing to the horizon.

"Take a look, Edward." Buckley pointed to an observer balloon launched by an intelligence unit. "Like I told you, Edward. When the balloon goes up."

Rooney looked at the large airship on the horizon and shrugged. "Well it sure as shit went up, didn't it?"

CHAPTER 14

Chateau Thierry, Crossing the Ourcq River, July 25, 1918

———

ON JULY 18, 1918, THE American 26th "Yankee Division," as part of the AEF's massive effort to counter the German army's Operation Michael, pushed the feared German storm troop divisions out of Chateau Thierry, with some of the fighting hand-to-hand. On July 26, the 42nd Rainbow Division relieved the 26th Yankee Division and continued the American push, attacking the Germans across the Ourcq River (Ork). The 165th Irish Regiment's Kilo Company of the 42nd Rainbow Division led the Ourcq River charge, losing more than two hundred out of 250 men during the two-day offensive. Seventeen hundred of the 165th Regiment's three thousand infantrymen were injured.

———

Regiments of the 42nd Division departed the Champagne-Marne battlefield and spent the next two weeks regrouping under the Vadenay woodland canopy east of Reims. The 42nd Division was now under the command of I-Corps, the US Army's premier combat corps, and the

42nd Division received its orders to replace the French 167th Division and the American 26th and 3rd Divisions inside the savagely embattled Chateau Thierry sector. The 26th and 3rd Divisions and a battalion of US Marines in Belleau Wood were bogged down in desperate casualties-fueled fighting and needed relief.

The 42nd Division's two brigades were ordered to split up again and depart the Vadenay woods on staggered schedules. The 84th Brigade was first to go, its two regiments leaving one company at a time and slipping out in the dark night hours to board trains for Chateau Thierry. Two days later on July 24, soon after sunset and natural light was gone, the 83rd Brigade emerged from under the leafy woodland canopy and marched to the rail depot.

The trip was a ten-hour overnight ride, and by now rumors spiked with gory details of bloody hand-to-hand fighting outside Chateau Thierry and Belleau Wood had passed down to the troops.

Word was that US Marines in Belleau Wood had demolished the Krauts by bayonetting one storm trooper at a time for two straight weeks. German soldiers taken prisoner kept referring to the hard-fighting US Marines as "Devil Dogs," and that name stuck. The 42nd men also heard about 3rd Division's "Rock of the Marne"—machine gun companies that staved off a German division singlehandedly and held an important bridge into Chateau Thierry.

Envious of others' heroics and stories of glory, some of the newbies audaciously stood up inside the rocking Chateau Thierry bound train, stout with confident swagger (or maybe great ignorance), and spouted that they too were eager to take a crack at the Krauts. Old-timers lay silent, saying nothing, but they scoffed. They didn't hear stories from Chateau Thierry like the newbies did. Savage bayonet fighting and rushing the Kraut line sounded ominous, even dangerous, to them. Chateau Thierry would be the real deal for sure, and all the old-timers knew any fighting up to this point had been mere practice.

Rolling toward Chateau Thierry, John knew he was charging head-long into a ravenous belly of the beast. Boisterous cheers proclaiming easy victory echoed hollow to him. He had formed much more profound convictions since he arrived in France, and was now sure he would surrender life and limb to defend his beloved America.

"Life, Liberty, and the Pursuit of Happiness" had become almost spiritual words; providential words filled with God-given truth. John had witnessed Life and Liberty firsthand; they were cherished ideals to be lived hour by hour, for in the flash of a split second, God-given freedom and the joy of being a free man on this Earth could be snatched away, taken by a bullet fired for the love of the kaiser.

The infantrymen weren't crammed together in the Hommes trains this time. Every man had room to stretch out and get comfortable. Warm summer air circulated through the wood-slatted cars, and the train rocked and rattled noisily. Nevertheless, the ride across the Champagne countryside to Chateau Thierry was peaceful. John propped his head up against his backpack and stretched his legs flat across the train's floor next to Ed Rooney.

"Do'ya think God'll ever forgive us fer killin' so many Krauts, Roons?" John asked him.

"He put us here in His grand garden fer some reason, Johnny," said Rooney. Rooney then rolled to his side and fell asleep.

Seeing how exceptionally comfortable John and Rooney looked, Daniel Buckley joined them, as did Bergs Morgan. Each man, so completely fatigued and exhausted, closed his eyes and surrendered to the gentle sway of the rocking train. Soon, each of them was fast asleep, getting much-needed rest before hitting the ground at Chateau Thierry and its carnage-filled battlefields.

———

The enormous US Army supply depot camp outside Chateau Thierry village was a harried, confusing place. Supply trucks loaded with mess provisions, regiments hauling thousands of artillery pieces, combat engineers operating heavy road-building equipment, trucks, cranes, and earth-moving plows interspersed with slower, horse-drawn carts and men moving afoot, all mashed together on sparse, narrow roadways in and around the small village, creating a massive gridlock.

Inside the camp near the train depot, a two hundred-truck convoy loaded with artillery shells for the front had lined up and was ready to roll, but it didn't budge an inch. Roadways between the camp and the front line were too jammed.

The Chaumont HQ conceived battle plan ordering eight divisions to move to one location at one time demonstrated a startling lack of planning. Essential materials needed to support frontline troops weren't delivered, and what did make it to the front arrived piecemeal.

French officers observed the American carnival-like disarray and got a usual high-minded laugh. The Americans were always stepping on themselves, but despite the chaos and unlike the French, the Americans eventually got the job done and never managed to miss a fight.

Shamrock Battalion's train arrived outside the Chateau Thierry camp at dawn and sat idle in the depot as the debarkation process proceeded slowly. Division sergeants assigned to get men off trains and onto trucks seemed hell-bent not to fall prey to the huge camp's disorganization, and the sergeants emptied each boxcar one at a time.

A sergeant careened down the platform barking orders and unlatched and slid open John and Buckley's door. John was first to jump down on the concrete, cautious not to drop his weapon. Daniel Buckley followed, he too protecting his rifle. Next was Ed Rooney and then Bergan Morgan.

John looked about, struck by the thousands of men, trucks, horse-drawn carts, and artillery cannons he saw lined up ready to move. He couldn't believe the massive size of the American camp and how it overflowed with men and machines.

"Rumor says we're at eight hundred thousand now," said Buckley.

"Looks like everybody's here, all right. Don't it?" said Rooney.

No matter which direction the squad mates looked, all they could see was khaki brown from the edge of the train tracks all the way into the horizon. The camp teemed with uniformed doughboys, every man wearing a Campaign hat and holding an Enfield rifle.

"Looks like a scene from a movin' picture," John imagined.

Buckley had it about right. By late July 1918, the Americans moved eight hundred thousand soldiers across the Atlantic and more were arriving each day, but the throng of men and machines filling the American Chateau Thierry camp was no way near the total American Expeditionary Force in France. They saw about two hundred thousand men, mostly I-Corps, and everyone and everything they did see was slated to ship west to the Marne River front.

On the platform, John handed Buckley his Chauchat, then tugged on the straps of his backpack to lift the sack off the ground and onto his mid-back. He lunged forward to get his legs beneath the eighty-pound weight, and he pulled on the straps again, this time to get the pack up to his shoulders. Once he could stand upright stably, Buckley handed John his Chauchat and pulled John's pack straps taught. Once John was finished, he helped Buckley get his pack on the same way. After Bergan Morgan and Ed Rooney got their packs fastened, the four men walked to the edge of the roadway and boarded one of the fifty trucks lined up along the depot's dirt road.

The four-wheeled flatbeds carried twenty men each, and once the entire train was emptied and all of 3rd Battalion had transferred packs and all onto the heavy 4x4s, the convoy was ready for the drive to Villers sur Fere, two miles beyond Chateau Thierry.

While crawling up onto the truck, Ed Rooney casually eyeballed the driver. The driver was a tiny man dark skinned, no more than five feet tall, probably Asian, certainly not a Frenchmen.

Every man climbing into the truck eyeballed the driver, but they were way too preoccupied balancing a heavy pack and thinking about the coming faceoff with the Krauts. No one gave much thought to the small Asian man. The squad mates got seated, and the truck's diesel engine rumbled to life. The weighty 4x4 vehicle, grind into gear. Ed Rooney looked down the two bench rows and shouted loud enough for every man to hear him.

"I've been on the road to hell for some time now, lads," he said with a wide grin, "but I never knew my driver was a Chinaman."

The squad mates burst with laughter. Everyone had noticed the driver. Chinese, Japanese, Korean; it didn't matter. The sight of an Asian man in the middle of war-ravaged France was so insanely odd. How in hell did *he* get here? The men thought up a thousand crazy answers, but in the end, they chalked the whole thing up to war's insanity.

It turns out that all the truck drivers were Vietnamese men enlisted from halfway around the globe to help mother France. The French called on all hands from her colonies, and everyone was pressed into service to defend the homeland.

Once the convoy got under way and made it out onto the narrow roadway and away from the massive American supply depot, it didn't take long before the entire line of trucks came to a grinding halt. Traffic was at a complete standstill, and 3rd Battalion was now caught in the middle of massive motor vehicle gridlock.

Shamrock commander Major McKenna and a group of his company captains slid down from the idling trucks and hastily conferred in a football-style huddle on the side of the road. The battalion had four miles to go before reaching Chateau Thierry and two miles more before reaching the French 167th Division transfer point in Villers-sur-Fere.

Time was running short, and Major McKenna refused to be late for his official changeover. He needed to gather as much intelligence on the

Krauts as possible, and he thought that keeping his French counterpart waiting showed very bad form.

The Shamrock officers hashed out an impromptu plan, and Major McKenna made a quick decision. He ordered his entire battalion to disembark from the 4x4s and fall into formation on the side of the road. The remainder of the journey, the six-mile trek to the village of Villers-sur-Fere would be made by foot.

In short order, one thousand men, the entire Shamrock Battalion, began to cascade off the high trucks and fall into neat rows along the narrow roadway. Once the battalion regained full formation, Major McKenna led the way and set a proper pace, singing cadence himself.

McKenna shouted a vigorous verse of "Garry Owen," and soon his four company captains joined in. Hearing the regimental ditty waft from the front, squad lieutenants began to sing and soon all the sergeants sang. Finally, every rank-and-file man was singing gleefully, arms swaying and legs now moving in unison, heal-foot, heal-foot, with perfect synchronicity.

> Our hearts so stout have got us fame
> For soon 'tis know from whence we came
> Where'er we go they dread the name
> Of Garry Owen, in glory

The 3rd Battalion jovially cruised past all the idled trucks and halted cannons and left the massive traffic jam behind, proud as ever to be the Irish Shamrock Battalion of New York City.

———

The boisterous journey soon degraded into a sloppy, mud-filled mess. As 3rd Battalion proceeded toward Chateau Thierry, the loose muck underfoot turned putrid and the air around them fell foul—a malodorous mix of rotting flesh and animal waste.

Out on the roadway lay thousands of dead German soldiers strewn across the pavement. They lay shoulder to shoulder, side to side, or piled atop one another, entombed inside shell-cratered holes. The scene was ghoulish and hellish. Dead men covered every inch of the sludgy ground, and maggot-borne flies swarmed by the thousands. It was impossible not to step on a decaying body. The stench was overwhelming. Many men fell ill, unable to breathe. Some donned gas masks.

The singing had long stopped, but the battalion still needed to make ground. They moved over the killing field, silently taking note of the 26th Yankee Division's handiwork. On this very ground five days earlier, a gruesome clash had occurred between these half-buried Germans and the American 26th Division, the Boston Irish. All was fought until it disintegrated into a horrific hand-to-hand, bloody knife fighting that ended in victory for the Americans.

Captain Hurley allowed his Kilo men to break rank and fall out of formation to avoid stepping on a body, American or German. The smell was sickening, but 3rd Battalion and its four companies were expected to arrive in Villers-sur-Fere and relieve the French 167th Division on time, and Major McKenna made his men press on.

Compounding the growing sense of unease, 3rd Battalion drew ever closer to the crashing sounds of enemy artillery fire. The 167th Alabama Regiment and the 168th Iowans had relieved the 26th Yankee Division a day before, and both regiments were now under heavy artillery attack at La Croix Rouge Farm outside Chateau Thierry.

German artillery shells pounded the 167th Alabamans' position hard. Projectiles landed one after the other. Fireball-fueled shockwaves blasted across the open field. Trees were ripped out by the roots and tossed like matchsticks, some trees bursting aflame before landing back in the forest and igniting more fires.

A few shells landed off-target and uncomfortably close to Shamrock Battalion. One shell started a large fire in the nearby line of trees. Suddenly, a series of shells landed even closer, and every man in the battalion had to flee and dive for cover.

Daniel Buckley lunged headfirst and eyes closed into a nearby shell crater, landing in a pool of loose mud just as a huge concussive blast blew past his body.

The intense heat frightened him, and he frantically scooped the loose ground. He began to panic after a second hot flash blew past, and he feared a shell would hit him. He clawed harder until he moved enough dirt to form a shallow trench, and he burrowed down. He kept clawing until he reached hard clay and could dig no deeper. Buckley then opened his eyes and saw the face of an entombed soldier staring directly back at him.

Buckley fixated on the distorted face as a wave of panic rolled over his body. He saw that the soldier had burned to death, and Buckley was convinced that he too would burn. He became paralyzed by fear, unable to move. His heart raced, his chest pounded, and his breathing quickened. He felt hopeless as he succumbed to the terror.

Buckley lay bunched in the muddy hole praying to God, begging for strength. He asked the Lord to shield him from the ghouls of sin as shells exploded all around, and slowly Buckley grew calm. An inner voice demanded he be brave, and his eyes welled full. Buckley thought himself a coward again, and he couldn't bear the shame. Tears streamed down his face, and he rolled toward the clear blue sky above and pleaded to God aloud, "Please do not forsake me!"

The men remained hunkered in the mud but could hear the growl of American artillery returning fire. 155 mm howitzers began to pound

the Krauts on the La Croix Rouge farm. The Shamrock men spontaneously jumped up, losing all sense of fear, and then tossed their caps into
the air. Fritz was getting a taste of his own!

———

At Villers-sur-Fere, General Menoher, the 42nd Division's commanding
officer, ordered his senior division staff, including Brigade commanders
Lenihan and Brown and his four regimental commanders, to report to
his headquarters. The men huddled around a large wooden table inside
Menoher's farmhouse kitchen, a make-do battlefield command post.
Menoher laid out the division's preliminary attack plan for crossing the
Ourcq River.

The 42nd had never faced the enemy without first drawing up detailed battle plans and plying their sophisticated command and control
to keep units coordinated on the field. This time, the division was getting rushed and had no time to draw up elaborate plans. French V army
commander General Degoutte, who was calling the shots for the larger
Chateau Thierry operations, wanted his forces including the Americans
advancing quickly to keep the Germans on the run.

General Menoher placed a sheet of paper on the briefing table and
used a pencil to sketch the division's battlefield organization.

"Our attack zone is a giant square, gentlemen," he said, drawing on
a sheet of paper. "We are at the bottom of the square, and our objectives,
Meurcy Farm and the Bois Brule, are at the top. Bisecting our vector
of advance is the Ourcq River. That's Ork." He drew a line across the
square. "The river is approximately twenty-five feet wide and three foot
in depth, relatively shallow and easy to traverse.

"All four of our division's regiments shall participate in the assault.

Along the square's far left side, the One Sixty-Sixth Regiment shall
forge the river and attack through Bois Colas onto Bois Brule. The One

Sixty-Sixth shall clear the Bois Colas of all enemy resistance and continue north until securing and holding Bois Brule north of Meurcy Farm. The One Sixty-Eighth Regiment shall follow the One-Sixty-Sixth.

"The One Sixty-Fifth Regiment shall attack through the middle, cross the Ourcq River, and take control of its northern bank on the low ground below Meurcy Farm. The One Sixty-Fifth will proceed upslope, and capture and hold the Meurcy Farm plateau."

Colonel McCoy spied topographical maps Major Donovan's men had drawn, and now, hearing that his regiment was responsible for crossing the battlefield's most unforgiving ground, the colonel grew concerned.

Both sides of the Ourcq riverbank were completely wide open and unprotected. The ground from the riverbank to the Meurcy Farm plateau sloped upward and offered only sparse low brush for cover. On the regiment's far right flank was a steep ridge crawling with Kraut machine guns.

General Menoher continued. "The One Sixty-Seventh Regiment shall take position on the One Sixty-Fifth's right flank. The One Sixty-Seventh will suppress any enfilade fire from the high ridge and from Forest de Nesles."

McCoy's eyes opened even wider. The 167th was still hung up repelling the German 3rd Army on La Croix Rouge Farm, and the regiment's casualty list was long. The 167th might not be capable of flanking the 165th.

"The order to execute this attack can come at any moment, gentlemen," Menoher warned. "French General Degoutte is eager to move. Be ready."

———

Colonel McCoy positioned his 165th command post as close to the forward line as possible, and he constructed a high tower to keep an eye on the action. 165th battalion commanders Majors Donovan, Anderson, and McKenna finished running reconnoitering squads throughout the regiment's zone of responsibility, and McCoy's intelligence squad, including Sergeant Joyce Kilmer, drew up crude but useful maps.

Kilmer had gotten bored doing clerical intelligence work and was itching to get closer to the real action. He petitioned Lieutenant Colonel Donovan with a request to join 1st Battalion, and Donovan approved it. Kilmer had convinced his higher-ups that he'd be much more useful assessing actual battlefield action rather than collecting reports from others. Upon execution of the Ourcq River attack, Sergeant Joyce Kilmer was assigned to Donovan's 1st Battalion intelligence squad.

The night before the American attack, the 167th Alabama Regiment had not yet finished with the German 3rd Army, but the 167th had managed to push the Germans off La Croix Rouge Farm and north of the Ourcq River. The Alabamans suffered hundreds of casualties during that effort, and the regiment's battlefield capabilities had been dangerously eroded.

McCoy, keenly aware of the situation, kept his concerns to himself, but plotted to bolster his own regiment's effectiveness by requesting direct field-artillery support from 42nd Division HQ. McCoy dispatched a messenger to General Menoher with his formal request.

McCoy also made his regimental assignments and he placed Major Anderson's 2nd Battalion on the left side of the 165th's thrust line. Major McKenna's 3rd Battalion was placed at the center, and newly promoted Lieutenant Colonel Donovan's 1st Battalion was placed on the right side. Center positioned, Third Battalion's Kilo Company, commanded by Captain Hurley but led into the battlefield by Major McKenna, would lead the assault across the Ourcq River and up the slope to Meurcy Farm. Third Battalion's India Company would follow Kilo Company and carry the bulk of the light-infantry weapons like mortars and machine guns needed to bolster Kilo Company once on the battlefield.

———

Attack Order 51 arrived on Major General Menoher's desk at 42nd Division HQ on the evening of July 26. He quickly approved the order and moved to disseminate the action to his four regimental command posts using motorcycle couriers. Every regiment of the division was ordered to move at 0430 hours before dawn. The 165th Regiment would cross the Ourcq River and spearhead a charge up the middle. The 166th Regiment on the far left side would attack Bois Cola, and the 168th Regiment would follow. The 167th Regiment on the far right side would suppress any enfilade fire emanating from the Forest de Nesles,

At 0230 hours, on the 26th, two hours before the Ourcq River assault was to commence, General Degoutte dispatched a message citing a number of his French divisions had not yet reached position and were unable to comply with the 0430 assault hour. Degoutte delayed the attack until 0630 hours, and now the stealth predawn assault across the open Ourcq River would initiate after sunrise in broad daylight.

———

Colonel McCoy used the unseen delay to summon Major McKenna and Captain Hurley up to his command post. He informed his 3rd Battalion major and his Kilo Company captain that the 42nd Division's Field Artillery Regiment was still stuck in traffic outside Chateau Thierry and would not be available. There would be no preassault softening of German machine-gun positions across the Ourcq River, and he also informed them they should not expect any friendly artillery support to counter German FAR from Forest de Nesles.

Major McKenna accepted Colonel McCoy's situation report stoically and decided to concentrate on victory rather than on the deficiencies that assured defeat. McKenna relayed to Colonel McCoy how Father Duffy had spent the night with his Kilo Company and how Duffy's very presence calmed the men and helped many find the fortitude needed to get the difficult job done.

"Father heard many confessions," McKenna added, "and he blessed us all. The men were deeply grateful. I believe Kilo Company is ready, Colonel."

———

At the break of daylight, Kilo Company lined up parallel to the Ourcq River's embankment. The company's officers managed to keep all five platoons, 250 men, out of sight behind a dense tree line. Once the attack was on, however, the infantrymen would be forced to career out into the open ground and charge down the river's flat, mud-packed riverbank.

As launch time neared, Kilo Company edged closer to the river, but still under the tree-filled wood line, and waited for Captain Hurley's signal to charge. John peered over at Buckley and unfurled Buckley's bound-up emerald armband.

"Ready, Roons?" John asked.

"Kill or die, Johnny."

"Trench knife?"

"Yep."

"You?"

"Yep." John ran his finger down the blade edge.

The sun was now up and shining brightly. The natural light glimmered on the river's gentle motion. The sky was clear; not a cloud. From the wooded edge, Kilo's infantrymen could see across the riverbank and up to the far side. They knew that German machine gunners lie in wait and that they'd face a curtain of hot lead. Murmured prayers could be heard up and down the line. John patted and pressed on Anna's rosary in his jacket pocket.

The order to execute the attack came via courier, and Major McKenna hacked his time clock to Captain Hurley's and gave the captain the OK to execute the "go" signal when ready.

At exactly 0630 hours, Captain Hurley raised his arm and fired three shots.

"Game's on, Johnny!" Rooney shouted while running out of the woods.

Along the tree line, weapons drawn, 250 men swarmed from under the protective tree cover and rushed to the river's edge. Adrenaline gushed as men fearlessly charged head-on to confront the enemy.

German machine gunners, all well trained, didn't shoot "knee-jerk." They waited and observed, holding fire until absolutely sure they'd inflict maximum damage.

John sped down the embankment, his adrenalin pumping. The ground under his feet was mostly firm, but as soon as he reached the river's edge, his foot sank deep into wet mud, and he panicked that he might get stuck. He turned to his right and saw Buckley, and suddenly he was startled by a deafening *rat-ta-tat-tat* clack coming from the far right side. German machine gunners had unleashed a dense wall of high-speed, razor-sharp bullets that began to hit the Americans.

Rat-ta-tat-tat! Rat-ta-tat-tat! The guns growled. John peered down the river and saw a giant cloud of sulfur smoke settling atop what looked like a million splashes pelting the surface of the river. Then he saw scores of Kilo men fall flat, their bodies splashing lifelessly into the water.

"Faster, Bucks!" John reached back and pulled on Buckley's jacket.

"I'm weighted down!" Buckley cried. He was carrying all of John's extra ammunition.

John pressed to the northern bank, his heart pounding out of his chest and his breathing deep and labored. He was scared out of his mind but managed to keep his wits and hold his Chauchat above the water.

Kraut Maxim machine guns sliced into the far right side of the line, tearing scores of men to shreds. Infantrymen, next in the line of fire, began to panic and abandoned their fallen squad mates, whose bodies now floated lifelessly on the blood-red river. German gunners aimed and fired mercilessly, mowing down everything in their path.

The American infantrymen acted crazed and undisciplined. They bunched behind one another, which only made it easier for German gunners to hit a large target. Squad lieutenants and sergeants tried to stop the bunching, but they too were struck down dead.

Major McKenna was the first to emerge from the water, and as he ran up the northern bank and dived for cover behind the low brush, he was hit by a torrent of machine-gun bullets. His body twisted wildly, bullets tearing grotesque holes in his chest and shattering his lower leg. The major collapsed dead in front of everyone.

Captain Hurley instantly took command.

"Charge, men! Charge!" he shouted.

His squad lieutenants echoed his order, as did his sergeants. All of Kilo's officers and NCOs began to shout full-throated, "Charge, men! Charge!"

Kilo Company roared to life as men sloshed even harder through the water and past the machine-gun fire. At first, ten men made it, then twenty, then forty. Eighty men made it to the low brush. Then 160 and finally two hundred of the company's 250 men made the crossing. Fifty fell to the guns.

If anyone dared to look back, they'd see a river darkened red. Filled with the blood of brave young American men.

"McKay! Rooney!" the squad sergeant beckoned. Both men rolled through the brush up to the sergeant's position.

"Follow Squad Three and leapfrog with them. They'll give you fire protection. When our grenadiers hit that machine-gun nest..." He pointed to the target. "…and those Kraut fuckers start to run, I want you to mow them down. McKay, you're left. Rooney, you're right."

"Yessir," John and Rooney answered nervously.

Buckley tossed John ten extra clips, and Bergs Morgan gave Rooney the same. The four riflemen led the way, crawling on their bellies from the squad line with John and Rooney following. The team was comprised of old-timers, and John knew each man by name. He was confident they'd come through OK.

The riflemen fanned out, putting distance between their positions. If a Kraut machine-gun nest opened fire on one rifleman, the other three would take aim and suppress it. John and Rooney would use that suppression fire to leapfrog closer to the target.

John got within three hundred feet of the machine-gun nest, and a few minutes later Rooney was abeam his position. Rooney gave John a silent thumbs-up and John returned the same. Both men were ready. One of the four riflemen shot three quick, successive shots—a signal for the grenadier team to fire.

"Clear!" yelled the grenadier leader, and his team volleyed a series of grenades, hammering the ground around the nest. John was close enough to feel the blasts but knew not to get distracted or nervous. He kept his eyes on the Kraut gunners.

American grenadiers closed in on the target nest, and John could hear the German gunners begin to shout anxiously at one another. John signaled to Rooney that it was time to stand just as one last grenade hit the Kraut nest spot-on and the German gunners jumped to flee. John and Rooney stood up, opened fire, and shot them all dead.

This time, the temperamental French automatic did its job and the Kraut machine gunners responsible for murdering dozens of Americans crossing the Ourcq River dropped lifeless to the ground. It didn't take but a moment for backup machine gunners hidden deep in the dense brush to open fire, but by that time John and Rooney were back down flat and crawling away.

———

At the 165th command post, Colonel McCoy followed Kilo's advance. He received reports that Major McKenna was KIA and Kilo Company had thus far suffered fifty casualties crossing the Ourcq River. McCoy was ready to send India Company, the backup, but was deeply dispirited, believing India Company would only get it worse. He knew Kilo Company needed the mortars and machine guns—he ordered India Company to attack and cross the Ourcq.

———

At the river's edge, Captain Hurley advanced his company's line using a series of ground signals. Hurley was able to move his entire company away from the open uncovered river embankment and up slope to a better defensive position, one that offered slightly better protection. Hurley then ordered his men to disperse as widely as possible and spread out. While being briefed for the Ourcq River assault by 42nd Division intelligence officers, Hurley was told about a hidden roadway running along the top edge of the sloping ground just below the Meurcy Farm plateau. Division intel said the sunken roadway's drainage ditches formed a natural berm trench and that Kilo Company should seek it for defense.

Hurley expected to see India Company close in on his rear flank, but as daylight waned and darkness fell, India Company was still pinned down, taking heavy machine-gun fire on the Ourcq riverbank. Hurley was desperate for artillery cover, but there was no support. The captain had to adapt, and he reconsidered his primary objective: take and hold

Meurcy Farm. Stalwartly and almost singlehandedly, Hurley advanced his men all the way up to the hidden roadway below Meurcy Farm without any outside artillery support or light or heavy infantry. His men methodically leapfrogged up slope as little as ten feet at a time, eventually reaching the reconnoitered roadway.

Lieutenant Colonel Donovan had made better progress than expected and was able to move his company north abeam Kilo Company's right flank using a roadway that ran along the battlefield's lower ground. Major Anderson, assigned to advance on Kilo Company's left flank, had thus far failed to provide Colonel McCoy with a situation report.

German commanders charged with keeping the American attack thwarted became alarmed when they learned one American company had managed to advance to the roadway ten short meters below the Meurcy Farm plateau. The Germans called on their long-range field-artillery support inside Forest de Nesles, believing a short burst of heavy artillery would be enough to force the lone American infantry company into retreat.

German enfilade began to pour down on top of Captain Hurley's men, but thankfully most shells impacted the ground, falling far off target. Kilo Company was able to spread out and take adequate cover along the roadway berm trench and none of the shelling proved effective.

———

Sometime after midnight, German 3rd Army units finished repositioning their heavy Maxim guns closer to the Meurcy Farm plateau, and at 0300 hours, the Germans initiated a full-frontal machine-gun assault and light mortar attack on Kilo's protected roadway position.

The machine gun-fire was intense and withering, but Kilo's infantrymen hunkered down and withstood the massive two-hour assault.

Maxim guns ripped up and pelted the edge of the roadway's berm, but nothing worse than loose dirt and rocks flicked down onto the infantrymen. Every man maintained his cool and every man stayed out of sight. German gunners expended thousands of rounds of valuable ammunition pointlessly. Captain Hurley calculated that it was simply a matter of time before the fast-firing Maxim guns would overheat and need cooling.

The machine-gun assault ceased before sunrise on day two, and an eerie calm took hold over the battlefield. Captain Hurley dispatched a reconnoitering squad to try to determine the Krauts' next move, but after only a few minutes, the squad men were back at the roadway trench. They reported a line of German storm troops—at least five hundred, they told Hurley—were rushing toward their position. Kilo Company was under attack.

Hurley had no options. He removed his revolver from his holster, pointed his pistol straight to the sky, and fired one single shot. Hearing the signal, his entire infantry line, five platoons total, took to foot and aimed their weapons at the charging Germans.

"Ready, Roons?" John shouted. He saw hundreds of Krauts coming up the shallow pitch heading at him, but this time the Germans had no protection from the American guns.

Capt. Hurley fired two successive pistol shots, and his company's infantrymen opened fire.

John and Rooney each squeezed the Chauchat trigger, spraying a torrent of bullets at the charging Germans. To John's right, he could see the entire infantry line erupt, spitting a wall of lead.

Grenades began to fly by the hundreds, launched or tossed. Grenade men aimed at the middle of the swarm and blew a huge, blood-soaked hole at its center. Men fell and body parts flew. From behind Kilo's rifle line, mortars began to launch: *thwump, thwump, thwump*. They nailed the attacking line, killing men by the score.

Bullets flew the shooting was so intense that a dense, sulfur smoke cloud settled atop the berm.

The cloudbank made it difficult for the New Yorkers to take good aim. Riflemen's vision became obscured, but Kilo Company kept firing; it was life or death. Bullets, grenades, and mortars tore across the terrain, and German soldiers fell dead into the scrub brush by the scores. But as fast as one Kraut dropped, another took his place.

John was quickly expending his ammo mags and could feel his Chauchat was getting dangerously hot. He fretted that the temperamental automatic might jam, but he had no choice but keep firing or he'd be overrun. Kilo Company was holding, but ammunition was dwindling fast. Most of the reserve ammo was gone. John had only three more mags and Rooney was on his last.

Earlier, Lieutenant Colonel Donovan moved his three infantry companies across the Ourcq River and advanced his force mostly unopposed, well inside Kilo Company's operational sector. Donovan took position on a low road below and abeam Kilo Company, and from that roadway vantage point Donovan could monitor both Kilo's and India Company's movements.

Donovan received a situation report from Colonel McCoy stating that India Company was bogged down at the river's edge and unable to advance. Donovan observed Kilo Company's position at the high roadway and believed Captain Hurley, in a desperate effort to seek a suitable defensive position, had moved his company too far up the slope and had become vulnerable to German attack.

Donovan was hesitant to move. The ground between his battalion's low-ground position and Kilo Company's high-ground position was rife with Kraut machine-gun nests. Donovan ordered two reconnaissance squads, two top captains, and two top lieutenants, plus his newly acquired 42nd staff sergeant, Joyce Kilmer, to get a read on the Germans. Donovan wanted real-time situation reports and knew that Kilmer would provide many excellent details. Donovan was loath to make any rash decisions and exercised extreme caution before he'd move his men.

But less than thirty minutes after the reconnaissance squads had departed, spotters at the farthest edge of 1st Battalion's defensive perimeter saw a recon team returning. The men were dragging a body. The spotters ran out to help the recon squad and learned that it was Sergeant Joyce Kilmer who had taken a sniper's bullet to the head. The world-famous poet was killed instantly.

The reconnaissance squads reported to Donovan a dire situation was unfolding for Kilo Company up on the roadway below Meurcy Farm. Captain Hurley's men were in deep distress and were being overrun by a slew of storm troops. The Shamrock men were outgunned and outmanned, then the recon team leader informed Donovan that the ground between his 1st Battalion position and Kilo Company was loaded with snipers and machine-gun nests.

Donovan feared the broader mission was about to fail, and he made an on-the-spot decision. He ordered all four of his 1st Battalion companies to attack the flank of the German force. Donovan fired a single white flare into the dark sky and, in a matter of moments, his entire force of one thousand men began to charge across the low brush and plow directly into the German flank.

On the high ground along the Kilo roadway berm, infantrymen in the 4th and 5th Platoons on the far left side of Kilo's line, far away from John and Rooney, were shot dead, hit by bullets coming from above and behind the roadway. The shooters: German snipers perched high up on Meurcy Farm were picking off Kilo men below.

Captain Hurley needed to secure the farm's high ground. He dispatched his 3rd Platoon, John's platoon, to scale the steep slope and attack the snipers.

"No prisoners!" Hurley shouted to his lieutenant as 3rd Platoon departed the trench.

Thirty of 3rd Platoon's fifty men still remained, and the platoon lieutenant was cognizant that most of his men were low on ammunition. He advised the infantrymen to leave their rifles at the berm.

"Bayonets and trench knives, men!" he yelled.

John dropped his Chauchat next to Rooney's and ran to the steep-sloping, earthen wall with Buckley.

On the lower ground two full squads of Donovan's attack force, a group of men led by lanky Sgt. Dick O'Neil, charged full-speed at a pack of unsuspecting Krauts. O'Neil's two squads quickly tangled and enmeshed with the Germans, punching, kicking, and wrestling until men fell to the ground, impaled by a bayonet.

O'Neil fired his rifle with great skill. He killed many Kraut soldiers, but O'Neil's exuberance also got the best of him. Struck by mortar shrapnel, his body was tossed into the air. On the way down O'Neil was shot at point-blank range by a German officer.

O'Neil suffered five wounds during the melee and he bled profusely, but company medics got to him and dressed his wounds. O'Neil never quit leading his squads. Even when near death, he successfully stopped the German assault. Before O'Neil was evacuated off the battlefield, he insisted on seeing Donovan face to face, and he passed to Donovan what proved to be essential intelligence information.

For his actions, bravery, and leadership, Richard "Dick" O'Neil was awarded the National Medal of Honor—one of only thirty-four hundred medals ever awarded to a US soldier in battle.

John crawled to the top of the plateau just behind Ed Rooney and brandished his trench knife. Buckley closed in behind John still carrying his Enfield. Buckley had ammunition. The two men joined Rooney and Bergs Morgan and the men reported to the platoon lieutenant.

The lieutenant believed that the Germans were hiding inside the dilapidated buildings scattered around the farm, and he split his platoon into three ad hoc squads, ten men each, and dispersed them around the farm perimeter.

———

On the low ground below the Kilo Company roadway berm position, Donovan's battalion smashed the Krauts, but not before two hundred storm troops broke away and made haste toward Kilo Company.

Kilo Company's four remaining platoons had depleted all their ammunition stores and the men had now resorted to positioning themselves shoulder to shoulder, bayonets, and trench knives drawn, ready to defend the berm. Captain Hurley ordered his men to crouch down, bayonets pointed high toward the sky. Any Kraut who dared stick his neck over the trench edge was sure to get impaled by the sharp blade.

The storm troops rushed the Kilo berm with orders not to shoot until they could see the faces of the enemy. The Germans got to the edge of the roadway berm and fired at point-blank range on the Americans, and the Americans could do little but lunge back with bayonets or grab the storm troopers by the ankles, drag them into the berm and pummel them to death.

Atop, on the plateau, Ed Rooney led a ten-man squad and rushed into a barn. As he and his men burst through the doors, a Kraut sniper lunged at Rooney. After a brief scuffle, Rooney and a group of squad mates plunged their trench knives into the sniper's side, killing him. John ran after a second soldier, who fled the barn as soon as he saw Americans coming and Daniel Buckley took guard position at the rear door with his rifle.

The sudden burst of chaos inside the barn quieted, but out of the darkness, Buckley could hear a rumbling noise and he realized the plateau farm was under attack.

"Run!" he shouted at the top of his lungs as he stormed back into the barn. Buckley waved his arms wildly, motioning for John and Rooney to get out. "Go! Go! Go!" he demanded.

Bergan Morgan flew like a gazelle and Rooney ran as fast as he could. Buckley saw the mob of Krauts soldiers crashing toward the barn and he too ran.

Shots rang out from every direction. John hunched down and ran from the barn as fast as he could, desperate to stay out of the line of fire. It was pitch dark and John could barely see the ground beneath his feet. He ran from the barn toward the plateau's edge, toward his platoon's re-group location, but suddenly, directly in his path, he saw the rim of a ditch—a trash pit. He couldn't stop his momentum, and he fell crashing down into the hole.

John didn't know a German soldier had trailed him.

He got on his feet and made his way across the refuse, but had trouble maintaining his footing. He wasn't injured, but he ended up having to crawl across the debris to the pit's edge. John had no idea the Kraut trooper behind him had now cocked his rifle and was taking aim.

John lifted his head and peered out over the brim of the pit's edge just as a deafening piercing eruption exploded above him. A rifle bullet cracked from its barrel and whooshed passed his head. John heard a man behind him gasp, then he heard a loud crashing sound as that man fell into the pit.

Out of the darkness, Daniel Buckley still holding his Enfield called down to John and offered his hand. Buckley pulled John out of the pit.

———

Although ultimately victorious, the 42nd Division was so badly decimated after the Ourcq River attack it needed relief in the field immediately. The New York 77th Division replaced the 42nd Division, and the American army continued its aggressive push against the Germans into the Bois Brule north of the Ourcq.

The decimated 165th Regiment retreated to a camp outside Chateau Thierry, far behind the line. Men could light fires to heat rations or shave. Ed Rooney used his cleanest foot stocking and filled it with some coffee grounds that Buckley had managed to scrounge up. He dipped the sock up and down in a can of hot water.

John tossed Buckley a pack of smokes, lit a cigarette, and passed the lit butt to Buckley. Buckley used it to light his own, and he threw the pack over to Rooney.

"Our charmed life," said Rooney.

He lifted the coffee can from the flame and poured the hot brew into each man's tin cup.

John squeezed his cigarette between his lips and reached inside his jacket lapel to unfasten the two pins Anna had sent him. He held the American flag pin in his hand.

"Hey, Bucks," John called out and all the squad mates around the campfire fell quiet. "Daniel Buckley," he said, "I salute you,"

John raised his tin cup of coffee, and the others followed.

"You are a great American hero, Daniel Buckley. As brave as any man I've ever known."

"Here, here," said Rooney.

"And Bucks." John brandished the American flag. "This flag is very important to me; hopefully it'll be important to you." John got up and went over to Buckley and pinned the American flag on his lapel.

Buckley swallowed hard and said, "I'll wear it proudly, John."

———

O'NEIL, RICHARD W.

Rank and organization: Sergeant, US Army, Company D, 165th Infantry, 42d Division

* Place and date: On the Ourcq River, France, 30 July 1918
* Entered service at: New York, N.Y.
* GO No.: thirty, WD, 1921

Citation: In advance of an assaulting line, he attacked a detachment of about twenty-five of the enemy. In the ensuing hand-to-hand encounter he sustained pistol wounds, but heroically continued in the advance, during which he received additional wounds: but, with great physical effort, he remained in active command of his detachment. Being again wounded, he was forced by weakness and loss of blood to be evacuated, but insisted upon being taken first to the battalion commander in order to transmit to him valuable information relative to enemy positions and the disposition of our men.

CHAPTER 15

Saint Mihiel Offensive, August 1918

———

ON SEPTEMBER 13, 1918, AMERICAN IV Corps tank commander Lt. Col. George S. Patton was called to provide backup for the Fighting Irish Regiment led by Lt. Col. Wild Bill Donovan. Together, Donovan and Patton led a brigade of tanks and the 165th Regiment to assault the German stronghold at Pannes village inside the Saint Mihiel salient.

Patton and Donovan ripped through German defenses and made rapid advances until ordered to stop by IV-Corps commanders. The ground captured by Patton and Donovan in September 1918 is the same ground Patton captured again during the Battle of the Bulge during WWII.

———

The Ourcq River attack was a quick and bloody business. The 42nd Division engaged in combat operations for nine days but paid a very steep price for victory. Of the 12,800 combat infantry officers and men assigned to the 42nd at the onset of the Ourcq River attack, only 8,155 remained. In one week's time, 4,669 Rainbow men had either been killed in action or severely wounded.

No individual regiment escaped high casualties, but the Iowa 168th and the Alabama 167th got it the worst. Both regiments counted a staggering 1,350 dead or wounded, almost one-half of each regiment's normal complement of men. The 166th Ohio Regiment totaled 819 casualties, and the Irish 165th Regiment counted 1,150 dead or wounded. As for Kilo Company, John's company, only fifty of its 250 men walked off the battlefield.

Casualty rates for the enemy were four times greater, a staggering loss of manpower that the German 3rd Army could ill afford. Supreme Allied Commander General Foch's policy to chase and rout the retreating German army was working. General Ludendorff was forced to abandon Operation Michael outright, and by July 20 of 1918, he cancelled all offensive operations against British Expeditionary Force in Flanders. Ludendorff had to redeploy his reserves and shore up defenses.

On August 7, the New York 77th Division replaced the 42nd Division inside Bois Brule and at Meurcy Farm. The 42nd was so badly degraded that it was no longer combat capable. Until the division was assigned further orders, the Rainbow was relegated to sit idle at Foret de Fere on reserve.

At Command HQ in Chantilly, Allied generals concluded that Ludendorff's Operation Michael was over and Allied commander Foch was eager to initiate his next phase of the war. Foch ordered AEF, BEF, and French army forces to reposition and attack at each sector's salient, the last German strongholds inside France.

First to advance was the BEF, attacking on August 8, 1918, along the Amiens salient in the northwest sector. After two days of fighting, the British 4th Army, ten divisions total, captured seventeen thousand German soldiers and killed or wounded thirty thousand more. Some sixty-five hundred BEF men died or went missing.

On August 18, French armed forces attacked at Noyons, a village located halfway between Amiens and Reims in the middle sector. After three days of fighting, the French pushed the German 3rd Army back thirty-five miles. Both BEF and French army forces continued pushing, and throughout the month of August the Allies methodically cleared out the Amiens and Reims salients of all enemies. By late September, the German army was pushed back to the original Hindenburg Line and all of Ludendorff's spring offensive Operation Michael gains had been lost.

As for the Americans in the southeast Lorraine sector, General Pershing hesitated. His army was still mired in readiness problems. Pershing needed to move I-Corps out of Chateau Thierry and train and organize his newly formed 1st Army. He convinced General Foch that the Americans should delay the Lorraine sector Saint Mihiel salient attack for at least one month, and Foch agreed. The American offensive in the Lorraine sector salient was slated for September 12, 1918.

———

US Army truck drivers rolling in and out of 42nd Division's Foret de Fere camp were full of stories. They claimed a massive buildup was "going down" inside the Lorraine sector. "Engineers are building roads," they said, "and they're laying ammo tracks." To a man, each driver ended up making the same claim. "All the shit loaded for Chateau Thierry is now rollin' to Saint Mihiel."

Hearing of a big assault in the Lorraine, 42nd Division men began to itch, and rumors ran wild. Everyone was sure the division would join the fight. They'd board trains and head for St Mihiel any day, but orders to the front line never materialized. The 42nd Division was nowhere near combat-ready, and Chaumont's staff officers had other plans.

Six thousand replacement doughboys fresh off transports awaited the 42nd at the Bourment training facility. Instead of chasing Krauts back to Berlin, the Rainbow Division detached from the prestigious frontline I-Corps and went to collect its recruits. Once done, the division proceeded to the Neufchateau Primary Training Facility inside the Lorraine.

Needless to say, receiving training orders and not combat orders came as a big blow for the proud Rainbow men. The 42nd was the first AEF division ordered to take a second run through primary training—a distinction many men didn't welcome. Nevertheless, the division had lost so much manpower that it simply couldn't absorb another six thousand fresh troops and head back into the field. The division needed to regroup and retrain.

———

One week later, the list of Chateau Thierry dead and wounded got tacked up on a post outside the 165th mess tent at Neufchateau. Everybody rushed to read it and get a glimpse. Most wanted to see if the rumors about Sergeant Joyce Kilmer were true and if his name was among men KIA. Somehow, before the list even went up, Daniel Buckley got a look at it. He saw Dick O'Neil's name under "Wounded."

On an off-day from training, Buckley and John strolled over to 1st Battalion's camp and found one of the old-timers from the armory days who remembered O'Neil. He told John and Buckley how O'Neil had gotten "shot up real bad" and how he almost bled to death. "He had five wounds," the man told them, adding, "Lieutenant Colonel Donovan is writing O'Neil up for a Medal of Honor."

John and Buckley thanked him for the info and made their way back to Kilo Camp. Buckley decided that he'd write Mrs. Hickey a letter and tell her about O'Neil. Buckley and Mrs. Hickey had traded a slew of correspondence since Buckley left New York. He kept her apprised of all things Fighting Irish and penned lengthy letters filled with details of camp life in France. Mrs. Hickey never ended a letter without first asking how John McKay and Dick O'Neil fared. "I pray for you boys," she wrote. "I pray every day."

———

The 42nd Division wrapped up its Neufchateau training period in the first week of September and was recertified to be combat-ready. The training was primary training, not much different than Langeau. The men learned the basics: command and control signals, sharpshooting, bayonet handling, and gas masks. They spent little time digging trenches or learning trench warfare tactics. Instruction centered on using natural barriers like road berms, edifices, or the rolling French terrain. They spent a lot of time desensitizing new recruits. More than once, newbies got to crawl under stretched barbed wire and slither through mud pits as howitzers thundered and pummeled the nearby ground.

At Neufchateau, the 42nd Division also made organizational changes.

The division commander was now General Mann. Commander Brigadier General Douglas MacArthur took the reins of 84th Brigade and Colonel McCoy, commander of the 165th Regiment, left for Washington, DC, replaced by Col. Harry Mitchell. Shamrock Battalion's much-loved Maj. James McKenna who was killed on the banks of the Ourcq River, was replaced by Maj. James Reilly.

On September 9, 1918, the 42nd departed Neufchateau by foot and headed out to take a position at the Saint Mihiel salient and join the rest of the American 1st Army. The 42nd Division was now assigned to IV Corps.

Some 350,000 American troops loaded with supplies and artillery pieces were en route to Saint Mihiel. The night allowed only covert movement, and moving three complete corps was a monumental task for any army, but Saint Mihiel was America's first go at it. Some 125,000 I-Corps troops—including the 2nd, 5th, 78th, and 90th Divisions—arrived by train from the west. In addition, one hundred thousand IV-Corps troops—including the 1st, 3rd, 42nd, and 89th Divisions—traveled by foot from the east, and 150,000 V-Corps troops—including the 26th, 4th, 35th, 80th, and 91st Divisions—moved via truck from the south.

Pershing formed his three-corps-size 1st Army, determined he'd demonstrate America's military prowess, and he was just as determined he'd command that army himself. Pershing had been in France exactly one year, and during that time he had stalwartly held his ground, opposing force amalgamation, and he struggled at times in vain to garner respect from his Allied contemporaries. The American Saint Mihiel attack was the culmination of everything Pershing endeavored to achieve in France, and now he had to prove to his Chantilly contemporaries that the American army would get it right. Perhaps as a gesture of generosity, General Foch detached a forty-eight-thousand-man Colonial Corps Division and placed it under Pershing's 1st Army command. Pershing's Saint Mihiel attack force grew to four hundred thousand men.

In place and ready to confront Pershing's American army, was Germany's Detachment Charlie, eight divisions totaling ninety thousand men. The Germans held the Saint Mihiel salient since the first days of the war and, unlike Amiens or Reims, the Germans used that time to fortify and strengthen it. German army Detachment Charlie was not General Ludendorff's strongest fighting force, but the Germans could rely on Saint Mihiel's deep and layered defenses to hold back and repel the larger American force.

Pershing mounted over three thousand field-artillery pieces, planning to bombard the German salient from two opposing directions. Pershing also deployed 1,500 Allied attack aircraft—the largest air force ever flown to date. He put his air operations in the hands of Col. Billy Mitchell. Mitchell kept his plan simple: Shoot down opposition aircraft, strafe and bomb enemy ground positions, and conduct intelligence operations. Air operations in direct support of ground troop movement had not yet been developed. Finally, Pershing created a mechanized infantry Tank Brigade commanded by Lt. Col. George S. Patton. Pershing gave Patton 144 Renault French tanks and supplied him with an additional 275 tanks operated by French army personnel.

The American and French attack force formed a V shape that pinched the Saint Mihiel salient. IV-Corps positioned its four divisions along a line running northeast out of Saint Mihiel village toward the city of Metz. Combined with I-Corps's four divisions, the two-corps force formed the American eastern front opposing the German Saint Mihiel salient. The western front, manned by V-Corps and three aviation battalions, ran northwest out of Saint Mihiel to Verdun.

The French Colonial Corps Division took position outside Saint Mihiel proper, where the western front line and the eastern front line converged. Somehow, the Germans never took notice as four hundred thousand American troops placed a deadly vise grip on the salient.

The American 1st Army's lead logistic planner and General Pershing's new right-hand man in Chaumont was Col. George C. Marshall. Marshall greatly improved the AEF's planning capabilities since Chateau Thierry. He widened all southern roadway approaches into Saint Mihiel. Roads could now handle two opposing trucks, and large convoys no longer conflicted. He made engineering regiments labor twenty-four-hour shifts and lay miles of narrow gage rail track to expedite ammunition shipments. Engineers also leveled acres of hilltops and mounted the heavy artillery guns.

General Pershing asked General Foch for one extra month's time, and Gen. Pershing used every day of it. Col. George Marshall drew up the final attack plan, fully cognizant that the "new" American 1st Army was an exceptionally large force conducting an exceptionally large assault over an exceptionally large zone of action. Marshall developed new battle terminology to keep Pershing's widely disparate army unified and coordinated.

The scheduled attack was September 12, a date Marshall's plan termed "D-Day." General Pershing ordered the assault to commence at 0100 hours, a time Marshall's plan termed "H-Hour." Every unit of the 1st Army was assigned its responsibility, movement, and objectives based on D-Day time, plus or minus days, and H-Hour time, plus or minus hours. The giant American army operated off one common timeline.

———

At midnight on September 12, the weather across the Saint Mihiel salient was closed in and dense. A low cloud layer lingered a mere fifty feet above the troops. Occasionally, the thick clouds dropped down to the surface and a few of the divisions disappeared behind an opaque curtain of fog. The damp, dense air also blanketed and softened the normal harsh noises of men and machines readying for attack. Everything at the front sounded muted, soft, and muffled.

But at exactly 0100 hours, H-Hour, the muted quiet gave way to an intense, angry clamor. American artillery shells tore across the black night sky, wailing their telltale whistle before careening down and crashing into German positions inside the Saint Mihiel salient. Three thousand American artillery guns roared at once, making the low clouds and opaque fog flash white-hot.

Thousands of shells soared above the American infantry line and over no-man's-land before slamming down and exploding. The detonations were so powerful that a giant heat wave evaporated the fog. Towering flames lunged at the night sky, and a curtain of fire took hold from one edge of the horizon to the other. The diabolic inferno scorched everything in its blaze.

John whispered, "It's like hell…" His face lit bright from the flames and flashes. Nighttime had changed to day.

"We'll know soon enough," said Rooney.

"Remember Champagne?" Buckley asked.

How could they forget? German artillery crashed down on them for four hours.

"The Hun's getting it tonight," said Bergan Morgan.

"The Chaumont boys sure got their shit together for this one," Donovan yelled over the crashing booms. He, Major Anderson, and Major Reilly watched the Armageddon-like display with awe. The raging conflagration burned horrifically. How any man could survive such a firestorm? It was impossible to imagine.

For three hours, American artillery guns pounded German defenses. Every Kraut fortification was smashed to bits. The German 10th Division, positioned directly across from the 165th, was in the middle of a full retreat when the shelling started and men were caught completely off guard. Many stood unprotected on open roadways, unable to take cover, and ended up incinerated in the violent explosions. Drivers dived down and abandoned their trucks, laden with ammunition, and those trucks exploded like tinderboxes. The massive American artillery barrage obliterated everything.

At H-Hour plus 3:45, the enfilade assault halted for a few minutes and the thunderous booms over the Saint Mihiel battlefield ended, but the guns soon roared again and this time American FAR laid down a rolling barrage aimed directly at the German front line. As promulgated in Pershing's battle plan, when the rolling barrage commenced, hundreds of machine gunners and mortar squads from every division should join the attack.

The 165th had orders to snake up a narrow roadway toward Pannes village and take control of a key bridge crossing the narrow but deep Rupt de Mad River at Essey-et-Maizerias. The bridge was the only paved road that the 42nd's support tanks and supply vehicles could use to advance.

Intel scouts reported that the bridge was heavily defended, but Lieutenant Colonel Donovan had formed a plan. He put all his Chauchat riflemen at the lead, and behind them, he put teams of mobile machine gunners and mortar squads.

At H-Hour plus 4:05, the rolling barrage ebbed, and the peppering mortar fire and machine guns quieted. Two hundred thousand infantrymen stood ready to storm the German line. Inside the 165th Battalion, all three regiment commanders raised pistols high to the sky and fired three shots.

"Game's on, Johnny!"

John and Rooney's fifty-man "wolf pack" squad of Chauchat riflemen led the charge, running down the narrow roadway toward the river crossing.

Pop-pop-pop! Rata-tat-tat! Pop-pop!

The lead wolf pack rifleman was under attack, and the entire squad behind him instinctively dropped to the ground and spread out. No one could believe that a Kraut machine-gun nest was positioned so close to the American line. That was sure suicide.

John heard shouts for a medic and saw Rooney lying on the ground a few feet away. He gave Rooney a once-over and saw that he was OK, then ran his hands up and down his own legs to make sure he wasn't hit.

"Buckley, Morgan, O'Hara!" The platoon lieutenant barked. "Recovery!" Four Chauchat gunners lay dead in the roadway and the lieutenant wanted them removed.

Buckley ran onto the roadway just as two mortar squads blasted the nearby enemy machine-gun nest and suppressed its fire. John's squad used the suppression to advance and they took cover behind a roadway berm. Eventually, most of the fifty-man team got to the berm, helped by a continuous peppering fire on the German machine gun-nest. Soon, all the mobile machine gun-teams and mortar teams got to the berm.

"Rooney, McKay, Brady, O'Brien," the lieutenant shouted, pointing left. "Take the left flank. Hurley, Moran, Mooney, and Sweet, take the right." The lieutenant wanted his automatic riflemen to sweep around and attack the Kraut nest from the sides, and he called for his machine gunners to lay down suppression fire.

John raced through the low brush behind Rooney. He saw the Kraut nest but was running too fast to take good aim. The German Maxim gunners and the American Hotchkiss gunners got in a wild shootout, blasting at one another with abandon. Neither Americans nor Germans were willing to cede and take protective cover.

The 165th mortar teams continued to pepper the Kraut nest as the lead Chauchat wolf pack men got within a hundred feet. The squad leader dispersed them, and they took position, forming an arcing perimeter. Thirty seconds later, he yelled "Fire!" and the Chauchat riflemen opened up and spewed hundreds of bullets at the German gun nest. The Chauchat riflemen burned through mag after mag and singed the low, grassy brush, but when finished, every Kraut machine gunner lay dead.

———

In the northern areas of the salient, the American attack quickly trans-
formed from offensive assault to wholesale disarming of the enemy.
I-Corps's four divisions advanced rapidly, taking the village Thiacourt.
I-Corps's Divisions practically rampaged across the northern sector, taking
thousands of German prisoners and capturing tons of heavy equipment.
German soldiers put down their rifles; seemingly they had had enough.
I-Corps's infantrymen, almost giddy, rounded up and arrested German
soldiers, the I-Corps men believing the American army unstoppable.

As for V-Corps on the opposite or northwest front, the American 26th
Infantry Division successfully captured the key village of Hattonchatel.
At daybreak, V-Corps attempted to launch its armada of aircraft, but
the weather remained closed in. Not until later in the morning did the
skies clear enough for aircraft of the Aero Divisions to take wing, but
by D-Day plus three, all German airborne resistance disappeared and
allied warplanes ruled the skies.

———

Lieutenant Colonel Donovan led his 1st Battalion up the roadway to the
heavily defended Essey-et-Maizerias Bridge. The sun had risen, giving
the Germans the benefit of daylight, so Donovan dispatched a two-man
recon team to spy the bridge before his men approached.

As his unit advanced closer, Donovan dispersed two machine-gun
squads to the bridge's left quadrant, one machine-gun team at center,
and two more teams at the right side. He then backed up his gunners
with mortar squads. Donovan planned to rush the middle of the bridge
using his fifty Chauchat automatic gunners plus two hundred riflemen.

Donovan's assault plan had a time hack. At H-Hour plus 07:15, the
wolf pack team of Chauchat gunners and two hundred riflemen plus
the mortar and mobile machine gunners would commence attack on
the bridge. Fifteen minutes later at 0730 hours, the remaining 165th

Infantry would charge to the river's edge and overwhelm any remaining German resistance.

Donovan peered at his wristwatch and silently counted down. "Four...three...two...one..."

At exactly 07:15, Donovan's machine guns ripped open and mortars nailed German machine-gun nests tucked behind the bridge abutments. The Krauts returned fire, shooting wildly swinging arcs, unable to determine the direction of enemy fire. American mortar teams, on their game, blasted the nests and hit them spot-on. German gun nests burst afire and the gunners leaped to flee, but as they ran, American riflemen cut them down.

Donovan ordered his wolf pack team to rush the bridge, and the Chauchat squads burst past waning Kraut resistance and took control of the bridge's approach. On the far side, across the narrow Rupt de Mad River, German machine gun-nests, still intact, attempted to halt the American raid and opened fire on the Americans.

At H-Hour plus 07:30, the remaining 165th infantrymen heard the three-consecutive-pistol-shot signal and charged forward, rushing the German line. The Irish quickly cleared all ground and advanced to the river's edge.

Donovan moved his mobile machine teams forward to the riverbank on either side of the bridge's approach and unleashed a ferocious machine-gun and mortar attack on German nests across the river. Chauchat teams continued to press up the middle, clearing the bridge's narrow pass. The Chauchat men couldn't determine if the Krauts were killed or if they abandoned post and ran, but resistance lessened as they moved forward.

By midmorning, Donovan's squads took control of the key Rupt-de-Mad bridge, and by early afternoon Engineering Division 4x4s and Patton's tanks began to cross the Rupt de Mad River and roll deeper into the Saint Mihiel salient.

Donovan put a perimeter defense around the bridge and conferred with Majors Anderson and Reilly to decide on how to proceed next. Engineering hadn't finished rigging telephone wires, and 165th commander Col. Harry Mitchell and 83th Brigade HQ were still relying on foot messengers for timely reports. Donovan saw no need to get out ahead of his command and control and demanded that the telephone lines be stretched as far as possible. The three regiment commanders agreed to remain in position abeam the bridge and move to attack Pannes village at daybreak.

The following morning, Donovan led his 1st Battalion up the Pannes roadway and made good progress, having met only intermittent resistance. During the overnight hours, he disbanded the special wolf pack squad, and John and Rooney returned to Kilo Company. Donovan chose to proceed into Pannes as lead battalion, relying on 1st Battalion's firepower.

But when approaching Pannes, the three regiment commanders stopped to confer once again. The commanders observed that Pannes was populated by many building structures and believed that Kraut soldiers would most likely be hiding inside them. French reports said that Kraut snipers had a penchant for church steeples, and British intelligence said the Krauts used many explosive tripwires at Amiens. There was no reason for Donovan, Anderson, or Reilly to think Pannes village would be different.

American engineers finished unrolling their telephone cables, and Donovan telephoned 165th Regiment commander Colonel Mitchell to request direct tank support. Mitchell cleared the request through Brigadier General Lenihan at 83rd HQ, and then returned Donovan's call to inform him that a fifty-tank brigade of FTs would arrive by the hour.

Donovan, Anderson, and Reilly made good use of the short delay and revised their Pannes assault plan. They decided to place the mechanized infantry tanks at lead and disperse company infantrymen in between and behind the vehicles. Donovan wasn't so much concerned about an organized German resistance as he was by booby-traps and machine-gun ambushes.

Within the hour, as Colonel Mitchell promised, a single line of Renault tanks rumbled down the Pannes roadway and approached the 165th Regiment position. The two-man vehicle moved at a pace no faster than a man's brisk walk as Lt. Col. George Patton strode abreast his tank drivers, barking commands.

"Halt!" Patton shouted, and the mechanized infantry column came to a stop.

He stood at attention and saluted Donovan. "Lt. Col. George Patton," he said.

Donovan saluted back.

"Lt. Col. William Donovan, 1st Battalion, 165th Infantry. This is Major Anderson, 2nd Battalion, and Major Reilly, Shamrock."

"Good Lord," Patton rumbled. "The goddamned Irish!"

"The goddamned Fighting Irish!" Donovan bellowed.

Patton shook Donovan's hand then Anderson's and Reilly's. The men shared a good-natured laugh.

"I was with the 69th in '16," Patton said. "The 69th are good men."

Donovan shared his strategy with Patton, detailing his concerns about the large number of buildings in the village and, when he finished, Patton responded tersely.

"I got plenty of gas," he said, "and I'm ready for any bullshit the Krauts can throw."

The tank and infantry squads crept into Pannes. Patton barked directions to his drivers and Donovan took position at the rear with his men. The 2nd Battalion advanced on 1st Battalion's left flank, and 3rd Battalion advanced on the right.

At the edge road, Patton ordered his crews to spread out and give cover to all the regiment infantrymen. After his tanks rolled into position, Donovan fired his pistol, signaling for the attack to begin.

Tanks led the way, shimmying down narrow paths followed by squads of infantrymen who entered and cleared each building one at a time. If a squad thought Kraut soldiers might be holed up inside a building, tank crews blasted the structure and collapsed it. German soldiers had no heavy defenses and carried only rifles. When they spotted American mechanized infantry tanks approaching, they dropped their rifles and surrendered. The 165th took thousands of prisoners.

After Pannes village was cleared, neither Patton nor Donovan saw any good reason to stop the advance. The two lieutenant colonels pressed on, and by day's end they captured the village Beney-en-Woevre and Vigneulles. The 165th Regiment advanced ten miles into the German salient. Not until the morning of the 14th, D-Day plus three days did the two ambitious light colonels get reined in by IV-Corps's staff.

On D-Day plus four days, the American 1st Army captured more than thirteen thousand German soldiers and five hundred artillery pieces and lost only eight thousand men out of four hundred thousand. The entire Saint Mihiel salient fell into American hands and the Germans retreated, moving farther north into the heavily fortified and extremely well defended Argonne sector.

———

American soldier morale shot sky-high. At ground level, division officers and infantrymen beamed confidence. The American army was a force to be reckoned with, and the vaulted German army was on its last legs. The Americans at Saint Mihiel saw German soldiers throw down their guns and surrender en masse.

At command level, however, the American army was collapsing under its own weight. General Pershing promised Foch that he'd hurriedly move the American army from Saint Mihiel and regroup in the Argonne sector, sixty miles to the west. Foch insisted Pershing commence a push north toward the Kriemhilde Stellung there.

All at once, just like during the Chateau Thierry offensive, six hundred thousand 1st Army troops, the entire American army, plus four thousand artillery pieces packed up and dumped onto the Lorraine sector's sparse narrow roadways. Major traffic snarls ensued. Col. George Marshall had no time to draw up organizational plans, and none of the roadways between Saint Mihiel and the Argonne had been upgraded and widened. Infantry personnel, construction engineers, artillery pieces, food, ammunition, and even ambulances laden with badly wounded came to a grinding stop.

Complicating the traffic quagmire, German FAR batteries controlled the high ground terrain above the Meuse River valley, and they mercilessly blasted American convoys. Unlike Saint Mihiel, Luftwaffe pilots still owned the skies over the Argonne, and they readily shot down any enemy aircraft that strayed into the sector.

Newly arrived American divisions having recently completed basic primary training were immediately deployed to the Argonne battlefield en masse. Pershing's Chaumont staff officers rushed to comply with General Foch's order: conduct a full frontal attack on the Kriemhilde Stellung inside the Argonne Forest.

Chaos reigned. Pershing's staff officers threw together the newly trained divisions and created entire corps without any consideration of battlefield experience. They also diluted the effectiveness of existing battle-tested corps by mixing them with many newly formed divisions. Command and control suffered greatly as inexperienced, poorly commanded divisions ended up occupying critical points along the Argonne Forest front line.

At the same time, commanders reeling from battlefield injuries and the much worse Spanish flu and TB clamored for more replacement troops. Still playing their old game, Pershing's staff, callously cannibalized arriving units, recently disembarked at the Brest piers. Tens of thousands of untrained infantrymen, many in uniform for less than forty days, were sent directly to the front line and into a combat division. There became the group of "stragglers": nearly ten thousand men who avoided the fight and the brutality of the front line by not reporting for duty. They wandered the Argonne woodlands until caught.

Meanwhile inside the Argonne Forest, Pershing placed three American corps units, I-Corps, V-Corps, and the newly created III-Corps, nine divisions total, along the southern edge of the Argonne Forest. Farthest to the west was I-Corps, made up from the New York 77th, the Pennsylvania 28th, and the Kansas/Missouri 35th. The 35th was one of the newly trained, zero-battlefield-experience divisions. In the midsection opposite the Argonne's highest ground, named Montfaucon, a ridgeline crawling with Kraut infantry, the US Army's V-Corps—the 91st, 37th, and 79th Divisions—took position.

The 79th Division, none its officers or infantrymen having any battlefield experience landed directly in front of Montfaucon and were assigned the most critically important job of capturing and holding the well-defended high-ground ridge. Montfaucon's capture was essential for future American successes, so the question of how its capture landed on the lap of the 79th—a division that never fought one single battle—had no good answer.

In the east of the Argonne along the Meuse River valley, III-Corps—including the 4th, 80th, and 33rd Divisions—took a position on the low ground directly beneath German FAR batteries.

American divisions in the Argonne ended up pinched between heavy long-range German gun batteries perched on the high hills east above the Meuse River and west in the high ridge crest above the Argonne Forest. American units spread out on the lower Argonne valley and used its smallish forests to provide ground cover.

Although heavy German guns bore down on the Americans from east and west, General Pershing ordered his three corps force, lined up along the southern edge of the Argonne Forest, to attack up the middle and clear the high ground, Montfaucon.

At 0500 hours on September 27, all nine American divisions along the Argonne's southern tier advanced northward. Regiments of infantrymen rushed downhill into a low valley, completely obfuscated by dense fog. Confusion quickly set in and American commanders found themselves unable to coordinate attacks. Inexperienced division and brigade commanders failed to meet even the most basic objectives, and other regiments flailed hopelessly on the battlefield. I-Corps's 35th Division and V-Corps's 79th Division, both responsible for storming the high ground Montfaucon ridge line failed to gain a single objective, and by the second day of fighting, both divisions disintegrated into chaos and failure. German General Gallwitz, who led the opposing German force at Montfaucon, moved five reserve German divisions and shored up his high ground defenses. After that action, the American Montfaucon assault as well as the larger Argonne Forest assault came to a complete standstill.

At the far west side of the American battle line, battalions inside Pennsylvania's 28th Division advanced deep into the dense Argonne Forest, but the 28th proceeded without any flanking support from the French army and the American 77th Division as planned. The 28th's 1st Battalion got trapped inside the Argonne woods and American newspapers quickly dubbed the trapped 28th Division men, the "Lost Battalion."

Battle hardened General Liggett, commander of the premier American I-Corps positioned at the far west end of the American assault line, moved to control the damage caused by 35th Division's and 79th Division's complete collapse. General Liggett enlisted the help of another battle tested general, 1st Division's General Summerall, and both generals Liggett and Summerall quickly reorganized their American forces and blasted through German defense fortifications and made advances by pushing northward into the Argonne Forest.

Liggett and Summerall convinced Pershing that German long-range artillery guns perched atop the Argonne's high hills had to be eliminated before any American division could advance farther into the Argonne Forest. Pershing therefore ordered Gen. Liggett's I-Corps, to include Gen. Summerall's 1st Division, to close in on the Argonne Forest hills from the west as V-Corps, bolstered by the Illinois's 82nd Division, a division that received five thousand replacement troops directly from a transport ship one week prior, was ordered to attack the opposite side of the high hill ridge from the east.

In a relatively short time the Americans were able to pinch the German FAR batteries and chase the Germans out of the Argonne Forest's high ridge. I-Corps also found and rescued the "Lost Battalion." At Hill 223, on the Argonne Forest's eastern ridge slope, Sergeant York, an infantryman assigned to the Illinois 82nd Division captured 132 German soldiers, single handedly.

Finally, American divisions were poised to advance into the lower Argonne valley, no longer threatened by German guns up on the high ridgeline.

On October 4, American I-Corps, V-Corps, and III-Corps mounted a second massive assault on the German line charging into the Argonne, but this time the Americans met a steep resistance. The Americans quickly realized the Argonne terrain was deeply layered with German defense fortifications and it was difficult to traverse. Only General Summerall's 1st Division made significant advances.

Summerall's 1st Division advanced ten miles in seven days, but that modest move forward cost his 1st Division an astonishing nine thousand casualties. Summerall was unfazed by the carnage he unleashed, and he continued to push his division north until he reached the tiny French village, Sommerance, two miles shy of the Kriemhilde Stellung's barbed wire and pillbox defenses. The Americans had finally reached within striking range of Germany's last defensive line.

———

General Pershing remained commander of American Expeditionary Forces and promoted Gen. Hunter Liggett as commander of the 1st Army. The 2nd Army was assigned to General Brown and on defense of the southern Lorraine sector.

General Liggett moved quickly to restructure the failing Argonne Forest V-Corps and promoted his hard charging Gen. Charles P. Summerall as its commander. Summerall's badly degraded 1st Division, no longer able to fight, was rotated to the rear and replaced by the 42nd Rainbow Division. The 42nd Division took position in the tiny village of Sommerance inside the Argonne and was poised to attack the Kriemhilde Stellung wires.

Liggett intended to use his V-Corps to break through the Kremhilde Stellung at Landres-et-Saint-Georges, two miles north of Sommerance. He wanted an aggressive commander to get the job done, and casualty-indifferent Gen. Charles P. Summerall was his man.

———

A Kilo Company sergeant poked his head inside John and Rooney's tent and barked out names.

"McKay, Rooney, Buckley, Morgan," he said. "Collect your packs and report to Captain Delacour, pronto. You're in Machine Gun Company now."

CHAPTER 16

The Meuse-Argonne, October 13–15, 1918

—

ON OCTOBER 14, 1918, JOHN McKay and his Hotchkiss machine-gun crew charged up this roadway out of Sommerance and entered the Meuse-Argonne battlefield. Standing in a steady rain atop a low bluff behind the church was Father Duffy. Duffy blessed each man of the 165th's Kilo Company as they passed and headed to the fight. October 15, 1918, would soon prove to be one of the deadliest days in the Fighting Irish Regiment's bold history. In the background is the ridgeline beginning at Montfaucon running north to the Cote de Chatillon.

———

October 13, 1918

"McKay!" a voice shouted from outside the barn out on the muddy roadway.

"McKay!" he shouted again.

John was fast asleep atop a pile of wet hay.

"McKay!" the voice boomed once more, but this time John was awake.

"What," he yelled back, not wanting to get up.

"A feller out here says he's your brother."

John bolted to his feet and ran out of the barn, careful to step on the wood boards over the mud.

"Arch!" he cried, not believing that Archie had made it all the way to tiny Sommerance.

"Johnny!" Archie gushed, and the two brothers hugged in the middle of the roadway.

"You look good, Arch."

"Yeah, yeah," Archie murmured, but he pulled back and coughed uncontrollably.

"This goddamn rain," he cursed, wiping his mouth.

"You don't want the TB, Arch."

"I don't got no TB." But he wheezed, coughed, and spit up a glob of phlegm.

"How in hell did ya find me?"

"We're movin' all kinds of shit. They're lots of divisions comin' up this way. Everything's moving to the front. Anyway, I heard some guy say the Irish is in these parts, so I asked around."

"You look good, brother."

"You too." But Archie's brow furrowed, and he frowned. "Anna tells me you're seein' lots of action. That true?"

"We're front line, Arch. We go where the Huns go." John pointed to the wooded hillside behind Archie. "That's the Cote de Chatillon up there," he said. "If it wasn't for this rain and drizzle, you'd see Fritz plain and clear."

Archie shuddered. "I saw the quartermasters south of here. They're digging graves for thousands."

"Most of them is Krauts. 1st Division mowed 'em down."

"Well, don't get too brave, brother. We're rounding up thousands of stragglers roamin' the forest behind you, here. There're hidin' in the trees and won't go to the front. Get your ass home. Like you promised."

"We're movin' to the wire tomorrow," said John. "And I'm on the Hotchkiss now—a machine gun."

"Word is Krauts aim for gunners."

"Not if you get 'em first."

"Wonderful." Archie shook his head.

"This war's almost over, Arch. The Krauts put down their rifles in Saint Mihiel. They don't want to fight us no more. So stop your worry."

"Well, it ain't like we're sippin' tea and sailin' for New York. You've done your job here, John. You don't owe no-body, nothing no more. Besides," Archie blurted, "I talked to Anna before I left. Ma's very sick, John. If something happens here, I don't if she'll ever survive it."

"There's nothin' I can do, Arch. Everyone relies on the gunner. I can't just shirk my duty, now."

A voice called out from inside the barn. It was Daniel Buckley.

"The machine gun arrived, John, as has the ammo truck. I'm going to fetch our load."

"I'll catch up, Bucks," John yelled, and then he turned to Archie. "I'm going, Arch. Sorry."

———

Newly minted V-Corps commander Charles P. Summerall decided that capturing the villages Saint Georges and Landres-et-Saint-Georges inside the Kriemhilde Stellung line was now his corps's primary objective. Destruction of the densely fortified Kriemhilde Stellung would set the stage for an assault on the city of Sedan farther inland—a key rail depot for German logistical operations. Summerall set the Saint Georges and Landres-et-Saint-Georges assault date for October 14, and he assigned his 42nd Division, one of his V-Corps divisions, to spearhead the attack.

Summerall expected great things from the 42nd. He wanted the Rainbow men to press hard against the German line, break it wide open, and he expected its officers to accept high casualties if need be. The war was now at a critical phase. General Ludendorff was in direct communication with the Wilson administration. Ludendorff was representing Kaiser Wilhelm and Germany's newly appointed chancellor, Prince Max von Baden. The men had great interest in President Wilson's recently published "Fourteen Points," and pursued them to find conditions that they could accept before signing any cessation of hostilities pact. In mid-October, however, Ludendorff rejected President Wilson's insistence that Kaiser Wilhelm must abdicate, and he threatened to rattle Germany's saber even harder.

The Meuse-Argonne offensive is the largest battle in American history to date. Some 1.2 million Americans lined up along the Kriemhilde Stellung/Hindenburg Line, as did one million British and 2.5 million French army forces. From July to October 1918, General Foch led his offensive operations against the German army by destroying every German salient in France. Now in October 1918, he had the Germans backed up against the Belgium and German border, and the Meuse-Argonne offensive, October through November of 1918, was his last big push. The attack line began at the farthest northwest Allied position at Ypres in Flanders and ran all the way southeast to Basal in Switzerland. In the cities of Ghent, Mons, Cambrai, Sedan, and Verdun, the Allies conducted ferocious attacks and maintained a high tempo of operations until Germany finally capitulated. This period from late July 1918 to November 11, 1918, was later titled the "one hundred days of war."

V-Corps, including 42nd Division had forty-eight hours to determine their Meuse-Argonne objectives. Saint George village to the west, Landres-et-Saint-Georges village at the center, and a high-ground ridge defining the Kriemhilde Stellung's eastern boundary, named Cote de Chatillon, were the obvious targets.

At 0300 hours, the 42nd Division would commence attack starting with a three-hour field-artillery preparation to soften hardened targets, followed by a 0600, H-Hour, daylight full-assault raid by Gen. Douglas MacArthur's 84th Brigade (the 167th and 168th Regiments) against the Cote de Chatillon. Three hours later at H-Hour plus three hours, companies of the 165th New York Regiment would charge up the Sommerance to Landres-et-Saint-Georges roadway and charge across the low ground battlefield toward the Kriemhilde Stellung wire. The 166th Ohio Regiment would charge across open farm fields and attack Saint George village.

At the onset, the V-Corps led, 42nd Division executed attack plan was overly optimistic, but no senior officer in the 42nd Division challenged it. General MacArthur's 84th Brigade (167th and 168th Regiments) had to capture and hold Cote de Chatillon's high hill in less than three hours and, regardless of success or failure, at H-Hour plus three hours, 83rd Brigade (165th and 166th Regiments) would charge northward to

Saint Georges village and Landres-et-Saint-Georges, streaming thousands of lightly armed men directly under the eyes and guns of Cote de Chatillon heavily fortified hills.

If the Cote de Chatillon didn't fall into American hands within the three-hour limit, 83rd Brigade would advance under withering machine-gun and mortar fire. Kraut guns would rip up the Americans. However, during an impromptu meeting called in the pouring rain by General Summerall at the nearby village of Exermont the day before the attack, not one 42nd Division officer voiced objection. At this very meeting, Summerall bullied Douglas MacArthur and goaded him into accepting the obviously flawed field order.

"Give me the Cote de Chatillon!" Summerall shouted from across the room. "Or give me a casualty list of five thousand."

MacArthur was nonplussed. He refused to cede an inch to the egotistic and antagonistic Summerall. After all, a few months earlier, Summerall was a junior field-artillery commander assigned to support the 42nd Division. Summerall took *his* orders from MacArthur.

"I'll give you Cote de Chatillon," MacArthur calmly claimed, "or I'll give you a casualty list with my name at the top."

October 14, 1918, 9:00 a.m.

Buckley lingered at the front of the formation near the church wearing his messenger armband and going completely unnoticed in the nonstop heavy rain. India and Mike Companies had set out up the low road to Landres-et-Saint-Georges thirty minutes earlier, and Buckley knew that messengers and ammo carriers would be back with reports. He wanted to hear what they said.

General Summerall's Field Order #36 was being executed exactly as written. At 0300 hours, a preassault artillery barrage bombarded enemy positions that were mostly on the Cote de Chatillon. The 155 mm long-range guns pounded rows of barbed wire at the Kreimhilde Stellung, and both the shorter-ranged 75 mm and 155 mm took aim at the Cote de Chatillon machine gun and mortars, nestled on the high-ridge hillside.

Although the American shelling persisted three full hours, none of the Kriemhilde Stellung's rows of barbed wire or machine-gun pillboxes guarding Landres-et-Saint-Georges village were degraded enough to be made passable. Companies of the 165th Regiment would have to take on those defensive fortifications alone with grenades and mortars.

At the 0600 H-Hour, infantry regiments of the 84th Brigade began to scale the Cote's steep slopes, and the 167th Alabama and 168th Iowa Regiment men quickly confronted a much sturdier German resistance than expected. At H-Hour plus three hours, the very time General MacArthur's 84th Brigade was supposed to have captured and taken control of the entire Cote de Chatillon, no ground had been gained by the 84th Brigade's two regiments and no advances were made by the Americans. All of Cote de Chatillon remained in German hands, machine-gun and mortar nests intact.

The 165th Regiment, assigned to cross the low battlefield ground below the Cote de Chatillon and attack Landres et Saint Georges' barbed wire and pillbox defenses, proceeded as planned, regardless.

Kilo Company was next in line, ready to head up the Sommerance to the Landres-et-Saint-Georges roadway. The company stretched itself thin, putting two men abreast to slide up the narrow roadway. On the 165th's far left, or western, side, west of Sommerance village, the Ohio 166th Regiment readied for its charge across the muddy, flat farmland to Saint Georges village two klicks ahead.

Kilo Company planned to move up the Sommerance/Landres roadway about one and a half klicks, then cut right eastward and cross the muddy field heading directly for the Kriemhilde Stellung wire and the pill boxes protecting Landres-et-Saint-Georges. The Ohio 166th would move straight north but eventually spread out and fill in behind the 165th along its western edge.

At 0900 hours, H-Hour plus three hours, Brigadier General Lenihan, inside 83rd Brigade HQ with battlefield reports in hand, learned that not only did MacArthur's 84th Brigade fail to capture Cote de Chatillon, but that the 84th Brigade had made little or no headway toward reaching its objective.

83rd Brigade's Ohio 166th Regiment commander, Colonel Hough, although farthest away from the Cote de Chatillon ridge, determined that a head-on attack on Saint Georges village would expose the 166th to direct frontal attack, over-the-horizon enfilade, and rear-quartering machine-gun and mortar fire from the Cote de Chatillon's high hills. He made a battlefield decision to keep his men in place and not attack.

The 165th Regiment, led by Major Reilly's Shamrock Battalion, India, and Mike Companies, but directly commanded by Lt. Col. William Donovan, somehow managed to disregard the 84th Brigade's dire warning, and they continued the attack as planned.

———

"Ready up!"

Kilo Company's men snapped into two tight rows. The men dressed lightly, no heavy packs—rifle, bayonet, trench knife, and entrenchment tool only. The officers expected a rapid move to the wire.

John and Rooney grabbed the ends of the Hotchkiss barrel, and Bergan Morgan lifted the heavy tripod and carried it himself. Buckley, now back in formation, took four ammo canisters.

"The machine guns are firing strongly," Buckley warned, repeating what he'd heard up front. "Mike Company took casualties. One of the runners said it was best to get off the paved roadway and remain down in the drainage berm."

The night before the attack, John nervously mulled over what Archie had told him about their mother. John had no idea his ma was sick, but now he wished he didn't know. He recalled the story the Meeker Avenue streetcar conductor once told him, about the fireman who ran into the Penny Bridge fire and died. That fireman did his duty, John considered; and now John knew what was expected of him. He wouldn't try and hide from danger. God would keep him safe.

Kilo Company lunged forward, and once abeam the old church, every man made an abrupt left turn and ran up the roadway's shallow incline. John spotted Father Duffy standing on a bluff over the road. He wasn't wearing a helmet. He wanted every man to see his face, but he donned a long raincoat and his leg puttees were wrapped tight around his boots and up past his knees. He blessed everyone who passed and called out a name or two if he recognized a face. Mostly, he knew the old-timers.

"God's speed, Daniel Buckley," Father shouted. He pointed to Buckley and made the sign of the cross. Buckley, moving at a double-time pace and with his hands full, moved his head up and down and then side to side. Duffy looked directly at John and blessed him, too. "God be with you, John McKay."

John raised his free hand, placed it over his chest pocket, and pressed down on Anna's rosary. The night before, he gave his confession and took Holy Communion from a French priest. Now, seeing Father Duffy on the bluff standing in the cold rain, he felt great pride: proud he was Shamrock, proud he was a 69er, and ever more proud that he was an American. He had to be brave and face his fear. Too many men relied on him.

As soon as the Kilo men emerged from the inclined road about a hundred feet past the old church, all hell broke loose. Kraut machine-gun fire ripped up the road, tossing dirt and rocks everywhere. Razor-sharp bullets ricocheted off the pavement and flung into the ranks of men packed so tightly together that they were unable to flee. They fell, their blood splattering on the road but quickly washing away in the heavy rain. Mike and November companies had made it out and taken casualties, but the Germans seemed more ready this time, and they took deadly aim on Kilo Company.

Men leaped for cover, landing in the drainage ditches on either side of the roadway. They became bogged down, unable to move.

"Set up here?" John shouted to Rooney.

"No. No. No. We'll attract fire."

Nobody dared peer over the roadway's edge. Kilo Company was held down in the ditches for about thirty minutes before battalion officers managed to coordinate some 155 mm field-artillery suppression. Most guns concentrated their fire on the Cote de Chatillon.

Eventually, the American 155 mms laid down a wall of suppression enfilade long enough for Kilo Company to get up out of the berms and make their way up the Sommerance road to a wooded area at the midsection. The woodland covering was small and in the middle of an open field, but it offered enough protection and space for the machine-gun squads to set up.

John, Rooney, and Bergan Morgan got off the road and ran across the loose mud to a tree line. Buckley raced in from behind.

John pointed to a natural clump, a mound of moss growing over fallen tree trunks.

"Here, Bergan!" He pointed.

Morgan popped open the tripod and jammed the legs into the mud as John and Rooney carefully placed the barrel over the pivot screw. Rooney turned his wrench and locked the barrel to the tripod, and John swung it side to side to test the travel. Buckley arrived behind the mound, quickly pried open the ammo canisters, and collected any loose ammo clips that each man carried into the field. Earlier, Bergan Morgan won the coin toss, and he chose to be first runner, but that was before conditions on the Sommerance road had worsened.

"Always the lucky one, Buckley, aren't you?" he snapped. He put his helmet on, tightened the straps, and ran back toward the roadway.

John took lead gunner position and Rooney spotted. Buckley piled up the ammo clips and fed the breach.

Rooney scanned the horizon, looking for any motion in the field. On his left side, he saw the narrowing and downward-sloping terrain leading to the Kriemhilde Stellung wires. Directly across from him was the Cote de Chatillon's high ridge, and off to his right was tiny Sommerance village. Rooney could hardly see any of Mike Company or India Company's men. They'd spread out and were heads down, taking cover inside foxholes. Nobody dared get up, or they'd be instantly shot. Rooney then spotted a squad of Kilo men running along the narrow pathway and into the downward-sloping terrain and out of sight of the Cote de Chatillon gun crews. They'd managed to move in close enough to the Kriemhilde Stellung to cut the wires. An engineer assigned to the infantry squad who specialized in using the wire-cutting tool got to the wire, but as he reached up to cut it, a German machine gunner hidden in a low pillbox on the other side of the wire eviscerated him. Then that same gunner turned his aim on the cutter's support squad. Blood splattered everywhere and all the men fell dead.

Brazenly, a second Kilo Company squad moved to the wire and a second engineer began snapping his cutter tool. From seemingly every direction, German machine-gun fire bore down on him and ripped his body to shreds. He lay lifeless, his body sprawled hanging on the wire. He served as a perfect warning. Any American who dared approach the line would be shot dead.

The American Cote de Chatillon attack was not going well. Not only did the 84th Brigade fail to take the high ground in three hours, the Americans now faced a possible defeat. All field artillery turned to the Cote de Chatillon and the Germans took a ferocious pounding, but they would not yield. Brigadier General MacArthur wound up needing three full days to vanquish the Germans on Cote de Chatillon, not an abysmally short three hours.

All day long on October 14, American soldiers lay prostrate in the mud, hunkered down inside make-do craters or foxhole trenches they'd dug. German machine gunners picked off any American who dared move, and the dead and injured toll quickly began to mount. It was virtually impossible to get an injured man off the battlefield and to a dressing station. The 165th's Mike, India, and Kilo Companies had become completely pinned down, not in a desperate firefight, but rather a desperate bid for survival.

The 3rd Battalion, the Shamrocks, had come under great strain. By 1300 hours, midday on the fourteenth, over half the infantrymen and officers had been hit by machine-gun fire or shrapnel fragments.

———

"That's Sergeant Hogan," yelled Rooney. He spotted one of Kilo Company's platoon sergeants running down the low road to the pill-boxes. Sergeant Hogan had a squad of men with him. This time, the squad carried mortars.

Buckley crawled into the nest and dropped his ammo canisters. "We're ordered to lay down nonstop suppression fire," he said, breathing hard.

"Says who?" demanded Rooney.

"Captain Delacour. A squad from Kilo Company is going to attack the wire."

The order made sense. Buckley put the canisters under Bergan Morgan and crawled back to the roadway to get more.

"Ready, guys?" said John.

He squeezed the trigger and opened fire. He couldn't see what he aimed at. From his vantage point, the ground rolled downward and out of sight, ending at a small creek. The barbed wire stretched across the ground, and pillboxes were scattered on the other side of the creek. Not able to see anything, John attempted to spray the enemy with bullets, anyway. He noticed that Sergeant Hogan's mortar men had opened fire, and he followed their lead, shooting in the same direction.

A wild crisscross exchange filled the sky overhead as German gunners up high on the Cote bore down on the forward-firing American machine-gun nests.

"Fuck, now they know where we are!" Rooney screamed.

John swung the barrel around toward the high ridge, and he picked off a Kraut gunner. The German took a spectacular fall to the low ground and, for a moment, some Kilo men believed they had a chance once their machine gunners found targets.

The violent crisscrossing exchange intensified and American infantrymen, lying flat in the field, hunkered down below the deflecting bullets and tracers and began to panic. Many crawled out of the foxholes and rushed across the field, falling in behind the perceived safety of a machine-gun nest.

The sergeants tried to stop them. Bunching of soldiers only created a larger target for enemy mortars, artillery, and machine gunners, but there was no way to halt the terror-stricken, tide of men. Few maintained proper battlefield discipline.

Sergeant Hogan's squad advanced to the wire. He stood at the top edge of the descending terrain, singlehandedly directing the aim of mortar teams and machine gunners toward the German pillboxes below. Hogan lasted for only a few minutes before he too was shot in the hand. He dropped to the ground, bleeding profusely but unable to leave the battlefield.

The crisscrossing firefight abated, and the afternoon overcast gave way to a patchy cloudy dusk. Immediately, Luftwaffe pilots swooned down to surveil the Americans. Some pilots flew low and threw mortar bombs at the groups of clustered infantrymen. Other pilots strafed trapped men using airborne machine guns. Earlier, when the skies had lifted, the 42nd Division launched an over-the-horizon balloon to assess battlefield conditions, but Luftwaffe pilots immediately located the hydrogen-filled airfoil and torpedoed it with gunfire. The American balloon basket fell to the ground, and its spotter managed to jump out and deploy his parachute to escape the fire. But on the spotter's fall to the ground, German pilots swarmed in and shot him dead. All on the ground bore witness to the horrific act.

The German pilots returned to base and provided targeting information for the long-range field artillery. A Bavarian division had finally taken position north of the Meuse-Argonne valley out of range of American FAR.

Heavy rain began to fall again, and the intense small-arms exchanges on the Meuse battlefield had lessened, but the morale of the men trapped in the shallow muddy foxholes on the blood-soaked battlefield was shattered.

German FAR began to slam down atop the three isolated Shamrock battalion companies spread out between Sommerance village and Landres-et-Saint Georges. The situation grew so dire that American runners couldn't get in and relay essential messages to captains, lieutenants, and sergeants, and badly injured men couldn't get out and make it to the field hospital. Lieutenant Colonel Donovan took charge and navigated his way through the hellish terrain. Battle ribbons conspicuously pinned to his chest, he attempted to calm the men.

The Bavarian field artillery laid down steady enfilade, and that forced the trapped American infantrymen to bunch up even more. The artillery then switched to a rolling barrage, and that slow incremen-tally moving line of exploding artillery shells inched ever closer to the rear echelon of men hunkered in the foxholes. Soon, those men were left with no choice but to abandon their positions, risk being shot by German machine gunners up on the Cote de Chatillon, and make a frantic run toward some perceived safer ground, but there was none. As soon as a man stood, a wall of bullets met him, and he was shot dead. The battlefield became a death trap. Hundreds of frightened in-fantrymen attempted to escape the massive artillery explosions only to be summarily executed. The incessant shelling turned an intolerable situation into a desperate killing field.

"I'm going back!" yelled Buckley. John and Rooney tried to dissuade him, but it was no use. The machine-gun team needed more ammuni-tion, and Buckley was determined he'd get it. Artillery shells blasted the ground all around him and shockwaves shook the muddy earth beneath his feet, knocking him to his knees. High-explosive flashes fluttered like a violent thunderstorm, but Daniel Buckley managed to make his way to the ammo depot.

At the machine-gun nest, Ed Rooney heard a voice from behind his position.

"Keep calm, men," the commanding voice boomed. Ed Rooney turned around and saw Lieutenant Colonel Donovan crouched down in the mud at his side, Donovan's face illuminated by the shell bursts.

"We're fucked," Rooney shouted as he turned to John. He knew if Donovan was out with them, things were going horribly wrong. Donovan was out there to keep his officers cool and collected.

A shell landed very close to the nest, the closest detonation so far, and John saw a bunch of infantrymen leap to their feet and run toward him. He turned his gun toward them and shot overhead, trying to hold them back, but it was useless.

Five men scooted in behind John and Rooney, and when Rooney looked to his side again, Lieutenant Colonel Donovan was gone. He had moved up closer to the wire.

"We can't have these guys bunching behind us," Rooney yelled to John. "They'll get us killed." There was nothing they could do to stop the scores of men crouching in on them. The next shell landed in front of the nest. John, Rooney, and Morgan felt the hard thud and reflexively ducked, but there was a fantastic brilliant flash and an enormous concussive hot flash. Bergan Morgan's body instantly shattered to pieces. Ed Rooney's legs ripped away from his body, and his torso was thrown into the air, landing lifeless on the ground twenty feet away. John flew backward toward the roadway and landed face-up in the mud. He was in shock. His lower-left leg shattered. His left foot clung to his leg by only mere shreds of skin. He was bleeding out.

Daniel Buckley witnessed the explosion and ran to John.

"Can you hear me, John? John? John!" he pleaded and yelled.

Buckley saw that John had lost his front tooth and rocks and dirt were imbedded in his face. He scanned John's torso and legs and saw John's bad injury. He unbuckled John's belt and pulled it free. He then wrapped the belt around John's left thigh and pulled it tight to stop the bleeding.

John opened his eyes and saw Buckley peering down, working on him. He knew he'd been badly injured, but he felt no pain. Loud ringing filled his ears, and he was deafened. He felt Buckley grab his hand and place it on the belt Buckley had wrapped around his thigh. Buckley pulled the belt taut.

"Hold on to it tight," Buckley pleaded to John. "Hold on to it tight, John." But John couldn't hear him.

Buckley pulled John's body across the mud to the roadway. "I'll get you to the dressing station!" he yelled. Then, a single shot rang out, and

Daniel Buckley fell to the ground. He'd been hit in the head, and he was dead.

John saw the lifeless stare in Buckley's eyes, and he panicked. He felt a sudden urge to escape. He kicked the wet mud beneath him with his good foot but went nowhere. A chill came over his body, and he could feel the rain hit his face. The violent artillery booming and brilliant flashes seemed so far away. They began to dim and John's body began to shake. He shivered with cold. John peered up and focused on the low, dark, overcast clouds above, and he could see Anna's face. Then he saw Archie's and Catherine and her beautiful babies. Oh, God, the babies. John thought of his mother and then his father, and he began to cry. He had let his ma down. He wouldn't make it home. Then he let go of the belt, unable to hold it tight, and he pressed his hand over Anna's rosary.

The raging war faded away. John bled out and died.

CHAPTER 17

November 1918-September 1921

———

When Johnny comes marching home again,
Hurrah! Hurrah!
We'll give him a hearty welcome then
Hurrah! Hurrah!
The men will cheer and the boys will shout
The ladies they will all turn out
And we'll all feel gay when Johnny comes marching home.

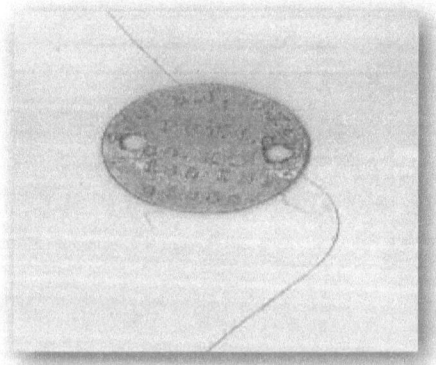

A US Army quartermaster tugged on the impaled Enfield and tossed the rifle into the mud. Then, he crouched down over the soldier's remains and untied the dog tags.

"How many is this?" he asked the team leader.

"One hundred and seventy-three. Any markings?"

"Missing right front tooth. Shrapnel wound, lower left leg. Mark as cause of death." He reached into the jacket pocket. "All these Irish got them worry beads," he said.

"Leave 'em. Anything else?"

"No."

"Tag?"

"John J. McKay. PVT 1/C, 165th Inf. K Co. 91539."

"I thought these guys were machine gunners."

"HQ will figure it out."

The quartermaster slipped one dog tag into John's mouth and shut it closed, and he handed the other dog tag to the grave marker. The grave marker then removed his heated branding rods from a wood fire and seared John's name, rank, serial number, and a large "165" onto a wooden cross, then he hammered the round dog tag into a doweled groove.

The team leader quartermaster filled out the army's ten-lined form, each item a specific detail of John's death and burial. Three other quartermasters dug out a shallow, flat-bottomed ditch about three feet in depth, then wrapped John's remains in burlap and placed him at the center. They waited for a Catholic chaplain to give burial rites before they put dirt over the grave. While waiting, the lead quartermaster notated the grave's location, writing down the longitude and latitude, and then he wrote in plain language, "PFC John McKay 91539, edge of the Sommerance to Landres-et-Saint-Georges roadway at Sommerance/Landres border. 1115 hours November 3rd 1918."

Father Duffy emerged from the lower roadway and climbed over the shallow berm. He stood over John's grave and whispered a rote version of the Catholic Rite of Committal, then blessed the dead soldier without ever noting the name. There were too many names. Duffy signaled that he was finished, and the quartermasters shoveled dirt over John's body. Duffy moved to the next man, Daniel Buckley.

———

Ferocious fighting on the Meuse-Argonne battlefield had been so stalemated and deadlocked that John, Daniel Buckley, Edward Rooney, and two hundred other Shamrock officers and infantrymen lay dead in the mud, their bodies uncovered for two weeks. The fighting was too fierce for recovery operations. The 42nd Division managed to hold its ground outside Landres-et-Saint-Georges but stayed trapped under withering machine-gun fire and over-the-horizon enfilade. Not until November 1 did the 42nd manage to reposition a more robust field artillery and close in on the Kriemhilde Stellung wires and pillboxes. The Rainbow men broke through the line on November 1 but were relieved in the field on November 3, replaced by the US Marines.

During the overnight hours of October 14 into the 15th, General Summerall flew into a rage. He was dissatisfied with the 165th Regiment's progress, and he relieved Brigadier General Lenihan, commander of the 83rd Brigade, and Col. Harry Mitchell, commander of the 165th Regiment, on the spot. Summerall insisted that if Lenihan and Mitchell had been more aggressive and attacked the Kriemhilde Stellung's line more forcefully, Shamrock Battalion's casualties count would be much higher and the dead infantrymen should have been found at the wires and not bunched together midfield, pummeled by enfilade.

Earlier the same night, sensing that conditions were quickly deteriorating and Shamrock Battalion's officers and infantrymen, trapped in the shallow foxholes short of the Landres-et-Saint-Georges wires, were failing, Lieutenant Colonel Donovan left the relative safety of Sommerance village. He navigated his way up the heavily shelled Sommerance to the Landres-et-Saint-Georges roadway and made his way to the machine-gun line. Donovan stayed with the machine gunners only momentarily, then scurried out under heavy enemy fire and ordnance and slipped onto the battlefield.

Donovan wore a brave face and conspicuously donned his war medals, attempting to bring hope to the hopeless. Shamrock infantrymen were locked down, unable to move backward or forward, and if German artillery forced a man to flee his foxhole, machine gunners were poised, ready to mow him down. Donovan assured his junior officers that victory was still attainable, and he swore that Cote de Chatillon's machine guns would soon be silenced.

After mere minutes hunkered down with the men under the blistering fusillade, Donovan too was hit in the leg by a German machine-gun bullet. He was incapacitated and bled profusely, trapped in a foxhole.

Donovan didn't stop leading his men, and he continued to direct Shamrock Battalion, maintaining command and control on the battlefield. He was finally evacuated during the predawn hours of the 15th.

For his bravery and action overnight on the Meuse-Argonne battlefield, October 15, 1918, William Donovan was awarded the National Medal of Honor.

When relieving General Lenihan and Colonel Mitchell, General Summerall didn't give much consideration to General MacArthur's failure. The 84th Brigade needed three days to capture the Cote de Chatillon, not three hours. Summerall also didn't give much consideration to the 83rd Brigade's 166th Ohio Regiment commander, Hough, who refused to advance his force and support the 165th's western flank outside Landres-et-Saint-Georges.

Summerall only cared about V-Corps's primary objective: penetrate the wires at Landres-et-Saint-Georges, and that assignment went to the 165th Regiment. General Lenihan and Colonel Mitchell failed to gain ground on the nights of the 14th and into the 15th, and they got the ax.

East of 42nd Division, over the Cote de Chatillon hills in the Meuse River valley, V-Corps's 32nd Division was first to break through the Kriemhilde Stellung line. Next, V-Corps's New York 77th Division on the corps's far-western boundary broke through the wires, and finally on November 1, 1918, the 42nd Rainbow Division plowed through the middle at Landres-et-Saint-Georges. The race to Sedan was on; the end of the war was in sight.

On the eleventh hour of the eleventh day of the eleventh month, 1918, Kaiser Wilhelm's government ceased hostilities and signed an armistice agreement inside a railcar at the Forest Compiegne on the Belgian border.

November 12, 1918, newspaper headlines across the world announced the Allied victory.

Spontaneous celebrations took hold all around Greenpoint, and Father McGolrick held an impromptu Mass celebration at Saint Cecilia's. Greenpoint citizens and anyone who ever knew a man in uniform filled the chapel pews. Men, women, and children spilled out the doors and onto the streets. Celebrations broke out all over Brooklyn and New York City.

Back in July 1918, American army casualty lists started to swell ever larger, and the numbers of American dead and injured began to resemble European casualty lists from 1916. Direct American combat operations began in July 1918 and lasted until November 11, 1918. In that relatively short period of one hundred days, later dubbed the "100 Days War," America counted over one hundred thousand dead—fifty-five thousand in combat and fifty thousand due to illness. Two hundred thousand men were injured. Tens of thousands more came home infected with tuberculosis or Spanish flu, or reeled from gas wounds, and later died.

———

Not until November 22, 1918, eleven days after the European war's official end and the jubilant and spontaneous street celebrations finally ebbed, a sorrowful, sober reality landed on every household doorstep or was distributed by newsboys on every street corner across the country. The US Army had released the Meuse-Argonne battle casualty list. The names of the dead and injured were not only to be published in the morning newspapers, but the army provided telegrams to Western Union as official notice from the US government. The cost for winning the month-long Meuse-Argonne battle was extraordinarily high. Twenty-six thousand men were killed in action and ninety-five thousand men were wounded. Brooklyn and Manhattan newspapers printed the horrific long casualty list in the morning edition.

McKay, John J.,
416 Meeker Ave, Bklyn.
Pvt., M. G. Co., 165th Inf.
Killed in action, October 15, 1918

Big William was first to read the news. He'd been scouring every newspaper article since John left for France. He found John's name crammed in the middle column of the paper. His name was printed in very small type in order to make room for all the names of KIA and WIA. There were thousands of local men. William had reconciled that his brother-in-law saw the heaviest action and understood John's chance of being killed was greater than most men's, but seeing his young brother-in-law's name printed starkly in the morning paper…he was shocked.

William sat at the kitchen table, his head buried in his hands; he prayed. He recalled the boys standing in the McKay parlor a year earlier with their uniforms donned for the first time, their lives so bright and beaming confidently. He thought of his sickly mother-in-law; she'd been so ill since John left for France that he worried the news of John's death might kill her. He'd have to get Catherine over to the McKay house before the Western Union messenger showed up with the army's official notice. Catherine needed to be with her mother.

"Goddamn this war!" he cursed. How would he tell Catherine? She was still in the bedroom getting dressed. He got up from the table and walked down the short hall just as Catherine opened the door. His eyes were deep red and swollen, and Catherine immediately discerned that something was horribly wrong. She could tell a crushing pain bore down on her husband. His stiff, upper-lip stoicism was gone, and he looked deeply saddened.

"Catherine," he cried.

Catherine gasped and covered her mouth, then screamed.

"Johnny! Not Johnny!"

William grabbed Catherine and held her tight. The young couple stood in the hallway embracing and crying, neither of them, wanting to hold back a single tear.

———

William had to explain to his wife that the official telegram from the US Army would be arriving this morning and, as he thought, Catherine's grief immediately turned to worry. She and William packed up the children and made haste up Russell Street to her parents' apartment, entering the home without knocking, but they saw it was too late. Mary was seated, motionless in her parlor chair, and Alex didn't move, either. Two Western Union telegram envelopes were laid on the table between them; one had been opened, and the other remained sealed.

"They have the wrong McKay family," said Mary. "They have the wrong house. When Johnny was injured, the telegram said 'Mrs. Mary McKay.'" She pointed at the telegram envelopes. "Look, right there. This new telegram says 'Mrs. McKay,' not Mrs. Mary McKay. It's not for me. There must be a thousand Mrs. McKays in New York."

Alex looked to Catherine, then William, and said nothing. He knew it was John, but he dared not say anything aloud. Mary's health was too fragile.

"Mother." Catherine reached down and held her hand. "The telegram might be from Archibald's regiment. Perhaps William should read what it says."

"No, no," Mary insisted. "Let them be."

———

A week later, a *New York Herald* reporter came to the house. By coincidence, he happened to be the same *Herald* reporter who had interviewed Alex McKay and family on Thanksgiving Day, 1911. When the reporter entered the McKay apartment, he immediately recognized Alex McKay and his daughters, Catherine and Anna. His heart sank. *What horror this war has wrought,* he thought. He fondly recalled the McKay household from that Thanksgiving Day—youthful and brimming with natural warmth and joy. Now, seeing this beautiful family under these horrible circumstances, the reporter was sickened. He asked to use the washroom, and when he got inside, he ran cold water over his hands and doused his face.

He clearly recalled that Thanksgiving Day in 1911, and he remembered when the Irish immigrant father, Alex McKay, proudly boasted that he was grateful for all that America had given his family. *How life's fate can turn so fast,* the reporter mulled. Irish immigrant Alex McKay's handsome family had now given everything to America.

"The army says my son is dead," Mary said, once the reporter's interview began. It was the first time she'd acknowledged John's death. "I have to believe our government," she added, "but there's a chance my Johnny is alive, and I would like the army to find him."

She told the reporter why she believed the telegram was a mistake, but at the same time, she said she'd accept the army's final word.

Alex promised to send letters and see what the army could do. Perhaps the nice people at the 69th Regiment Armory could help.

As weak and sickly as Mary was, she remained stalwart and driven. Her John could be roaming the French countryside, shell-shocked. He could be injured and was being nursed to health by a kind French family. Mary had to hold on. She'd heard wondrous stories of soldiers who found their way back home, and she desperately clung to those tales. They gave her the strength she needed. She was determined to get her Johnny back.

Pvt. John J. McKay.

Pvt. John J. McKay, 23 years old, who was killed in action on October 15, was the son of Mrs. Mary McKay of 418 Meeker ave. Mrs. McKay does not believe that her son is dead. When her son was gassed, on March 21 last, the Government's telegram was addressed to "Mrs. Mary McKay." When a week ago a messenger brought another telegram announcing officially the death of Pvt. John J. McKay, it was addressed simply "Mrs. McKay."

Pvt. McKay was born in the Eastern District. He was graduated from St. Cecilia's Parochial School. After leaving school he was apprenticed to the steamfitter's trade. When the United States declared war against Germany Pvt. McKay was in the employ of the Standard Oil Company. He enlisted in the old 69th Regt., and went to Camp Mills. There he was assigned to Co. K, 165th Inf. Pvt. McKay had seen much service, according to his letters

The 53rd Regiment ship, loaded with thousands of doughboys, pulled alongside the crowded Hoboken Terminal pier under much fanfare and celebration in the spring of 1919. Parents, wives, children, girlfriends, and extended family members waited for the ship to berth and for the heavy ropes to be tied up and secured to the pier and for the returning doughboys to flood down the gangplanks.

Archie never told his family that he was on his way back. He never gave them an arrival date. When the ship docked, Archie was immediately quarantined, removed from the ship by stretcher, and sent by ferryboat and special Long Island Rail Road train out to the Camp Mills Base Hospital on Long Island. Like 15 percent of all American soldiers in France, Archie had contracted tuberculosis.

After about a week, Archie was able to make a phone call, and he spoke to Anna. A month later, Anna was permitted to visit Archie at Camp Mills, and she broke the news about John.

"He can't be killed on the fifteenth," Archie insisted, shaking his head side to side. "I saw him on the sixteenth. The army gets things wrong, Anna. I've seen it for myself!" But Archie had his dates mixed up. He saw John on the thirteenth of October, before the Meuse-Argonne battle, not on the sixteenth.

Anna told Archie how their ma agreed with him and how their dah had written letters, asking the army to investigate. She explained the different telegrams and the possible mix-up.

"He ain't dead, Anna!" Archie pounded the bed frame. "When I get out of here, I'll get to the bottom of it. You'll see."

Anna left for home, and Archie lay in his bed, stewing. He wanted to get out of the hospital and now, hearing about his brother missing and his ma being very sick, he got antsy. He thought he should get up and just leave, but then his heart pounded and unexplainable feelings of panic and despair rolled through his body. He'd told the nurses about his attacks, but nobody listened to him. Nobody seemed to care.

The nurses hardly came around. They kept him confined from the other patients, and no one from the 53rd Pioneer Regiment ever came by to visit. No officers or sergeants came by to tell him what he should expect. The doctors never said a word.

Archie stayed at the Camp Mills hospital for two months, confined to his room and agonizing over his missing brother and ill mother. His panic attacks came more frequently, and he grew fraught that he couldn't control his anxiety. He couldn't understand what was happening. He never had these kinds of attacks before, not even in France. Why was he having them now? He craved a drink and thought a little booze would calm his nerves. He needed to get out of the hospital. The whole US Army was disbanding and everyone went home. He was being held captive for no reason.

———

In July 1919, the US Army quartermasters came back to the Meuse-Argonne battlefield, this time to exhume the graves dug and reinter the remains of American soldiers into the newly commissioned Meuse-Argonne National Cemetery. The Meuse-Argonne National Cemetery became the resting place for thirty thousand Americans.

Five cemeteries were established in France, all named after a major American battle. First was the Aisne-Marne Cemetery, then the Oise-Marne, Saint Mihiel, Somme, and Meuse-Argonne Cemeteries. At the end of the war, 110,000 American soldiers were officially interred, and the names of the missing were etched onto memorial walls.

Mothers and fathers of the dead were not satisfied, however; they didn't want to leave their sons in a faraway place like France. American parents wanted their children returned to the United States and buried with them and other family children in a family plot.

The clamor grew louder and louder. At first, the French government flatly refused, arguing that resources needed to ship one hundred thousand dead men by train and cargo ship were too great for a nation recovering from war. The US government wasn't very eager, either, and Theodore Roosevelt and his wife, Anita, traveled the country, telling Gold Star parents, "We should let the boys be." Quentin Roosevelt's body remained interred in Champagne.

On September 10, 1919, the 42nd Rainbow Division, including the 165th Regiment, once again called the 69th Fighting Irish Regiment of New York, paraded down Fifth Avenue in an enormous patriotic display celebrating victory in Europe. The avenue was jam-packed with revelers and spectators. Men, women, and children waved American flags and Irish 69th banners. They cheered the triumphant soldiers as they passed.

Few knew that virtually none of the original men who had enlisted into the 69th Regiment on June 4, 1917, marched in the victory parade. All those young men were dead. Officers William Donovan and Father Duffy survived, as did about 5 percent of the original infantrymen—one hundred men, and that was because those infantrymen were badly injured earlier in the war and convalesced in hospitals.

Medal of Honor honoree Dick O'Neil was an exception. He was badly injured during the Ourqc River battle, but he recovered and reported back to his company to fight in the Meuse-Argonne. At the finish of the Fifth Avenue parade, O'Neil and his new bride, Estelle, visited Mrs. Hickey's boardinghouse on West Eleventh. O'Neil was sure he had the right address, as Mrs. Hickey's green 69th Regiment flag was still flying next to her Stars and Stripes. O'Neil explained how John and Daniel Buckley had been killed during a violent battle and told her that they were both laid to rest in France. Mrs. Hickey said that she knew the boys had been killed. She, like so many, scoured the newspapers every day and saw Johnny McKay and Daniel Buckley's names on the lists.

O'Neil gave Mrs. Hickey a loving hug, and they shared a teary good-bye. Then, he and Estelle crossed the East River and knocked on the McKay family door in Greenpoint. Both Alex and Mary were at home and the McKay's welcomed the highly decorated soldier in full uniform and his wife into their house. All four sat in the parlor.

Dick O'Neil never said John was dead. Instead, he told Mary and Alex how John was the bravest of men, a good soldier, and a man who always did his duty. O'Neil said that the men in John's platoon greatly respected him and that the McKay family should be very proud. O'Neil handed Alex and Mary the two photographs he had taken at Camp Mills. One picture was John sitting with O'Neil, Rooney, and McSweeney, and the other picture was John standing alone on a pedestal outside the New York Guarantee Trust building in Mineola.

"I, for one, will never forget your son," O'Neil said, and he added, "No American should ever forget your son."

——

Archie slipped out of the Camp Mills hospital and made his way to Greenpoint, not telling anyone he had returned. He didn't feel like explaining anything to his family, so he used some saved-up money and rented a flophouse room along Metropolitan Avenue; this way, he could do what he wanted with no questions asked. He felt free again, liberated, and just like he thought he'd feel, a little sip of whiskey soothed his nerves just right.

No officials from the army came looking for Archie. No one from the hospital seemed to care that he had gone missing. The US Army and the reserve guard outfits had all demobilized. Archie went in and out of his rented room, frequenting Greenpoint's gin mills as he pleased, and nobody asked him any questions.

One afternoon at McGee's bar, a group of soldiers from the New York 77th Division came in for drinks. They were a boisterous group, reliving wartime exploits and recalling stories of bravery while in France. They purposely spoke loudly enough so that everyone in the bar could hear.

"Men of the 77th are the boldest and bravest," they shouted. "We broke the wire at the Meuse-Argonne, not the mighty Irish."

In Greenpoint, at McGee's, that kind of talk and those kinds of boasts were fighting words, but nobody in McGee's took the rambunctious ex-77th soldiers to task. Archie heard the braggarts, too, but he held his tongue. Archie held it as best as he could. After an hour of having to listen to those 77th Division punks disparage the Irish 69th, however, the 77th being men who didn't even belong in Greenpoint, Archie decided he had heard enough.

He got up from his barstool and confronted them.

"My brother was a Sixty-Niner," Archie spewed in a man's face, "and he's a tougher son of a bitch than *any* of you pissants."

"Keep your slobber off me, you syphilitic little shit. No one who's anything like you can be tough. Yer brother was probably a drunken fool like you."

Archie took a swing at the man but missed. "My brother fought in the Sixty-Ninth!" Archie yelled across the bar. "He's an American hero!"

The 77th men looked to one another, and they circled around Archie. They hustled him, pushed him out the front door, and shoved him onto the sidewalk. One of the men knocked him down to the gutter, and they began to kick him.

Each man took a turn. The heavy kicks to his chest inflamed his lungs, and Archie could hardly breathe.

"My brother's an American hero!" Archie kept shouting, and the men hit him harder.

"Bullshit!" they yelled back.

A police officer saw the scuffle down the avenue and made his way up toward McGee's. The 77th men scattered into the side streets and disappeared, and Archie lay on the sidewalk coughing and gasping, his arms wrapped around his chest.

"My brother's a hero," he whimpered. "My brother's a hero."

A paddy wagon rolled up and two cops picked Archie up off the street and took him downtown to the Adams Street jail.

Later that night, a policeman knocked on the McKay door. The officers knew this was a Gold Star home, and they showed great respect toward father Alex McKay, but they had to tell him that his son, Archibald, had been arrested for vagrancy and public intoxication, and he was being held in the downtown jail. Someone had to claim Archibald.

————

By January 1920, the US Army's investigation into the death of John McKay was complete. The army determined that PFC John J. McKay, serial number 91539, was hit by shrapnel and killed in action on October 15, 1918 inside the Meuse-Argonne Forest. The army now needed to know if the young private had a wife or dependent children. The US government was ready to pay the McKay family the $10,000 survivor benefit.

John had never married, had no dependents, and, as stipulated on his enlistment papers the day he joined the 69th Regiment, Alex and Mary were his sole beneficiaries.

The McKays received $10,000 from the US government, and they did two things with the money. First, they purchased a family grave inside Calvary Cemetery. The plot selection wasn't a random grave. Any family looking to purchase a grave in Calvary by 1920 had to buy a plot in the "New Calvary" cemetery, a sprawling section far to the north of Greenpoint. Alex and Mary enlisted the help of Father McGolrick and were able to purchase a plot inside the "Old Calvary" cemetery inside a section that had been closed since before the turn of the century. The McKays selected a special site, one on the south-facing, downward-sloping ground, overlooking the Newtown Creek and Meeker Avenue Bridge. The plot could be seen from Greenpoint on the opposite side of the creek.

The McKay's then purchased a standalone house at the end of Meeker Avenue for $5,000, a house not far from the Old Dutch Colonial that they had rented from Standard Oil in 1911. From the vantage point of the new home's front windows, Mary could see straight across the Newtown Creek and view the sunlit sloping south lawn—the place her Johnny would eventually rest forever.

By mid-1920, the clamor from American families, demanding their sons and fathers be returned to the United States, reached a tipping point, and both the French and American governments finally gave in. American KIA interred in France, upon family request, would be exhumed and shipped back to the United States, beginning in the spring of 1921. The McKay's immediately requested John's body be returned. Fifty thousand of the one hundred thousand dead were returned.

———

In April 1921, General Pershing stood on a Hoboken pier, awaiting the SS *Wheaton* to dock. Some 7,200 KIA American doughboys had been exhumed from France's National Cemeteries and placed in transfer cases for shipment back to the United States. The Hoboken arrival ceremony was solemn and quiet, and only a handful of dignitaries joined General Pershing to acknowledge the returning soldiers. Very few reporters covered the story.

Once the ship docked, General Pershing said a few words, thanking the brave young men for their service to country, he then departed.

The job of moving seventy-two hundred transfer cases onto the pier and making sure every case went to the proper claimant was under way.

The SS *Wheaton* served as the sole transfer ship, and John's body returned to the United States aboard the *Wheaton* on August 31, 1921. By that time, no dignitaries waited on the pier, and only one newspaper reporter covered the story of the ship's arrival. The McKay family requested a local funeral director to claim the transfer case. The funeral director arranged to move John's body via boat, sailing a similar route that John sailed on the day he departed for France—around lower Manhattan, past the Statue of Liberty, up the East River, under the spanned bridges, and into the Newtown Creek to Meeker Avenue, Greenpoint.

John's funeral Mass was scheduled for September 1, 1921, at Saint Cecilia's, and Father McGolrick insisted that he be the sole celebrant. Ennis O'Shea attended the Mass, as did Dick O'Neil and his wife. It seemed as if all of Greenpoint turned out for John: people the McKays knew well and many others they didn't know at all.

Mary was too frail to walk, and Catherine had recently given birth to her third child, a son they named John Francis. Mother and daughter, baby John Francis, Little William, and Kitty rode in a horse-drawn carriage behind John's two-wheeled caisson, provided by the 69th Regiment. His casket was draped with an American flag, and a 69th Regiment honor guard led the procession. Alex, Archie, Anna, and Big William walked behind the carriage from the steps of Saint Cecilia's Church, down Meeker Avenue, across the Newtown Creek to the Penny Bridge rail station, and into the south gate of the cemetery.

At graveside, Mary peered across the creek to her home, and she was satisfied. She had her Johnny back.

Ten days later, after John's funeral Mass and burial, Mary McKay fell desperately ill. Her kidneys stopped functioning, and she lay bed-ridden, unconscious. She was under a doctor's care, but there was little the physician could do. Mary's blood pressure hadn't been under control for years, and the damage to her organs was already done. Now her blood pressure had climbed dangerously high again.

Mary had waited three long years before she got her son back. As ill and weak as she had been all that time, she could never let go and succumb to her illness, not before her John was safe home. Be he dead or alive, Mary could never abandon her beloved son and leave him adrift in the world. She had to have him back.

Now Mary had her son, and she knew where he rested. She took great comfort in knowing that she could see his place every day. This time, when her blood pressure flared high again and her kidneys failed, Mary no longer had the will to fight back. She no longer had a reason to stay strong. On September 11, 1921, Mary McKay finally let go and died at age fifty-three, a young mother who was forever left broken-hearted—an unknown casualty of the Great War.

———

Mary sat quietly in her seat, riding the Meeker Avenue trolley back to her home. As the streetcar neared the last stop, she saw the conductor tug on the cord to ring the trolley's bell.

Clang, the bell sounded, and the conductor stoutly shouted, "End of the line. Cross over for the cemetery."

It was time for Mary to get out. She stepped off the trolley car and heard a distant but clear whispering voice. A man said aloud, "Ma's home."

She turned to look across Meeker Avenue Bridge toward the Penny Bridge train station and Calvary Cemetery on the far side and felt a powerful energy—the aura of an angel who was standing at the middle of the span. Mary saw the angel, a young man who wore a soldier's uniform and a campaign hat. His eyes shone bright and magnificently, beaming a soothing, comforting light. His face was aglow, filled with natural love and eternal peace. He had the kindest, most welcoming face Mary had ever seen.

Mary then realized that the powerful angelic force standing before her was her own son, John, and instantly Mary's spirit was infused with a profound peace and a great joy. Her broken heart instantly healed and filled with unconditional love.

The angel raised his arm and beckoned her, and then he took hold of her delicate hand.

"Come, Ma," he said. "It's not the end of the line."

———

PETER MCHALE IS A PROFESSIONAL airline pilot and ex–US Navy pilot and naval officer. McHale is a graduate from Villanova University.

Greenpoint Doughboy is McHale's first book and is based on the adventures of his great-uncle John McKay during World War I.

www.ingramcontent.com/pod-product-compliance
Lightning Source LLC
Chambersburg PA
CBHW031254170626
46807CB00001B/146